COCHIN FALL

LIZ HARRIS

HEYWOOD PRESS

1

British Cochin, South India,
    Thursday evening, September, 1934

CLARA RAN THROUGH HER BEDROOM, filled with excitement, and out on to the wooden verandah that encircled the upper storey of the house.

Smiling happily, she stared out at the view that since a very small child, she'd looked at last thing each night before going to bed.

Her gaze swept across the darkened garden to the broad stretch of sand, bone-white beneath the light of the moon, and to the glittering ribbon of ebony water that lay beyond. On either side of the garden, framing the sand and the sea, stood slender coconut palms, their dark fronds spiking the indigo sky.

The night air was alive with the sound of water lapping against the shore, the relentless clicking of cicadas, the occasional bark of a distant dog, and with the haunting tones of the Indian music that rose from the town that lay behind their house.

She sighed deeply. At last she was home!

And what a return it had been!

She'd only been home for a few hours, yet so much had happened.

And it had all been perfect.

She couldn't have wished for a better homecoming.

And that was thanks to her father, she thought in affection. He'd never been able to keep a secret, and that evening had been no exception.

Not that it was a secret as such—it was something that had been decided between her parents and their good friends, the Goddards, the parents of Lizzie and George, but she wasn't supposed to have been told so soon after her return.

Her father, however, hadn't been able to resist, and now she was beside herself with joy.

What a wonderful start to the next stage of her life!

Hugging herself in delight, she leaned against the balustrade and thought back to the events of the evening.

As THEIR MEAL had drawn to a close, her father had inched his chair back from the long rosewood table where they'd been dining, and had rung the small brass bell at the side of his plate. Taking his pipe from the pocket of his jacket, he'd smiled at her and her mother, Mary, as he waited for the head servant, Amit, to appear.

'I'm pleased to see you've settled so quickly back into the routine of home, Clara,' he'd said, tapping his pipe against a glass ashtray. 'It's good to have you back—the house has seemed very quiet since your sister left.'

'Thank you, Papa. I can't tell you how pleased I am to be home.'

Mary put her white napkin on the table, and stood up. 'If you'll excuse me, Henry, I think I'll leave you both to catch up with the past few years and go to bed now. I'm still somewhat tired after the journey home. Not to mention the heat here, which is so much greater than that in England.'

'Of course, my dear. That's completely understandable. And it'll be a busy day tomorrow. I know that Tilly's expecting you in the morning.'

Clara rose as if to follow her mother.

With a wave of his hand, Henry indicated that she should stay where she was, and she sat again.

'Why don't you keep me company for a little longer, Clara?' he'd said. He turned to the head servant, who'd come to his side. 'I'll have a brandy, Amit, please.'

Amit crossed to the sideboard, poured out a brandy and brought the snifter to the table on a silver salver. Taking the drink from the salver, Henry signalled that Amit could leave, and he'd turned his attention back to Clara. 'After all, you've not yet finished your coffee, Clara, and I thought it would be nice to talk for a bit.'

'Of course, Papa,' she said with a smile. 'Were you thinking about any particular subject?'

'Oh, no,' he said quickly. 'Not at all. Indeed, not at all.' And he gave a slight cough.

That was far too swiftly uttered, she thought, and she sat a little straighter. Her father most certainly *did* have something he wanted to say, but was clearly reticent to do so.

'No, I just thought it would be nice to have some general conversation,' he went on. 'But first things first,' he said, taking a tin of tobacco from his pocket. 'Just give me a moment.' He half-filled the bowl of the pipe with tobacco, pressed it lightly down, and added more tobacco.

While he went through the procedure she remembered so well, she'd glanced idly around the room, enjoying the spicy aroma of tea, cardamom and sandalwood, which was laced with a hint of the sea. It was a combination of scents that had been ingrained in both the wood and her memory for as long as she could recall.

And in her heart.

While her father had been testing the draw of his pipe, she'd glanced above his head to the gilt-framed family photographs that hung above the buffet sideboard, and along the row of pallid faces that stared unsmilingly from their sepia backgrounds, some captured on celluloid in England, and some in Cochin—the faces of family members long gone.

A rhythmic breeze brushed her cheeks, and she looked up at the central electric fan. Whirring with a steady rhythm, it was fluttering the frill that hung from the long wooden pole suspended across the ceiling.

The *punkahwallah* must be overjoyed that her parents now had an electric fan in every room, she thought, as well as the frilled *punkah*. He'd no longer have to lie on the verandah outside the window all night, continually moving the cloth fan backwards and forwards by pulling on a rope, one end of which was tied to the cloth-bearing pole inside the room, and the other to his toe.

As a child, she'd always been worried that he might fall asleep during the night, and then the *punkah* stop would stop moving. If that had happened, she'd been sure that her face would become a meal for mosquitoes, and her feet food for sandflies. But such an anxiety felt a long time ago.

It *was* a long time ago.

It was six years, and she hadn't been home in those six years.

She'd been twelve years of age when she'd left the Sree Rama Varma High School in Cochin and instead of being transferred to the college attached to the school, had been sent like most of the children of the British to a school in England.

She and Lizzie had gone to the same school, and had travelled together on the boat, accompanied by her mother. Her mother had used the occasion to visit her family in England and to make the holiday arrangements for Clara. She had also ensured that Lizzie's accommodation during the school holidays was what Lizzie's father, Albert Goddard, thought he'd organised.

After that, her mother had travelled further north to check that Lizzie's brother, George, was comfortably settled in the school in which he'd started the year before, and wasn't in need of anything. And then she'd returned to India.

Her mother had been so lucky to see George.

And now, she, too, would surely see him soon. She could hardly wait.

Her father's chair sounded loud on the terracotta-tiled floor, and she sensed his eyes on her. She glanced at him. He'd adjusted the angle of his chair and was surveying her. With one hand he was swirling his brandy around the sides of the snifter, and with the other he held his pipe.

She felt a sudden nervousness beneath the directness of his gaze, and she reached up and tightened the ribbon into which she'd gathered her long hair at the nape of her neck.

'What shall we talk about, Papa?' she said, annoyed to hear the note of anxiety in her voice. 'Perhaps you'd like to tell me about the company, and how it's getting on. I'm sure that would interest me.'

He smiled at her. 'And I'm sure it wouldn't. No, there'll be many more interesting topics than that, I'm sure.' He cleared his throat.

Her anxiety increased.

'I may have been away for a good while, Papa, but I remember clearly how you used to cough, and clear your throat, whenever you were nervous.' She tried to smile. 'It was usually when you knew you had to tell me off, but you were going to hate doing so. What are you trying to tell me now that you'd rather not have to say?'

'Nothing at all, Clara. You're mistaken. There's nothing I plan to tell you. At least, not on the first night you're home.'

'I shall never sleep tonight, Papa, if you don't tell me what you're talking about. I shall think the most fearsome things.'

'You mustn't do that,' he said anxiously. 'There really is no cause for alarm.'

She leaned forward. 'Then tell me, dear Papa,' she said cajolingly. 'I promise not to tell Mama that you've told me,' she added conspiratorially.

He chuckled. 'You've always been able to get around me, you and Tilly. The number of times you've twisted me round your little finger.'

'Please tell me, Papa.'

He shook his head in resignation. 'I suppose I'll have to, having got this far. I was going to tell you tomorrow, anyway.' He cleared his throat.

'You've grown into a lovely young woman, Clara,' he began. 'In fact, you remind me of your mother at the same age. It was the age at which Mary and I married. I, of course, was some years older, as ideally it should be.' He straightened up. 'But not necessarily so,' he added, and he gave a slight cough.

She swallowed hard.

'What are you saying, Papa?' she asked, a tremor in her voice.

He reached quickly across and patted her hand. 'I'm not telling you who you're to marry, my dear, if that's what you're thinking,' he said. 'Indeed, no. A number of my friends at the club have chosen a husband for their daughter, but I don't propose to do that. I'm trusting you'll make a wise decision, and not disappoint your mother and me. We've given you the best possible start by sending you to a school in England, but the rest is up to you.'

She felt herself relax.

'Thank you, Papa,' she said tremulously. 'I promise I won't be rash. After all, my future happiness depends upon it.'

'That's very true, my dear.' He hesitated, and cleared his throat again. 'I know you've been back a very short time, and must still, like your mother, be feeling the effects of the journey, but I wonder if I might be so bold—and I leave your choice entirely up to you, you understand—but since you're at an age now to be thinking of marriage, might I suggest a direction in which you could look?'

'A direction?' she echoed questioningly.

Her stomach churned.

'Yes. Just further along the road, in fact—to the Goddard family. To young George.'

Relief coursed through her.

She beamed at him.

George must still be free of any attachment! If he wasn't, her father would never have proposed him as a husband.

'I realise that George is only a year older than you,'

Henry continued, 'and in the light of what I said moments ago about the desirability of a disparity in age, it might seem strange that I'm asking you to consider a man so close to you in years.'

'Not so, Papa,' she said quickly.

'But George is a mature young man,' he continued. 'He's now been working with his father for a year, and Albert says he shows a real flair for the business. He's confident that Goddard & Son will be in safe hands when George eventually takes over from him.'

'George has always wanted to follow his father into the business.'

'Just so. And with their interest being in the coconut trade, and mine in peppers and spices, and with both our companies having offices, boats and warehouses near each other in Muttancherry, a union between you and George would make good business sense.'

'How romantic you make it sound, Papa,' she said in amusement.

He laughed. 'I suppose I could have expressed it better. But you and George have long been good friends. It's one of the reasons why a little while ago, with the gossip in town being that Albert was thinking about a trading colleague's daughter for George, I raised the possibility with Albert and Julia of you and George. Since then, I've heard no further mention of the other girl.'

She frowned. 'A girl here in Cochin, someone I might know?'

Henry shook his head. 'No, in Calicut. But it could well have been a rumour that lacked any substance. You know how these things get around.'

'They did at school, too.'

'And I'm sure Lizzie would be delighted if you married

her brother. It's why I thought you might be prepared to consider this.' He paused. 'Well, my dear?' he prompted. 'Will you give this some thought?'

She looked at him, her face glowing. 'Thank you, Papa. Obviously, it's years since I've seen George, but we've written to each other, and as you say, we're already good friends. I'm very much looking forward to seeing him again.'

He gave her a sheepish smile. 'Well, you won't have to wait too long—it just so happens that the Goddards will be dining with us tomorrow evening. That's why I'd intended to suggest such a line of thought before the evening began.'

'They sound as bad as you!' she exclaimed with a laugh. 'But I didn't realise that you and Mr Goddard were as friendly. Our two families didn't really see much of each other when we were little, even though they live close by.'

'Things change. Some time ago, we both started going more regularly to The English Club on Wednesday evenings. Apart from the other traders like us, highly placed officials from companies such as Pierce Leslie and Aspinwall often go there, too, and it's good to be part of such a group.'

She smiled. 'I'm sure it is.'

'As a result, Albert and I got to know each other better, and moved from being fellow traders to being friends. And the fact that I can help with a concern he has, and he can help with one I have, has brought us even closer.'

Her brow wrinkled. 'What concern has he got?'

He smiled. 'That George has the right wife. That's so important for an ambitious man, and Albert has ambitions both for himself and for George. But he's anxious that George's focus doesn't move from the business to a search for a wife.'

'You and he sound very alike,' she murmured.

He laughed. 'That's probably true. But as I haven't a son,

it's my dearest wish that you marry a man familiar with trading. I inherited Saunders & Co from your grandfather, and it would be a relief to know that there was someone in the family who could take it on when the time came. Mathilda has married well, but Michael's career is with the colonial administration, and he hasn't the slightest interest in the export trade.'

'I understand, Papa.'

'But it isn't only about business, of course,' he added hurriedly. 'Albert and Julia were as confident that George would want to marry you as your mother and I were about your feelings for George. Or rather, your mother was. I may know the exact moment when pepper berries are ready to be harvested, when they're still green and haven't yet turned to red, but the workings of the female mind are completely beyond me. I leave that sort of thing to your mother.'

'I'll certainly think about marrying George, Papa. Assuming he wants to marry me, that is. Thank you for your kindness in leaving the decision to me. Not every father would have done that, and I'm very grateful to you.'

He nodded. 'You're a good girl, Clara. All your school reports have said this, and so, too, did your mother every time she returned from visiting you. We want you to be as happy as Mathilda is with Michael. Which you'll see for yourself tomorrow when you and your mother go there for coffee. I believe you're staying for lunch, too.'

'I can't wait to see Tilly again!'

'And she's very much looking forward to seeing you, too. I expect you mother told you that Mathilda and Michael wanted to come over tonight, but we thought your first evening at home should be a quiet one. Michael's a good man, but perhaps not the easiest man to talk to.'

'I look forward to seeing him again. Thank you again, Papa, for being so kind.'

He waved her gratitude away, finished his brandy and stood up. 'I'm off to bed now. I imagine you'll want to do the same as you must be tired, and with Tilly's in the morning, and the Goddards coming here in the evening, tomorrow's going to be a busy day.'

She rose, went impulsively up to her father, flung her arms around him and kissed him on the cheek.

'Thank you for making my first day home so pleasant, Papa,' she said, and smiling broadly, she went through the arched doorway and out into the hall.

THE WHOLE EVENING had been perfect. There was nothing at all standing in the way of her happiness and George's, she thought as she stared at the view. Leaning against the wooden balustrade, she let herself be drawn into the beauty of the scene.

A twig snapped.

It seemed to come from somewhere to her right. She frowned, and glanced in that direction.

But there was no movement at all among the shadows.

Shrugging, she returned to the view.

Then she heard it again. Followed by silence.

Her skin prickled and goosebumps ran along her arm.

She wasn't alone.

There was someone out there, hidden in the velvet darkness of night, watching her. She could sense their presence.

Straightening up, she pulled her shawl more tightly around her shoulders.

Could it be George, she wondered.

She glanced to the left, to the narrow path that separated the tall palm trees from the sand.

George's house being only fifteen minutes' walk along the path—less if he ran—many a time as they'd grown older, he would secretly slip out after dinner, run along to her house, and call quietly up to her. She'd throw something over her nightdress, creep down the stairs, and go out to him, giggling.

Together, they'd sit on the lower verandah, their cane chairs touching, their heads close, sharing the dreams they'd tell no one else.

So could it be George out there, eager to see her on her first night home?

Smoothing down her auburn hair, she stared to the left, waiting.

Nothing.

Then it couldn't be George, she realised. He wouldn't have hidden away for so long. He would never have done something that he'd know would scare her. And the sound she'd heard had come from the wrong side of the garden, anyway.

Maybe one of their servants was taking a late night walk. In sudden hope, she ran to the far corner of the house and stared down into the garden.

But the godowns where their servants lived, and where their cook prepared her family's meals, were in darkness. She couldn't see behind them to the jetty and godown in which her father's private launch was kept because the trees hid them from sight, but there'd be no one there at that time of night.

And why *would* there be anyone out there, cloaked in darkness?

It'll have been a small animal or a bird. Nothing more

alarming than that, she thought, and walking back along the verandah, she scolded herself for being so fanciful. She'd been away for so long that she'd forgotten the many sounds in an Indian night.

And with one final glance at the glistening dark water, she went back into her bedroom, into the warm amber glow thrown out by the lamps, and pulled the shutters tightly closed behind her.

A FEW MOMENTS LATER, a dark figure emerged from the shadow of the tallest coconut tree on the right, paused, and stared up at the deserted verandah.

His eyes glittered, reflecting the light of the moon as he stood there, motionless.

Then he turned away, and walked back into the gaping mouth of darkness.

2

T he following morning

CLARA LAY IN BED, staring at the *punkah* that stretched motionless across the ceiling, thinking happily back to her father's words the night before.

She didn't know why it had taken her by surprise—a very pleasant surprise, but a surprise no less—that he was keen for her to marry George. For as long as she could remember, she'd known how important it was to her father that there was someone in his family in whose hands he could leave Saunders & Co.

Many a time he'd recounted to her the story of his father, her grandfather, who'd left London to work as a representative of an important trading firm in Cochin, which engaged in businesses sponsored by the East India Company. Her grandfather had assumed that eventually he'd return to England, her father had told her, but he hadn't.

Instead, a few years later, when restlessness had set in, he'd moved into one of the offices in Muttancherry that had been vacated by the East India Company and, using the contacts he'd made, he'd started a trading business of his own.

Saunders & Co had been successful from the outset, and at the end of his first year of trading, confident of being able to provide for a family, he'd started looking for a wife to run his household, and to give him a son and heir.

Soon after that, at a social gathering, he'd been introduced to the daughter of a British official working for the Resident, the man who advised the Maharajah of Cochin on the administration of the state, and it had been love at first sight on both sides.

They'd married ten weeks later.

It had been an extremely happy marriage, but one that was far too short-lived. To her grandfather's great distress, his beloved wife had died a few hours after giving birth to their first child, Henry, her father.

Tortured by grief, her grandfather had refused to consider marrying again, preferring thereafter to share his life with a bottle. Encouraged by concerned trader friends, he'd sent Henry, who was effectively being brought up by his *ayah*, to school in England.

When Henry returned to Cochin at eighteen years of age, he'd been shocked at the sad condition of his father. And the only surprise felt by anyone a year later, when her grandfather was found dead in his bed, was that he'd lived so long.

Her father had promptly set about building up the

company, which had been in rapid decline owing to its neglect. And after ten years of hard work, he found himself presiding over a thriving business, and in a position to think about marriage.

From that point on, he'd started to look for a suitable woman, he'd tell her, glancing slyly at her mother as he spoke. When a fellow trader introduced him to Mary Forndyce-Brown, the attractive daughter of an English banker who was visiting Cochin with his family, he embarked upon a whirlwind courtship, and Mary had finally agreed to become his wife.

Tilly had been born a year later, and seven years after that, after two miscarriages, Clara had been born. There'd been no more children.

No wonder he was anxious that she marry someone keen on, and knowledgeable about, the trading business.

And she wanted that, too, given that the someone he'd suggested was George.

Her parents had known that she and George were good friends, but they couldn't have known how much they loved each other. She'd loved George for as long as she could remember, and during her years away at school, had missed him more than she'd ever have believed possible!

On the ship from England, getting closer to Cochin each day, her excitement had mounted at the thought of soon seeing George again.

What would he look like now, she'd wondered every morning when she woke, and every night before she went to sleep.

And what would he think of her now?

Would he still think her beautiful, as he'd told her he did seven years ago, his face very serious, on the day before he'd set sail for England the year ahead of her? The day they'd promised to love each other for all eternity, and to marry each other and no one else.

She straightened up, and took a deep breath.

It would be unwise to place too much reliance on what they'd said as eleven- and twelve-year olds. He'd been back in Cochin for a whole year, and could easily have met someone since he'd returned, someone about whom his parents had as yet no knowledge.

After all, he'd been extremely good-looking at twelve, and was probably even more so now. With his looks, and a secure future, he'd be seen as a catch by every unmarried young woman in Cochin.

She must be prepared for that.

But if he *had* transferred his affections, she didn't know what she'd do.

She pushed back her sudden anxiety.

He wouldn't have done that. Not George.

He would still be feeling about her as she felt about him.

They might not have seen each other in the intervening years, their schools being some distance apart, and having to stay with their respective relatives during the holidays, but they'd written to each other. Not often, it was true, but with sufficient frequency for her to be confident that his feelings for her had remained unchanged.

And he'd written once since he'd returned to Cochin. Admittedly, that was almost six months ago. But she'd have been able to tell if he'd met someone else.

She was worrying needlessly. And she was going to stop.

The whole day ahead of her was going to be wonderful, starting with her visit to Tilly, and ending with George's family coming to dinner at her house, and she was going to wipe any baseless concern from her mind.

.   .   .

SHE FOLLOWED her mother through the gate into the gravelled courtyard, and stopped abruptly.

'It's lovely!' she exclaimed, looking around her.

The low walls of the courtyard were covered in clusters of red hibiscus and a mass of pink and white begonias, and at the foot of the enclosing wall, pink periwinkle bloomed. In the far corner of the courtyard, near the short flight of steps that led up to the large house, a drooping neem tree was veiled in a haze of small white flowers.

'What a wonderful mass of colour!' she exclaimed, hurrying after her mother who'd continued walking across to the house. 'Lucky Tilly,' she said when she caught up with her.

'And you, too, will be just as lucky.' Smiling, her mother reached across and gave her a hug.

'I do hope you're right,' Clara said, staring at Tilly's house in excitement.

Her mother had told her during their rickshaw ride that Tilly's husband, Michael, would be staying at home until they arrived as he wanted to say hello, but after that he would have to leave for work.

Good, she'd thought. She hardly knew Michael, and it would be so much easier to get to know Tilly again without him there.

Not that she'd be getting to know Tilly again—she'd never really known her in the first place.

She'd always looked up to Tilly, but the seven-year difference in age meant that they'd never been close. But now that she was eighteen, and might even be married before too long, the gap between them would seem far less, and she couldn't wait to meet her sister again.

Deepak, Tilly's head servant, was already holding open

the front door when they reached the entrance, and he ushered them into the house. As they went into the cool interior, Clara glanced at the row of *topis* hanging from the wooden hooks on the wall to the right of the door, and saw from the number there that they might not be the only guests that morning.

Darn, she thought, as she handed her straw cloche to Deepak.

After not seeing her sister for so long, she'd hoped they'd have time to talk that morning, and it was disappointing to think that she might have to share Tilly not only with their mother, but also with visitors. The need for social niceties would inevitably inhibit any sisterly conversation.

With luck, though, she and her mother would be the only ones staying for lunch.

'Clara!' a voice shrieked in delight.

Before Clara knew what was happening, her sister had run into the hall, her dark brown hair flying wildly behind her, and was pulling her into an enthusiastic embrace. Then she released Clara, held her at arm's length, and stared at her.

'Look at you, Clara!' she exclaimed. 'You're all grown up.' And she hugged her again.

'I'm so pleased to see you, Tilly,' Clara said, returning the hug.

To her horror, tears of emotion rolled down her cheeks.

'Ignore me,' she sobbed, smiling through her tears. She wiped her face with her gloved hands. 'It's just that so much seems to have happened so quickly—what Papa said last night, and seeing you now, and seeing George later today.'

'I understand,' Tilly said, laughing.

'I haven't seen him for seven years. I feel as if I'm

standing on the edge of my destiny, if that doesn't sound too silly for words. I'm not a fanciful person, but that's how it feels. And just seeing you has made me so happy.'

Tilly hugged her again. 'You're going to have a wonderful life, dear Clara. I'm sure of it.'

3

M oments later

'GOOD GRACIOUS ME! Could this beautiful young woman be our little bridesmaid?'

Clara turned towards Tilly's husband as he came and stood next to his wife, smiling warmly at Clara.

She blushed. 'Hello, Michael,' she said shyly. 'It's lovely to see you again.'

Tilly tucked her arm into Clara's. 'Come on. We're outside.'

'Who's the we?' Mary asked as she and Michael followed Tilly and Clara across the sitting room to the verandah.

Tilly glanced over her shoulder at her mother. 'We've two visitors, and you know both of them. Michael's boss, Edward Harrington, and also Father's company agent.'

'Lewis Mackenzie!' Mary exclaimed. 'What's he doing here?'

Tilly shrugged. 'To be honest, I haven't a clue,' she said, and they went out on to the wide verandah that surrounded the house.

To Clara's delight, the heavy green bamboo *tattis*, which were frequently pulled down from the verandah roof to protect against the onslaught of the sun, were still rolled up, and a panoramic view greeted her.

She disentangled her arm from Tilly's and took a step forward.

'It's as lovely at the back of the house as it is in the front,' she said.

Her gaze followed the brightly coloured flowers that grew in the pots in the corners of the wide steps leading down to the lush green garden, to the groves of tall graceful coconut trees at the end of the lawn, their fronds a glossy deep green beneath the dazzling blue sky, and beyond them to the sapphire sea that shone in the gaps between the trees.

'You probably take it for granted as you see it every day,' she went on, her eyes still on the view, 'but it's as if I'm seeing it for the first time. And I probably am. I was so young when I left that I wouldn't have noticed the scenery around me. But after years in England, which is greyer and less dramatic, everything here seems so vivid.'

'You're fortunate with the weather,' Tilly remarked. 'Even though the monsoon's passed, we still get quite a lot of rain in September and October. But not today. You're lucky to be seeing the house and garden for the first time when it's sunny, and rain's not falling in sheets.'

'By the sound of it, you've no regrets about leaving England and returning to Cochin. Or have you?' Michael asked as she turned away from the view.

She shook her head. 'No, none at all. I was ready to come back. It wasn't because I didn't enjoy my six years at the school, because I did. And I was happy enough to stay with my English cousins during the holidays, but England never felt like home.'

She glanced towards Tilly and Michael's visitors. The two men had risen from their wicker chairs, which had been grouped around a small table.

Tilly took Clara's arm. 'Let me introduce you to Edward Harrington, Clara. Edward's one of the principal aides to the British Resident, who advises the Maharajah of Cochin. Michael helps Edward in his work. They work on Bolghotty Island, in Bolghotty Palace, which is where the Resident lives. That's the capital of British Cochin, and we tend to refer to the palace as The Residency. Edward, meet my sister, Clara.'

'I'm pleased to meet you, Mr Harrington,' Clara said, shaking his hand.

'The feeling is mutual, Miss Saunders,' he said, inclining his head towards her.

The thought sped through her mind that while he wasn't unpleasant in his appearance, one couldn't describe him as good-looking. And his light brown hair was decidedly flecked with grey.

'And let me introduce you to Lewis Mackenzie, Father's company agent, Clara,' Tilly said, indicating the tall man with sun-bleached hair who was standing next to Edward. 'Lewis has been Father's agent for the past four years. That's right, isn't it, Lewis?'

'Indeed it is,' Lewis said, leaning forward to take Clara's hand. 'It's a pleasure to meet you, Miss Saunders.'

'And for me, too,' she said, colouring slightly as she saw how very attractive he was.

'Both of you know my mother,' Tilly said, moving forward. 'So, now that we all know each other, we can sit down and have some refreshment.' She indicated that Clara should sit on the closest chair.

Michael glanced at Edward. 'Will there be time, or would you prefer us to leave right away?'

'Oh, I'm sure we've time for a coffee first. Michael,' Edward said, sitting down and unbuttoning his lightweight suit jacket.

Lewis sat down again, his chair opposite Clara's, and Michael and Mary took a seat, too.

Tilly indicated to the servant standing in the doorway that they were ready for refreshment.

'It's a very pleasant surprise to see you today, Mr Harrington,' Mary said with a smile.

'It's kind of you to say so, Mrs Saunders. Michael and I will be accompanying a group of visitors who're being taken around the Maharajah's College this afternoon,' Edward told Mary.

He glanced across the table at Clara. 'Forgive me if I'm telling you what you already know, Miss Saunders, but the college is said to be one of the oldest in India, and it has a prestigious collection of rare literature in its library. This afternoon's visitors are extremely interested in the collection, and much of our time will be spent among fairly ancient books.'

'It sounds fascinating,' Clara said politely.

Lewis gave a slight cough. Glancing across at him, she met an amused smile, followed by an almost imperceptible rolling of eyes.

Quelling the urge to giggle, she clasped her hands firmly in her lap.

'Our visitors always expect to be told a little of the history of the area,' Edward continued. 'To be honest, at times I get tired of telling it. As you, too, must have done in

England, I imagine, Miss Saunders. I expect your English friends wanted to learn all about Cochin.' He smiled at Clara.

She nodded. 'I did have to relate the history a number of times. But I virtually know it by heart—we were taught it every year in the school I went to here before going to England. My teachers would have been proud of me as I don't think I missed a thing.'

Counting the events on her fingers, she raised her thumb as she started with Cochin having long been a prosperous spice-trading port, which other countries were eager to rule.

She held up her index finger for the Portuguese being the first to set up a base in Cochin, back in the fifteen hundreds, and doing a lot that was good, such as building a fort and planting coconut trees for trading purposes, but they had a poor administration system.

She raised her middle finger for the Dutch taking control about a hundred years later, and proving to be very extravagant and, like the Portuguese, poor rulers. Ambitious to control a larger area, they were in constant conflict with other rulers, until, at the beginning of the nineteenth century, worried there might be an attack on their nation, they signed a treaty with the British, giving Cochin to the British in exchange for a place in Indonesia.

Her fourth finger was for the British rule, which was only over the small area of Fort Cochin and British Ernakulam.

'Well, how did I do?' she asked with a laugh.

'Admirably, Miss Saunders,' Edward said with a smile. 'When it all becomes too wearisome for Michael and me, we know upon whom to call.'

She laughed again.

'The danger would be,' Lewis said smoothly, 'that the visitors would be so enchanted by Miss Saunders that they wouldn't hear a word of her delivery.'

Tilly glanced at her mother, and imperceptibly raised her eyebrows.

Clara blushed, and fixed her gaze on the marble inlay in the wicker table.

'I expect Cochin looks somewhat different from when you were last here, Clara,' Michael said. 'Instead of British Cochin being separated from mainland Ernakulam by a small island, there's now a large island there, built with the mud dredged from the sea. With the channels on both sides of the island deep enough for all sea-going vessels, Cochin is well on the way to becoming a major seaport. That can't have been much more than a dream at the time you left.'

'It was a little more than that,' she said with a smile. 'The island had been built, but it wasn't yet called Willingdon Island. But coming into the port as it is today was very exciting.'

Michael nodded. 'I imagine it would be.'

'I knew Father had been very worried that with all the changes, companies like his might lose their existing back-water traffic,' she went on. 'But Mother wrote recently that his fears had proved unfounded. Didn't you, Mama?'

'That's right,' Mary said. 'I can't tell you what a relief that is.'

'I echo that.' Lewis told Clara. 'There are numerous berthing facilities alongside the channels on both sides of the island—and not just berths, but godowns and other warehouses, and jetties and stream moorings. And it's still just as easy to get from Muttancherry into the backwaters. In fact, trade has never been better.'

'I was really surprised that the view as you come into the

harbour is still as attractive,' Clara said. 'With the large bamboo fishing nets. And the Flagstaff, and white Court-house behind them. And all the white, yellow and grey Dutch houses, even though they're small.'

Edward nodded. 'The Dutch houses are certainly very different from the spacious, airy bungalows with their long verandahs that we British seek out.'

Lewis leaned forward. 'You're obviously interested in all the changes around you, Miss Saunders. I know how busy your father is, and I wonder if you'd like me to take you around our premises in Muttancherry, and tell you a little about our work these days.'

Clara blushed, and glanced questioningly at her mother.

'The invitation obviously extends to you, too, Mrs Saun-ders,' Lewis added quickly.

Clara looked back at Lewis. Grey eyes dancing with teasing playfulness met her green eyes. He gave her a slight smile. She felt herself colour more deeply.

'Thank you. If Mother is agreeable to our going,' she said, 'I'd enjoy that very much.'

'That's a lovely idea, Lewis. I might even join you,' Tilly said brightly. 'Michael is always so busy that we rarely go further than St Francis and The English Club. And Father's always far too involved in his latest deal to want to stop and tell us about his day-to-day work. Yes, I think I'd enjoy such a trip. Ah, here's our refreshment!' she exclaimed as Deepak appeared, followed by two house servants, each of them carrying a large tray.

'We won't stay long after lunch,' Mary said as Deepak placed a banana leaf on the table in front of each person, put a dish with chunks of pineapple, mango and banana in the centre of the table, and poured their coffees.

'The Goddards are dining with us this evening,' Mary

continued. 'George Goddard and Clara grew up together, Lewis. I'm sure he's looking forward to seeing Clara tonight as much as she's looking forward to seeing him again.'

Lewis inclined his head towards Mary.

'George has grown into a fine young man. But I expect you know that, Lewis, as the Goddards' office isn't far from Henry's,' her mother went on. 'Albert took him to meet the Resident last week. I joined them and Edward for a very pleasant lunch afterwards.'

'Indeed,' Lewis murmured.

Clara felt herself colouring with embarrassment at her mother's blatancy.

Edward would know from Michael of her parents' hopes regarding George, so this will have been for Lewis's benefit. She glanced at Lewis, hoping he hadn't realised what her mother was clearly telling him.

Lewis sat back in his chair, and gave her a long lazy smile.

He obviously had.

Inwardly cringing, she went a deeper shade of red.

If she hadn't loved George as much as she did, she could have easily found herself attracted to Lewis, she realised. He really was very handsome, and his grey eyes were quite striking.

The object of her thoughts turned to say something to Edward, and she studied him from beneath her long dark eyelashes.

Bronzed skin like his, a testament to a life spent more often outside than in, was so much more attractive than pale skin, like Mr Harrington had. And it was much more inviting, she thought, although she wasn't quite sure what it invited. And he was the perfect build for a man—taller than she was, and not too fat, not too thin.

Her school friends had always giggled when they'd tried to imagine what men and women did when they were married, which they knew involved a bed. If anyone was married to someone like Lewis Mackenzie, they'd be sure to enjoy finding out.

'Clara,' her mother prompted. 'Edward was asking you a question.'

'I'm so sorry,' Clara said apologetically. 'I was thinking about bed.' She felt Lewis's eyes jump to her face. 'About the mosquitoes whining on the other side of the net last night. I'd forgotten how much I hated that sound,' she added hastily. 'Would you be kind enough to repeat the question, please, Mr Harrington?'

'After the praise you've heaped on Cochin in the short amount of time you've been back,' Mary said, a note of reproof in her voice, 'Edward asked if there was anything negative that had struck you.'

'I must be a prophet,' Clara said, smiling brightly. 'I answered Edward's question before I'd even heard it.'

'I sympathise, Miss Saunders,' Edward said warmly. 'I, too, dislike mosquitoes.'

THE LUNCH OVER, Clara and Tilly settled down on the verandah, their cane seats side by side so that they faced the coconut groves, a glass of lemonade for each on the table between them.

Clara glanced towards the sitting room. 'Will Mother mind being in there by herself?'

'Not at all! I know she said she was going to read,' Tilly said with a laugh, 'but if she gets as far as the second word on the page, I'd be amazed. She always closes her eyes after lunch.'

Clara smiled. 'I see.'

'So, Clara, how is everything? Are you as happy to be back as you sound?'

'Absolutely. I couldn't be happier.' She beamed at Tilly. 'I'm sure you knew what Papa was going to say to me last night. About George, I mean.'

Tilly nodded. 'We all think it an excellent idea. We thought you would, too.'

'Oh, I do. George and I have been friends for years. Don't tell Mama and Papa, but before he left for England, we actually promised to marry each other. I'm so happy that this is what Father wants.'

'So what was this morning about, then?' Tilly asked steadily.

Clara coloured. 'What d'you mean?'

'You know perfectly well. The thing with Lewis.'

'There wasn't a thing with Lewis, as you put it.'

'We aren't blind, Clara,' Tilly said quietly. 'And we're not stupid. We know what we saw. I dread to think what Edward must have thought at such blatant flirtation. He's Michael's superior, and a highly respected British aide. When he visits, which he doesn't do very often, we try to show the family at its best.'

'I suppose we might have joked around a little. But that's all it was—a bit of fun. It didn't mean anything. It's George I love, and you know it.'

'I certainly hope that's true,' Tilly said, her face serious. 'Lewis is a man of the world, and you're straight out of school. And he works for your father, so it could be said that he isn't our equal.'

'It wasn't serious, Tilly.'

'Well, I'm glad to hear it. Although we're in India, we've a lot of values in common with England, which is not surprising when you think about it. The colonial appointments here are made by the British, and a lot of traders like Father, although born in Cochin, had parents who came over from England, and who sent their children back to England to be educated. Like we were. It means we share the same values with those in England. And status matters to the British.'

'I realise that,' Clara said with a touch of impatience.

'I wonder if you *do*, though. The British community here has turned itself into a typical little English village. Consider how we spend our weekends. It's cricket at the Parade Ground every weekend, and croquet, bowls, billiards and tennis at The English Club. We tend to dine either at the club or at the home of a friend. And we have frequent bridge parties and the like. We could just as easily be in England, as in British Cochin.'

'I understand.'

'It's important that you *do*, Clara. The colonial administrators here, like Michael and Edward, and the traders with origins in England, like our parents and the Goddards, don't just *act* like the people in England, they *think* like them. Obviously, Lewis's background makes him a little different, and also the job he does.'

'I know that.'

'He'd never be considered a suitable match for you, the daughter of a respectable trader with a highly successful company, who was educated in England. What's more, you could jeopardise a marriage with George by such antics if the knowledge of such behaviour got around. The Goddards take social status very seriously, and they would've been appalled by your behaviour today.'

'I'm sorry, Tilly,' Clara said, her voice little more than a whisper. 'I wasn't thinking.'

Tilly hesitated, and then smiled. 'I won't say anything more about it, then. Lewis obviously appreciated you, and that must have been very flattering, so it's not really so surprising that you responded.'

'That's all it was,' Clara said gratefully.

'He'd clearly intended his invitation to be for you only. Mother was added as an afterthought, when it suddenly dawned on him that you wouldn't be allowed out without a chaperone. No unmarried woman from a family of good standing would be seen alone with a man. It'd be very easy to lose your good reputation in a small community like ours, and very hard to win it back. And the Indians, too, would think badly of anyone acting in such an unsuitable manner. Indian men and women don't even hold hands in public.'

'Is this you not saying any more about it?' Clara asked with a wry smile.

Tilly laughed. 'That's a fair point.' She reached across and squeezed her sister's hand. 'We'll change to a more congenial subject. In a few hours you'll be seeing George again. You must be very excited. You can tell me what you're planning to wear this evening.'

4

———

L ater that morning

So, thought Lewis as he stepped off the company launch on to a wooden jetty that jutted out into the water at a point some distance south of Muttancherry.

The densely packed houses and shops that lined the narrow streets in the area around the Muttancherry wharves had given way to coconut groves, and to bright green paddy fields, which hosted a myriad of slender white egrets.

So Clara Saunders was destined for George Goddard, was she, he thought as he moored the boat on the wooden jetty, and started along the dusty path that led to the small boatyard and godown that he owned.

At least, that's what her family was hoping for Clara.

For someone who was supposed to be keen on marrying George Goddard, whom, Henry had confided in him, was widely believed by them all to be the choice that Clara would want to make, she'd been remarkably responsive to the very slight interest he'd shown in her that morning.

And as he intended to show her an even greater interest in the future, her family's belief was going to be put severely to the test.

Because, as of that morning, he'd decided that he, not George Goddard, was going to marry Clara Saunders.

That hadn't been his intention when he'd first seen her the night before, nor when he'd set out from his home that morning.

The night before, under the cover of darkness, he'd been taking the boating equipment, which he'd borrowed without asking, back to the godown at the end of Henry's garden where Henry kept his launch. After padlocking the godown door, he was going up the jetty to the sandy path that would take him back to the road, when he'd glanced up at the Saunders's house, which was just visible through the gaps in the screen of dark green trees in front of him.

Clara had been standing on the verandah, an ethereal figure bathed in moonlight.

He'd moved swiftly to the closest coconut tree and, shielded from sight, had stared up at her.

So that was the woman intended for George Goddard, he thought.

Lucky George.

Not only had he been given a top position in his father's successful trading company without having to earn it by working his way up from the bottom, but now he was also being provided with a suitable companion for life.

Perhaps he, too, should think about getting married, he mused as he watched Clara. Apart from the obvious advantages a wife would bring, he needed someone to supervise his household.

The servants were cheating him, he was sure, and he didn't really have the time to deal with it.

He'd attempted on several occasions to get his head servant to extract a detailed account of the weekly expenditure from his cook, but he'd yet to receive anything that came even close to the truth, and it had become pretty obvious that the head servant was taking a cut of the various scams going on in the Dutch house he was renting.

However, there was no point in replacing any of the servants as the replacement, too, would be almost certain to cheat him. Or even worse, he might turn out like a cook he'd heard about, who was found to be running a brothel out of the servants' quarters.

Having a wife to keep a close check on what was happening in his house could save him a considerable sum each month.

So far, however, the only woman he'd met whom he wouldn't mind having around all the time was Gulika, the Indian girl who looked after the small house owned by the company that he used on his trips to the backwaters, and who was always ready to warm his bed in the most pleasant of ways.

But as having an Indian wife was now frowned upon by the British ruling class, who not so many years ago, in the absence of sufficient English women, had encouraged the new arrivals from England to take an Indian wife, Gulika would have to remain where she was. Given his ambitions, the last thing he intended to do was alienate the very people with whom he hoped to do business.

But it really was time he took a wife, he'd thought as he'd gazed up at the verandah.

He hadn't yet determined at that time, however, that Clara would be that wife. That idea didn't strike him until the visit to the Wakefields.

When he'd woken up that morning, it had occurred to him that it might be interesting to see Henry's daughter in daylight, and, needing to drop in on a trader who was based in Cochin, anyway, he'd decided to call on the Wakefields first, knowing from Henry that Clara would be visiting her sister.

That Clara had liked him had been instantly apparent. He could tell that Mathilda thought so, too, and was far from pleased about it. And that spurred him on to go out of his way to charm Clara.

It was only later when heading down the coast to his boatyard that he'd thought back to his morning visit, and to how Clara had blushed every time she'd looked up at him from beneath her extremely long eyelashes, and at how flirtatious and coy she'd been, giggling at his throwaway comments, no matter how banal, that he'd suddenly taken a great leap of imagination.

A heart-stopping leap.

He'd sat up sharply in the boat. Why shouldn't Clara be his wife?

In fact, it was the perfect solution to everything.

It wasn't that he loved her, because he didn't—he didn't know her. And from what he'd seen of her, she wasn't the sort of woman who attracted him, being just out of school, obviously innocent and prone to easy embarrassment.

He liked a bit of fire in his bedroom activities, such as Gulika provided, and from the short amount of time he'd spent with Clara, he was pretty sure that she'd never be the sort of woman who'd rush to light the flame.

But she was easy enough on the eye, and in fact was

quite pretty, he'd told himself. He couldn't foresee any difficulty in getting along with her. And it wasn't as if he wouldn't be able to continue enjoying a pleasant few hours with Gulika during his every visit to the backwaters.

He reached the bamboo gate that led to his yard and to the godown behind it, and stood there, his hand on the gate, lost in thought as the sun beat down on his *topi*.

Of course, Clara finding him attractive and good company was a long way from her wanting to marry him.

Transferring her affections from George Goddard to him would require patience and effort. To do so, he'd need to spend time with her, and that was going to be a problem.

Her parents wanted her to marry George, so they'd never allow him to court her officially. And Tilly had already shown her displeasure at the sight of him charming her sister, so she wouldn't help him at all. Quite the opposite, in fact. And as Clara would always have to be chaperoned when she left the house, it wasn't going to be easy to spend sufficient time with her to capture her affections.

But he'd find a way, that was sure.

Not because his interest was in her as a person. Oh, no.

It was in her for what she would bring with her. She would bring something of far greater value to him than improved household management and the conjugal ministrations of a wife.

She would bring Saunders & Co.

Henry didn't have a son. One day, he'd need someone to run the company when he no longer could, and that would be the attraction of George Goddard as a son-in-law. But George wasn't the only person who could step into that role.

Henry had said on more than one occasion that Lewis had become like a son to him. Well, he was going to fight tooth and nail to make that a reality. As Henry's son-in-law, he would be the man to whom the business would one day inevitably pass.

This would be a hitherto undreamed-of shortcut to having a company of his own.

Even before he'd stepped ashore in Cochin, he'd wanted to have his own trading company. And from the moment that he'd arrived in the town, he'd worked hard to make his dream come true.

But if he married Clara, he'd as good as have his own company, not immediately, but before too long.

He felt a rising sense of excitement.

What's more, it would be the best thing for the company all round if he were to become the boss. Henry Saunders was stuck in his ways, and wasn't interested in developing the great potential that surrounded them.

Every time he approached Saunders with a way of enhancing their income—perhaps a new route, or a new product to export—he was gently reminded that this was how Henry's father had run the business, and those were the items he'd chosen to export, and those the areas to which he'd chosen to send them, and that was how it was going to stay.

At times, he'd wanted to scream his frustration.

It was true that the company was making a pleasing profit all the same, but even if a company was doing well, they shouldn't become complacent. Every employee in Saunders & Co would benefit if the company expanded.

Other companies were doing just that.

They were grasping the new opportunities with both hands, and they could soon be overtaking Saunders & Co with their volume of trade and monetary returns.

If that happened, Saunders & Co would find itself slipping from its position as one of the top trading companies in Cochin, and potential new customers, seeing the downward spiral of their fortunes, would take their business elsewhere.

But Henry didn't seem to appreciate that.

It seemed to have escaped him that Cochin had become a major international port, with limitless potential for traders, who were now able to trade with places with which they'd never before attempted to trade, and who were dealing in commodities they'd never before handled.

If he, Lewis, took over the running of the company, the company's horizons would widen.

Looking back, he realised that he'd been preparing for this moment for years.

WHEN AS A TINY child in England, he used to help his fisherman father to haul in the nets, and listen to his father tell him that one day the boat would belong to him and his brother, he'd mentally retort that his brother could keep it. It was a legacy he didn't intend to accept.

Just as soon as he was old enough to finish with school, he was going to leave Newlyn.

But he wouldn't be turning his back on the sea.

Ever since he'd first listened, wide-eyed and open-mouthed, to the tales of daring and adventure that his father's fellow fishermen used to relate—tales of spices, sandalwood and silk, carried across the ocean from exciting destinations far and wide, with the sailors forced to battle on the way against pirates and monsters and whirlpools and hidden rocks—he'd wanted to be a trader.

The sea would provide for him, he'd thought with confidence, but in a way that was very different from that of his father, and grandfather before him. He'd no intention of following in their footsteps and staying in Cornwall, wallowing in pilchards for the rest of his life.

And his intention had never faltered.

When he was close to leaving school, he'd told his parents and brother what he intended to do. They didn't attempt to dissuade him.

On the contrary, while they said they were sad at the thought of seeing him go, they couldn't hide their relief. It would have been a struggle for his father's fishing business to have supported more than his parents and the family of one of their sons, and his brother was clearly interested in fishing in a way that he, Lewis, wasn't.

With their blessing, he'd packed a bag and gone to Tilbury Docks, which he knew to be the destination of many cargo-laden boats arriving from overseas, and also the starting point for a number of passenger liners heading for distant parts.

For the first couple of weeks, he'd hung around the docks, listening to what the sailors were saying about the places they'd visited and the places to which they'd be going, and the things he'd heard about British Cochin had appealed to him.

None of the sailors had actually been to Cochin— Bombay had been their port of call on the west coast of India—but they'd carried on board officials and company representatives, who'd disembarked at Bombay and headed south for Cochin.

It was from them that the sailors had learnt about the small seaport that was the centre of the spice trade.

And when he heard that Cochin was governed by the British, and that the residents there spoke English, including the local people, and that it was home to a number of established offices representing the interests of

British trading firms, he'd decided that Cochin was the place for him.

He knew himself well enough to know that he'd never have the patience to follow the traditional route of applying to a British firm based in England, which had a trading office in Cochin, and to work for them in the hope of one day being transferred to Cochin. And then, when in Cochin, to branch out on his own after a suitable period of time.

No, that was much too slow a path for him, with too many uncertainties.

The best way of learning the export business was going to be by working in the heart of the place from which he'd be exporting, he'd decided from the outset.

If he did that, by the time he felt ready to start up on his own, he'd have a thorough knowledge of the area, and of what he could and couldn't supply, and he'd have a list of contacts and potential customers, and he'd know the different sea routes for the various commodities.

With that in mind, he'd applied to join the crew of a liner heading for Australia, and was taken on. The attraction was not Australia—it was that the liner would stop on the way at Bombay.

When they reached Bombay and were allowed to go ashore, he'd disappeared into the crowd, and had stayed disappeared. When the ship had continued its journey, it had been without him—he was already on the first of the trains that would eventually bring him to British Cochin.

Upon his arrival, he'd found a modest Dutch house to rent, and he'd started going around the trading offices in Muttancherry, asking if they needed help.

When he reached the office of Saunders & Co, he struck gold. Only a few days earlier, Henry's company agent had been found drunk once too often, and had been dismissed. Lewis became his replacement.

That had been four years ago.

In that time, never forgetting his goal was to be a boss himself, he'd worked hard for Henry, spent little of his wages and built up modest savings.

And then, two years after starting as Henry's agent, a friendship he'd struck with a village contact in the backwaters, had resulted in him being given an opportunity for the company to make an additional sum of money.

A great deal of money.

Suppressing his excitement, he'd indirectly sounded out Henry, but he'd fast realised that this would never be of interest to him.

After a moment's dejection, he'd decided to take advantage of the proposal himself.

His first steps had been to buy a small, run-down thatched-roof boatyard some distance south of Muttancherry, which was on his route from the Muttancherry wharves to the backwaters, and then to buy a launch and his own *kettuvallam.*

He needed the rice boat as well as a launch as it could carry large, heavy loads, the cargo being well protected by the width of palm-leaf and split bamboo that arched from one side of the boat to the other.

And the identical spiral curve at both the bow end and the stern meant that *kettuvallams* could travel with equal facility in either direction. It made them perfect for navigating the narrow stretches of backwater that connected the lakes and rivers.

It was true that a launch was faster on open water, but it lacked the versatility of a rice boat that could be sailed, poled or rowed, or even be pushed by crew members who'd jump overboard where the water was particularly shallow. And launches didn't have the same capacity.

The attraction of the boatyard was the godown behind it, and as soon as he'd made the purchase, he'd found local men upon whom he could call should he need extra help with his shipments, and who would watch the godown when it was full of stock.

And the last thing he'd done was to start paying Sanjay, one of Saunders's employees on the wharves, to work for him as well as for Henry.

With all that established, the next time he'd gone into the backwaters to collect the fruits of the pepper harvest for Saunders & Co, which was part of his job, he'd agreed a deal with the village man—him personally, not on behalf of Saunders & Co—for the man to collect certain products for shipping and to deliver them to the *kettuvallam* that had brought him there, a deal that was not part of his job.

The village man had a link with a factory that was local to him, from which he collected regularly the goods for a number of different destinations.

Any goods that Lewis could ship through Saunders & Co would yield him a very high reward.

Those destined for places to which the company didn't ship, would have to be delivered to an address that the village man would give Lewis when he gave him the consignment.

Since he'd be no more than a delivery man for those transactions, he'd earn considerably less. It was in his interest, therefore, to send as much through the company as he could.

And Henry was completely unaware of any of this.

No one, apart from Sanjay, had any idea of what he'd been doing for the past two years, and not even Sanjay knew how much extra he'd been making. And to ensure that it stayed that way, and that he continued to escape detection, he'd forced himself to curb his impatience and had refrained from officially setting up on his own.

To have started what would be a relatively small trading company would have been unwise. His company would have stood out among the larger companies, and should there be any suspicion of illegal activity in the area, his boats and godowns were bound to be among the first to be searched, and searched with a thoroughness not accorded to the long-established houses.

He'd reluctantly accepted, therefore, that frustrating though it was, for the foreseeable future he would have to continue operating under the protection of Saunders & Co.

But from the moment he'd realised that Clara was attracted to him, everything had changed.

By marrying her, he was certain to be allowed more say in the way the company was run as Henry would know that ultimately he, Lewis, would be in control.

He'd be able to start being more adventurous in what he did, knowing that the reputation of Saunders & Co would give him all the cover he needed for his activities to remain invisible.

So marry her, he would.

With a smile of great satisfaction, he pushed the gate open and went into his yard.

F*riday evening*

AT THE SOUND of voices down in the hall, followed by move-ment into the drawing room, Clara slid her silver bangles on to her wrist, went across to the rosewood-framed full-length mirror that stood in the corner of her bedroom, and studied her appearance.

The sleeveless black floral dress that she'd bought in England created exactly the effect she'd wanted. Her mother had glanced at it earlier, raised an eyebrow and remarked that something pink might have been more suitable, or a green dress that would have matched her eyes.

She didn't want to look like a girl who'd just returned from school, she'd told her mother very firmly. She wanted to look like an adult, like someone sufficiently grown up to be married. Lizzie wouldn't be dressed as a baby, and she didn't want to be thus clad, either. And anyway, she'd added, the large red and cream flowers broke up the black background and made the dress very suitable for her age.

She ran her hand up the back of her head, caught a few stray hairs and tucked them into the loose coil on the top of her head. Despite her dark auburn hair having a natural curl, she'd never been tempted to wear her hair short and tightly waved, and for the past couple of years, she'd stood out in her class as being the only girl who'd kept her hair long.

Quickly pinching her cheeks to give them more colour, she picked up her matching bolero, and stared once more in the mirror.

In a few moments, she'd be seeing George again after six long years away from him. And this was what he would see when he looked at her.

Butterflies fluttered wildly in her stomach.

She pinched her cheeks again, took a deep breath at the thought of George, and went out of the room and started down the stairs.

Halfway down, she saw George emerge from the drawing room and look up at the landing. Seeing her, he stopped abruptly, and stared.

Her heart pounding, she walked as steadily as she could down the last few stairs, her eyes never leaving George's face. When she reached the bottom stair, she paused.

For a long moment, neither moved.

Then George took a step forward, and Clara jumped from the last stair and flung herself into his arms.

They stood there, hugging.

'You're so beautiful, Clara,' he whispered into her ear, holding her tight. 'You're even more beautiful than you were, and that's saying something.'

'Amit has called us into dinner,' they heard Mary say from close by.

They jumped apart.

Each stared at the other with glistening eyes.

'I think we can take it that you're pleased to see each other again,' Mary said drily, and then her face broke out into a warm smile. 'We're having a drink in the drawing room at the moment, Clara. Lizzie's looking forward to seeing you again, but we thought the first moment should go to George.'

Clara beamed at George.

'I should warn you, you won't be sitting next to each other at the dining table,' Mary said firmly. 'Albert and Julia are keen to know what you thought of England, Clara, so you'll be sitting next to Julia. And Henry is very interested in hearing how you're getting on, George, so you'll be sitting next to him.'

Acutely aware of George in a physical way that was different from anything she'd ever before experienced, Clara followed her mother into the drawing room, surreptitiously glancing sideways at George.

His shoulders were wider now, and the way he walked—it was the walk of a man. And the appreciation in his eyes the moment he'd seen her. It had made her feel quite weak at the knees.

If she'd entertained any lingering thoughts about Lewis Mackenzie, they'd disappeared the moment she set eyes on George.

LED BY HENRY AND MARY, they went into the dining room and took the seats indicated by small white place cards.

The long dining table was covered with a heavy white

cloth. Ferns entwined with red roses lined the middle of the table, in the centre of which stood a silver bowl filled with red roses. Between the ferns had been placed small silver dishes filled with stuffed dates, pickled ginger and crystallised fruit.

Every place setting had an array of silver cutlery, carefully polished and laid out by the table steward who'd been with the family since Clara's birth. A small floral-embroidered doily had been placed at the tip of each dinner knife, and on top of the doily stood a finger bowl in which floated a sweet-scented red geranium. A starched white napkin, folded into a peak, had been arranged in the centre of each place setting.

In the light thrown out by the wall lamps, the silverware and the crystal wine glasses sparkled the length of the table.

'In honour of Clara's return,' Henry said as Amit moved silently around the table, filling the glasses with white wine, 'we're having Indian dishes only this evening. All Clara's favourites. At least, they were her favourites when she was eleven. Let's hope her tastes haven't changed.'

'Hear, hear!' Albert echoed with enthusiasm.

Both he and Henry smiled broadly at Clara.

George glanced at her and grinned, and Lizzie giggled.

She went pink.

To her relief, the table steward entered the dining room, causing a distraction. He was followed by the cook's kitchen assistants, each of whom was carrying a tray with plates of layered flatbreads made of flour, and bowls of beef chunks cooked with ground spices, black pepper, coconut and chillies.

Clara clapped her hands in delight. 'I love *parottas*. Fancy you remembering, Papa.'

'And wait till you taste the *biryani*. Cook insisted you

liked *biryani* made with chicken better than with mutton or beef, so that's what we're having,' her father said, looking very pleased with himself, Unfolding his napkin, he tucked it into his collar.

'Cook's right. Thank you, Papa. You've been really thoughtful.'

'We must credit your mother, too,' Henry said, and he smiled down the table at Mary, who sat at the far end, facing him.

They waited until all the dishes had been placed on the table, and the servants had withdrawn, and then they picked up their glasses.

'How are you getting on with Tamil, George?' Henry asked.

George pulled a face. 'Not that well, despite having been learning it for almost a year. And I'm not that good at Hindi, either.'

Albert smiled at him. 'I would say you're doing pleasingly well, George. It's hard enough to pick up one new language, let alone two, but it's an advantage if we traders can do so. And George is learning about the business at the same time, Clara.'

'I thought everyone spoke English,' she said in surprise. 'All the servants do. We've never had to learn their languages.'

'But that isn't true of all parts of India,' Albert told her, 'and we trade with other Indian states, as well as with overseas countries. Our British community here is very limited in area. Not even the people in the neighbouring states can be relied upon to know English, but we need to be able to converse with everyone.'

Clara pulled a face. 'Poor George. I didn't enjoy my

French lessons as school. Thank goodness I don't have to learn Tamil and Hindi, too.'

'So, Clara,' Albert went on, spooning the spicy beef mixture into the centre of his *parotta*. 'Tell us about the school friends you made. Lizzie said that you and she were friendly with different people. I imagine that like Lizzie's friends, yours also came from a similar background to you, which is so important.'

With an inward sigh, Clara abandoned any hope of an interesting conversation. She'd been dying to hear from Lizzie if George had been excited about meeting her again, but that would have to wait until they could leave the men to their after-dinner drinks.

'I think they did,' she said, 'but I don't really know. Lizzie and I were the only two from Cochin in our year.'

'And what was your favourite subject?' he asked, as he raised his *parotta* to his lips. 'We can assume it wasn't French.'

AT THE END of the meal, the women stayed for a few minutes after the port and Madeira had been brought out, and then withdrew to the drawing room for coffee.

'What did you and Mrs Saunders do today, Clara?' Lizzie asked politely. She lowered her voice. 'We'll have to catch up another time on the things you'd never tell your parents, and when we do, the more salacious and gossipy the better.'

Clara giggled.

'Lizzie!' Julia Goddard exclaimed. 'I heard that! That's no way for a young lady to talk.'

'Oh, I don't think we have to worry, Julia. If they're telling their mothers that they know something unsuitable, you can be pretty sure that they don't,' Mary said, looking at Lizzie in amusement.

Clara and Lizzie exchanged glances, and smiled.

'I was going to ask when you'd arranged for the *durzi* to drop by,' Julia asked, angling herself slightly towards Mary. 'I'd like to have one of my dresses copied.'

'We'll have to get together at some point, Lizzie, or we'll never be able to talk. I know we'll meet on Sunday after church,' Clara said, edging forward in her chair, 'and at The English Club afterwards, but we won't be able to talk properly in either place. There'll be lots of people around, and they'll all want to say hello as we've been away for so long.'

'I know,' Lizzie said gloomily. 'How many times do you want to tell someone your favourite school subject? I'm sorry about Papa. He's got a complete lack of imagination.'

Clara waved dismissively. 'It was nice of him to want to talk. And what else is there to talk about but school?'

'I suppose so.'

'I know we can always go round to each other, but why don't we meet on Monday morning? It'll be nice to get out of the house,' Clara said. 'If we persuaded Tilly to come with us, we wouldn't need either of our mothers. We could leave before it was too hot, take a rickshaw to the Chinese fishing nets, watch them for a bit and then walk from there as far as the church and the Parade Ground. And then go up Princess Street to Tower Road, and have a coffee in Old Harbour House. If there's nothing you have to do, that is.'

'I haven't. And it's a lovely idea. I know we've only been home for two days, but I've got so used to having someone to talk to every day that I miss it.'

Clara nodded. 'Me, too.'

Lizzie inched closer. 'What did you think of George when you saw him? Did you come over all goose-pimply?

Do you like him in the way you know I mean? I'm dying to know,' she whispered.

'It's extremely rude to whisper in company, Lizzie,' Julia said, clearly displeased. 'Your conversation should be suitable for all of us.'

'I'm sorry, Mama,' Lizzie said, and she sat back in her chair.

'I'll tell you on Sunday,' Clara hissed under her breath. 'But the answer's yes.' And she, too, sat back.

A few minutes later, the three men returned, closely followed by Amit with a tray on which there was a whisky and soda for each.

'We thought we'd join you,' Henry said, sitting down. He picked up a box of Light of Asia cigars from the small table next to his chair, and offered them to Albert. Albert took one, and sat down on the chair next to him.

George remained standing.

'Would anyone mind if I stepped out on to the verandah for some fresh air?' George asked.

'I need some air, too,' Clara said quickly, and she stood up. 'I always love the warm evenings here. This time of year in England, it's turning quite chilly.'

The two sets of parents glanced at each other.

'I don't see why not,' Henry said slowly. 'But stay in the light, where we can see you. We haven't forgotten what it's like to be young,' he added, and he laughed.

'They're so embarrassing,' Clara muttered as she and George went quickly through the door and out on to the verandah.

Together, they went across to the balustrade, and leaned against it, gazing into the darkness, their arms touching.

The air around them was heavy with longing.

'The first thing I did when I got to my room on my first

night back,' she said at last, 'was go out on to the verandah and look at the view. It was only then that I felt truly home. I missed Cochin so much.'

'So did I,' he said, and he turned to her. 'And not just Cochin. All the time I was in England, I missed you, Clara. And I've missed you every day of the year that I've been back.'

'Have you really, George?'

He nodded.

'I'm glad because I've missed you just as badly,' she said. 'I used to torture myself that in your final year at school, you'd go to a dance at a girls' school and meet someone else, someone who'd make you forget about me. Or that you'd meet someone at the club after you'd returned. After all, we were so young when we made that promise to each other.'

'I could never forget you, Clara. I've always loved you, and I always will. You know that.'

'The sort of love you feel when you're eleven or twelve is different from the love you feel when you're older. Do you feel that different sort of love?' she asked, and she blushed.

'Yes, I do.' He hesitated. 'And d'you feel that way about me?'

'Oh, yes, I do,' she breathed, and she found herself moving closer to him. He put his hands on her shoulders, and she tilted her face to his.

'George!' his father called. 'We'll be leaving soon.'

Without moving, they smiled at each other. Then he dropped his arms, and they turned again to the view.

'It was very strange last night,' she said. 'When I was on the verandah before going to bed, I had the strongest feeling that someone was watching me. I wondered if it was you.' She glanced at him. 'Was it?'

He frowned slightly. 'No, it wasn't. I'd have called up to you.'

'That's what I thought. I expect I imagined it,' she said dismissively. 'Tell me what you've been doing. How are you finding it, working for your father?'

'The work's really interesting, but I hate having to go to Muttancherry so often. Why our fathers have offices there, I don't know.'

'Could it be that they're traders,' she said lightly, 'and that Muttancherry is in the heart of the business area, and can be approached by road and water? Or perhaps it's that all along the shoreline, there are wharves and jetties and everything else a trader could need, and that it faces Willingdon Island, where the main port is situated? Or that the backwaters are easily accessed from Muttancherry? Could it be for any of those reasons, do you think?'

He laughed. 'I suppose it could be. And I suppose I'll get to love the noise and the dirt of Bazaar Road. Father seems to, after all. And what does it matter that the area is dust-laden and fly infested, and that no one worth knowing would ever go there if they didn't have to for work?'

She pulled a face. 'When you put it like that, it doesn't exactly sound wonderful.'

'It isn't,' he said, moving closer to her, and gazing down at her. 'But you are. Just the thought of coming home to you every evening will lift me out of my surroundings and raise my spirits. I love you very much, Clara—much more than I did when we were children.'

She gazed up into his face. 'And I feel the same about you, George. I can't wait to be in our home, able to close the door on the world, and it to be just us.'

He shook his head gravely. 'I'm afraid our parents are going to lecture us every day for the coming month,' he said.

She looked at him in surprise. 'What about?'

'About this.' He took her by the arms, pulled her to him and brought his lips hard down on hers. After the momentary shock, she melted into his arms, wound her arms around him and kissed him back with the same passion as he was kissing her.

'That's enough, George!' thundered Albert. Red in the face, he stood at the doorway to the verandah, radiating anger. 'You forget yourself, son. You'll apologise to Henry and Mary, and to Clara, too. And then we'll go home.'

Her eyes shining, her hair in disarray, Clara drew apart from George.

'I apologise, Clara,' George said with exaggerated remorse. 'I forgot myself.'

She nodded, her gaze on the verandah floor. 'I accept your apology,' she said, trying not to laugh.

Keeping a straight face with difficulty, George turned and followed his father into the drawing room.

Clara trailed after him, dreading how her parents might respond. They'd risen to their feet and were glaring at the pair of them.

She silently groaned.

George went up to Henry. 'It was most disrespectful to you and Clara, sir. I don't know what came over me.'

Henry growled something indistinguishable.

Clara glanced at Lizzie. Lizzie had her hand in front of her mouth, and was clearly trying to hide her amusement.

She looked quickly away, lest she, too, gave way to the mirth and happiness that were bubbling up inside her.

Standing quietly next to her mother, she waited patiently while the two families said a goodnight to each other that was punctuated with apologies on both sides, desperately longing to be able to escape to her room and give way to the glee and explosion of joy she'd felt as George's arms had surrounded her.

SITTING IN THE DRAWING ROOM, their guests having gone, Henry and Mary faced Clara.

'Albert and Julia are agreed about this,' Henry said. 'And George is being told the same thing this evening. If you and George *do* decide that you want to marry, both families would prefer you to wait for about six months before there's any official engagement announcement.'

He heart sank, and she stared at her parents in dismay. 'But why?'

'Because you both need time to find out how you truly feel about each other,' Henry said. 'Your mother and I married for love, as did Tilly, and we want you to do the same. You and George are young enough not to have to rush at this.' He paused. 'Of course,' he added, 'there'd be no reason why you couldn't marry six weeks after the announcement.'

'Well, I won't pretend I'm not disappointed, Papa, because I am. I wanted to marry George as soon as possible. And I'm sure he feels the same.'

'Believe me, it's for the best darling,' Mary said gently. 'You're clearly strongly attracted to each other, but he's no longer a boy, and you don't really know the man he's become. You need time to do that. And just think, the wedding would be next March, which is comfortably before the monsoon months, and which is a lovely month in which to get married.'

'I suppose so,' she said dejectedly. Feeling close to tears of disappointment, she stood up. 'If you'll excuse me, I'll go to bed now.'

·   ·   ·

As Henry and Mary made their way up the stairs to their bedroom a few minutes after Clara, Mary turned to Albert.

'I don't like seeing her so sad, but it's the right decision. I'm sure, though, darling, that Clara and George *will* get married. This will put your mind at rest about the company, I hope.'

'It does. But if tonight's anything to go by, we're going to have to start organising our days so that we can be extra vigilant.'

'What you mean is, *I* shall have to start organising my day so that I'm free to chaperone them if they want to meet up when George isn't working.'

He smiled. 'Just so. You, or Tilly, or Clara's *ayah*—it doesn't really matter who it is, as long as she has someone with her. We don't want any more episodes like this evening. And we'll invite the Goddards to dinner on a more regular basis.'

'I realise that they behaved badly, Henry, but it's under-standable—they hadn't seen each other for so long. But Clara's not the sort of girl one needs to worry about.'

'One can't be too careful, my dear.'

6

T*he following Monday morning*

THE TANG of the sea was strong as Clara, Lizzie and Tilly sat in a rickshaw, being pulled along narrow cobblestoned streets towards the tree-lined promenade that ran alongside the beach where they'd find the Chinese fishing nets.

They'd been surprised to see the number of small road-side shrines that had sprung up over the years, some set between two very large stones, others crouching among the roots of glossy-leaved banyan trees.

'You certainly know you're back in India,' Clara said in amusement as a cow ambled along at their side for a short distance, and then drew away to graze on tuffs of grass that were growing at the edge of the walkway.

Before long, the street opened out on to a wider sandy track that teemed with a mass of people—*ayahs* tending to the children in their care, merchants carrying their wares on their heads, hawkers with overflowing trays of brightly coloured bangles and beads, some people dawdling along as they took the air, and others scurrying to and fro, a sense of purpose to their movement.

On the beach side of the walkway, a melee of fishermen stood at their stalls, some shouting out the prices of the daily catch, others haggling with buyers over a purchase. Crouching at their feet, beggars sat, their hands open.

And towering behind it all were the huge Chinese fishing nets that fringed the upper part of the beach. After not seeing them for so long, at her first glimpse of the tall graceful structures made of teak wood and bamboo poles, she grasped the side of the rickshaw, leaned forward, and stared.

Lizzie did the same.

'I'd forgotten how dramatic they are,' Lizzie said, her gaze on the nets.

Clara nodded. 'Me, too.'

Tilly smiled at their excitement.

Motionless, the nets hung from the horizontal arm of each structure, like a row of giant hammocks suspended above the sea.

The coolie pulling the rickshaw slowed to let them watch as a man started walking along the horizontal arm of the nets, which had been carefully balanced so that as he walked forward, the net began a slow descent into the sea.

The man knew just when to stop, and how long to leave the net in the water before four or five other men raised it by pulling rhythmically on ropes of different lengths, each of which was weighted with large stones that ensured the correct balance.

'If you like, we'll come one evening when the sun's about to set,' Tilly told them. 'Most of the fishing is done in the

morning and early evening, but the evening is best as the
nets are silhouetted against the sunset. No matter how many
times I witness the sight, I find it breathtaking.'

'I'd like that,' Clara said, sitting back as they reached the
end of the line of fishing nets.

The rickshaw halted. Tilly paid the coolie, and they got
down, and wandered across to the last of the nets, where
they stood watching the fishermen at work.

'Come on,' Tilly said after a few minutes, 'or it'll be too
hot for even a short walk.'

Turning back to the walkway, they walked south as the
beach gradually opened out and they saw St Francis Church
to the left.

Across the road from the church was The English Club
to which her parents had belonged since before she was
born. The long, low building with a red-tiled roof, and a line
of arch-styled windows that ran for the length of the building, and the extensive gardens, were surrounded by a hedge.

They went as far as the drive leading to the main
entrance to the club, which was almost opposite St Francis
Church, and then they crossed the road to the church.

'When we went to church yesterday, I thought it looked
as if it had seen better days,' Clara remarked, staring up at
the weather-worn stone porch and columns, and above
them to the arched windows and tall gable.

'You would, too, if you'd been here since the sixteenth
century, being battered daily by sea winds,' Tilly said. 'Personally, I think it looks impressive and full of old world
charm. And so's the inside, too. You must admit, the wood
carvings on the pulpit and confessional are magnificent.
Don't you think?'

Clara and Lizzie looked at each other and giggled.

'Philistines!' Tilly exclaimed with a laugh. 'Right, let's

continue walking, then. I don't know about the two of you, but I'm ready for coffee.'

Sitting round one of the small tables in the courtyard of Old Harbour House, shaded by mango trees and reddish-brown jackfruit trees, Clara and Lizzie kept throwing each other looks of despair, longing for Tilly to give them some time alone.

Finally, Tilly finished her coffee, picked up her bag and smiled at the two girls. 'I haven't forgotten what it's like to be young and single,' she said, 'even though you think I might have. I'm sure you're dying to talk by yourselves.'

'Not at all,' Lizzie said politely.

Clara laughed. 'Don't listen to her, Tilly. Yes, we are. Thank you for realising that.'

'I'm going to go and look for some silk. The *durzi* will be coming next week and I want him to make me three dresses. He's going to you, too, Clara, and probably also to you, Lizzie.'

'I've a couple of dresses I'd like him to copy, but in material of a different colour,' Clara said.

'Be warned,' Tilly said, waggling her finger in the air. 'I once gave the *durzi* an old dress of mine that I loved so much that I'd worn it to death. It had even been patched a couple of times. I asked him to make me one just like that. And he did.' She laughed. 'Right down to the two patches!'

'Ouch!' Lizzie exclaimed.

'Before he comes, I suggest you talk to your mothers about what you might need in your wardrobe. Because of Michael's work, we frequently get invited to functions at The Residency. And Edward often kindly extends the invitations to Mother and Father, and to your family, too, Lizzie.'

'That's kind of him,' Lizzie said with a smile.

Tilly stood up. 'So both of you will need a suitable frock for any such occasion, and hats and gloves. And when you choose the material, remember that it's much warmer here than in England.' She pulled her gloves on. 'I'll be off now. You'll stay here, won't you? It wouldn't be appropriate for you to go anywhere on your own. I'll not be long. Order another coffee if you wish, or a mango juice.'

And she headed for the large arched entrance, and out to the street.

'I thought she'd never go,' Clara said, slumping.

'I know. I've been dying to talk to you,' Lizzie said. She leaned forward. 'Well?' she asked eagerly. 'What did you think of George? Obviously, I've got some idea after that display at your house—both our families have— but that could have been mainly on George's side. After all, he would have pounced on you, not the other way round. Or was it?'

Clara giggled. 'I wouldn't say there was any pouncing involved. George kissed me, and I kissed him back.'

Lizzie grimaced. 'The idea of someone kissing your brother is a bit sickly. But I suppose it's got to happen if you're going to become my sister, and I certainly hope you are. I'd much rather have you as my sister than some girl from Calicut.'

Clara sat up straight. 'That's funny. Papa mentioned a girl in Calicut. Who is she?'

Lizzie waved her hand dismissively. 'It was an idea of Father's not long after George returned from England. Father had got friendly with a spice merchant there, and there was some suggestion that the man's daughter and George might marry.'

'What did George say about that?'

Lizzie shrugged. 'I wouldn't know—I was still in

England, wasn't I? But Papa and your father came up with a much better idea, and Calicut died a death. Knowing George, though, I imagine he'd have fallen in with Father's suggestion. He gets more like him every day. But he obviously loves you, and if you like him—'

'I *do* like him, Lizzie; ever so much. I always have done, and I still do. I like him even more than I used to.'

With a mock-severe expression, Lizzie held up her hand. 'I think we'll stop there, or I really will be sick.'

Both laughed.

'What about you, Lizzie? Have your parents hinted at any plans for you? After all, they had a plan for George—two plans, by the sound of it—so they're bound to have been thinking about your future, too.'

'Father said something about a man in Madras. His name's John Lansdowne. Apparently, he's high up in the colonial administration there. Father met him when he went to Madras to sign a contract to supply a Madras factory with coir—you know, the fibre from the outer husk of the coconut. I've said I'll meet the man at some point, but that I want to get used to being back in India first.'

'Aren't you excited about meeting him? I would be.'

Lizzie shrugged. 'Anyone Father chooses is bound to be stuffy. He's only interested in a person's income, background and status. Whereas I'm more interested in the way they look.'

'You'd need to know that they can support you, too, though, otherwise they'd soon stop looking good,' Clara remarked. And then her face fell. 'But you'd have to move away if you married your Mr Lansdowne, wouldn't you?'

'That's one of the reasons why I'm not as excited as I might have been.'

'I do hope you meet someone here then, and soon. Before your father's plans are too far advanced.'

'Fortunately, he doesn't seem in a rush about it. He's talked more about George's visit to The Residency, which was apparently very pleasant and not unduly formal.'

'You're father's met the Resident before, though, hasn't he?'

'Several times. Papa's hoping to be elected to the Legislative Assembly, so he's been meeting lots of important people. But George hadn't met him before. Apparently, these days you no longer have to drop a calling card into The Residency—you just sign the visitors' book.'

'And what happens then?'

'You're invited to at least one event. Rumour has it that one of the Resident's assistants types out each name under a particular heading, such as Cocktails or Buffet Lunch for the less important, or Luncheon or Dinner, for those higher up the social ladder. Younger people are invited to Tea and Tennis or Croquet.'

'I take it George was invited to tea.'

Lizzie nodded. 'That's right. Last year, Father was invited to Luncheon, and George said he's been full of it ever since. George thought the tea very good and the Resident charming. And that was it. It was mildly interesting when I heard it the first time, but after the twentieth time, any interest had gone.'

'If he's so busy getting George noticed, you've time to see if there's anyone in Cochin you'd like to marry. I do hope there is. I like the idea of us both living here.'

'So do I,' Lizzie said with a smile.

Clara took a sip of her coffee. 'We must take Tilly's advice and get the *durzi* to make us a few lovely dresses so that we're ready for any social functions. Me, so that George doesn't look at anyone else. And you, so that when you meet a tall, dark, handsome man, whom you instantly like, he'll fall madly in love with you. He must live in Cochin, though, not in Madras.'

Lizzie gave her a sly smile. 'There's no need,' she said. 'I wasn't going to say anything today, but I find I can't hold it in any longer. I've already met the man I want to marry. And it's not John Lansdowne.'

She sat back, and smiled at the astonishment on Clara's face.

Clara frowned, perplexed. 'But we've not even been back a week! The only places you've visited are our house, St Francis Church and The English Club. Did you meet someone at the club yesterday? Is that it?'

Lizzie shook her head. 'No. It was before that. Think back to the church.'

Clara frowned more deeply. 'I'm trying to think, but I can't come up with anyone. All I can remember is George being dragged away by your father to meet someone, and you and me standing next to our mothers, responding politely to every exclamation of delight at us being back, and us answering endless questions about school, while doing our best to disguise our boredom. I don't remember any attractive men coming over.'

'That's because you kept trying to see what George was doing and who he was talking to. You had your back to me most of the time.'

'I was hoping that George and I would get a moment or two together, despite being closely watched by our parents to ensure that there was no second act of gross impropriety, as they called it. Of deliciousness, as I'd call it.'

'Ugh!' Lizzie exclaimed.

'But we didn't get a single moment together, thanks to

their relentless efforts. So, did they introduce you to some-one, then?'

'Not exactly,' Lizzie said with a giggle. 'I was standing there by myself, bored stiff, desperately hoping we'd soon go across to the club, by which time the worthy people of Cochin should have exhausted their supply of predictable questions, when all of a sudden, someone behind me said something about the sterling work of the *punkah* coolies throughout the service. It was a man's voice, so I turned to him.'

'Naturally,' Clara said lightly. 'So, who was it?'

'I didn't know then, did I? But to say that he was attrac-tive doesn't do him justice. He said he'd been so fascinated watching the *punkahwallahs* sitting cross-legged in the open arches down the side of the church, pulling the *punkah* ropes as if their lives depended upon it, that he hadn't heard a word of the service. Then he apologised for not waiting to be introduced, and said his name was Lewis Mackenzie.'

'Father's company agent!' Clara exclaimed. 'Well, I'm amazed! I met him on Friday morning at Tilly's. I didn't see him in church, nor at the club afterwards, but then I didn't actually look for him as I wouldn't have expected him to be there. Or at least, not at the church.'

'He said he couldn't go to the club yesterday—he had things to do in advance of a trip he's got to make this week. But I'm surprised you didn't notice him outside the church —I saw him staring at you a few times.'

'That'll be because we'd met on Friday. He might have intended to say hello again, but that would've been difficult with the cavalry at my side.' She paused. 'So it's Mr Mackenzie you think would make a good husband, is it, rather than Mr Lansdowne?'

Lizzie smiled broadly. 'That's right. Imagine it, Clara,

having someone like that coming home to you each evening.'

'You don't think your father might be against it?' Clara said, looking worried. 'After all, Mr Mackenzie's an employee, not a boss, and that sort of thing matters to fathers. If your father withheld his consent, you'd have to wait till you were twenty-one.'

'He'd be worth waiting for. But you're jumping too far ahead. He might not want to marry me.'

'I'm sure he will. You're really pretty, Lizzie, and you've got lovely blonde hair and blue eyes. When we used to go to the boys' school for dances, you were always being asked to dance.'

'No more than you.' Lizzie sat back and studied Clara. 'So you saw Mr Mackenzie on Friday, did you? What did you think of him?'

Clara hesitated. 'The same as you. I thought he seemed very pleasant, and yes, he was very attractive.'

Lizzie bit her lip. 'As attractive as George?'

Clara laughed. 'Of course not. I love George, don't I? I could never feel about anyone else the way I feel about George.'

Lizzie's shoulders slumped. 'That's a relief. I wouldn't want us to like the same man. You and George aren't yet engaged, after all.'

'But we're going to be. Anyway, back to Mr Mackenzie. How are you going to go about seeing him again? I doubt it'll be easy as he must frequently go off on trips, which could last a few days. For example, Papa said Mr Mackenzie was going to the backwaters this week to check that the pepper vines aren't too waterlogged after the last downfall of rain. Apparently, they're prone to a fungal disease that could kill the vines. I wasn't really listening, but I think he said Mr Mackenzie wouldn't be back till Thursday.'

Lizzie shrugged. 'Our parents used to go to the club most weekends, didn't they? I'm sure they still do. They certainly went yesterday after church, and we went with them. I'd be amazed if Mr Mackenzie doesn't go, too, whenever he's in Cochin. So I'll see him there.'

Clara looked doubtful. 'But when we go there, we're under the watchful eye of our parents. Yours will be doubly vigilant as there's someone lined up for you in Madras.'

Lizzie frowned. 'All right then, what about this? If we see Lewis again on a Sunday morning, we could drop him a hint that we plan to come here for coffee on a certain day. If he knows that, he might join us. Tilly would probably come with us like she has today. If he turned up, it would show he was interested in me, wouldn't it?'

'I suppose so.' She hesitated. 'We must be careful what we say, though. Tilly would never agree if she thought that either of us was angling for Mr Mackenzie.'

'You don't know that for sure, but anyway, we wouldn't tell her. If she saw him with us, she'd think it a chance meeting. Or better still, if you could cleverly find out from your father when Mr Mackenzie—or Lewis, as I now think of him—will be in Muttancherry, we could find an excuse to go to your father's office and see him. You'll help me, won't you, Clara?'

'Of course, I will. I suppose my *ayah* could accompany us to Muttancherry. Neither our mothers nor Tilly would.' Clara leaned forward, her face anxious. 'I know you like Mr Mackenzie, but don't make any big decisions yet, Lizzie. You'll meet people at colonial functions, and you might meet someone you'd find even more attractive than Mr Mackenzie.'

'I could say the same about you and George,' Lizzie retorted. 'Not that you need to worry—George clearly adores you. And it's just as well for me that he does as I wouldn't want to be in competition with you for Lewis.'

They both laughed.

7

Late Monday morning

Struggling to control his impatience to get to the Muttancherry wharves, and thence to his boat-yard, Lewis cursed as he was continually forced to weave his car between the pull-carts, plethora of rickshaws, the people on foot, and the occasional cow that blocked Bazaar Road.

Street traders lined both sides of the narrow road, at times overflowing on to the dusty track itself: shoe repairers sitting cross-legged on the litter-strewn ground; street tailors working their ancient machines; barbers plying their trade, and spice ladies squatting behind woven mats that were covered with mounds of spice of every imaginable colour.

Behind them gaped the open-fronted shops of well-to do merchants—hardware shops, spice stalls, jewellery kiosks, shops selling every variety of silk and material, and stalls piled high with fruits and vegetables. Every so often, the row of shops was broken by a colourful red and gold temple complex, fronted by ragged-clothed beggars, hopeful of coins from worshippers.

At last, he reached the wharf near the office of Saunders

& Co. He left his car, and hurried down to the edge of the wharf, hoping that Sanjay had left the company's launch in the place where he'd asked.

As he neared the water, he anxiously scanned the rows of *kettuvallams* lined up by the jetty, some of which were Henry's rice boats, and others those of rival traders, and the tugs and workboats, trawlers and barges, ancient floating dredges and small fishing boats that crowded the strip of sea between Willingdon Island and Muttancherry.

The launch was in position, he saw in relief—he had a lot to do that day—and he hurried across to its mooring.

HAVING REACHED his destination and secured the launch, Lewis walked along the short wooden jetty to the dusty path that led to his boatyard. As he did so, he glanced down at the launch that was moored securely at the top of the sloping ramp next to the jetty—the launch that *he* owned, not the company.

But he wouldn't be going by launch the following day, not his, not the company's. Rather, he'd be in one of the company's *kettuvallams*.

He and Sanjay would be setting out from the Muttancherry wharf nearest Henry's office, and at the end of the trip, they'd return to the same wharf. But unknown to Henry, they'd be making a short stop at Lewis's boatyard on the way back to unload those of the goods that were to be delivered elsewhere.

After that, they'd continue to Muttancherry, where they'd unload the rest of the goods.

He was pretty certain that the number of trips to the backwaters was going to increase in the future, and knowing that the security of his godown needed to be improved, he'd brought with him that morning several strong metal padlocks.

He'd also arranged for his men to join him at the yard as he wanted to talk to them about shoring up the walls of the godown.

He lifted the latch, pushed the gate open, and went across the yard to the open-fronted building where several men in white shirts were standing talking, each of whom was wearing a skirt-like *lungi* wrapped around his waist.

To the right of the building, between its wall and a tall mesh fence that paralleled the water's edge, a narrow path led to the godown.

He stared with dislike at the *bidis* the men were smoking, and at the discarded butts on the ground.

When he'd first arrived in Cochin, and had wanted to fit in, he'd taken one of the small *bidis* offered to him by a company worker, who'd explained that it was a hand-rolled cigarette made of tobacco, wrapped in *tendu* leaves and tied with string at one end.

He'd lit it, and promptly choked. He hadn't even been able to finish it. How they could smoke them, he didn't know, especially as they had to be frequently drawn to keep them alight, and that required effort.

He shook off the distaste he always felt when he saw the men with their *bidis*. The trip that week promised to pay him well, and that was all that mattered.

Most of the following day would be taken up with travelling through the silent backwaters to the village house owned by Saunders & Co. Gulika would be at the house when he got there, which was a very pleasant thought, but she was a treat that would have to wait till later.

His first task when he reached the village would be to alert his contact to his arrival, and when they met, to give him the orders for Saunders & Co, most of which were for consignments of peppercorns that were ready for shipping, having been dried in the sun for six days, and there was also an order for cardamom.

When they'd loaded his orders on to the *kettuvallam*, they'd put into a separate part of the boat the goods for destinations other than Saunders & Co, a small number of which would be shipped through the company, and the rest he'd be delivering to an address given him by his contact.

For doing this, he was going to be paid very well.

But good as it was now, it was going to get better, much better.

He walked across the dusty yard to the men who worked for him. As he neared them, he saw them straighten up in deference.

He smiled to himself in satisfaction.

8

T he following Sunday,
    the beginning of October

AS THE CHURCH bells chimed loudly in the stillness of a town where everyone abstained from work on a Sunday, natives and British alike, the congregation swarmed out of the Church of St Francis and gathered in groups in front of the arched entrance.

Emerging ahead of her parents, Clara moved swiftly to stand beneath one of the two pinnacles constructed on either side of the stone façade, where George would be certain to see her.

A moment later, he hurried from the church, glanced quickly around, and saw her. Smiling broadly, he went towards her.

Her heart leapt, and she half-ran towards him.

Just as they reached each other, his father called his name.

Both stopped. They stared at each other in consternation.

Glancing over George's shoulder, she saw that his parents and Lizzie were standing at the other side of the doorway with a couple of men she presumed were traders.

She groaned loudly. 'I think your father wants you to meet some people.'

Annoyance clouded George's face.

His father called again.

With a slight shrug, and a rueful smile, George went back to his parents.

Lizzie caught her eye.

Assuming an expression of helplessness, Lizzie indicated her parents and the people with them, signalling the impossibility of walking away from them. She pulled a face, and turned back to the group with obvious reluctance.

Her mother and father had stopped to talk to the vicar, she noticed, and she decided to wait for them to join her.

Looking around, her gaze came to rest on the cenotaph in the middle of the lawn, which had been built as a memorial to the people of British Cochin who'd died in the war. The sight of it made her think back to what some of the girls in her class had been saying during their last year of school.

When they'd returned to school after their half-term holiday, several of them had said that people were talking about the possibility of another world war.

She'd fervently hoped they were mistaken, and surrounded by the loveliness of Cochin, with the brilliant blue sky above her, the greenery all around her, and beyond The English Club, a band of shining yellow sand and an aquamarine sea, she was sure that they must have been.

But what if they were right? Would that affect George?

She felt a sudden alarm.

'Miss Saunders.' The sound of her name cut through her thoughts, and she turned towards the owner of the voice.

'Mr Mackenzie!' she exclaimed with a smile, and she looked quickly to see where Lizzie was, but people were blocking her view. 'How nice to see you again,' she said. 'I trust your trip went well last week.'

'How gratifying that you know my movements well enough to be aware that I was, indeed, away from Cochin. It was highly successful, thank you.'

'Papa must have been pleased.'

He inclined his head to her.

'This is going to sound very rude of me, I'm sure,' she said, her eyes dancing with amusement, 'and it's not really something to be said outside a church, but I gather from my friend, Lizzie Goddard, that you were at church last week, too. I wouldn't have thought of you as a person with an interest in the spiritual.'

He laughed. 'Well, that depends upon the sort of spirits you're talking about! Which brings me neatly on to The English Club. I presume you're going there after you've been here for an acceptable period of time, once you've made sure that Saunders & Co has been seen by the entire congregation.'

'Are you always this cynical?'

He pretended to think for a moment. 'I would say so, yes.'

She giggled, and then put her hand to her mouth. 'Don't make me laugh. I've already been in trouble since I returned about my behaviour. I don't want another lecture.'

'Just to prove how spiritual I truly am, isn't there some-thing in the Bible about one person not judging another, less that person be judged, and about a person not condemning another, less that person be condemned? You could quote that in the future, if again chastised.'

'Now I'm really impressed.'

'Your father's joined Albert for a moment,' Mary said, coming across to Clara. 'What are you so impressed about, Clara?'

'Mr Mackenzie has been quoting Scripture to me.'

'Then that makes two of us who are impressed, Lewis. And to be honest, surprised, too. Apart from last Sunday, I can't remember the last time I saw you at church.'

He laughed. 'I'm afraid I've been found out, Miss Saunders. The scriptural knowledge comes from school, not from St Francis. I came last week, and also today, as I'm keen to win a contract on behalf of the company, and I was pretty sure that the other party might be here. I thought that presenting myself as a churchgoer might help me to secure the deal.'

'And did it?' Clara asked.

'So far, no. Annoyingly, he wasn't here on either occasion. It means that I've endured two sermons of utter tedium for no good reason.'

Clara and Mary exchanged smiles.

'Maybe some good has rubbed off on you, nevertheless,' Mary remarked.

'Perish the thought! I do hope it hasn't,' Lewis countered with speed, and all three laughed.

'Hello, Mother.' Tilly appeared at her mother's elbow.

'No Michael, I see,' Mary said, glancing over Tilly's shoulder.

'He'll meet us at the club. He's gone for a short stroll with Edward. They've something to discuss that couldn't wait. Edward is joining us at the club, too.'

'Sounds intriguing,' Lewis murmured.

Tilly smiled politely, and then turned to her mother. 'I'll walk over with you and Clara, if I may?'

Mary nodded. 'Of course. You don't have to ask.' She glanced towards Henry. 'It looks as if your father's just about finished his discussion. You can be sure it was all about work and nothing to do with this morning's service.' She turned back to Lewis. 'I imagine we'll see you at the club, Lewis. Now that's a place I do recall seeing you on a Sunday morning.'

He grinned at her. 'You imagine correctly, Mrs Saunders. But I need to have a word with a friend first. I'll see you there.' With a smile at Clara, he moved away.

'I'll get your father,' Mary said. 'You girls start walking.' And she went across to Henry.

'Mr Mackenzie always goes to the club on Sundays,' Tilly said, tucking her arm into Clara's as they started walking in the direction of the Parade Ground, which was opposite the entrance to the drive leading to the club building. 'He's one of those who rolls up at about midday, ostensibly for casual conversation, drinks and billiards, which he plays well, but in reality hoping to be asked back to lunch by one of the married couples.'

'What happens if no one invites him back?'

'Either he ends up in one of the chummeries, I suppose, eating scrambled eggs and washing them down with gin or beer, or he'd go home.'

Clara's forehead wrinkled. 'What's a chummery?'

'A boarding house or a bachelor mess. It used to be where unmarried British army officers were quartered, but you don't have to be one of the soldiers now to go to a chummery.'

'I doubt Mr Mackenzie will have to resort to that,' Clara

said firmly. 'I'm sure he can talk himself into anything, and that someone's bound to ask him to lunch.'

'Who are you talking about?' Mary asked, catching up with her daughters as they crossed the road.

'Lewis Mackenzie,' Tilly said. 'I was telling Clara that he'll be hoping for an invitation to lunch somewhere.'

'I'm sure you're right,' Mary said.

'Do you ever invite him to our house?' Clara asked.

Mary shook her head. 'Rarely. He's your father's employee, which would somewhat inhibit conversation. And any conversation would be about work. Your father talks about work six days of the week, as well as on Sunday mornings, as you'll have seen. The last thing I want is traders' conversation over Sunday lunch, too. As for today, the Goddards are lunching with us, including George, and I hope, Clara—'

'What were you saying about no traders' talk at lunch?' Clara interrupted brightly. 'You should be safe. After all, Papa and Mr Goddard wouldn't dream of talking about work at lunch, would they?' Her voice rose in amused incredulity.

Mary smiled. 'You're not going to deflect me from saying that I trust you'll remember how you and George should be comporting yourselves.'

'The scripture that Mr Mackenzie quoted was a caution against one person judging or condemning another, lest that person be judged or condemned himself,' Clara said with mock gravity. 'Or herself.'

'Mr Mackenzie said that?' Tilly exclaimed. She laughed. 'Mind you, I can definitely see Lewis wanting to deter anyone from judging him. It wouldn't surprise me at all if his transgressions weren't large in number.'

'What makes you say that about Lewis?' Clara asked

Tilly as they turned down the drive and headed for the club building. Beyond its red-tiled roof, the deep blue sea sparkled.

'Instinct tells me that in matters to do with work, he could sail a little close to the wind. But he's an excellent company agent, and I'm sure that Father has the measure of him.'

Clara nodded. 'I see.'

They reached the three red stone steps that led to the entrance. Unlinking their arms, Tilly went ahead into the building with her mother.

Clara paused. She looked up and sniffed the air. The salty scent of the sea was strong. She inhaled more deeply with pleasure, and then followed the others inside.

In a matter of minutes, she and George would be together again, she thought happily as she passed a sign advertising the club's amateur dramatic society, and she swallowed her desire to shout with glee. With luck, they'd manage a few minutes to themselves.

Since she'd been home, she'd had no more than the occasional glimpse of George, apart from at the dinner with his parents, and that wasn't enough. They'd so much to talk about—what they'd been doing, their plans for the future, their feelings for each other—and for that they needed some quiet time together.

She looked back at the people behind her, but there was no sign of George, so she followed her mother and Tilly through the anteroom, past the men sitting in armchairs reading newspapers and magazines, and out into the garden.

They chose one of the groups of cane chairs that had been set around a table that was shaded by a large dark umbrella, a number of which had been placed at intervals across the garden, and sat down.

Immediately, two servants clad in white, wearing white turbans, placed an iced drink in front of each of them, and asked for their order. Her mother and Tilly both ordered a pink gin, and she asked for a lime juice.

She removed the straw hat encircled with a cornflower blue ribbon that matched the colour of her cotton dress, pushed her hair behind her ears, and glanced towards the people playing croquet further down on the lawn.

A sudden rush of air next to her made her turn, and she saw to her delight that George had sat in the chair next to hers.

'Is it all right to sit here?' he asked. 'Or were you saving it for someone else?'

'Let me think,' she said, adopting a thoughtful pose. 'No, I think it'll be all right for you to sit there.' And she laughed.

Then she saw the expression on his face, and her laughter died away.

She frowned. 'You weren't being serious, were you? You must know I've been longing to talk to you. Who else would I want next to me?'

'Lewis Mackenzie.'

She stared at him in amazement. 'Why would I want to sit next to him and not you?'

'You tell me. All I know is that when I saw the two of you outside the church this morning, you seemed to be getting on extremely well.'

'He works for Father, so he'll obviously go out of the way to get on with Father's family. He's got a pleasant manner, and is easy to talk to. But it's aimless talk and doesn't mean a thing. I love you, George. You know that.'

'But I don't know that. You talked to him for long enough.'

'Because you were talking to your father's friends!' she retorted. 'And so was Lizzie. And my parents were some-where else. Mr Mackenzie probably saw that I was alone, assumed I'd be feeling uncomfortable standing there by myself, and came over to join me. It was a kindness on his part, but nothing more.'

She saw his features relax. 'You're right. I'm just being silly. I'm sorry, Clara. It's just that you're so lovely that I'm terrified of losing you to someone else.'

'And I couldn't bear to lose you. The answer's simple' she said lightly. 'We must get our parents to agree to a wedding sooner than they want. I can't wait to marry you.'

He edged his chair closer to hers, and took hold of her hand. 'Nor me you. You and me together for the rest of our lives. Oh, Clara. You've no idea what that thought is doing to me.'

Their heads moved closer.

'I think that's far enough, don't you?' Julia said coming up to the table. She sat down opposite Clara and George, who drew apart with reluctance. 'Your father's arranging for our drinks, George. I'm not sure where Lizzie's got to. She was here a moment ago.'

'I'm here,' Lizzie said, coming up behind her mother's chair. 'I thought of taking a short walk by the beach, and I wondered if you'd like to come with me, Clara.'

Clara glanced at George, and then back at Lizzie. 'Couldn't we take a walk in a little while? We've only just sat down and I want to talk to George.'

'It won't be for long. You'll still be here when we get back, George, won't you? And you won't let anyone sit on Clara's chair, will you?' Lizzie commanded.

George glared at Lizzie, and then looked back at Clara. 'I know that tone of voice. Lizzie won't give us a minute's peace if you don't go. It's easier to give in. Don't be long, though, will you?'

'Just a short walk, then, Lizzie,' Clara said in visible irritation.

'It will be,' Lizzie said tersely.

And Clara got up and went with Lizzie across the garden to the path that led to the sea.

'Why did you take me away from George?' Clara asked as they walked between the hedges on either side of the path. 'You know how little time we've had together since I got home.'

'You had enough time to talk to someone else, though, didn't you? You and Mr Mackenzie had quite a lot to say to each other this morning. I was watching you.'

Clara saw that Lizzie's eyes were glistening.

'Not you, too,' she said, with more than a trace of annoyance. 'I'm not at all interested in Mr Mackenzie, Lizzie,' she added firmly. 'As I told George, he was keeping me company because I was by myself. It was George I wanted to talk to, but your father had other ideas. And you didn't come over.'

'Father wanted us there as a family. He's just struck a deal with a man who was there, who's got a factory in Alleppey where they make all sorts of mats and carpets. We're going to be shipping a lot of our coir to them.'

'I'm not saying that you should've been with me and not your family. I'm just pointing out that I was on my own till Mr Mackenzie spoke to me.'

'There wasn't that much speaking from what I could see. You were both laughing and joking.'

'Oh, I see,' Clara said. She stopped at the edge of the sand, and turned to Lizzie. 'So it would have been all right if it was a heavy conversation, or we were boring each other to death, would it, but not if it was pleasant? Just because I love George, and I do, I'm not going to stop talking to other people, too, Lizzie.'

'I don't expect you to,' Lizzie said quickly.

'Well, it sounds as if you do. Even talking to the man Michael works for, Edward Harrington, would have been better than standing much longer on my own. Although I suppose I could've forced myself into a conversation I wasn't interested in, with people who bored me. Perhaps you would have liked that better.'

Lizzie leaned forward and hugged Clara. 'I'm sorry,' she said. 'I'm being silly.'

She tucked her arm into Clara's and they started along the narrow walkway at the edge of the sand. 'It's just that I really like what I've seen of Mr Mackenzie. Even if there were boatloads of eligible men in Cochin, I'd still want to know him better.' She gave an awkward laugh. 'Of course, he might not feel the same about me.'

'I'm sure he does,' Clara said. 'I can't imagine him not liking you.' She hesitated. 'I'm wondering, though,' she started, and then stopped.

Lizzie faced her in anxiety. 'What're you wondering?'

'It's something Mama said earlier on. She said we wouldn't invite Mr Mackenzie to lunch at our home because he's an employee. Unless it's to do with work, obviously.'

'He's your employee, not ours!' Lizzie snapped.

'And Tilly said he wasn't our equal. That wouldn't matter to you and me, I know, but your father's even keener on status than mine.'

'My parents just want me to be happy. George is working for the business, and will take it over, so it doesn't really matter who I marry.'

Clara smiled at her. 'Well, you know your parents better than I do. It would certainly be fun if we were both marrying and starting a family at the same time.'

'I'd like that, too.' Lizzie stopped walking and turned to Clara. 'Promise me that you'll keep away from Lewis, but that if you *do* talk to him because it'd be rude not to, you try to bring the conversation round to me. You could try to find out if he likes me.'

'You're wrong if you think he's any interest in me. For a start, he knows I'm marrying George.'

'Promise me.' Lizzie's voice was sharp.

Clara shrugged. 'All right, I promise.'

9

T *he following Friday evening*

IN A VIVID BLAZE OF CRIMSON, orange and yellow, the sun sank slowly into the horizon, sending forth a dazzling pathway of gold that tapered across the ebony water to the shore.

Clara stood with her parents, their backs to the town, and stared at the tall slender structures of the Chinese fishing nets, stark silhouettes against a flame-red sky.

Then they turned away and started walking slowly down the promenade, glancing idly at the many tables from which fishermen were selling fresh fish.

In between the fishermen were stalls laden with fruit and vegetables, rolls of fabric, medicines, brass and tin-ware, and kiosks displaying brightly coloured trinkets and bangles, which reflected the red-gold blush of the dying day.

All around them, they could hear the rhythmic pulsation of stringed sitars, the high-pitched barking of feral dogs, the clamour of hawkers selling their wares, the bartering between vendor and customer, the creaking of rickshaw wheels, the wailing of children and the laughter of young and old alike.

She sighed loudly with contentment. 'Tilly was right. This is the time of day to come.'

'It is, isn't it?' agreed a voice from behind her.

All three turned instantly.

'Edward!' Mary exclaimed with pleasure. 'How lovely to see you.'

'Like you, I thought I'd join those on the walkway and catch the sunset at its most glorious. I don't come here often enough. But it captures the essence of Cochin, I always think. I suspect you feel the same, Miss Saunders. I saw your face in profile as you stared at the view, and I saw how you relished it.'

She put her hand to her cheeks. 'Am I such an open book?'

He smiled at her. 'In this matter, yes. But who wouldn't be, especially someone who's just returned to the town after several years away? England has many wonderful sights to offer, but few can compare with Cochin at sunset.'

'You're right, Mr Harrington. My face spoke the truth—it's absolutely lovely. I can see myself coming here on as many evenings as possible.'

Mary pulled her light shawl around her shoulders. 'We thought to continue as far as the Parade Ground, Edward. If you'd like to walk with us, you'd be very welcome.'

Henry nodded. 'Indeed you would,' he said. 'I've been wanting to ask you about the Silver Jubilee for George V. Michael said you'd already started working on this, even though it isn't until next May.'

'I forbid you to talk about anything to do with work, Henry, yours or Edward's,' Mary said as they resumed walking, the four of them in a line, with Henry on the outside at one end, and Edward at the other. 'The evening walk is for relaxation. It would be most unfair on Edward.'

She leaned slightly in front of Clara to address Edward. 'You must ignore Henry, Edward, if he says anything at all that relates to your job or his.'

'I don't know about ignoring Henry,' Edward said with mock gravity, 'but I'd do my best to deflect the conversation to a different topic.'

'That's good enough for me,' Mary said with a laugh. 'You're known for your tact and diplomacy, and I'm sure you've deflected many a conversation in the past.'

'I think we'd be wise to move quickly to a different topic, or Miss Saunders will be analysing everything I say to her, wondering if I'm responding to what she's said, or if I'm trying to steer us in a different direction.' He glanced sideways at Clara and smiled.

She laughed. 'I promise I won't do that. You said just now that you love the view, but don't often come here in the evenings. I'm wondering why not.'

'You can blame it on my work, I suppose. I have to balance two somewhat incompatible things—I have to be accessible to the public, and I have to maintain the dignity of my office. If I put myself in the position of being waylaid on a regular basis in the street, it could be difficult to sustain the necessary level of respect for the position I hold.' He gave her a wry smile. 'I'm afraid that sounds very pompous. I do apologise.'

'No, it doesn't,' she said quickly.

They glanced at each other, and both burst out laughing.

'Well, maybe it does. But only a little bit,' she said in amusement.

The increasing number of people walking along the promenade made it more difficult to walk four abreast, and she and Edward fell back and walked behind her parents.

'From what Mama said,' she went on, 'you're so good at changing the subject that I'd never be able to spot you doing it, so there'd be no point in even trying.'

He smiled. 'To ensure that you can completely relax while we're talking, I suggest you choose a subject, and I promise to stick to it faithfully. Even if you've initiated a discussion about the minutiae of ladies' fashions.'

'Well, it won't be anything to do with sewing or knitting as I intensely dislike both, and I won't be talking horse as I'm not keen on riding. I could make a fair attempt at saying something about tennis as I play it, although indifferently, but I don't know that it would be particularly interesting. The trouble is, I'm in a difficult position, Mr Harrington,' Clara said, turning to him, her eyes laughing.

'Is that so? Perhaps you'd like to explain your dilemma.'

'None of the above possibilities appeals to me. I do have something I'd like to ask, however. But Mother said we mustn't talk about your work as that would be unfair to you. It's a question about your work, though. Do you see the problem?'

'Indeed I do,' he said with feigned seriousness. 'If you deliberately ignore your mother's prohibition, which we both heard, you'll risk offending both me and her. This means that you don't feel able to ask the question, and so will have to struggle consciously to hold it in, which could have a detrimental effect upon our conversation.'

'That's right! So what do you advise?'

'That you disregard what your mother said, and that I

mentally fortify myself against a feeling of being wronged. As your mother remarked, diplomats are possessed of tact and diplomacy, at least they like to think so. She omitted one other very important characteristic—namely, they have the hide of a rhinoceros.'

Clara glanced very obviously from the top of his head to his toes, and giggled. 'I must say, it's well disguised. All right, then. I'm really curious about the Silver Jubilee that Papa mentioned. Would you tell me about it, please?'

'Certainly. Next year, the Resident will be hosting a special celebration in honour of the King in The Residency. There'll be a lot of important people there, councillors and members of various committees, and work on it will begin very early. It'll be a grand affair, but perhaps not quite the sort of event you were hoping it might be.'

'It sounds very pleasant,' she said doubtfully.

'But?' he prompted.

'But a little bit stuffy.' She giggled. 'Does that make me sound horribly lightweight?'

'Not at all,' he said cheerfully. 'I would have thought that tennis parties, lawn parties and dances were more your choice of activity—the sort of activities put on by the club.'

'You're right.'

'To let you into a secret—I agree with you. And because of that, there's going to be an event to which your father didn't refer, and much earlier in the year. I'm planning to host a party in my house. Ostensibly, it'll be in honour of the king, but really it's because it's about time I did so. I was thinking about early in February. The New Year celebrations at the club will be long over by then, and February's one of the most beautiful months of the year, being dry and warm, without being overly humid.'

Clara stared at him in excitement. 'You mean in the palace?'

He shook his head. 'That's not my house—that's where the Resident lives. I have a couple of rooms there as I frequently need to be on hand, and I sometimes work until late in the day. When I do, I wouldn't want to have to travel back from Bolghotty Island to Cochin in the dark. And for the same reason, Michael, too, has a room. No, I have a house just south of The English Club, and it's there I intend to hold the party.'

She beamed at him. 'How exciting for everyone who's invited. But how alarming for your wife to have such a responsibility. At school we were taught the basics of organising social events, and planning a party sounded very complicated. There was so much to think about. Your wife must be very skilled.'

'There is no wife. I'm not married.'

'Why not?' She felt herself go scarlet, and she put her hand to her mouth. 'I'm really sorry, Mr Harrington. That was rude of me. It's none of my business.'

'It's quite all right,' he said mildly. 'It's understandable that you'd assume that someone of my venerable age would have a wife. No,' he said quickly, holding up his hand to stop her from speaking. 'There's no need for a prettily uttered speech about how I'm not at all old, and if I am, how I don't look it.'

She burst out laughing.

'But to answer your question,' he continued. 'I've never met the right person. My career occupied my early years, and by the time I'd reached a point at which I could think about marriage, there was no one in my line of vision I wanted to marry.'

'Is that because you're abnormally fussy?'

He smiled. 'As I don't know what normal is, I can't really answer that. But I do know that I want more than just a handsome woman who's a skilled organiser and who has the art of social conversation. There are a lot of British women of that type in India.'

She looked at him in surprise. 'Surely such a woman would be the perfect wife for a diplomat. What else would you want?'

'I can't really say. But when I meet the right woman for me, I'll know it at once. She'll be someone who, by sharing my life with me, will enhance it.'

'Well, I hope you find her before too long,' she said. She grimaced. 'Ouch,' she said. 'I'm sorry. That sounded as if I was suggesting you were so old that you might soon be too old to marry. I didn't mean that, of course.'

He smiled at her. 'I feel your distress, so I think that now I shall change the subject, and very obviously so. It occurs to me that if you've had lessons in how to organise parties, you might be kind enough to give me some advice. I'm not the sort of person to want to leave anything to the last minute. February isn't that far away so I'd like to make a start on the planning quite soon.'

'Me?' she exclaimed.

'Just so. This will be the first time I've opened the house to so many people. While I'm used to organising grand events at The Residency, I'm less *au fait* with the sort of event I'd like my party to be. While my house servants are very capable, in this they might benefit from some guidance.'

'You're just being kind, and trying to make me feel better for expressing myself so badly.'

'I'm afraid you're crediting me with more noble motives than I actually have,' he said with a smile. 'I'm just hoping to take advantage of someone young enough to know how to prevent the evening from feeling like a scaled down palace affair. I don't want it to be what you'd term stuffy.'

'Well,' she said slowly, 'if you really think I could help, I should be happy to try. After all, it would ensure that I got an invitation,' she added with a laugh. 'Oh, look, Mama and Papa have stopped to wait for us. They must have been galloping along, or we've been walking quite slowly. Is your party a secret, or is it something I can talk about with Lizzie, for example?'

'Thank you for asking that, Clara. Perhaps it would be better not to go out of the way to talk about it for a week or so. Certainly until a date has been decided. I need to have invitations made, and before that, I'd like to decide upon a theme. Perhaps that's something upon which you can advise me.'

'I shall start thinking at once,' she said happily. 'Of course, fancy dress parties are always very popular. Everyone loves them.'

'That's true,' he said. 'But do you think there's a danger that with it being in honour of the King's Silver Jubilee, all the men would come dressed as George V and all the women as Queen Mary. Or vice versa.'

She laughed.

He smiled at her. 'If you and your parents would come to my house one evening next week—Thursday, shall we say? —we can discuss the party over dinner. If you've had a few thoughts by then, we'll be able to run through them.'

'I'd like that,' she said shyly.

He smiled. 'Then I'll issue an invitation to them before we go our separate ways.'

.   .   .

THEIR EVENING MEAL OVER, Henry and Mary sat side by side on the verandah, staring beyond the expanse of darkened lawn to the stark white sand that bordered the sea. A hazy film shimmered above the water's surface, imbuing a sense of the unearthly to the scene.

The coconut trees that towered on either side of the garden were trapping the fragrance from the nearby frangipani trees, and their aroma was mingling with the sweet scent from the white jasmine that grew at the foot of the wooden steps leading down to the garden.

As they sat in companionable silence, they could hear Clara moving around on the verandah above them, and then they heard her return to her bedroom, and close the door behind her.

Amit came through the doorway with a small tray on which there was a *chota peg* of brandy with soda water and ice, and a gin gimlet. He put the brandy on the table next to Henry, and the gin gimlet next to Mary. Then he took a step back, and stood with the tray in his hands.

Henry indicated that Amit should leave. Then he leaned forward and picked up his glass. 'So, Mary,' he said, taking a drink. 'What are your thoughts about our walk this evening?'

'I was sorry that with Edward and Clara so busy talking, it wasn't really possible to get our customary bowl of fish curry. I've come to anticipate our Friday evening treat with pleasure.'

He shook his head impatiently. 'I'm not talking about food, am I?'

'Then, is this about Edward inviting us to dinner on Thursday? Or that he's planning to hold a party in February? Obviously, I realise that both are connected.'

'I'm talking about him and Clara, of course, and about

him asking for her help with the party. I mean, what does she know about organising such an event?'

'I believe they had some instructions at school, preparing them for what they might need to know in the future.'

He made a noise of dismissal.

She frowned. 'If you're trying to suggest that Edward has designs on Clara, I'm sure you're mistaken. Apart from the fact that he's bound to know that she and George are virtually engaged—Michael sees him daily and will have told him—Edward is years older than Clara.'

'Twelve years. That hardly puts him in his dotage. It's an age when an unmarried man, who's established a career, thinks about getting married. And yes, Clara will be getting engaged, but there's no official engagement as yet.' He took a sip of his drink. 'I think I'll speak to Albert about possibly bringing forward the date of the announcement.'

She raised her eyebrows. 'I'm afraid I don't agree. George and Clara need to spend more time together—they've hardly seen each other since she got back. Both are now grown up. and they need to know if they still truly want to marry each other. I think it better to stick with our original intention.'

'All right, then,' he said impatiently, and he took a sip of his drink. 'But as they're clearly very fond of each other, it would be sensible to have something ready to post in *The Malabar Herald* and *The Cochin Argus*. It would signal to Albert and Julia our continued interest. I haven't forgotten that they considered a girl in Calicut for George.'

'I realise that you're thinking of the business, darling. Just go cautiously is all I ask,' Mary said, stirring her gimlet. She paused and looked thoughtfully at Henry. 'Do you really believe that Edward's thinking of Clara with a view to marriage?'

He shrugged. 'It's possible. Such a thing wouldn't have occurred to me before this evening, but I must admit I do wonder now.'

She frowned slightly. 'Wouldn't such an alliance please you? I realise you've an understanding with Albert, but there's nothing formal between George and Clara yet. If she preferred to marry Edward, would that be so unacceptable? And don't mention the age difference—you're some years older than I am.'

'It would be an excellent alliance for Clara, Edward being so well established and respected, and with a secure future, but a union between her and George would give me infinitely more pleasure. Albert and I have become good friends, and it's vital to me that there's someone who'll take over the company in years to come. George would oversee both their company and mine. '

'Is that the only reason?'

He hesitated. 'I'm a simple man, Mary. Albert and I speak the same language, and move in the same world. As does George. Michael and Edward effectively speak a different language, and move in a different world, one that doesn't interest me. I already have one son-in-law for whom the colonial administration is his future, and I don't want another.'

'You say you speak the same language as Albert, but he's keen on becoming a member of the Legislative Assembly. You've never shown any interest in this.'

'That's because I have none. I'm aware of Albert's ambitions, but I'd still much prefer an evening with him to an evening with Edward, pleasant though the man is.'

'Thinking about it, given Albert's ambitions, I'm

surprised it hasn't yet occurred to Albert to push Lizzie into Edward's line of vision. Julia said that Albert has his eye on someone in Madras for her, but there's nothing definite yet. I would have thought that the idea of Lizzie married to Edward would have a stronger appeal.'

Henry stopped abruptly, his glass midway to his mouth. His face creased into a broad smile. 'Now that's an idea!' he exclaimed. 'Thank you, Mary, for seeing what I didn't. Lizzie will have had those same lessons as Clara. And she's an undeniably pretty girl. I don't know how advanced the Madras thing is, but it wouldn't hurt to drop a hint about Edward to Albert next week. Yes, I'll do that.'

10

T*he following Tuesday*

CLARA AND LIZZIE stepped down from the rickshaw, followed by Clara's *ayah,* and all three stood on the edge of the betel-stained pavement and stared across the road at the street that led down to the office of Saunders & Co.

'I hope Father's not furious at us for disturbing him,' Clara said anxiously to Lizzie.

'He won't be,' Lizzie replied airily. 'He'll be pleased that you're interested in seeing what he does in the day.'

'I hope you're right.'

'And it's not as if we want your father to show us around —absolutely not—we're hoping Lewis will. He was the one who suggested this, after all.'

Clara bit her lip. 'But suppose he's not there? He wasn't at the church or the club on Sunday. Perhaps it wasn't so wise to decide to come here today. I only said that I thought

I heard Papa tell Mama that Lewis would be in the office this week, and not on a trip. And I assumed he'd be there in the mornings, as they all stop for a sleep in the afternoon. If we'd had more time to talk on Sunday, we might have come up with a better idea.'

'But we might not. If he's not there, we're going to have one of the most boring mornings of our lives, and for no reason, but it's still worth a try. Nothing else has occurred to us, has it?' Lizzie said.

'I suppose not.'

They stood there for few more minutes, plucking up the courage to cross Bazaar Road and go down to the office, while in front of them, coolies wove their way to the market in Jew Town, some balancing sacks of rice on their heads, others baskets of vegetables, all of them dodging the rickshaws that were being pulled to and from the market.

Behind them streamed a river of colour as women in bright saris, and men wearing a shirt and a patterned cotton *lungi* tied around the waist, were making their way along the narrow gap between the open-fronted shops and the street-traders who lined the side of the road.

The air was saturated with vanilla, black pepper and cumin, and reeked with the pungency of ghee, and the acrid smells of sweat on bodies that milled in the heat and of hair slicked down with coconut oil. Pervading all was the stench of rotting fish and the scent of the sea.

'Well, are we going then?' Lizzie asked in impatience. 'It's hardly pleasant here, and it's getting hotter and stickier by the minute—I don't remember it being this clammy in October. If Lewis is there, he might not be there for long.'

'I warned you, he might not be there at all,' Clara said as they crossed the road, the *ayah* trailing behind them.

'Well, I certainly hope we're not wasting our time,' Lizzie said sulkily.

'If there's no one there, we could always go to Goddard & Son. It isn't far from here.'

Lizzie gave a sharp exclamation of dismissal. 'Not likely! There's no way I want to spend the morning watching you and my brother gaze at each other.'

Clara put her gloved finger under her chin and assumed a thoughtful pose. 'Hm. I'm now wondering if we should go there, rather than to Papa's. Your father's office suddenly sounds utterly irresistible.'

Lizzie exclaimed in annoyance.

'Don't worry,' Clara said with a giggle. 'I'm teasing you. This morning is about you and Lewis and no one else. And George probably wouldn't have been there, anyway,' she added. 'Let's go, then.'

Making their way past stone houses with flowerpots hanging from the windows, and past the godowns where grain and produce from the backwaters were stored, they headed in the direction of the riverfront wharves.

When they reached the office of Saunders & Co, they stopped outside and glanced nervously at each other.

'D'you want to go in first?' Clara asked.

'He's your father,' Lizzie said, and propelled her forward.

Having asked the *ayah* to remain outside, Clara pushed the door open and went into the office.

The shuttered room was dark apart from the right hand corner, where an open doorway framed a rectangle of bright light from a small courtyard. The stone wall at the far end of the courtyard was covered with an abundance of yellow mimosa and red hibiscus.

At the back of the office on the left-hand side, there was an arched doorway covered by a beaded screen.

Clara moved further in, her eyes accustoming to the darkness, with Lizzie following closely behind.

The whir of the electric fan in the centre of the high ceiling was loud above them, and there was a rhythmic flutter from the papers caught in the movement of air.

There were three wooden desks inside the office. The largest desk was at the back of the room. It was Henry's desk, and he was sitting there, his head bent over a ledger.

On the opposite side of the desk from Henry there were two wooden chairs, their backs to the door.

A smaller desk stood on either side of the office, the papers on each trapped beneath a quantity of paperweights.

A man in a turban and white cotton shirt sat at the desk on the left, but the high-backed wooden chair behind the desk on the right of the room was empty.

Clara glanced at the empty chair, and gestured despair at Lizzie.

'Why, Clara!' Henry exclaimed, suddenly looking up. 'And Lizzie, too.' He stared at them both in surprise.

Then smiling broadly, he pushed the schedule he'd been reading to one side, rose to his feet, and pulled on his jacket. 'What a pleasure to see you both!'

She looked at the ledger he'd been holding, and at the pile of papers in front of him, and at the trays that lined the front of the desk, each tray overflowing with documents.

One tray was labelled pepper shipments, and there were similar trays for sandalwood, cardamom, coconut products and silk. Another tray was filled with documents relating to the goods that had been processed for shipping. There was a tray headed shipping schedules, and next to it, trays labelled regulations, registration papers, clearances, certificates and general documentation.

A box of files headed customers and shipping agents sat on one corner of the desk, and a large clock on the other.

A wave of guilt shot through her.

'I'm sorry, Papa. You look so busy. We shouldn't have disturbed you.'

'I'd never be too busy to see you, my dear. And you, too, Lizzie. Why don't we ask Nitesh to bring us some refreshment in the courtyard?' Without waiting for a reply, he signalled to his clerk.

'Of course, *sahib*,' Nitesh said. He rose from his chair, padded across to the beaded screen, his feet bare, pushed the screen aside and disappeared through the arched doorway into a room at the back.

'Your visit is timely, Clara,' Henry said, moving towards the courtyard. 'There was something I wanted to ask you about Edward's invitation.'

'We didn't mean to take you from your work,' Clara said, following her father into the courtyard. 'Quite the opposite, in fact. We were interested in learning what you did in the day. But we can see that you've so much to do, this would not be a good time, and we'll leave when we've had our refreshment. We can come again another time, when you're less busy.'

Henry beamed at them both. 'I'm highly gratified at your interest, my dears,' he said. 'We're always busy—we don't just trade in Indian produce—we're shippers and forwarders, too, you know. But I will never be too busy to see you. Now sit, sit.' He waved his hands in the direction of six rattan chairs set around a table in the centre of the courtyard.

'What was that about an invitation from Edward?' Lizzie whispered to Clara.

'We're going to his house for dinner on Thursday. To *his*

house, not to The Residency,' Clara told her as she sat down where her father had indicated.

Throwing her a look of amazement, Lizzie took the seat next to her. 'I want to hear about Edward's later,' she said under her breath. 'What bad luck Lewis isn't here.'

They settled down, endeavouring not to show their disappointment, and almost immediately, Nitesh appeared with a tray on which there was a cup of sweet milky tea, and two glasses of lime and ginger soda into which mint leaves had been crushed. There were several banana leaves, and a plate piled high with chunks of pineapple, mango, passion fruit and breadfruit.

He put the tea in front of Henry, and gave a lime juice to Clara and Lizzie. Then he put the pile of banana leaves and the fruit in the centre of the table, and turned to leave.

'Those juices look very good, Nitesh. Could you bring me one, too?' a voice asked.

Clara and Lizzie turned sharply towards the owner of the voice.

Lewis was crossing the courtyard, coming towards them.

Both imperceptibly smoothed their skirt.

Clara went pink with relief and sent a sly smile in Lizzie's direction.

'If this is a family thing, Henry,' Lewis said, hovering a little way back from the table, 'just say, and I'll have the juice at my desk. It would be no bad thing as I've paperwork to catch up on. I'd hate to intrude.'

'You wouldn't be intruding at all, dear boy. In fact, your arrival couldn't have been better timed. The girls have just been telling me that they'd like to understand a little of the business. I can't think of anyone better than you at being able to explain what we do. I would've done so myself, but I've an appointment that I'll shortly need to get off to.'

Lewis came and sat down at the table.

'I noticed your *ayah* outside, Clara. Nitesh will see that she, too, has some refreshment,' Henry said, sitting back and stretching out his legs under the table. He took a sip of his drink. 'Now, what exactly are you girls interested in knowing? It would probably be helpful for Lewis to know.'

Clara and Lizzie looked at each other. Clara bit her lip, and Lizzie coughed.

Lewis moved closer to the edge of his seat. 'I imagine it must be quite difficult to pinpoint any one thing that interests you ladies, isn't it?' he said smoothly. 'After all, you won't as yet know the different facets of our work. I imagine you'd like a general idea of what happens to the goods we bring to our wharves, how we process them, and the procedure for their export.'

Two pairs of eyes looked at him in gratitude.

'That's right,' Clara said. 'We just wanted a general idea of your day, Papa. After all, it's what supports the family, isn't it?'

Lewis gave a suppressed laugh, which he swiftly changed to a cough.

'I suggest that I take them through the key points in the office, Henry,' he said, 'and explain how we co-ordinate the import of the goods, ensuring they've been properly reviewed and documented. And I could then run through the process for exporting them. If you like, I'll also explain how we track our shipments and communicate delays, damage, and other problems.'

Henry nodded. 'Excellent, Lewis.'

Another pair of eyes looked at him in gratitude, this time from beneath bushy brows.

'When I've done that,' Lewis went on, 'we could go to the wharves, and perhaps look into a couple of our godowns on the way. You might be interested, ladies, in how we store the various goods to be exported.'

Clara and Lizzie exchanged glances and murmured something meant to be taken as assent.

'And one last suggestion—we're so close to Goddard & Son that we could finish up at your father's office, Miss Goddard. He might appreciate a visit from you. If he wanted you to stay until he was ready to leave for home, and return with him, I could always ensure that Miss Saunders and her *ayah* got safely home.'

'That's a very kind thought, Mr Mackenzie,' Lizzie said hastily, 'but I seem to recall Father mentioning at dinner last night that he wouldn't be in the office today. Clara and I will visit him on another occasion.'

Lewis smiled. 'Of course.'

Henry nodded. 'If I've not yet returned when Lewis brings you back here, you girls can wait for me. We can leave you at your house on the way home, Lizzie.'

'Thank you, Mr Saunders,' Lizzie said, dimpling.

Henry nodded. 'That's decided then,' he said. 'It's all planned. Now we'd better drink up before the ice melts.' And he picked up his glass of juice.

11

That went very well, Lewis thought in satisfaction as he moved back from the car that was to take the girls, the *ayah* and Henry home. He gave them a slight wave, and then headed across the road to the office.

What luck he'd returned the moment he had!

Any later, and it would have been Henry who'd have had to explain the office procedure to the girls, a task that Henry wouldn't have enjoyed, and which he'd clearly been delighted to hand over.

And he, Lewis, couldn't have been more pleased to help out.

If he'd had any doubts about Clara's interest in him, her visit that morning had banished them.

As he'd approached the courtyard table, he'd seen the smile that Clara had given Lizzie. It was unmistakably a smile of delight, and there'd been a touch of triumph about it. He'd known in that instant that they'd been talking about him before he'd turned up at the office.

In fact, seeing him might have been the reason they were there in the first place.

Indeed, the more he thought about it, the more certain he was that he *was* the reason for their visit to Muttancherry.

When the girls had been asked what interested them about the business, they hadn't been able to come up with a single thing. Their lack of any real interest had been reinforced by the gratitude in Clara's face when he'd promptly stepped in with some suggestions.

Yes, they'd gone there because Clara had wanted to see him again.

What other reason could there have been?

Her blushing, and her giggling, and her obvious attempts at feigned interest in everything he'd shown them, reinforced that.

And Lizzie, undoubtedly aware of Clara's interest in him, was just as bad as Clara, frequently going red and glancing at him as if to determine if he was looking at Clara, and if so, with what expression.

Mentally, he hugged himself in delight.

And that morning wasn't going to be the end of it, he thought gleefully as he pushed open the office door and went inside.

When he'd been a little way back from Lizzie and Clara while they were standing on one of the wharves closest to Saunders's office, staring at the small fishing boats weaving a path between the deep sea freighters that were passing along the channel between Muttancherry and Willingdon Island, he'd heard Lizzie suggest to Clara in an unnaturally loud voice that they have coffee on Friday morning at Old Harbour House.

The key thing she'd want to hear about, she'd added, would be the dinner that Clara's family would have had the evening before with Edward Harrington in his house. She'd want a full description of his house when they met on the Friday.

He'd been immensely surprised when he'd heard about the dinner. And extremely pleased.

Edward Harrington regularly invited people to The Residency—indeed, one of his administrative tasks was to help with the entertaining of the Resident's guests—but he didn't invite them to his own home.

On one occasion in The English Club, he'd overheard someone ask Harrington why he never invited his friends to his house, and he'd said very firmly that he did a lot of entertaining in The Residency, and hosted personal dinners at The English Club, but that he preferred to keep his home as a haven away from all that.

Yet he'd invited Clara and her family there for dinner. It showed that he must consider them special friends.

And that wasn't too hard to understand.

Henry Saunders was a sound businessman, and affable enough, and Mary was a gracious woman. And as their son-in-law was one of Harrington's assistants, and supposedly destined for promotion in the British administration, the Saunders family had a special link with Harrington.

It meant that Harrington's friendship would almost certainly translate into support for Saunders & Co, should such support ever be needed.

And that could stand him in good stead in the future.

It would be more likely that he'd be given Harrington's backing, for example, if, once he was married to Clara and running the company, he decided to go after a seat on the Legislative Assembly.

Albert Goddard certainly thought it would be a worthwhile position to hold. And he was a shrewd man. And ambitious, too, in a way that Henry Saunders would never be.

Had Goddard & Son not been destined for the son, he might have been tempted to consider Lizzie as a possible wife. He sensed that Lizzie was more of a kindred spirit. But Albert Goddard had a son, so the advantages of marrying Clara eclipsed anything that a union with Lizzie could give him.

And moreover, he was realistic enough to know that Goddard would never allow his daughter to marry a man like him.

The gossipmongers had spread the belief that Goddard was hoping for a marriage between his daughter and a man who was highly placed in the British administration in Madras. Apparently, he'd met the man when he'd been there to conclude a deal, and had seen the man as a possible husband for Lizzie.

Knowing Albert Goddard, he would have been greatly impressed by the man's standing in Madras society, seen the potential benefit to himself, and would have gone out of the way to strike up a friendship with him.

But toadying to people in government wasn't his way, Lewis thought with a degree of contempt.

Furthermore, if Goddard had asked his opinion, which he hadn't, he would have told him that he could well be wasting his time, trying to advance himself in such a way.

The British raj was surely in its final days.

A lot of the British seemed blind to what had been happening in recent years, but the reality was that a number of Indians were already playing an important role in running their country, and if rumour was right, that role was soon to get larger.

The word was that India was going to be divided into

self-ruling territories, a sort of united federation along the same lines as Australia or Canada, but without the same level of independence.

But the Indians weren't going to be happy with such a situation for long, and they were likely to become even more vocal about wanting the British out. And as they were certain to persist in this, the days of the British rule must surely be numbered.

But there would always be a local assembly, and being a member of the assembly, or even a municipal councillor, would furnish him with invaluable knowledge, both about what was happening in Cochin, and more importantly, about plans projected for the future. Such plans could have a great effect on trading, so a seat on the assembly would be worth pursuing.

And obviously Albert Goddard thought so, too. It would be why he was pressing his suit to anyone who'd listen, and why he'd dragged his son off to a completely unnecessary meeting with the Resident.

Yes, having a closer relationship with Edward Harrington would be an unexpected bonus of marrying Clara, he decided as he unlocked the drawer in his desk.

And joining her for coffee at the Old Harbour House would be a step towards that.

It was clear that she hoped he'd be there, or Lizzie wouldn't have done what Clara would have been too embarrassed to do—made sure that he knew where he'd find them the following Friday morning.

Indeed, in the light of that, it would be churlish of him not to join them.

Smiling to himself, he took a sheath of signed documents from the drawer, locked the drawer and pocketed the key. Then he went across to Henry's desk, pulled one of the trays towards him, and slid his documents between those that had already been processed for shipping.

Friday morning it is, then, he said to himself, and he pushed the tray back into line with the others and turned away.

STANDING in her bedroom in front of the tall mirror that stood in the corner of the room, Lizzie tightened the linen belt around the waist of her short-sleeved blue and white polka dot dress, and adjusted the skirt which fell to just below her knees.

Lingering there, she allowed herself a moment or two before going downstairs to join her family for dinner.

The day had been an outstanding success, she thought, mentally congratulating herself. After all, it had been her idea to go to the Saunders office on a pretext, in the hope that Lewis would be there.

And the gamble had paid off handsomely. He'd been thoroughly charming and extremely friendly. And very informative.

Company agent he might be at the moment, but he wouldn't be that for long. Of that she was sure. Lewis was ambitious. Thinly veiled his ambition might be, but she'd sensed it from the moment she'd met him.

Or at least, soon after she'd registered how attractive he was.

And no one could be better than she at recognising ambition, living in a house where ambition reigned supreme.

Her father made no secret of his hopes for the future. The owner of a prosperous trading company, he was now to become a member of the Legislative Assembly, which would add to his prestige in the community and give him power beyond the confines of his company.

And he was also ambitious for George, who'd take over the company, and who, by marrying Clara, would also one day be in control of Saunders & Co. When that came about, George was bound to merge it with Goddard & Son, and that would make them one of the strongest trading companies in Muttancherry.

It was all going to work out well for George.

And her father was ambitious, too, for her. That was obvious from the fact that they were promoting an alliance between her and the man in Madras.

She'd learnt a little more about John Lansdowne since her father had first raised the subject of such a marriage.

After Mr Lansdowne, in his official capacity, had been a signatory on the lucrative deal between Goddard & Son and a carpet factory in Madras, her father and Mr Lansdowne had sat over a *chota peg* or two.

During their friendly conversation, her father had learnt that the man's wife had died in childbirth, and the baby, too, and that having had the pleasure of a short but happy marriage, he was keen to marry again, although obviously not till his period of mourning was over.

Her father had remarked that his daughter, now of marriageable age, would shortly be returning from school in England. No more had been said, but there was a tacit understanding about what might happen in the future.

When a few days after her return from England, her parents had told her about Mr Lansdowne in great excitement, she'd agreed to meet him at the appropriate time. After all, she was going to have to get married before too long—there wasn't much else she could do, and she'd be unwise to wait any great length of time, or men might think her too old to marry.

Her father had been delighted at her willingness to please him, and had said that the next time he had business in Madras, the whole family would go, too.

But things had changed since then.

They'd changed the minute she'd met Lewis Mackenzie, and had known instantly that this was the man she wanted to marry.

She'd realised then, too, that although she hadn't long been back in Cochin, it wasn't only Clara who wanted her to remain in the town—she, too, wanted to stay. She'd been back long enough to know that.

She and Clara had always got on well, even though they'd mixed with different people at school. Clara would be staying in Cochin, and the thought of being married to Lewis, settled in the same town as Clara, and being part of what was a small but lively community, was an immensely appealing one.

Far more appealing than moving miles away to live in a place where she knew no one.

It was much too soon to share her thoughts with her parents, though.

She'd need to prepare the ground first.

What she'd do was occasionally slip a positive comment about Lewis into the conversation over the family dinner, and then, when the time felt right, and she was certain that Lewis reciprocated her feelings, she'd say something to them.

Of course, if they suddenly advanced the situation with the man in Madras, she'd have to say something sooner than that.

And to her great joy, something that could make a start towards moving her father away from the idea of a union between her and John Lansdowne had landed unexpectedly in her lap that morning. It was the news that the Saunders family had been invited to dine with Edward Harrington in his home.

Her father was going to be very interested in that. And as surprised as she had been.

And very pleased.

That George would be marrying someone whose family was as close as they obviously were with Edward Harrington, could be of great benefit to Goddard & Son.

And that being so, and it being in her father's nature to want close ties, in as many ways as possible, with a family whose standing in the community was rising, the pressure on her to marry Mr Lansdowne was likely to be reduced in view of the advantages gained by her remaining in Cochin, able to continue her friendship with Clara.

So by the time she'd passed on to her father everything that Clara would be telling her over coffee on Friday morning, she'd have moved considerably closer to being able to marry Lewis.

With a lightness in her step, and a smile on her face, she swept out of her bedroom and made her way to the dining room.

12

T*he following Thursday morning*

'MR GODDARD IS HERE, *MEMSAHIB*,' Amit announced, standing in the doorway that led to the verandah.

Clara and her mother glanced at each other in surprise.

'Did you say Mr Goddard, Amit?' Mary asked. 'At this time of day?'

'Young Mr Goddard,' Amit explained.

'Oh, it's George!' Clara exclaimed in delight. Dropping her book on the table, she pinched some colour into her cheeks.

'Do ask him to come in,' Mary said, putting her crochet to one side.

Amit stepped back into the sitting room, and a few minutes later, returned with George.

'How lovely to see you, George,' Mary said, as he came

forward, smiling broadly. 'Do sit down. You'll have some refreshment, won't you?'

'A coffee would be very welcome,' George said. 'Thank you.'

'We'll all have coffee, please,' Mary told Amit, who was hovering at her side.

As he settled into his seat opposite Clara, George grinned at her, and then, assuming a contrite face, he turned his attention to Mary. 'I must apologise, Mrs Saunders, for turning up without an invitation.'

She laughed. 'You're always welcome, George, with or without an invitation, and without prior notice. As you must surely know.'

'That's very kind of you, Mrs Saunders. It's just that an unexpected chance to see Clara came up, and I couldn't not seize it with both hands.' He smiled at Clara.

'I take it your father doesn't need you today,' Mary said.

'That's right. He's gone to some of our coconut planta-tions in the low-lying areas. They're planting seedlings now that the heavy rains have passed. I'll be going early tomorrow to some of the paddy fields to oversee the two-crop rice. The first crop's already been harvested, and we're about to plant the seedlings for the second crop. I have to check the fields they'll be planted in, and make sure they're sufficiently well manured, among other things.'

'Good gracious, George!' Mary exclaimed. 'That's quite a responsibility. Your father obviously has great faith in you.'

He laughed. 'It sounds more important than it actually is. The workers have been doing this for years, and they know far more about it than I do, and probably always will. It's more for the effect it has, seeing Father or me there. I'll adopt a knowledgeable face, and walk around grunting like Father does. I'll prod the ground in several places, take a keen interest in a plant or two, and be liberal with my words of praise. In reality, my presence will be completely unnecessary, and everyone knows it, but it looks good.'

'I'm sure you're being too modest,' Mary said with a smile. 'We know how highly Albert thinks of you.'

'I do hope you're right. Father's ambitions are catching, and I want the company to do even better than it's already doing. But to come back to today, as he and I will be away in our different locations until the weekend, he suggested I take the morning off. And here I am.'

He paused as Amit appeared with their coffees, and put them on the table, with a plate of small coconut cakes.

Clara beamed at George. 'I'm so glad you came,' she said. 'You'll take my mind off this evening. We're having dinner with Mr Harrington, you know? At his house, not in the club.'

George nodded. 'Lizzie mentioned that a couple of days ago. Father was most impressed.'

'When you arrived, I was talking with Mama about what to wear.'

'You could wear a sack made out of coconut coir, Clara, and you'd look absolutely beautiful,' he said warmly.

Clara blushed.

Mary glanced from one to the other. 'I don't think I'll have a cake this morning, so I'll take my coffee and crochet into the sitting room.' She stood up. 'You two can stay out here and talk. But I'll be where I can see you, and I don't want to see a repeat performance of what happened when your family came to dinner, George.'

'You won't, Mrs Saunders,' George assured her with feigned meekness.

Clara smothered a laugh.

Mary picked up her crochet and hook.

'There's no need to call Amit,' George said hastily. 'Let me take your coffee for you.' He scrambled to his feet.

'That's kind of you, George; thank you,' Mary said, and she went into the sitting room, followed by George. He put the coffee on the occasional table next to the armchair on which she'd sat down, and then went back to Clara.

'I notice your mother's chosen the chair that gives her the best view of what we're doing,' he murmured, sitting down on the chair vacated by Mary, which put him closer to Clara. 'I don't suppose there's any likelihood of her taking a *siesta* before lunch as well as after?'

She laughed. 'I'm afraid not.'

'I thought as much. Sadly, we don't seem to be getting any time by ourselves.' He leaned towards her. 'Every minute of the day, I long to be with you, Clara.'

'And I feel the same about you, George. I can't wait for us to be married.'

'I'd thought that at least when we were in The English Club, we'd be able to spend some time with each other, but Father seems to see this as a chance to introduce me to anyone and everyone. If things don't improve, we'll have to resume our midnight get-togethers. Come to think of it...' He inched his chair closer to hers.

She giggled. 'It might come to that as I don't think it's going to get any better until we're married.' She paused. 'Is your father still set on making us wait for six months?'

'He is,' he said mournfully. 'I keep on suggesting that I ask your father for his permission. We could then make an announcement and perhaps fix a date that was a bit sooner than originally planned. After all, both sets of parents agree, and we know what we feel, so there's no point in such a long wait.'

'I know. It doesn't make sense. What does he say when you ask him?'

'Just that it's a difficult time, with me learning about the company, and him teaching me, and trying to get on to the assembly at the same time.'

She stared at him in dismay. 'But it's always going to be busy. I'd so wanted us to be engaged by Mr Harrington's party, and that's in early February.'

'What's this about a party?' he asked in surprise.

'He hasn't made it widely known yet, and the preparations haven't begun. It's why we're going to dinner this evening—to discuss it. Can't you persuade your father to consider an earlier date?'

'I'll certainly try.' He paused. 'But I'm not sure that the refusal to shorten the time isn't actually down to Mother.'

'Your mother,' she echoed, frowning. 'Why d'you think that?'

'She pulled me aside one day last week after she heard me badgering Father again. She said that I shouldn't be in such a hurry—I needed to be absolutely certain how I felt. I gather she's afraid that we might have a romanticised view of each other, left over from before we went to school, and not see each other as we actually are.'

She looked at George in sudden alarm. 'Are you sure that's all it is, and they aren't still thinking about the girl in Calicut?'

He shook his head, and smiled. 'No, they're not. Absolutely not. That idea was dropped the minute they realised that the perfect wife for me was you.'

'Who is she, that girl?'

'The daughter of a merchant there. He'd moved from Madras to Calicut some years earlier, leased land for his godowns and office, and gone into the coffee curing business. Then he gradually started exporting coir and coir products, also cashew nuts, timber and ginger. That's how he met Father —it was through the coconut connection. He's keen to open up an office in Cochin, now that Cochin's become a major port, as he wants to expand his range of shipping services.'

'Have you met his daughter?'

'No, and I've no interest in doing so. I love you, Clara,' he said quietly.

'And I love you, George. It isn't romanticised, but I love you romantically.'

'And I can say the same. Feel my heart.' He took her hand and placed it against his chest. 'It's racing, just being near you. I want us to be married as soon as possible.'

'Oh, George, so do I.' She slid her fingers between the buttons of his shirt, and touched his bare skin. 'So do I,' she breathed.

'Clara,' her mother called sharply. 'Move back from George so that I can see you.'

His eyes on her face, and hers on his, George pressed her hand hard against his chest, left it there a moment, and then let her remove it. Both turned to look at the sea.

'And really, when you think about it,' he said after a moment or two, 'a year ago, my parents were thinking of rushing me into an engagement with someone in Calicut. I wouldn't have known her at all. You and I have known each other for almost all of our lives. Having to wait six months is ridiculous.'

'I think so, too.'

'I can still feel where you touched me,' he said softly. 'I'm going to talk to Father at the weekend, and you talk to yours, too,' he said. 'It makes sense to be married before the monsoon hits again.'

'That's what I think,' she said happily.

'It would certainly make the monsoon more bearable. You might not remember what the monsoon season's like, with the build-up of pressure, and then the heavy rains, day after day. It's like living beneath a continual waterfall. And the risk of lightning rain strikes. And all the creatures coming out of the ground, rain having flooded the holes and burrows that have been their home for months. We'd be stuck indoors, but it would be wonderful to be stuck indoors together, just you and me.'

'I want that, too,' she said, flushing. 'I'll speak to Papa tomorrow. We'll get tonight over with first, though.' She glanced over her shoulder towards the sitting room. 'We'd better change the subject. Mother's giving us a very strange look. I've an awful feeling that she might decide to join us again.'

He edged his chair slightly away from her. 'Tell me about yesterday, then. Lizzie said the two of you went to Saunders & Co as you were interested in seeing what your father did all day.' He grinned at her. 'None of us believed that, of course. Mother said you were probably just bored and wanted something different to do. So what did you think of it?'

She pulled a face. 'To be honest, it was a bit dull. Well, more than a bit. Mr Mackenzie did his best, but details about the export of pepper and spice aren't exactly riveting.'

'Lewis? Did he take you around?' he asked. 'From what Lizzie said, I thought your father showed you around. I must've misunderstood. In that case, I'm amazed you found it dull. I would've thought Lewis could make just about anything interesting. Father once described him as irreverent, and that seems to fit. Women are supposed to like irreverence.'

'Is that so?' she said lightly.

'You must come to Goddard & Son next time. I'll be the one to show you around, and when we get behind a gigantic pile of fibrous husks, I'll show you how delightful irreverence can be. And I promise, you won't be bored for a minute.'

'Why do I think we're returning to the same topic?' she said in amusement.

He raised his palms in the air in helplessness. 'It's one of those things that happen when I'm with you.'

She glanced back at her mother, and pulled a face. 'Mama's gathering her things together. We *are* about to have company.'

'I thought I'd join you,' Mary said a moment later, coming up to the table and sitting down. George made a move to get up. 'Stay where you are, George. I'll be fine here. You'll stay to lunch, won't you? We're just having something light as we're dining with Edward Harrington this evening?'

'Father is extremely envious. It's quite an honour to be asked to dinner by Mr Harrington, let alone to his house. I'll be expecting a minute-by-minute account from you. In fact, given what we were talking about earlier, Clara, I think that might give me some leverage with Father.'

Mary raised an eyebrow. 'How cryptic, George.'

He smiled. 'The hibiscus are particularly beautiful at this time of year, Mrs Saunders, are they not?'

13

T *hursday evening*

'I LOVE YOUR HOME, MR HARRINGTON!' Clara exclaimed as she walked beside her parents and Edward from the dining room and up the teak stairs.

'Clara's right, Edward; it's quite wonderful,' Mary said, as they went through an arched doorway into the drawing room. 'I've long admired it from the outside as the combination of the Dutch and Portuguese styles is most pleasing to the eye. To see the inside is a real pleasure. The carved doors are simply beautiful, and so is the wood panelling on the ground floor ceiling. And on this ceiling, too,' she added, glancing up at the high vaulted ceiling.

He nodded. 'The house is practical, too, which is of even greater importance. The air has space to circulate, so the house is cool even in the summer months, despite the sunlight pouring through the skylights. I thought we'd sit outside, though, as it's a beautiful evening.'

As they made their way across the drawing room, they passed a number of pieces of teak furniture, and two informal sofas, one placed opposite the other on either side of a low rosewood table.

'I tend to sit on the side facing the sea,' he said as they went out on to the verandah.

He indicated that Clara, Mary and Henry should take a seat on one of the rattan chairs around a table, each chair being angled so that the occupant was able to see the sea as well as the people at the table, and when they'd sat down, he, too, took a seat.

'I've been known to sit so long in the evening at the end of a particularly busy day, enjoying the swift descent of dusk and the cooling off of the day which brings with it the loveliest of scents,' he said, staring at the violet-blue scene in front of him, 'that not only do I see the sun set, but I also watch the sky move gently towards the dawn.'

'You must be exhausted the following day,' Henry remarked.

Edward smiled at him. 'If I am, I always feel it was worth it.'

'I can understand that,' Clara said. 'It's the sort of thing I'd do. Watching the sea is mesmerising, especially when the waves are touched by moonlight. We, too, have a lovely view of the sea. We're both so lucky to have waterfront houses.'

He smiled warmly at her. 'We are, aren't we?'

Henry gave a slight cough. 'It was a delicious meal,' he said. 'Quite delicious.'

Edward's smile widened to include Henry and Mary. 'I'm

glad you enjoyed it. I think the simpler meals are often the best. The fish was netted on the incoming flood tide, the vegetables and fruit came from my garden, and the bread was baked by the nuns in one of our Cochin convents. But I can't take credit for any of the meal. My cook chose the fish and cooked the meal, his assistant went for the bread and the *mali* admirably tends the garden.'

'Well, it was all quite delicious,' Henry repeated. 'And we're most grateful for the invitation.'

'I'm the one who should be thanking you,' Edward said. 'You're allowing Miss Saunders to help me.'

He paused as his head servant, Kumar, appeared on the verandah with a tray on which there were two glasses of whisky, two cups of coffee, and a plate of mango chunks. After Kumar had set everything on the table, he left them.

Edward cleared his throat. 'With your daughter's permission and yours, too, Henry and Mary, I should like to ask Miss Saunders to call me Edward, and I'd like to call her Clara. As we'll be meeting on occasions to discuss the party, it would be pleasant to do so with an absence of formality. And the three of us have long dropped any formality.'

'Of course, Edward,' Henry said quickly. 'I've no objection, if Clara hasn't.'

Clara blushed. 'Thank you, Mr Harrington. I should be happy for you to call me, Clara.'

'And?' he asked with a smile.

She laughed. "And I should be happy to call you Edward, Mr Harrington.'

'I think we need to work on that,' he said, laughing.

'Well, we seem to have made a sound start on matters relating to the party,' Mary said. 'Wouldn't you agree, Edward?'

He turned his attention from Clara to Mary. 'Indeed I would, Mary. I think Clara's right that we'll be tired of donning fancy dress by the time the New Year is over, and we should rule out yet another such occasion.' He looked back at Clara. 'Your suggestion of having silver as a theme, thereby introducing the element of silver into the year that will see the Silver Jubilee, is a very good one.'

She smiled in gratitude. 'I just think people will be ready for something that's both informal and sparkling at the same time.'

'I'm sure you're right. So the next thing is to decide upon a date. And we need to think about the design of the invitations. Perhaps you'll help me with that,' he said. 'I don't want people to think this is going to be a small-scale version of a palace event, and with silver and white, which I imagine the invitation will be, there's a danger it could look that way.'

She thought for a moment. 'We could always introduce an element of black, for example.'

'Now that's an interesting idea,' he said slowly. 'Yes, I like it. It could be quite striking. Perhaps both of us could draw up some ideas, and discuss them one morning in a couple of weeks' time. We could fix on a date for the party at the same time. And perhaps think about whether or not it would be appropriate to have dance-programmes, given this won't be a ball as such, but there'll obviously be dancing.'

Clara clapped her hands in glee. 'I'm so pleased there'll be dancing!' she exclaimed.

'I've been told that the two-step and foxtrot are essentials for all successful parties. On a later occasion we could talk about how to decorate the house.' He glanced at Mary. 'Would you be able to accompany Clara one Saturday morning in a couple of weeks, Mary? If not, perhaps her *ayah* could come with her.'

'I'm sure there'll be no problem, Edward. There won't be anything I can't rearrange.'

'That's good then,' he said, sitting back. He glanced at Clara. 'I haven't yet asked you about your journey back from England? I hope the sea was smooth.'

'I prefer to forget about the ghastly part that wasn't,' she said with a laugh. 'I think Mother and I both enjoyed it, and so did Lizzie. It was a lovely ship. It even had a swimming pool. Mother spent most of her time with the wife of a man who worked in the Public Works Department, and Lizzie and I made friends with several girls who were returning from school, like we were. And also with some others who were on the way to marry their fiancés. Their fiancés were waiting for them on the docks in Bombay. It was very exciting.'

Her eyes shone as she remembered the trip.

Henry glanced at Edward's face, and saw that he was smiling with pleasure at Clara.

'Talking of engagements,' he said quickly. 'And I really shouldn't as there's nothing official as yet. But Clara and George Goddard will formalise their engagement before too long. We're waiting for the right moment.'

Edward hesitated imperceptibly.

'Then let me congratulate you, Clara. George seems a fine young man. And a very lucky young man, if I might say. I'm sure you'll be extremely happy together, and I certainly wish that for you.'

'Thank you, Mr Harrington.'

'Thank you, Edward,' he gently reminded her.

'Thank you, Edward,' she said with a smile. 'George and

I rather grew up together,' she went on. 'While I've always known Lizzie, it was George who was actually my best friend in the years before I went to England.'

'Friendship is certainly a good basis for marriage,' he said.

'It certainly is,' Henry commented. 'And when there's no son to take over a trading company, it's important, too, that friendship is joined by an interest in trading.'

'I can see that,' Edward said. 'Both you and Albert Goddard are quite unusual in the way that you're working to ensure that your businesses stay in the family. It's something we associate with Indian firms, who rely more on family ties than do the British. Most traders in Cochin tend to recruit from outside the family. From people like Lewis Mackenzie, for example.'

Henry nodded. 'We're very lucky with Lewis. He's hard-working and diligent, and has a genuine interest in the company. He's an ambitious man with plenty of ideas. Having him as our agent is a godsend.'

'He works quite a bit on his own, Michael was telling me. It's good that you can trust him in such a way.'

'How interesting that Michael knows that,' Henry said in surprise. 'But I suppose, in a small community, everyone knows everything about everyone else.'

'Or they think they do,' Edward said with a smile.

Henry laughed. 'That's certainly true. Yes, Lewis is free to make decisions on his own, and he can even enter into certain contracts on behalf of the company. But I have to approve everything before he completes the deal, and nothing is final till I've signed it off.'

Edward smiled. 'Which is just as it should be, even with a trusted employee.'

'To go back to Clara's engagement, Edward,' Mary said.

'I'm afraid that Henry was a little precipitate in talking about it. There's nothing official yet, and even though it's only a matter of time before there will be, it would probably have been better not to have mentioned it.'

He nodded. 'I understand. You can rest assured that I won't mention it to anyone. But when there's been a formal announcement, perhaps we can celebrate it in the time-honoured tradition.'

'That's good of you, Edward,' Henry said. 'Mary's right. I let my tongue run away with me. We've enjoyed the evening enormously. Perhaps you'll do us the honour of dining with us at some point in the future.'

'Most definitely. I look forward to it. And now, may I offer you further refreshment?'

EDWARD LEANED against the verandah balustrade and stared beyond the darkened lawn to the sea. Moonlight rippled in silver diamonds across the surface of the water.

Normally, the beauty of the scene before him would relax him, no matter how stressful his day had been. But that evening, the splendour of the night was failing dismally to lift his despondency.

And this was all his fault. At times, he surprised himself at quite how stupid he could be.

The first time he'd seen Clara, which had been at her sister's house, he'd felt an instant attraction to her, even though Clara had shown no interest in him at all. Quite the reverse. If her interest had lain anywhere, it had been with Mackenzie.

And why wouldn't it be?

The man was younger than he, and much better looking. Obviously, a girl like Clara, who could have her pick of the men in Cochin, would look beyond him to someone more pleasing to her in age and appearance. To a man such as Mackenzie.

And such as George Goddard.

So she was to marry George Goddard, was she?

Lucky George.

In every way he was suitable, so what better match for her could there be?

There'd been a reason why, some weeks before, he'd decided to get to know Henry Saunders better, and this had meant getting to know the family, too. But overwhelmed by an interest in Clara that he hadn't expected to feel, his focus had slipped from where it should have been.

Usually, he was so scrupulous in keeping interests of work separate from those of pleasure, and if there was a risk that one might impinge upon the other, he'd prioritise matters of work, and step back from anything else.

Not this time, though.

Asking Clara to help him had been inspired in view of his wish to get to know Henry Saunders better, but in terms of his personal happiness it couldn't have been a worse move.

He hadn't really needed her help—he had staff who could do everything for him—but the thought of having Clara's lovely head bent close to his on a regular basis as they discussed his party plans, had been irresistible.

Now that he knew her destiny had been decided, and that it didn't include him, it was going to be torture, seeing her over the weeks in order to make good his request.

And even though it would further his original intent, that felt poor compensation for the misery he suspected he was going to suffer.

Turning, he went slowly back into his house, a house

that had never failed to be a welcome retreat from the world when he needed one. But as he stood in the drawing room, bathed in a warm amber light, for the first time ever he felt himself surrounded not by the comforting embrace of the familiar, but by emptiness.

14

F*riday morning,*
      the end of October

LIZZIE TAPPED her fingers impatiently on the surface of the table as she sat in Old Harbour House, facing the entrance to the courtyard. While Clara talked on, she picked up her drink in an attempt to stop herself from showing her irritation.

She'd been interested in hearing about the dinner the night before, and her father even more so, but she would have preferred to have had all the details out of the way before Lewis arrived. And the longer Clara went on, the less likely that would be to happen.

But it had to.

Lewis was coming to see her, not for the party details.

He'd obviously listen politely to them, but he'd want to get on to something more personal, perhaps even ask if he might call upon her. But if Clara was still waxing forth about the dinner the night before, he might be unable to turn the conversation to a different subject.

She glanced anxiously towards the entrance, willing Clara to stop talking and for Lewis to appear.

And there was also Tilly to think about.

Delivering a message from Michael to the Post Office wouldn't take an indefinite amount of time, and even if she went slowly in order to give them more time together, she could be back quite soon.

The one hope was that she'd stop and look at the colourful stalls on the opposite side of the road. If she did so, it could keep her away for a little longer.

She glanced towards the entrance, dreading to see Tilly coming through it. But to her huge relief, there was no sign of her as yet.

She turned her attention back to Clara.

'Edward loved the idea of silver as a theme,' Clara was happily trilling. 'And before you say anything, yes, it was a pretty obvious idea, given it's the Silver Jubilee next year,' she added with a laugh. 'He wants me to go again in two weeks' time, and we're going to fix a date for the party. After that, we're—'

'He's here!' Lizzie hissed in excitement, cutting Clara off mid flow.

She straightened up, pinched her cheeks and moistened her lips as Lewis came through the wide opening that led out to the courtyard.

'Hello, ladies,' he said as he approached the table.

'Hello, Lewis. This *is* a surprise!' Clara exclaimed, glancing round at him. 'Do you often have morning coffee here?'

He went to the seat opposite her and sat down.

'I could lie,' he said, 'and say that I do. But I must own up to the fact it's your fault that I'm here, Lizzie.' He smiled broadly at Lizzie. 'On Tuesday, I heard you mentioning meeting here for coffee, and I couldn't resist the chance of spending some time in such charming company.' He glanced back at Clara. 'I hope you don't mind.'

Clara smiled. 'Of course, we don't. We're very glad that you're here. Aren't we, Lizzie.'

Lizzie beamed at him. 'Yes, we are.'

The waiter appeared at the side of the table. 'I'll have a coffee,' he said. 'Are the two of you ready for another drink?'

'Yes, please,' both said at the same time.

'We'll have the same again,' Lizzie told the waiter, and turned back to Lewis. 'I should warn you that Tilly might turn up at any moment. She's our chaperone today. So if there's anything you want to say before she gets here, now's the time,' she said lightly.

'I'm wracking my brains to think of something that would be suitable to be repeated in front of you two ladies that I wouldn't want an older sister to hear.' He pulled a woebegone face. 'I regret I can't come up with anything. Does that mean I have to leave?'

'Definitely not. Does it, Clara?' Lizzie said in a rush.

'Of course not. In fact, I've just had a brilliant idea, Lewis,' Clara said, smiling at him in delight. 'You're a man—'

'How gratifying that you've noticed,' he said smoothly.

Both girls giggled.

'Well.' Clara glanced quickly at Lizzie, and then back at Lewis. 'You might be able to help.'

'Now you've piqued my curiosity,' he said.

He paused to let the waiter put the coffees on the table,

and in the centre of the table a dish of small teacakes and one of mango, banana and pineapple slices.

'Whatever it is, I'll be pleased to help,' he said, picking up his coffee as the waiter left. 'So, now that I'm committed, you can tell me what I've let myself in for.'

'This isn't to be made widely known yet,' Clara said, 'but Mr Harrington is giving a party at the beginning of February.' And she told him what they'd discussed the evening before. 'I've got to try and come up with some ideas, and Lizzie's going to help.'

'I certainly am.' Lizzie smiled at Lewis.

'But it would be really good to have input from a man,' Clara went on. 'We want men to be comfortable there as well as women, so the decorations shouldn't be too pretty, and too feminine, if you see what I mean. With your help, we could see that they weren't.'

'Edward Harrington is a man,' he said, taking out a packet of Player's No. 3 and a box of Swan Vestas matches. 'Wouldn't he curb any excess of pink fluffiness?'

'He'd do his best, I'm sure, but The Residency events are usually stuffy. Which of course they have to be,' she added hastily. 'But for that reason, I don't trust his taste in decoration. Having another male viewpoint would be really helpful. I doubt that any of your ideas would be stuffy.'

He grinned at her. 'Of course, I'd be delighted to help.'

He widened his smile to include Lizzie. Lizzie sat back in her chair, satisfaction on her face.

'Shall we all meet here for coffee next Friday,' Clara suggested, 'if that's a good day for you, Lewis? I won't be seeing Mr Harrington till after that, so by the time I do, I might have had some good suggestions from both Lizzie and you.'

Lizzie and Lewis glanced at each other.

Two satisfied faces looked back at Clara.

'I'm sorry to have been so long,' Tilly called coming up to them. 'Lewis, what a nice surprise.' She sat down, called to the waiter that she'd like a coffee, and turned back to them. 'So, what have you been talking about?' she asked.

SHE'D DONE her best for Lizzie, Clara thought that afternoon as she sat on the verandah, her book unopened on her lap, her eyes on the tips of the coconut trees, where the fronds were green-gold in the afternoon light.

And Lizzie had obviously appreciated her efforts, and had been gleeful at the prospect of another morning meeting with Lewis.

She'd left Clara with the words that she and Clara should go to each other's houses during the week, and plan how Lizzie could get a few private minutes with Lewis, as she wanted to have something to suggest when she saw him again on the Friday.

But if Lewis was really serious about Lizzie—and Lizzie seemed convinced that he was—then he ought to speak to Lizzie's parents soon, and ask permission to walk out with her. There were only so many excuses they'd be able to conjure up for the three of them to meet together.

Lizzie ought to be sure what she truly thought about Lewis.

She couldn't possibly know that yet, the short amount of time she'd spent with him.

Even with a chaperone in the background, if she spent a morning or two with him, with her parents' permission, she'd have a chance to find out if there was more to her feelings than that she found Lewis extremely attractive.

And another reason why Lewis shouldn't leave it too long to speak to Lizzie's parents was the man in Madras.

Just as Mr Goddard had opened discussions with the man without Lizzie's knowledge, he could proceed with further arrangements in a similar manner. Fathers often acted on behalf of their daughters, and Lizzie had already expressed her willingness to meet the man, so that might well happen.

But would Lewis be acceptable to Lizzie's parents, she mused.

Even though Lewis was very pleasant, it was hard to believe that Mr Goddard would welcome the substitution of a company agent with limited means for a man with a promising career in the colonial administration.

She shrugged. Lizzie must know better than anyone how her parents would react, so she was surely worrying needlessly. And she opened her book.

LIZZIE SAT in the sitting room opposite her mother, who was embroidering the corner of a cushion, and her father, who was reading the *Cochin Argus*. Frowning, she stared at the embroidery that lay on her lap.

Lewis had gone to the café that morning solely because he'd wanted to see her. He'd made that clear as soon as he'd sat down.

In fact, he couldn't have made his feelings plainer.

If Clara hadn't been droning on about their evening at the Harrington house before Lewis arrived, she could have helped her work out a way of getting her alone with Lewis for a short period of time.

Getting him there that morning had been the first stage, but no more than that.

They needed time in which to talk to each other, just him and her, without any mention of parties and boring invitations—time which would give Lewis the chance to put his feelings for her into words.

It was what he'd been hoping to do that morning, she was sure.

But it wasn't going to be easy.

Clara couldn't leave her alone with Lewis in Old Harbour House.

In a small community, word would soon get around about such behaviour. Her parents would be certain to hear about it, and they might speed things up with John Lansdowne, which was the last thing she wanted.

That left the three of them at the table.

But Clara couldn't really be expected to put her hands over her ears and try not to hear her when she talked with Lewis, so she had to come up with something better than that if she and Lewis were ever going to have a chance to declare their feelings for each other.

The only thing she could think of was arranging to meet him under the cover of darkness.

She felt a shiver of expectation run through her.

She hadn't forgotten that Clara had once told her that George used to go along the beach path to her house after dinner, and Clara would creep downstairs and sit with him.

Lewis could come to her house in such a way.

It would take a couple of minutes only for her to suggest to him that he do so, or for him to come up with an alternative plan. And before the three of them met again next Friday, she'd talk to Clara about how best to get the few minutes they needed.

Perhaps Clara could draw Tilly away from the table, for example, by pretending to feel ill.

With Clara's help, it could be done.

Or perhaps she'd have a moment after church on Sunday, when everyone was talking to everyone else. That was a possibility, too.

She sighed. If she didn't manage to speak to him on Sunday, it was going to feel a very long week.

'Is anything wrong, Lizzie?' Julia asked. 'You seem distracted, darling.'

'Nothing's wrong,' Lizzie replied, picking up her needle. 'I'm just reminded, though, how boring embroidering is.'

THE MORNING HAD GONE WELL, Lewis thought as he sat on his verandah, a whisky at his side.

Clara didn't look or behave like a girl whose engagement was about to be announced. On the contrary, she'd clearly been delighted to learn that seeing her again had been his reason for going that morning.

The look she'd given Lizzie had told him that.

And if he'd had any doubts, which he hadn't, her invitation to him to join their discussion about the party decorations, had confirmed it.

She was bound to have realised that he wasn't remotely interested in decorating a house, and was unlikely to contribute to such a discussion, but she'd obviously wanted to see him again, and the party had given her an excuse for doing so.

But why had Harrington asked for Clara's help, he wondered.

For a party in Harrington's house, which would be subject to the scrutiny of the British community, most of whom had never before been inside the house, the decorations would without doubt be done by his experienced staff and would be chosen by him, whether or not Clara liked them.

It must be that Harrington enjoyed the company of her parents—after all, he'd seen them together several times at the club in recent months—and thought that by involving Clara in an aspect of Cochin life, it would help her to adjust to being back in the town, and that such a gesture would please them.

That morning had brought them all together around the table, and made sure that they'd meet again before too long, which was exactly what he'd wanted. But ideally, the next meeting would be the last in which a chaperone would be involved.

After that, when he met up with Clara, it should be just him and her.

And to further that, inconvenient though it was going to be, he'd be at Old Harbour House the following Friday.

Annoyingly, he had consignments that had to be collected during the week, so he'd now have to go to the backwaters two days earlier than planned, which meant he'd miss a Wednesday night at the club, and those Wednesday evenings were proving useful for making contacts.

But the pursuit of Clara was of prime importance at the moment.

After next Friday—and he didn't yet know quite how he'd do it—it would be just Clara and him.

It might be that he'd have to speak to her outside the church. With everyone intent on chatting to friends and acquaintances, they might be able to snatch a few minutes together. It wouldn't take long to let her know that her feelings were reciprocated. And then they could plan what next to do.

He pulled the bottle of whisky towards him, and poured another shot.

'Cheers,' he said, raising his glass to the high wall surrounding the courtyard. 'In anticipation.' And he emptied the glass in one go.

15

The following Friday morning

WHILE HER MOTHER sat on the sofa, glancing through the newspaper, Clara stood at the sitting room window and stared out at the stormy grey landscape.

Rain rattled relentlessly on the roof.

The rain had begun to fall in a torrents last Sunday as they were leaving St Francis Church, taking them quite by surprise, preventing any after-church conversation and sending them hurrying back to their homes, rather than across the road to The English Club.

Every morning since then, the sun had risen in a cloudless blue sky and shone down on a world washed anew in the night—a world in which every leaf was a bright glossy green and every flower a blaze of brilliant colour beneath a veil of sparkling raindrops.

And then, an hour or so later, a tiny cloud had appeared

in the distance, no more than a smudge in the wide expanse of blue, but that smudge had swollen at amazing speed, bringing with it a mist that shrouded the world in a sombre grey.

And rain had begun to fall in sheets, and had continued to fall until the following day.

There'd been a break of a couple of hours in the middle of the Wednesday, and her hope had risen that the worst was over and that Friday would be sufficiently dry for them to meet at the café as planned.

For those two hours, the air had been clear and fresh and filled with the songs from a multitude of birds, and she'd run out into the garden, stood on the lawn, the foliage on either side of her hidden beneath a cloud of fluttering butterflies, and she'd inhaled the sharp, sweet smell of wet grass.

But those two hours had been no more than a short respite from the relentless rain, which, when it returned, swept across the sea in a dense pillow of grey, releasing its load when it reached the land, and drowning all hope of any meeting on the Friday.

'Ah, here you are,' Henry said, coming into the room and going across to the sofa. He sat down next to Mary. 'According to Amit, we'll have seen the last of the rain for a while by Monday.'

Clara went and sat in the armchair opposite them.

She glared at the knitting needles and wool on the table beside her, and pushed them further away. 'I was surprised you went into the office today, Papa. It's awful outside— there's not been a break in the rain since I got up.'

'There were things that had to be done for next week's shipments, but you're right, it's not the most pleasant of days. The wind was blowing heavily from the south, and

Bazaar Road was a river of mud. As it's been all week. I felt quite sorry for Lewis, who had to go on a trip a few days ago.'

'To the backwaters?' Clara asked in surprise.

'That's right. I told him it wasn't necessary, that it could wait until the rain had stopped, but he was anxious to supervise a quantity of sandalwood he'd arranged to pick up.'

'I didn't realise you traded in sandalwood, Papa,' Clara said.

'I didn't until recently. That I do now is thanks to Lewis. He's entered into a contract for the company to convey sandalwood to a steam distillation factory. The wood had to be delivered to the factory this week, he said. He'd arranged for extra men to help and didn't want to let them down. He's a good man.'

'Why did he need extra help with a bit of wood?' Mary asked in surprise.

'Because they remove the whole tree. The wood from the stump and root possess a high level of sandalwood oil, you see, and that can be processed and sold. I'm very grateful to Lewis for getting us such a potentially lucrative contract. He only returned yesterday.'

'Was the trip successful?' Mary asked.

Henry nodded. 'Apparently, so. Despite the rain, he also picked up a couple of other consignments, I believe.'

'He's admirably conscientious,' Mary said. 'It's a shame he isn't married. A man like that has a lot to offer.'

'What about Lizzie for Lewis? She's not yet engaged,' Clara said lightly. She gave a slight laugh to suggest that she wasn't being entirely serious.

Henry snorted. 'I wouldn't want to be in her shoes if she ever presented that to Albert as a proposition. Even if he hadn't already set his sights on some man at the other side of the country, he wouldn't for one minute entertain the idea of his daughter marrying a company agent. Not Albert.'

'Clara wasn't being serious, darling,' Mary said with a smile. 'We all know how ambitious Albert is, and Julia, too, I suspect. And probably Lizzie, too.'

'Of course, I wasn't,' Clara said hastily. 'Lizzie's agreed to meet the man her father wants her to marry. I wouldn't call her ambitious, though.'

'Maybe that was the wrong word,' Mary said. 'Perhaps strong-willed is more accurate. My instinct tells me that Lizzie's the sort of girl who'd ignore all advice, if advice was given, and go after what she wanted with blinkered determination.'

Clara was silent for a moment. 'What about me?' she asked. 'Do you think I have the same blinkered determination as Lizzie?'

'No, I don't,' Mary said calmly. 'But I wasn't indicating that this is a characteristic to be admired. It isn't. You're good-natured, and you're more caring of the people around you than I suspect Lizzie is.'

'You make me sound boring,' Clara said sulkily.

'Nonsense,' Mary said with a laugh.

'To my mind, your mother's being a little hard on Lizzie,' Henry said. 'Lizzie has shown an admirable obedience to her father's wishes about her marriage. She seems a charming girl.'

'I like her,' Clara agreed. 'I wouldn't say we've ever been really close in the past, but since we got home, we've become closer. I'd be sorry if she moved away.'

'Well, don't suggest to her that she marries Lewis as a way of keeping her here, is all I can say!' Mary exclaimed, and she and Henry laughed. 'Now, what about that knitting you were going to do?'

'It was your idea that I do it, not mine. I'll never be any good at knitting. I hate it. I'd much rather read a book.'

'Knitting is a better attribute for a wife to have,' Mary said firmly. 'A lot of men would be put off a woman if she read too much. I should keep that preference to yourself.'

FOLDS of thunder rolled sonorously above the tiled roof of the Goddard house, and intermittent flashes of lightning illuminated the purple sea and lit up the tips of the palm tree fronds that stood out against the leaden sky.

Lizzie glared through the window at the drama that lay before her eyes.

This wasn't the way she'd hoped to be spending her Friday morning, stuck in the sitting room, listening to her mother tap pieces of her wooden jigsaw puzzle on the side of the table while she deliberated where she could place a piece.

Turning away from the stormy seascape, she flounced across the room and sat down in her favourite armchair.

Her father and George were working in the study, having decided against going into the office that day. And they wouldn't be the only ones who'd be staying indoors on such a day, she was sure. So, too, would Lewis.

If only she'd been able to see him that morning, she thought in despair.

But the horrendous weather had made that impossible, and she'd been reduced to sitting with her mother, surrounded by overly ornate pieces of carved furniture, fervently hoping that the rain would soon stop so that she and Clara could at least meet Lewis the following week.

But November could be almost as wet as October, so there was no certainty that the following Friday would be possible, or the one after that.

And even if the weather *did* clear before the following Friday, Lewis, like her father, would have a great deal of work to catch up on, and would be unlikely to think of going to the café on the off chance that they might be there.

There was always a risk, also, that if the ghastly weather continued for as long as two or three weeks, their advice for Edward's party would no longer be needed as he'd have gone ahead and asked his staff to do the necessary planning.

Clara had suggested silver as a theme, and as a sop for no longer needing her advice, he'd probably stick with that idea. It would be all that he and his staff would need to know in order to get things moving.

And if that, indeed, happened, they'd have no excuse for meeting Lewis.

It made it all the more imperative that she come up with another way of seeing him, so that she could invite him to come to her garden.

Ideally, it would be a plan that didn't rely upon anyone other than herself, and one that didn't depend upon too many other circumstances being met.

She sat bolt upright.

Lewis usually went to The English Club late on a Wednesday afternoon. Her father had mentioned seeing him there a few times.

Well, she could go there, too!

She could be accompanied by her *ayah.*

Admittedly, that wasn't ideal. Her *ayah* would feel a loyalty to her parents, who'd kept her on after Lizzie had gone to England, and the *ayah* would be sure to tell them if

Lizzie talked to a man. So she'd have to think of a way of temporarily getting rid of her.

She obviously couldn't go inside the club building—apart from the fact that she'd be unchaperoned in front of people who knew her parents, women weren't allowed in there by themselves—but she could wait for him, hidden beneath the trees across the road from the club, and then call to him when he arrived.

The only problem would be if he drove straight through the gate and up to the parking area next to the club building. She'd never be able to run up the drive to him as she'd surely be seen.

That meant she'd have to be close enough to the entrance that when she saw his Chevrolet Tourer slowing down to turn into the drive, she'd be able to manoeuvre herself so that he saw her. He'd then park the car and come back down the drive to her.

They wouldn't have long to talk, but all they needed was sufficient time for Lewis to declare his feelings, and for her to let him know they were reciprocated. And also for her to suggest, unless anything else occurred to her before then, that Lewis come to her garden late at night when her parents were in bed.

A sense of excitement fizzed through her at the thought of standing in the moonlit garden, close to Lewis, and it was all she could do to refrain from clapping her hands in delight at the thought that she'd soon be seeing him again.

She'd go to the club on the first Wednesday she could, and if that didn't work, she'd try to talk briefly to him outside the church, or at the The English Club afterwards, and she'd go to Old Harbour House with Tilly and Clara. She'd try everything until she found a way of talking to Lewis.

Nothing was going to stop her.

Her mother glanced up from her jigsaw puzzle. 'You seem very restless today, darling. I was going to suggest that when the weather improves, you learnt to play bridge. It's something you could be thinking about. Bridge parties are very popular here, and I'm sure they'd be even more so in Madras. To be a good player would be an excellent entrée into the social circles your husband will move in.'

'I've not even met the man yet,' she snapped.

'If when you'd met him, you chose not to marry him—though we hope you'll fall in with your father's wishes—a knowledge of bridge would be an excellent way of widening your circle of friends here. Please do think about it, Lizzie.'

'I will,' she said, without the slightest intention of doing so.

16

T*he Residency,*
    late afternoon, Monday

THE BREEZE FELL AWAY and the tide slackened.

The boats that had been moored at the end of the short wooden jetty at the southernmost tip of Bolghotty Island, bobbed up and down as a stillness settled on the afternoon.

Edward and Michael strolled across the lawn of The Residency towards a table set for them in the shade of one of the many trees planted in the gardens by the British some years before.

'I appreciate you staying over for a couple of nights,' Edward said. 'After last week, there're some things we need to catch up with, and it'll give us a couple of extra hours in the evening to do so.'

'I don't mind at all,' Michael said. 'Once we get all the urgent things done, we might even have time for a round of golf before we return to Cochin.'

'You must be a stickler for punishment,' Edward said in amusement. 'I'll never forget your attempt to hit the ball that had lodged in the grass close to the edge of the water. Your swing was something to behold. As was your follow through. As I recall, you swung around twice and landed in the water, leaving the golf ball where it had been at the start of your action.'

Both laughed.

'That wasn't my most impressive hour, I must admit,' Michael said ruefully as they sat down. 'I hope to have the chance to expunge that memory from your mind.'

Edward chuckled. 'We'll see.'

Moments later, one of the servants appeared with a tray on which there were two snifters, a bottle of brandy and a plate with some miniature curry puffs. He put everything on the table and silently withdrew.

Edward poured brandy into each of the snifters, and pushed one across to Michael.

They sat back, relaxing as they stared across the stretch of water that separated the long, narrow island from Cochin, which was shimmering in the haze of the late afternoon.

As the sun began to sink towards the horizon, two of the servants emerged from the palace's pillared entrance to begin the nightly ritual, walking solemnly along the path to the flagstaff.

Standing at the wide stone base of the flagstaff, they stood, halyards in hand, watching for the moment when the sun disappeared in a blaze of white light. At that exact moment, they pulled on the ropes and lowered the flag, and then folded it and returned to the quiet grandeur of The Residency.

'Tilly said that one of the things that struck Clara, now

that she's back,' Michael remarked, 'is how swiftly night falls here. It's very different in England.'

'I suppose it would seem strange.'

'That last hour of daylight is my favourite time of the day,' Michael went on. 'There's a quietness at that time that seldom exists before then.'

'It's an Indian sort of quietness,' Edward said with a smile. 'The birdsong and chatter of frogs and insects are always with us, but we don't really notice them. We notice them when they're not there, though. Such as during the monsoon when they're silenced.'

'The rain certainly washed out the last two weeks,' Michael remarked. 'You've not yet been able to meet Clara and Mary, have you? Tilly said Clara had been trying to come up with suggestions, and was pretty fed up with the rain.'

'I wouldn't want Clara to know this, but my staff have started on the preparations,' Edward said drily. 'I knew that the weather might put a damper on things—and I don't think the rains are quite over yet. Given that, and the fact that I'm going to be tied up with the Navy's visit for most of next week, I thought it best to make sure there'd be no last-minute rush.'

'I don't blame you. I saw the naval visit listed in the diary. Is there any purpose for it?'

'It seems they're interested in seeing the port and Willingdon Island. As much as anything, I think the visit's about proclaiming as widely as possible that they're no longer the Royal Indian Marine, but are now called the Royal Indian Navy. As each of their ships is now His Majesty's Indian Ship, they can entitle the ship HMIS. It's a source of great pride.'

'I see.'

'To come back to Clara, I didn't want my lack of free time to put pressure on her. I imagine she's more than enough to do with her engagement and wedding plans.'

'Because of the rain, there's not been any movement on either, as far as I know. But there's plenty of time. The six months that she and George are having to wait before there's an official announcement are nowhere near up.'

'George is a lucky man.'

Michael nodded. 'Yes, he is. She seems a very pleasant girl. Not that I've seen that much of her since she's been back. Work and all that. But Clara's lucky, too. She's being allowed to marry for love. As I understand it, Lizzie Goddard will be marrying a man she hasn't even met yet.'

He paused, and then went on. 'But talking about traders and their families, I've been meaning to ask if you'd got any further with your enquiries. Or were they, too, a casualty of the weather?'

'The weather and the sheer difficulty of finding out anything so secretive in nature. We know for certain that drugs are being shipped from Cochin to other parts of the world, but we still don't know who's responsible. There's always been such a trade, but not on the scale that's happening now.'

'Have you any idea yet how many people are involved?'

Edward shook his head. 'It's impossible to know. There'll be the person who sets up the deals, and the men who pick up the drugs, and those who secrete them on the outgoing ships. And the sailors who work on the ships have probably got a pretty good idea of the nature of their cargo.'

'What about offering a reward for information?' Michael asked.

Edward shrugged dismissively. 'It's not worth it. There's so much money to be made from drugs that everyone involved will be so well paid that they've no incentive to inform on the person paying them. On the contrary, it's in their interests to see that he isn't caught.'

'I can see that. Can the police and port authorities help?'

'We can't rely on them. Some of them will have been handsomely paid to turn a blind eye. And there's little point in checking the logbooks of suspect ships as the captain will almost certainly have falsified them. We're doing random checks, nevertheless, but without much success.'

'It sounds a bit of a lost cause.'

'It may seem it, but I refuse to give in. The damage that drugs can do is incalculable. I'm pinning my hopes on the men that for the past few months, we've been placing among those working on the wharves. With luck, one of them will come up with something that will point to the source of the problem.'

'I'll certainly do what I can to help. You only have to say.'

'Perhaps you and Tilly would come to dinner the week after next, and I'll invite the Saunders family, too. If anyone knows what's happening in Cochin and Muttancherry, it'll be Henry Saunders.'

Michael nodded. 'I think that's right.'

'As you know, with that in mind, I've now met him a few times, and found him very personable. But much as I hate to say it, we can't yet rule him out of any involvement.'

'I realise that, sir. I'm confident, though, that you'll come to believe he's above reproach. He'll know about the legitimate activities in Cochin, but not the illegal ones.'

Edward smiled at him. 'As he's both Clara's father and Tilly's, I'm sure you're right.'

Michael laughed. 'Fair enough. I'm bound to be prejudiced. But you'll see for yourself that it's justified. And I'll do my bit, too. I intend to make an effort to get closer to Lewis

Mackenzie. He's as likely as Henry to know what's happening in Cochin. Possibly, even more so. The company agents have lines of communication between themselves. If there's anything untoward at Saunders & Co, he'll certainly know about it. And he could even be responsible.'

'How will you go about it?'

'The traders go to The English Club for a couple of hours on Wednesdays from about four o'clock, and so do the company agents. I'm going to begin going there, too, at that time, ostensibly for a game of billiards. Not this week, of course, but I hope to start next week. It can't hurt.'

'It sounds a good idea. I wish you luck.'

'And perhaps I'll suggest to Tilly that we go with the Saunders to a Saturday evening at the club. I'm sure that Lewis goes on Saturdays, too. And if he and I have had a game of billiards earlier in the week, followed by an evening together, possibly with his agent friends, it would be natural for me to invite him to join our group.'

Edward nodded. 'I take it you think that convivial surroundings might loosen his tongue.'

Michael grinned. 'That's the plan.'

THE LAMPS inside The Residency had been lit, the doors and windows thrown open and the paths through the gardens watered to lay any residual dust.

With the scent of wet earth strong, Edward stood on the verandah in front of his palace bedroom and stared out across the lawn to the sea.

He very much hoped that Michael's trust in Henry Saunders wasn't misplaced, both for the sake of Michael, whom he liked enormously, and for Clara, for whom he regretfully still felt something very much stronger than liking.

But the rumours were that Henry Saunders was at the heart of the new drugs' trade, and that opium was the drug he was shipping out.

Poppies had never been widely grown in the Cochin area in the way that they had in Northern India, so if he could stamp out the trade at this early stage, there was a possibility that the shipping of opium through the port of Cochin could be brought to an end before it had seriously begun.

Not even Michael knew that he'd placed Jitu, one of his most trusted men, a man who was intelligent and literate, specifically to watch the practices in Saunders & Co.

This wasn't because he didn't trust Michael to remain silent, because he did. There was no man more loyal and reliable, of that he was sure. But there was always a risk that Michael might reveal in a family gathering, by word or deed, or simply by his expression, that the finger of suspicion was pointing at his wife's father.

As far as Michael was concerned, Jitu was just another of their undercover workers, who happened to be working on Henry's wharves.

Any check on Jitu's background would find that he'd been dismissed from his last job for suspected theft, and Edward was hoping that with the criminal past he'd given Jitu, the man would prove a magnet for illegal smugglers.

And if that smuggler was, indeed, Henry, well, it would cause Edward a huge amount of grief, but Henry would have to be arrested.

The very thought, though, was utterly distressing.

It was vitally important, therefore, for the sake of the Saunders family, that if the rumours were wrong, he found the person at fault. Only in that way would he free the family from any suspicion, and restore to Henry Saunders the reputation for honesty that he was in danger of losing, possibly without any justification.

In the meantime, his party was a mere two months away and when he returned to his house, he'd have to see how far his staff had got with their preparations.

At the thought of something connected with Clara, he found himself smiling.

But he shouldn't be thinking of her, he berated himself.

It was so infuriating that despite his best endeavours, he just couldn't get her out of his mind.

17

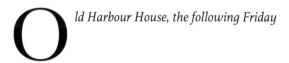

ld Harbour House, the following Friday

CLARA SMILED at George across the table.

'I'm so glad we were able to meet today,' she said happily. 'It was very kind of your father to give you the time off. It's worked out perfectly as I hadn't yet arranged to see Lizzie.'

'It wasn't really kindness—I was more than due a morning off,' George said. 'I haven't stopped working all week. And over last weekend, too. The minute the rain stopped, it was work, work and work. And it wasn't just in the office that I was needed—I had to visit the plantations to check the coconut seedlings we planted in September.'

'Father's been busy, too, so I knew it wouldn't be easy for us to meet. Seeing you today is a lovely surprise.'

'It's our mothers we have to thank. They decided we should get together, and Mother suggested to Father that I have the morning off. Suggested might be the wrong word. I think she told him that the two of us were going to have coffee together.'

'That was nice of them.' Clara turned and smiled at Mary and Julia, who were sitting a few tables away from them. Both mothers smiled back, and raised their cups in acknowledgement.

'Being stuck indoors for a couple of weeks, I had plenty of time to work out how little we've seen of each other since I got home,' Clara said, taking one of the banana cakes that had been brought with their coffees. 'I thought we'd have met more often by now. Our parents want us to get to know each other again, but how can we if we never meet?'

'The trouble is, I'm so tied up in the day. It's not that I don't want to see you, because I do. It's just that there doesn't seem to be any time. On the last few Saturdays before the rain, I went with Father to The Residency. He's found someone who can teach me golf. The Residency course is only small, but golf is increasingly popular, and Father thinks it's a game I should know.'

'D'you like it?'

'It's all right. I prefer cricket, though, and would much rather be taking part in a game on the Parade Ground. I've hardly had any occasion to wear my flannels this year because of the golf, but I'm certainly hoping to play more regularly next year.'

'I see,' she said quietly.

'And you know what it's like after church and in The English Club—there's never a moment when I'm not being called upon to talk to someone or other. It's been impossible to get together, even though I desperately want to. And I do,' he said, leaning slightly towards her, and taking her hands in his. 'I really do.'

'It sounds as if I come quite a long way down the list of things you want to do,' she said, trying to inject a bounce into her voice. 'You've got work, cricket, golf, important people to meet, and then, somewhere near the bottom, there's me.'

He released her hands, and sat back.

'That's not really fair,' he said. 'You know I'll be running the company one day, and a man can't start too soon to prepare for that. I've a great deal to learn. I'm doing this for us, Clara. I want to be able to make a lovely home for us, and to look after you as best I can.'

'I know you do, George,' she said. 'Ignore me. I love you, and I'm just feeling miserable that I've seen so little of you since I came home. But I know it's not your fault.'

'And I feel just the same, Clara.' He reached across the table and again took her hands in his. 'You mean everything to me,' he said, his voice thickening with emotion. 'And I must start showing you that, and telling you that, and not just assuming you realise it. I can't wait to marry you.'

'And I could never love anyone more than I love you. That's why I want to spend more time with you.'

'I'd love that. But what can we do?'

She felt herself blush. 'When we were little, you used to come to my garden after dark, and call up to me. I'd come down and we'd sit on the verandah and whisper to each other, telling each other everything. I used to love that time with you. Perhaps you could sometimes visit me again that way.'

He tightened his hold on her hands. 'That's an excellent idea!' he exclaimed in delight. 'That's what I'll do. I don't know why I didn't think of it myself.'

'It's because you're so busy. Don't tell Lizzie, though. She knows we used to meet that way, but she might not approve, not now we're older.' Hesitating, she went a deeper shade of red. 'I shall probably be in my nightdress when you come, with a shawl around me. If I changed from my customary routine, my parents might suspect something. We can kiss if you want.' She giggled with nervousness. 'But that's all.'

'I love and respect you, Clara. You know that,' he assured her, his face very serious. 'You're not the sort of woman to behave as a wife to a man who wasn't her husband. Not even if she was engaged. I know that.' He leaned closer. 'But stealing a few kisses, now that's a different matter,' he said, his words caressing her.

She beamed at him.

'We'll be leaving shortly,' Mary called across to their table.

Both turned and smiled at their mothers.

'Maybe Father will allow this again,' he said, turning back to Clara. 'After all, I can offer to work late one afternoon to make up for it, or give up the afternoon breaks that we have.'

'I'd like that,' she said. "But I'd also like it if we met on our own at times. Like I suggested. Without either of our parents, or Tilly, staring at us. Or Lizzie. What's Lizzie doing today, by the way?'

He shrugged. 'I don't know. She's been in a fairly awful mood for the past couple of weeks. It's quite a relief to be able to get out of the house. I take it you don't know what it's about.'

The image of Lewis's face sprang to her mind.

'Not really. She'd been going to think up ideas for Edward's party. Maybe it's that. Perhaps she can't think of anything and is worried about letting me down.'

George laughed. 'Whatever it is, it won't be that. For all of her life—and I'm assuming that her years at school were no different—the only person Lizzie has thought about is herself. I promise you, it'll be something Lizzie wants from Father, that isn't falling into her lap.'

There was a sound of scraping chairs. Glancing towards their mothers, they saw that Julia and Mary were standing up.

'We'll do this again as soon as we can,' George said quickly. 'And with luck, we might get a few minutes together after church, and possibly even at the club, too.'

She held up her hands, her fingers crossed. 'But try to come to my garden after dark, too, won't you?'

'I'll do my best. But you know what work's like. I need some sleep.'

She felt her spirits drop. 'You do want to come, don't you, George?'

'It's time to leave now,' Mary said, coming across to them. 'I think you'll both be pleased to hear that we've agreed that our two families will have dinner together at the club next Saturday, and we'll stay on for the evening's activities. The club's organising a sort of party. So you'll be seeing each other again before too long, and in a relaxed social setting.'

She smiled at them both.

How would George have replied if her mother hadn't come across when she had, she wondered as she lay in bed that night.

Looking back on their conversation, she couldn't avoid feeling a little disappointed at George's lack of enthusiasm at the idea of visiting her after dark. He'd said it was an excellent idea, but he hadn't said when he might do so. Nor that he definitely *would* do so.

Surely he could see, as she could, that lovely though it was to meet him and sit with him at the table as they'd done that morning, being under the watchful eye of a parent, sister or *ayah* meant that it wasn't the same as when he came to her under the cover of night and they were alone, truly alone.

Able to talk together about what mattered to them.

Able to kiss each other.

How she wanted to feel his arms around her again, his lips on hers!

There hadn't been any more kisses since that first night at their house, when he'd kissed her on the verandah—just professions about how much they loved each other and wanted it to be just the two of them together.

But if he wanted it to be just him and her, why hadn't he jumped at her invitation to come to her at a time when it would be just the two of them together?

Could his reluctance be, she suddenly thought, because no matter what he'd said, he knew that he'd find it difficult to hold himself in check, her being in her nightclothes, both of them being alone in the dark of night?

A warmth swept through her. That would be it. He was acting out of consideration for her, anxious to avoid any risk of compromising her.

She'd heard the girls at school say that men found it hard to hold back when they were with the woman they loved. And even when they were with a woman they didn't love, she'd also heard. They could be animals, the girls had told each other in hushed tones.

What sort of things did the men want to do, her class-mates had asked the older girls, who seemed to know so much more than they. And the older girls had told them.

So she had a vague idea about what to expect on her

wedding night, and she wouldn't mind George doing that to her as she loved him. But she also knew there was a connection between that act and having a baby, and she knew they must do nothing like that till they were married.

And George would know that, too.

He was trying to protect them both, she thought in a wave of happiness.

She'd very much liked the way his kiss had made her feel, and the sensation that had shot through her body when her fingers had touched his bare skin. And George would have responded to her touch in the same way as she had to his.

He was right that it would be wiser to avoid that happening again in case, loving each other as they did, he was carried away and she found it impossible to ask him to stop.

Dear George, was her last thought as she drifted into sleep.

18

W ednesday, late afternoon,
   almost two weeks later

AT JUST BEFORE FOUR o'clock in the afternoon, Lizzie pressed
herself close to the trunk of the breadfruit tree, the large,
thick leaves that hung low from its branches affording both
shade and cover from anyone who might be passing by.

She fervently hoped that she was right that Lewis, like
the other company and commissioning agents, went to the
club at the beginning of the hours that were sacred to the
traders.

Her father and traders like him tended to go later in the
day, and she'd have to be away long before then in case this
turned out to be one of the weeks in which either her father
or Clara's, or both, turned up.

And also, because of her *ayah*, she was limited in how
long she could stay there.

She and her *ayah* had taken a rickshaw to St Francis

Church, and there she'd told her *ayah* that she'd like to spend an hour and a half inside the church. That would give the *ayah* time to complete the errands she'd been given, Lizzie told her, and by then, she would have spent sufficient time in the church.

Her *ayah* had looked amazed at the idea of Lizzie voluntarily spending any time at all in the church, let alone an hour and a half, and clutching the list of purchases that she'd been asked to make, had been visibly reluctant to leave her.

Lizzie had made an effort to look coy and embarrassed, and had given the *ayah* to understand, without actually going as far as lying, that she was meeting the vicar to talk privately about one or two sensitive matters to do with marriage, now that her parents had found a possible husband for her.

She was anxious that her parents didn't know about this, though, she'd hastily told the *ayah*. Some things were a little too personal, and too delicate to be discussed with parents, she'd managed to indicate.

The *ayah*'s brow had cleared, and she'd nodded her enthusiastic willingness to be complicit in something that had the suggestion of romance, and had assured Lizzie that while she'd return in an hour and a half, it wouldn't be a moment sooner than that.

As soon as her *ayah* had disappeared, Lizzie had hurried from the porch of the church, run down the short drive and a little way along St Francis Church Road to the place that was opposite opposite the main entrance to the club. There, with the Parade Ground behind her, she'd stood in the shadows of one of the trees, waiting.

At first, she'd been confident that she'd have more than enough time to talk to Lewis, and then to get back to the church in order to emerge from the porch at the right moment.

But time was speeding by, and she was getting quite anxious. If Lewis didn't soon turn up, or if she failed to attract his attention when he arrived, the afternoon would have been a complete waste of time, and she'd have to go through the whole procedure again the following week.

She groaned.

Her *ayah* was romantic, but not stupid.

She couldn't use the same excuse a second time. She kicked at the trunk of the tree in frustration.

This could be her only chance of meeting Lewis when there was no one else around.

She kicked the tree again.

It was true that she was going to the club with her parents and George on the Saturday evening, and with Clara's family, too. And Lewis was certain to be there, as well. But she would be watched so closely by her parents that the chance of a quiet word on her own with Lewis was extremely unlikely.

In fact, she'd be wise to go out of her way to avoid him in case she unwittingly gave herself away.

She hadn't yet prepared them for the way she felt about Lewis—she could hardly do so before she'd spoken to Lewis —and at that point, if either her father or mother suspected that she had feelings for Lewis, they'd whisk her off to Madras in no time at all.

And she needed to be cautious about George, too.

He'd become much more strait-laced than she remembered him being. It was as if, because he was now working in the company that one day he'd run, he'd decided that it was appropriate to mould himself into a younger version of their father.

When she'd first realised the way that she and Lewis felt about each other, it had occurred to her to ask George to chaperone her on occasions. She would then have taken him into her confidence, and asked him to let her spend a little time with Lewis in the open somewhere, in broad daylight.

But instinct told her that while the old George would have readily agreed, the new George definitely would not.

So given his closeness to their father, it was as important that he knew nothing of her feelings for Lewis, as it was that her parents remained in ignorance.

Seeing Lewis on a Wednesday afternoon really was her best hope, she thought in despair. But it was beginning to look as if that wasn't going to be the Wednesday on which such a meeting took place.

And then she heard the hum of an approaching car.

Her heart leapt, and she stared down the road in the direction of the sound.

It was a pale yellow car, the colour of Lewis's car. Yes, it was Lewis!

She pulled her straw cloche firmly on to her head, and took a step forward.

And then she heard the sound of a second car.

'Darn!' she exclaimed aloud, and she stepped quickly back into the shadow of the tree.

The second car had pulled out of the road just south of the Parade Ground and had turned in her direction. With luck, it would go straight past the club and continue to the north of Cochin.

She saw Lewis's car reach the drive that led to the club building, and slow in preparation for turning right.

To her great frustration and dismay, the second car didn't drive past as she'd hoped, but slowed down, waiting for Lewis to turn on to the drive. Then it, too, turned on to the drive.

For a split second, she saw the face of the driver in the second car—Michael Wakefield.

What's he doing there, she thought in annoyed surprise.

Although he and Tilly went occasionally to the Saturday evenings at the club, he rarely went on Wednesdays, if ever. His work usually kept him in The Residency during the day. She knew that because her father had remarked one evening that it was surprising how rarely Michael went to the club.

He must have been visiting Edward Harrington, she decided. Edward lived south of The English Club, and that would explain why Michael had been coming from the south, rather than from his house, which was further north.

She glanced quickly around, but there was no one remotely close by—it was a little too early for the many people who came out for an evening stroll along the promenade. The road, too, was empty in both directions.

She couldn't resist taking a weeny chance.

She ran across the road and, shielded from sight by the hedge that surrounded the club, she stared along the drive at the two cars that had come to a stop in the parking area, one beside the other.

Lewis had got out of his car and was heading for the entrance to the club.

She saw Michael climb from his car, and heard him call to Lewis, who stopped walking and turned towards him.

Michael's body language expressed surprise at seeing Lewis there, but not displeasure.

That's funny, she thought. Lewis frequently went there on Wednesdays, and Michael didn't. It should be Lewis who was surprised at seeing Michael there, not the other way round.

Michael appeared to be smiling warmly as he went up to Lewis. They spoke briefly, and then the two men walked together towards the entrance, chatting as they went.

Shaking with fury at how it had all gone so wrong, she turned and ran back across the road to the trees.

How maddening that Michael had suddenly decided to go to the club mid-week, and how absolutely infuriating that he should have chosen to do so on that very same day, and at exactly the same time, as Lewis.

There was no chance now of speaking to Lewis.

She'd just have to hope that at the club on Saturday night, she and Lewis would be able to slip away for a short amount of time. Perhaps he'd ask her to dance, and instead of dancing, they'd run out of the building, go down to the beach and talk there, away from the beam of light thrown out from the clubhouse.

If they were quick, they could be safely back before the dance had ended.

But that was still a few days away.

More importantly now, how on earth was she going to fill the time before she had to emerge from the church to link up again with her *ayah*? She could hardly go round the shops on her own, and the idea of going inside the church was risible.

She felt like bursting into tears.

If only Clara had been more helpful when she'd had the chance, she thought bitterly as she started to walk slowly around the perimeter of the extensive Parade Ground, making sure that she kept in the shadows cast by the breadfruit trees. She wouldn't have had to struggle like this.

But it was as if Clara didn't take her feelings seriously.

The only feelings that seemed to matter to Clara, were her own!

It really was too bad of her, and utterly selfish.

Well, two could play at that game. And if ever she got a chance to hold back on something that might help Clara, she'd certainly take it.

19

T *he following Tuesday afternoon*

HAVING TOLD his driver that he'd probably be gone a couple of hours, Michael walked down the cobblestoned alley to Henry's office, and pushed open the door.

Henry looked up from his desk. 'Michael!' he exclaimed in surprise, and he got up and came round his desk towards him, his arms outstretched in welcome. 'What a pleasant surprise,' he said, shaking Michael's hand. 'Isn't it, Lewis?' he said, glancing towards Lewis's desk.

'It might be for Lewis,' Michael said, glancing at Lewis with a smile. 'But not so pleasant for me after the trouncing at billiards that Lewis gave me last Wednesday.'

They all laughed.

'What's brought you to these parts, then?' Henry asked. 'We rarely have the pleasure of seeing you here.'

'I've had to take a group of guests to Jew Town, and I've just left them at Muttancherry Palace. To my great relief, they wanted to have a look round it by themselves, and then do some shopping. The thought of showing again the musty coronation robes and roped-off palanquins wasn't something I'd been looking forward to. Not to mention the highly sensual murals. This was a group that comprised only women.'

Henry chuckled.

'When I saw the time, I realised you'd probably be about to have some tea, and I thought I'd join you. If I'm invited to do so, that is. And perhaps have a look at the wharves afterwards. As you say, it's a while since I've been here.'

'Of course you're invited to join us. Isn't he, Lewis? And you're quite correct about the timing. We were about to go outside for a few minutes with our tea. But if you'd like something stronger, just say.'

Michael smiled his refusal. 'Never before six,' he said. 'But don't let me stop you.'

'You won't be. Lewis and I follow the same routine as you.' He glanced at the desk opposite Lewis's. 'Some refreshments, Nitesh, please, there's a good chap. Are you coming outside with us, Lewis?'

Lewis half rose and gave them an apologetic smile. 'Regretfully, no. I'm off to the village tomorrow morning, if you recall,' he told Henry. 'As I want to get an early start, I must have everything ready tonight.'

Henry nodded in satisfaction. 'As you can see, Michael, Lewis is a good worker, and not just a skilled billiards player. Nitesh will bring your tea to your desk, Lewis. Come on, Michael. Let's leave Lewis to it and go outside.'

And Henry turned and led the way into the courtyard.

'Your hibiscus is beautiful,' Michael told him, sitting where Henry indicated. 'This is quite an oasis amid the teeming life outside.'

'It *is* very pleasant, yes,' Henry said with a smile as he sat down opposite Michael. 'Tell me, how was the group today? Was it the spice trade that interested them or the synagogue?'

'Definitely the synagogue. And the Rajah's Palace, of course. Jew Town's no longer the centre of the spice trade in the way that it used to be, and as they'd travelled widely throughout the region, I imagine they'd already found out everything there is know about spice.'

He paused as Nitesh came out with their cups of tea, and a plate of sliced banana and breadfruit. He put everything on to the table and left.

'They may look in on the Spice Market while they're here,' Michael went on, handing a cup of tea to Henry and taking the other himself, 'but it was the Paradesi Synagogue they really wanted to see. They'd heard about the glass chandeliers and the hand-painted blue and white porcelain floor tiles from Canton, with no two quite the same. Also the Great Scrolls of the Old Testament, of course. It's just a shame that after so many centuries here, the Jewish community has shrunk so much that one can see a time when there won't even be the ten people required for a service.'

Henry nodded. 'That would indeed be a shame.'

'You'll be pleased to know,' Michael said, with laughter in his voice, 'that I pushed the importance of pepper. They knew that spices such as pepper can give an acceptable taste to food of an inferior quality, and can even mask the stench of decay.'

Henry nodded. 'That's certainly true.'

'But they'd no idea that after a bad harvest, or during a cold winter, the heavily preserved meat that saved lives would have been preserved by salt, or very likely by pepper. And as there were never sufficient peppercorns, peppercorns came to be so valuable that they were used as money. They'd never heard that as far back as 408AD, the Visigoths demanded a bounty in gold, silver and pepper to call off their siege of Rome. Or that rents were often paid with peppercorns.'

'I can only hope that your efforts on our behalf this morning will increase the demand for our product,' Henry said in amusement. 'Tilly's all right, I take it?' he went on.

Michael smiled. 'She is. As you'll see for yourself at the end of the week. We're looking forward to the party at the club. The rain put a stop to a number of social occasions, and Tilly's delighted to have the chance to wear one of the dresses made by the *durzi* just before the weather broke.'

'I must say, I'm very glad she's your financial burden, not mine any longer,' Henry said with a laugh. 'Clara's enough of an expense as it is.'

'We're looking forward to seeing Clara again. Tilly very much enjoys chaperoning her and Lizzie. They mustn't hesitate to ask her again.'

'I'll pass that on,' Henry said. 'So you, too, are going to the club on Saturday, are you? It sounds as if we'll all be there.' He took a sip of tea and looked curiously at Michael above the rim of his cup. 'Lewis mentioned that he saw you at the club last Wednesday. I didn't realise you'd started going there.'

'I haven't. I happened to be working on some things at home, and on the spur of the moment, I decided to take a break. I knew that you traders often go on Wednesdays, and

I thought I would join you. Working in The Residency makes us seem quite remote, and both Edward and I are keen to avoid giving the impression that we're isolating ourselves from the British community out of choice.'

Henry nodded. 'It's no bad thing for you go there at times. After all, Edward has the ear of the Resident, and the Resident is meant to pass our concerns to the Diwan, so that he can inform the Maharajah of them. If you and Edward don't mix with the people who're the lifeblood of the community, you won't know their concerns.'

'That's exactly it, Henry,' Michael said. 'And apart from general interest, given how long it is since I've been to the wharves, it's another reason for deciding to take a stroll down to the water to look at the boats.'

'We'll go together when you've finished your tea. I imagine that you'll want to look in the godowns, too.'

'I'd like that.'

They smiled at each other.

'And I might pop into Goddard's as well,' Michael added, 'since they're so close by.'

'I've been wondering what that was all about,' Henry told Mary at the end of dinner, after Clara had gone to the sitting room with her book.

'You don't think it was just what he said—he was in the vicinity and decided that he might as well look in. You said yourself that it's a while since he's visited your office and walked around the wharves.'

'But he didn't just casually visit, he showed a keen interest in everything. Without realising it, I found myself telling him what he must have already known; namely, that I sign the contracts, and increasingly, Lewis does, too. Then the goods are collected by Lewis, brought back on a *kettuvallam* to Muttancherry, and stored in our godowns.'

'You're right—he will have known that. He was probably just being polite—he knows how much you like to talk about your work.'

He shook his head. 'I don't know, Mary. It felt more than that. We even got on to the paperwork, though I don't know how. How it was checked by me, and then filed in the relevant box. How Nitesh looked after the arrangements for shipping, and generally, how Sanjay and I supervised the goods being loaded and shipped. And Lewis, too, obviously. But it's basic stuff and Michael already knew all of it, so why come today?'

'You said he went to Albert's, too.'

'That's right, he did. So which of us, I wonder, was the purpose of the visit,' he mused. 'It would be interesting to know.'

Mary frowned. 'I can't believe that he would have had an ulterior motive for either visit.'

'I hope you're right. But the word on the wharves is that an increasing number of illegal drugs are now passing through Cochin. It's clearly a highly lucrative business, but both Lewis and I want no part of it. There's a risk, though, that when the rumours reach the customs people and the Resident, which they must have done by now, we'll all be under suspicion. I'm wondering if that was behind today's visit.'

'Surely Michael knows you well enough to be confident that you'd never participate in such a trade.'

'I'd like to think so. But all the same, I shall tell Lewis to be extra scrupulous about completing all the necessary forms.' He paused. 'Perhaps you could have a word with

Tilly, and see if you can get anything from her. Without it being obvious, of course.'

'I'll do my best, but Tilly isn't stupid. I imagine she'll see through me, and tell me as much as Michael has told her she can.'

'Anything at all you can find out would be of interest.' He stood up. 'But for now, let's go and join Clara, shall we?'

20

*S*aturday evening

THE GODDARDS and the Saunders reached the club's parking area at exactly the same moment.

With much laughter and talking, they climbed from their cars and went into the building together. There they settled themselves in the dining room, choosing a group of tables and chairs that was within easy reach of the room where the dancing would take place and where a late-evening buffet would be laid out.

'So this where you are,' Tilly said, coming up to them, with Michael behind her. Seeing a need for more chairs, Michael went to drag two extra chairs to the table.

'Here, let me help you,' Lewis said, materialising at his side the moment before a club servant could reach Michael.

He took the second of the chairs from Michael, posi-

tioned it in a space that had opened up at the table between
Lizzie and Tilly, and started to move away.

'Why don't you pull up a chair and join us, Lewis?'
Michael said as he sat down. 'Unless you're already attached
to a group, that is.'

'I'm not. I've only just arrived. Well, thank you, Michael.
I'd be happy to join you.' He indicated to the nearest servant
his need for a chair, and the servant swiftly placed a chair
between Michael and Tilly.

'Oh dear no!' Lewis exclaimed as he looked at the empty
chair. He laughed. 'Far be it from me to come between a
husband and wife.'

Smiling, Michael slid across to the chair next to Tilly,
and Lewis sat down between Michael and Lizzie.

Leaning slightly forward, Lizzie glanced beyond George,
who was on her other side, and smiled at Clara. Clara raised
her eyebrows, and then both turned their attention back to
the table, where a waiter was taking the order for drinks.

'It's good to see you again, George,' Lewis said, leaning
back in his chair and directing his comment behind Lizzie's
back to George. 'There was something I wanted to bring up
with you, but I won't do it now, not with this lovely rose
between us.'

Lizzie turned towards him. Straightening up as he
finished the sentence, he looked at Lizzie and smiled.

She smiled back.

'If we don't get a moment today, Lewis,' George said,
speaking across Lizzie, 'come into the office next week. Our
seating makes it difficult to talk at the moment. Although we
might get a chance later tonight.' He glanced at Lizzie. 'I'm
going to leave you to talk to Lewis, Lizzie, as I intend to turn
my back on you to take advantage of a rare opportunity to
speak to Clara.'

With a smile at them both, he turned to Clara and trailed his fingers down her cheek. She gazed lovingly back at him.

'You look absolutely beautiful,' he said, his voice breaking with emotion.

Pink with pleasure, she glanced down at her sleeveless sage green chiffon dress, and looked back at him. 'I'm glad you like it.'

'That's an understatement. I love it. And I love you.'

'And I love you. You've no idea how much I was hoping we'd be able to sit together tonight,' she said.

'Oh, yes, I have. Because I was hoping for that, too. Whenever I'm not with you, I'm thinking about you, and I've had far more thinking time than I'd have chosen. This wait seems interminable. And pointless. We both know what we want, don't we?'

'I know that I certainly do.'

'And me, too.'

Dragging his eyes from George and Clara, Lewis grinned at Lizzie. 'The seating has worked to my advantage,' he said warmly. 'It'll be my pleasure to talk to you. I hope you'll be able to say the same.'

Lizzie went red.

'Did you manage to get out to the vines to check the harvesting of the pepper, Lewis?' Henry called across the table, the waiter having left.

Throwing Lizzie a look of desperation, Lewis turned towards Henry and opened his mouth to answer.

From her seat across the table next to Henry, Mary raised her hand to prevent Lewis from answering. 'No, don't reply to that, Lewis,' she said firmly. 'Henry knows that all talk about work is banned this evening. We're here to enjoy ourselves.'

Henry turned slightly and stared at Mary in mock surprise. 'What could be more enjoyable than calling to mind a godown full of peppercorns that have been dried in the sun for a week and a half, their green berries blackening as they turn into the peppercorns we grind in our mills?' he asked.

With upturned palms, he expressed bewilderment.

Albert leaned forward. 'It just so happens, I can think of something, Henry. Take a massive pile of coir, for example, which is waiting to be shipped to factories here in India and overseas, to be made into mats and runners, carpets and rugs, and sacking. A prettier picture you'll never find.'

He sat back and beamed round the table in satisfaction.

They all laughed.

'We'll call it a draw, I think, Mary, don't you?' Julia said, as the waiter returned with a tray and began to circulate their drinks. Another waiter put some small bowls of cashew nuts, curry puffs and figs in the centre of the table. 'And you, too, Albert, are forbidden to talk about work. Oh, look! It's Edward.'

'Good evening,' Edward said, coming up to the table. 'I wonder if I might join you?'

'Please, do,' Henry and Albert chorused in unison.

A chair was brought to Edward. He asked the waiter for a snifter of *Rupee d'or* brandy, and sat down next to Mary, opposite Clara.

He turned to Mary. 'I'm delighted to see you today. I'm afraid that the rain rather prevented the visit I'd hoped you and Clara would be able to make,' he said, 'and I wanted to apologise for that. It was a little more than the light showers we normally expect at this time of year.'

'There's no apology needed, Edward. The plans of us all were affected by the rains,' Mary said. 'But Clara's been most anxious about your party. Haven't you, Clara?' she called across the table.

'I heard what you said, Mama, and the answer is yes.' Clara smiled apologetically at Edward. 'I feel awful, Edward. I suggested a theme, and then I somewhat disappeared.'

'No need to worry,' he told her with a smile. 'I saw that time passing and wasn't sure when we'd be able to get together, so I got some of my staff working on it. We're using your suggestion of silver, and my staff have taken it from there.'

She gave an audible sigh of relief. 'I must admit, that's a load off my mind. As Mother said, I was getting quite worried.'

'Then I'm pleased to have been able to restore your peace of mind.' Edward inclined his head to her, and then glanced at George. 'I'm delighted to see you again, George. The Resident and I both enjoyed the visit you paid with your father a while ago. How are you getting on?'

'He's doing extremely well,' Albert said with pride. 'He's a natural trader.'

George grinned at Edward. 'If Father's going to talk about me in such praiseworthy terms, I think I'll just sit back in future and let him continue to be my voice.'

They all laughed again.

'I do enjoy the work, though, sir. It's full of variety and challenge,' George went on. 'And as I can't see that changing, the future looks extremely bright.'

Edward nodded. 'That's good to hear. You're a lucky man, Albert, to have such an able son, who's so interested in the business.'

'And I know it,' Albert said, with obvious pride.

Edward then turned to Mary, and engaged her in conversation.

'It's almost December now,' Albert remarked to Henry, lowering his voice. 'We said we'd give it six months before announcing the engagement. But I think we can now safely say that both young people are certain that they *do* still want to marry.'

Henry nodded. 'I agree.'

'Six months will bring us up to February. Christmas is a busy period for everyone, so it would be better to wait till after it. Why doesn't George have a word with you at some point before Edward's party, and the two of them go there as an engaged couple? They could even announce their engagement at the party. I'm sure Edward wouldn't mind. He seems very well disposed towards your family.'

'Indeed, that does seem to be the case, and I'm extremely grateful for the kindness he's showing towards us. Whenever anyone from the Port Trust is down on the wharves, they invariably make a point of stopping and chatting, and show a real interest in the company. I put that down to Edward's goodwill,' Henry said. 'It's clear that apart from being a very pleasant man, he's a good friend to have. As are you, Albert.'

They smiled at each other, and then both men looked towards Clara and George, whose heads were bent close to each other.

'Therein lies the future for both of us,' Henry said quietly, and Albert nodded.

'I can't believe that it's only just over a week since we were in the Old Harbour House together,' George said to Clara. 'It feels so much longer than that.'

'It does to me, too,' Clara said. 'I can't wait to be able to spend every minute of every day together. Except for the minutes when you have to work,' she added with a laugh.

'And what will you do in those minutes when I'm slaving away somewhere else?'

'Read, maybe,' she said lightly.

He laughed. 'What else?'

'Knit, I suppose.'

'That's a good thing to do. I've heard you and Lizzie be very dismissive of it, though.'

'But if you have something to knit for. Or, rather, someone to knit for,' she added. 'I meant you,' she said quickly, and she blushed.

George took her hand in both of his. 'I can't wait to work on creating a little someone for whom you can knit.'

Clara went an even deeper shade of red.

He leaned forward and whispered, 'I shall be thinking of that throughout every dance we have this evening.'

'You're more likely to be thinking of your toes,' she countered with a laugh. 'I have to warn you, the dancing classes at school were good, but it was ballet rather than ballroom. I haven't a clue how to do the Charleston, for example. I'm best at a waltz, but that's only because it featured in an end-of-term play that I took part in at school.'

'All the better if you're unsure of the steps. I've the perfect excuse to hold you tight and lead you.'

Each smiled lovingly at the other.

While Lizzie was chatting on in an animated fashion, it occurred to Lewis that even if Lizzie didn't have a brother who was destined to inherit the family company, his inclination would have led him to Clara, rather than Lizzie.

A few months ago, he wouldn't have said that. But now that he'd determined to install Gulika in his home as soon as he was married, his instinct told him that he'd get more past Clara than he would past Lizzie, who appeared to be more demanding as a person.

He really must come up with a way of securing a private moment with Clara, he berated himself. But how to do so? He couldn't even see her from where he was sitting as George was blocking his view.

And then an idea struck!

His spirits lifted, and he turned his full attention on Lizzie.

'And what do you plan to do now that the rains have stopped and you're able to escape the confines of your home, Lizzie?' he asked when she'd paused for a moment to draw a breath.

She pouted. 'Not much. Women are so limited. You men are really lucky. You've opportunities open to you that are denied a woman.'

'What opportunities? Apart from joining the club, that is. That's obviously for men only.'

'I'm not sure what's obvious about it,' she said archly. 'Women should be free to be members, too. But it's not only that. Men can go where they want, when they want. They don't have to be chaperoned. Women do, though. And that's very limiting.'

'But having a chaperone doesn't really restrict where you go, does it? It stops you from going alone to wherever you want to go, but that's all. Look at us men, and how hard we have to work all day. Having to be chaperoned is considerably less of a restriction than having to put in the hours of labour that befall a man. And besides,' he added, moving his head closer to hers, and lowering his voice, 'I'm sure you ladies have ways of getting around the obligation of having a chaperone.'

'I suppose some of us must have,' she said, equally quietly, happiness flooding her.

'Well,' he prompted.

They stared at each other.

Lizzie was certain that he must be able to hear the loud beat of her heart.

'Lewis, old chap,' Albert called across the table.

Both turned swiftly to look at him.

'I understand from Michael that you're a pretty fair billiards player. I wonder if you'd like a game.'

Forcing a smile to his face, Lewis looked across at Albert and nodded. 'It'll be my pleasure,' he said. 'Perhaps George will play the winner. What d'you say, George?'

'Hm. I don't know about that. I'm in a difficult position,' George said with feigned concern. 'If my father beat you and I had to play him, I'd have to make sure that I lost the game. I wouldn't risk him withholding my salary, would I? And that wouldn't make for much of a game. Perhaps Henry should play the winner.'

Henry nodded. 'I'd be happy to do so. And then Michael could play the winner after me.'

'I'd be delighted to do so,' Michael said with a broad smile.

'And that's the truth,' Tilly said drily. 'All evening, he's been wondering how to getout of the dancing, and you've just given him the perfect escape.'

Julia raised her eyebrows. 'I'm now viewing my husband's suggestion of a game of billiards with great suspicion.'

Albert laughed. 'If you'd recently seen me play billiards, my dear, you'd know that I'll be back with you in a matter of minutes. I'll do my best, of course, but I'm afraid that poor

Lewis won't get much of a game.' He stood up. 'Shall we go now, then, Lewis?'

Lewis rose to his feet. He looked down at Lizzie, amusement in his eyes. 'We've an unfinished conversation, I believe, Lizzie. I won't forget.' And he followed Albert across the dining room to the billiards' room.

As she surreptitiously watched him go, Lizzie's heart beat rapidly in excitement.

When he was finally out of sight, she turned towards Clara, wanting to tell her at once what Lewis had said, and to describe his expression when he'd gazed into her eyes, but from what she could see of Clara, she was engrossed in conversation with George, and clearly wouldn't have welcomed such an interruption.

Swallowing her words, she sat back and strained to hear what George was saying to Clara.

'I think I'll sit in Lewis's chair while he's gone,' Mary said, standing up. 'I want to hear how you've been, Lizzie, and as Michael's talking to Tilly and Edward, this will be a good moment to do so.'

She came round the table, sat down on the chair that had been Lewis's and turned to Lizzie. 'So, Lizzie. How've you been? Bring me up to date, will you.'

Lizzie said a word to herself that her mother would have been shocked to know that she knew.

21

L*ater*

As THE BAND packed up for the evening, the club's table stewards finished laying out a lavish buffet-style breakfast of ham and eggs, imported sausages, toast and marmalade. At the far end of the table, they set out cups of tea and coffee.

Then they stood back against the wall behind the table, ready to replenish dishes as they emptied or to bring any item that might be requested.

Seeing the food laid out, and with the last dance over, people started gravitating towards the buffet table. Clara and George followed them. Without a reason to continue holding hands, each reluctantly released the other's hand.

Then there was a sudden flurry of movement, and she heard George exclaim in surprise.

Turning, she saw that two people had grabbed George by the arms and were stopping him from moving.

'What's going on?' she asked.

George glanced over his shoulder. 'I seem to be a prisoner of the cricket team,' he said, and he burst out laughing. Grinning broadly, they started dragging him towards the far side of the room. 'I'll be back, Clara,' he called.

Annoyed, Clara watched him go.

At that moment, Lewis came through the arched doorway. Seeing Clara on her own, and George being pulled into the distance, he made a beeline for her before she could be joined by anyone else.

'I see that George has been forcibly removed from your side,' he said with a smile when he reached her.

'I know. And I'm not too pleased about it,' she said, her back to him as she stared after George.

'I doubt that I would be, if I were you. But at least it's given me the chance to talk to you.'

She turned towards him. 'I'm being rude. I'm sorry.'

'There's no need to apologise. I'd be annoyed, too, if my young man didn't make any attempt to stay at my side.' They both looked again towards George. 'I wasn't able to claim you for a dance, I'm afraid,' he continued a moment later. 'Blame my omission on billiards.'

Clara turned back to him. 'I'm not sure that blame is the right word. You deserve credit for defeating them all. Michael had said you were a pretty fair player, but I gather that was something of an understatement, and you beat one after the other.'

'I was lucky,' he said.

'For one game, maybe, but not for all of them. I wouldn't be at all surprised,' she added with a laugh, 'if after what Tilly hinted at earlier about Michael being keen to avoid dancing, he didn't start practising billiards at once so that he's never again knocked out so soon.'

He smiled. 'He's a good player. He doesn't need to practise that much.'

'Tilly said that you and Michael met at the club on Wednesday, and that you played a game then.'

'We did indeed. We spent a pleasant couple of hours at the table, and plan to do so again on the next occasion that we're both there at the same time.'

A couple came towards them from the buffet table, each with a plate of food in their hands.

'That looks good,' she remarked as they passed by. She glanced in the direction that George had gone, but there was no sign of him. 'I won't wait for George, I don't think. I'll get some food and eat it next door. Have you see Lizzie recently?' she asked as they both started moving toward the table. 'I didn't see her dancing.'

He shook his head. 'I haven't, I'm afraid. I came straight here from the billiards' room.'

'She must be with the others, then. Are you staying in one of the guest rooms tonight?' she asked, taking the plate that was offered to her.

'Unfortunately not. I'd intended to do so, but I left it too late to book a room. Five guest rooms is insufficient on a night like this when a number of people want to stay. No, I'll go back to the house.'

'Have you a waterfront house, too?'

'No, one of the Dutch houses. It's not far from the water, though. You'd think I see enough water in the day to want to be as far away from it as possible when I'm not working,' he said wryly, 'but obviously not so.' He cleared his throat. 'There was something I asked Lizzie, but was called away before she could answer. As I'm not sure where she is, I wonder if I could ask you the same question.'

She looked up at him with a warm smile. 'You've really

piqued my interest. I'm intrigued. The ham and eggs can wait. What did you ask her?'

'Let's step away from the table, shall we? Better not to be overheard.' They moved a little to the side. 'We were comparing the burdens on a man with those on a woman. Lizzie said it was onerous to be obliged to have a chaperone whenever you went out or entertained anyone. I remarked that I was sure you ladies had found some ways around that. She was about to tell me what they were, but we were interrupted. Perhaps you can tell me.'

'I see.' She frowned slightly. 'I'm afraid that I don't really know what she would've said. Obviously, when Tilly, or either of our mothers, accompanies Lizzie and me, they usually run a few errands and we're left alone in the café. But I don't think you mean that, do you?'

He shook his head. 'Not really.'

'The only other thing I can think of is what George and I used to do in the days before we left for school. Lizzie and George live fairly close to us, so it was possible. But it wouldn't be possible for everyone.'

'Now I'm the one who's intrigued.'

'It's nothing much really. Every night when I go up to my room, I get ready for bed and then I go out on to the verandah and stare at the view. The sight of the dark sea glistening beneath the moon and the stars is beautiful, and I always sleep better for seeing it last thing at night.'

'I can understand that. It's a view that I, too, love.'

'Years ago, when we were younger, George took to coming along the path between the trees and the beach after dark. He'd come into the garden and call quietly up to my room if I wasn't already on the verandah. I'd go down and join him, and we'd sit and talk quietly to each other.

That's all. I can't think of any other way to escape one's chaperone.'

He stared at her, intensity in his gaze. 'So that'll be what Lizzie would have said, would it?'

She nodded. 'I think so; yes. Basically, it's go to the garden after dark and call up to the verandah. Keep in the shadows, though, and do so quietly, just in case someone hears you and investigates.'

'Clara.' Lizzie's voice sounded behind her.

Clara glanced over her shoulder, saw Lizzie and smiled. 'There you are, Lizzie! I assumed you were in the dining room. I was just getting something to eat, and then I was going to find you.'

Lizzie beamed at her. 'I came in search of food. I'm starving. But I thought you were in here with George.'

Clara gave a theatrical sigh. 'When the last dance ended, he was dragged off by his cricket friends. I'm sure he'll come back in a minute, though. I hope so, anyway.'

'I'm certain he will,' Lizzie said happily. 'He's not likely to stay away from you for any longer than necessary. Anyone can see that he's madly in love with you.'

'Now that you've answered my question, Clara,' Lewis said. 'I'll leave you ladies to talk. I'll get some food and join the rest of the party.' With a slight bow, he took the plate that the steward offered, and started to walk along the table.

Her eyes shining, Lizzie turned to Clara. She opened her mouth to speak. At that moment, Albert appeared at her side. She closed her mouth.

'What is it, Papa?' Lizzie asked in thinly veiled annoyance.

'I'd been looking for George, but you two will do. Our table is somewhat depleted. Since I doubt that we older ones are the company that Tilly and Michael would wish for, I'll wait while you get some food and go back with you.'

'Of course, Papa,' Lizzie said.

She exchanged a despairing glance with Clara.

'If I don't get a chance to speak to you later, or after church tomorrow, I'll come round on Monday morning. I've masses to tell you,' Clara said quickly.

'I'm afraid that Lizzie will be out with us on Monday, Clara,' Albert said. 'We're going to Bolghotty Island. Michael has very kindly invited us to The Residency. The ladies will have coffee, while we men play a round of golf.'

Lizzie looked at Clara and pulled a face.

Clara threw her a look of sympathy, and held out her plate for a portion of spiced chicken with basmati rice.

22

L *ater that night*

CLARA LAY in her bed and stared through the open shutters at the marbled face of the ivory crescent moon, which was low in the indigo sky.

It had been a really enjoyable evening, she thought, and a highly satisfying one, too.

The enjoyment had come from relaxing with her family and friends, and from having danced nearly every dance with George. That alone had made the evening a very special one.

And when she'd heard that their fathers had talked to each other about formalising their engagement a little earlier than planned, she'd been overjoyed.

And so had George.

Soon, very soon, their engagement would be official, and

so, too, would the longed-for day when she became George's wife.

That thought had made her so happy that she'd completely forgotten to chide George for leaving her side at the buffet, and for not yet coming to see her after dark.

When they were married, there'd no longer be a need to stand on the verandah, staring down into the darkened garden, desperately hoping that he would materialise out of the shadows. Instead, he'd come home to her at the end of every day. They'd spend the evening together, and then they'd go upstairs where they'd lie together in their bed, side by side.

It wouldn't be long now. A nervous thrill ran through her.

She turned over on to a cool patch of sheet.

And apart from it being a wonderful evening, it had also brought her the satisfaction of being able to help Lizzie. That had pleased her enormously.

It was a shame that she hadn't been able to pass on the good news to Lizzie.

Although Lizzie's father had interrupted their conversation, she'd still hoped to find a moment to take Lizzie aside before the end of the evening and tell her what Lewis had said. It would have made her so happy, and it would have prevented her from being taken by surprise when he went into Lizzie's garden and called up to her.

But Lizzie had been on the opposite side of the table next to her mother, and there hadn't been a moment to speak privately to her.

And as soon as they'd finished eating, Lizzie's parents had broken up the evening, her father thinking it time that they went home. And her parents, too, had said that they were ready to leave.

As she wouldn't be able to talk to Lizzie on Monday, it was essential that she speak to her the next morning after church. Unless, of course, Lewis was there. If so, he might be able to get the message to Lizzie himself. That would be the best thing of all as he could then tell her what time to expect him.

It would have to be after the church, or nothing.

Her parents had told her that they wouldn't be going to the club the following morning—they felt they'd seen enough of the place that weekend. And Lizzie's parents probably felt the same.

It meant that if she didn't see Lizzie after church, she wouldn't be able to alert her before Monday to the fact that Lewis might call on her as early as Monday night.

And it would quite likely be Monday, and not later in the week.

He'd seemed so keen, and the expression in his eyes when he'd said her name so warm. And she'd seen the hope on his face when she'd told him about her garden meetings with George. He'd drunk in her every word.

And the was if telling her to alert Lizzie.

A sudden bolt of alarm shot through her. She sat up.

What if George decided to run along the path to her house at exactly the moment as Lewis was arriving at George's house in search of Lizzie, and they met?

George would be torn between staying with Lizzie to protect her from possible dishonour, as he'd see it, or leaving Lizzie and continuing to her house. In such a situation, staying with Lizzie would have the greater claim on George.

And he'd be watching Lizzie thereafter, fearing another incursion by Lewis. If that happened, George wouldn't be making any more late night visits to her garden.

She frowned in anxiety.

Then her forehead cleared. She was getting upset about nothing.

She slid back beneath the sheet. The reality was that George had shown no real interest in reviving the midnight visits since she'd returned.

Admittedly, she did feel hurt about that. But at the same time, she was coming to appreciate the amount of work he had to do, and the demands his father made of him, and she could see that he needed to get some sleep at night. Life was now very different from the days when they'd been children, and able to ignore their *ayah* and lie late in bed in the mornings.

And it wasn't for much longer, anyway, not now that their fathers had advanced the date.

She turned back to look at the moon, and smiled.

LEWIS SAT on the cane chair in the corner of his bedroom, a glass of whisky in his hand.

He ought to get into bed, he knew, but with so much on his mind, he hadn't a prayer of a chance of sleeping.

He took another sip of his whisky.

His suspicions about Clara's feelings for him had been confirmed that evening, and he was ecstatic!

She'd clearly been overjoyed when he'd joined their group—he'd seen the way she'd beamed at Lizzie when he'd sat down. And later she'd said that he was better than pretty fair at billiards. She must have been talking about him to the others. She certainly hadn't seen him play—he'd been keeping his eye on the billiards' room door all evening.

And then, to top that, when he'd asked about dodging a

chaperone, she'd effectively told him to visit her at night in the way that George used to do.

Not in so many words, of course, though she might have done had Lizzie not turned up at that very moment, but her meaning couldn't have been clearer.

The irritation of the evening had been completely washed away by her words.

He'd been so fed up, and so frustrated, with the endless billiards' games, one after another, which were stopping him from asking Clara to dance, that he'd actually thought about deliberately losing a game. But when it came to it, he couldn't do that. He always played to win. That's just the way he was.

But as soon as the final game had been played and he'd been declared the overall winner, he'd gone quickly in the hope of having at least one dance with Clara. But he'd been too late—the band had already started packing up.

Worse still, he'd seen Clara standing close to George.

A wave of anger had shot through him, anger at himself for being unable to make himself lose a game, and anger at George for being at Clara's side, which was where he, Lewis, should be.

But before he could think of a way of separating Clara from George, the cricket team had done it for him. All he'd had to do was go across to her, and start talking. And that he'd done.

Until Lizzie had annoyingly put an end to their conversation.

But by then, he'd heard all he needed to hear.

And he wouldn't delay. He'd go and see Clara on Monday evening.

It would have been so tempting to go to her the following day, but she was sure to be tired after the lateness of the hour at which the club dance had ended, and prefer to sleep uninterrupted on the Sunday night. By Monday, though, she'd be looking for him.

Of that he was sure.

Why else would she have come so close to issuing a direct invitation to him?

The least he could do was not disappoint her.

But how should they proceed after that, he wondered.

They could hardly keep meeting in the garden. And Henry's godown wouldn't be much better. Although he had the key to it, and there was a boat inside where they could sit, it was damp and hardly a romantic setting.

No, he must encourage Clara to hint at home that she was no longer as certain that she wanted to marry George as she had been. And she couldn't be, or she'd never have encouraged him in the way she had.

And for his part, he must be extra cautious about everything he did without Henry's knowledge. He must never give Henry any reason to question the wisdom of allowing him to take over the running of the company when the time was right.

He finished his whisky, and stood up.

He was in danger of letting his thoughts run away with him, and he must rein himself in. He needed to focus on one step at a time, the first being to build on Clara's affection for him and make her desperate to marry him. And he must do that soon, before her engagement to George was announced.

After that, everything else would fall into place.

So Monday evening, it was.

. . .

THANK YOU, thank you, Clara, Lizzie thought, lying back in her bed and smiling up at the ceiling. What a wonderful friend Clara had proved to be.

Before her father had arrived in the buffet room, an unwelcome presence indeed, she'd heard enough to know that Clara had told Lewis that he could contact her by going along to the Goddard's garden after dark.

Lovely Clara had been giving Lewis the answer to the question that Lewis had asked her before they'd been so rudely interrupted by the billiards' games.

He had obviously been determined to find out that evening how he could meet her without a chaperone present, and as she hadn't been close at hand when the billiards had finally ended, he'd found out what he needed to know by asking Clara.

Thank goodness she'd overheard them talking. If she hadn't, she might not have known to be ready for him. Clara would have done her best to warn her, of course, but it was hard to see how she could have got through to her.

When they'd got back that evening, her father had told them that they wouldn't be going to church in the morning —he had some papers to go through with George as they wouldn't be able to do so on the Monday.

And her mother needed to decide what clothes they'd be asking the *durzi* to make when he came later in the week for his second visit that year. That could no longer be left until the Monday as her mother had originally intended.

She was absolutely certain that Lewis would come on the Monday evening.

He was unlikely to come on the Sunday night as they'd all be catching up with their sleep. No, it would be on the Monday.

A further thought struck her, and she put her hand to her mouth in sudden concern.

What if George decided to go and see Clara that evening!

He'd use the same path as Lewis. They might meet on the way!

She bit her lip.

Perhaps she should find out on the Monday whether George intended to go to Clara that evening. The only way she could really do that would be to ask him. Not outright, of course, but she could tell him playfully that she sympathised with Clara at seldom seeing him.

But if she did that, there'd be a risk that she'd put the idea of him going that evening into his head.

She might have to take that chance, though. The likelihood was that he had no intention of slipping out that night as he'd seen Clara so recently. But if she was going to be able to relax while she waited for Lewis, she needed George to confirm that.

Fortunately, he wouldn't think it strange that she was commenting thus as he'd told her more than once that Clara kept on chastising him for not going to see her more frequently.

And in her heart at the time, she'd agreed with Clara—it had been remiss of George.

At times, she'd even wondered if George was as enamoured with Clara as he said.

He'd seemed quite willing to marry the Calicut girl, after all. He certainly looked upon Clara as a really good friend, and he obviously thought her lovely to look at, but perhaps it was no more than that. She certainly hoped that he did love Clara as much as he said, she thought as she turned on her side, and that it was only volume of work, and fatigue at the end of the day, that kept him from visiting her more often.

As that evening had shown, and the earlier visits to the Old Harbour House, Clara had proved to be a really good friend, and would make a lovely sister. For everything that Clara had done on her behalf, she deserved to be as happy with George as she was going to be with Lewis.

23

T he Church of St Francis, the following morning

THE IVORY STONE of the church's façade gleamed white in the late morning sun as the congregation poured along the nave and out through the arched entrance.

As they stepped outside, Henry and Mary were hailed by friends of theirs. Not wanting to get tied up in a conversation of little interest to her, Clara moved slightly away. She'd already ascertained by surreptitiously looking around at the congregation during the service that Lizzie's family wasn't there, and there was no sign of Lewis, either.

It was another lost opportunity to acquaint Lizzie with what Lewis had said, and she kicked the dust with the toe of her shoe in disappointment.

'You're looking a little worried, Clara. Is it anything I can help with?'

At the sound of Edward's voice, Clara looked up from the ground, and smiled.

'Thank you, but I'm afraid not,' she said. 'I'd wanted to tell Lizzie something, but won't be able to do so now as she isn't here, and I can't tell her tomorrow as she's going to Bolghotty Island.'

'Well, I shall be at The Residency tomorrow, too. Can I take her a message? If it's private, you could write it down,' he suggested. 'I promise not to peek.'

She giggled.

'It's fine, thank you. It's not that important. She'll find out soon enough anyway.'

'How mysterious,' he remarked.

'I'm making it sound more interesting than it is.'

'Then to change the subject, which I'm doing openly if you recall an earlier conversation—'

'I do,' she said, and she giggled again.

'I wanted to apologise for going ahead with plans for the party without any further meetings between us. I didn't know how long the rain would last, and I was keen to avoid a rush at the last minute.'

'There's no need to apologise, Edward. I meant it when I said it was a relief that your staff had taken over. I'd asked Lizzie for ideas, and Lewis was going to have a think, too, but the rain stopped us from meeting more than a couple of times, so we hadn't really had time to come up with any ideas. I was so pleased when you said you'd got others working on it.'

He nodded. 'That's good. And it's not as if you haven't contributed, is it? The theme was your idea.'

She smiled at him. 'It's just like you to say something nice like that, but it was a little obvious, wasn't it, in the year of the Silver Jubilee?'

'Maybe,' he said in amusement. 'But you'll get your party invitation, anyway. So what have you been doing with yourself, given the bad weather? I would have asked you last night, but you were whisked away to the dance floor soon after our arrival, and I didn't see you again till the end of the evening.'

'Mainly resisting Mother's attempts at getting me interested in knitting and embroidery.' She pulled a face. 'I really hate anything like that.'

'What would you rather be doing, then, when you can't go outside?'

She adopted a secretive expression. 'I can't tell you, I'm afraid.'

'If you fear putting me to the blush, be assured that I'm a number of years past being shockable now,' he said cheerfully.

She laughed, and they started walking slowly towards the grassy verge around the cenotaph. 'It's nothing blushworthy, believe me. It's a matter of how I present myself.'

He exaggerated his mystification. 'What I see before me is a pretty young woman, in a most becoming green dress that's bringing out the green of her eyes. Her hair's curled up on top of her head, shining in the sun, but styled in a way that's frowned upon by the pundits of fashion. I have to say, I admire the way in which she presents herself.'

'That's because you don't think along the same lines as my mother.'

'I'm highly gratified that you've observed that there's a difference between your mother's thought processes and mine,' he said gravely.

They both laughed.

'All right, I'll tell you then,' she said. 'But I hope you

won't think the worst of me. I'd rather read a book than knit. There, I've said it!'

He stopped walking and looked surprised. 'But what's wrong with that?'

'According to Mother, a woman who aspires to be a wife one day should get down to her knitting rather than open a book.'

'Maybe that's why it's so difficult to meet women with whom you can have a conversation about matters that don't pertain to the household,' he said as they sat down on the low wall behind the cenotaph. 'If you're a man who's been known to read in his leisure time, it would be highly desirable to be able to engage in conversation with someone else who enjoys books.'

She nodded. 'That's what I would have thought.'

'Yet you continually meet people who say they don't read much literature because they work too hard, or because their books fall to pieces in the climate, or because there are so few bookshops. All these are just excuses. You can forgive people not being interested in talking about opera as they don't have the chance to see the great operas performed here. But reading is different.'

She smiled broadly at him. 'I think so, too. There's a limit to any conversation confined to knit one, pearl one, I would've thought.'

'So what have you been reading recently?' he asked.

'I've been working my way through Jane Austen. We read *Pride and Prejudice* at school, and I loved it. Half the class thought it wonderful, and half were bored stiff. Which half would you have been in?'

'The half that thought it wonderful,' he said. 'I've read all her books more than once. Each time, you find something you missed the first time round.'

'I agree,' she said in excitement. 'One of the first I read after school was *Persuasion*. I really enjoyed it, so I read it again, and I saw masses that I'd missed the first time. It's easy to miss things if a teacher isn't pointing them out.'

'What did you see the second time, then?'

'That she was highly critical of the aristocracy and gentry. In *Pride and Prejudice*, she'd been admiring of the gentry, which took the forms of Mr Darcy and Mr Bingley, but in *Persuasion*, Sir Walter Elliot and his daughter Elizabeth are absolutely ghastly. They're vain, pompous and disparaging of others. And she actually praises Admiral Croft, who was trade of a sort.'

'That's because her brother fought in the Napoleonic Wars, and returned home before she wrote that book. Listening to him, and to others like him, gave her a different perspective.'

'I didn't know that!' she exclaimed. 'Thank you. It explains a lot.' She paused. 'What are you reading now?'

'*David Copperfield*. It's by Charles Dickens. Did you come upon that at school?'

She shook her head. 'No. Is it good?'

'I think so. I've only just started it, but if it continues in the way it's begun, it'll be a most enjoyable book to read.' He hesitated. 'When you've finished with Jane Austen, I'd be happy to lend you something from my library if you were looking around for something else to read. You could even read *David Copperfield* if I've finished it by then, and we could discuss it after you'd read it.'

She smiled. 'I'd like that very much,' she said. She paused. 'George doesn't read a lot, you know. Not that it's his fault. He works so hard that at the end of the day he needs to relax. And that's not just an excuse. Not that *you* don't work hard, too,' she said quickly, blushing. 'Because you do.'

She blushed more deeply. 'I'm sorry. That sounded a bit rude of me.'

'Not at all. It's a fair comment. I do work hard, but it's a different sort of work. I work in a lovely building, meet interesting people more often than not, and I spend more time at a desk than George. Also, I've done this for some years now, so while each day offers variety and interest, I wouldn't describe it as a challenge in the way that learning the ins and outs of life as a trader must be. George is discovering what goes on behind the scenes as well as doing a full day's work. And I believe he's learning some Indian languages, too.'

She nodded vigorously. 'Yes, that's exactly it.'

'It's right that he relaxes in the evening, and avoids anything mentally stimulating.' He gave an awkward laugh. 'Now it's my turn to apologise. I've implied that talking to you wouldn't be mentally stimulating, but it would.'

'It's nice to know that you can put your foot in it, too.'

They smiled at each other, and then each turned to look across the road at the sea, a shining ribbon of sapphire that stretched from one side of the wide horizon to the other.

'I wonder,' he said after a moment or two. 'A few weeks ago, I'd suggested that you come to my house one morning with your mother so that we could talk about the party. That won't be necessary now. But perhaps you and your mother would like to come to coffee one morning, anyway, and have a look at my collection of books.'

'Thank you for the invitation,' she said slowly, 'but I don't think Mama would enjoy a discussion about books, so I'd better decline. It was a kind thought, though,' she added.

.   .   .

WITH HER BACK to the church, Mary allowed the conversation around her to wash over her as she stood watching Clara and Edward. She saw Clara turn towards Edward, and smile.

A formless anxiety swept through her.

'I'm sorry, Henry,' she said, turning to him, her look of apology embracing not only Henry, but also the people grouped around them. 'But I feel slightly under the weather. I wonder if we could leave now?'

'Of course,' he said in concern. 'Excuse me.' He took her arm, and moved them away from the group. 'I'm sorry you don't feel well, darling,' he said as they walked towards Clara. 'You must lie down as soon as we get home.'

'I'm fine, Henry,' she told him shortly. 'Clara and Edward have been talking together for long enough, and this was the only way I could think of breaking them up.'

Henry looked at her in surprise. 'But they're in full view of everyone. Surely, that's within the bounds of propriety.'

'It is. I just think they've talked enough. Call it a mother's instinct,' she said. As they approached Edward and Clara, she put her hand on her brow. 'Clara darling. I feel less than well. It's probably because of our exertions last night, but I should like to go home now.'

Clara stood up at once . 'Of course, Mama. I'm sorry you're feeling unwell.' She looked down at Edward. 'It was lovely talking to you, Edward. Enjoy the rest of your day.'

She tucked her arm into her mother's, and the three of them started walking in the direction of the Parade Ground and their car.

HOW COULD he have been so silly as to engage Clara in conversation that morning, he chastised himself as he strolled back to his house, and after he'd been so assiduous in avoiding spending time with her.

As soon as he'd learned that she was destined to marry George, who was so suitable for her, he'd resolved to pull back from her, and to keep a check on his feelings for her, which annoyingly strengthened each time he saw her.

If he didn't take control of his emotions, he knew he'd face certain heartbreak in the future.

And he'd done so well with his resolve.

He'd deliberately got his people working on the party in order to avoid the need to arrange any more meetings with Clara.

Furthermore, he'd refrained talking to her on the occasions he'd seen her at church, and he'd managed to keep his distance afterwards in the club.

It was true that he'd joined her table the evening before, but there were several other people at the table, too, and he didn't sit next to her, or speak to her. He'd deliberately prolonged his every conversation in order to prevent himself from being free to talk to her.

And he hadn't asked her to dance.

He'd loved to have done so, and he'd even been wondering if he could allow himself just one dance.

But when he'd seen the delight on her face when George had asked her to dance, and then her visible joy at having one dance after another with him, he knew that he mustn't separate them.

And not just for her sake, but also for his.

It would have been too painful to watch her trying to mask her disappointment at having been parted from George, and to have had to endure her polite responses to his remarks until their dance had ended and she could hurry back to George's side.

So why, after all the care he'd been taking over the weeks to keep away from her, had he gone up to her that morning, initiated a conversation and issued that coffee invitation?

Thank goodness she'd turned it down.

He was in a bad enough state over her as it was, and to have spent a morning with her would have made it only worse. The sad truth was that he was still deeply in love with a woman who was deeply in love with someone else.

24

M *onday evening*

CLARA PULLED her loose-weave shawl around her shoulders so that it covered most of her nightdress, moved closer to the wooden balustrade around the verandah and stared towards the coconut trees on the left hand side of the lawn.

As ever, they obscured her view of the path from George's house, the path that had brought him to her so many times in the past.

But that past felt a very long time ago.

She didn't really know why she'd hesitated as she was about to get into bed, and had turned and gone outside instead, and was now standing alone in the embrace of darkness.

Since her return to Cochin, she'd stood on the verandah so many nights, hoping that George would come to her as he used to, but her hopes had been in vain, and she'd stopped consciously waiting for him.

She didn't know why she'd thought that things might be different that night, but she had.

Yet she didn't even want him to come that evening. In fact, it would be disastrous if he did.

Lewis would be going to Lizzie, and he and George mustn't meet.

She leaned against the balustrade, and looked down at the garden.

The fronds of the silhouetted palm trees that reached up to the sky on both sides of the garden cast eerie shadows across the lawn. On either side of the darkened grass, silvery fireflies flickered and danced among the dense foliage.

It all looked so beautiful, she thought. It was the perfect night for Lewis to declare his love for Lizzie.

As she stared ahead, the darkness that surrounded the trees on the right moved.

She caught her breath and straightened up.

It moved again.

It's George, she thought joyfully. He was playing with her—surprising her by coming from the right, not the left.

She pulled her shawl around her more tightly still, and ran quietly to the steps that led down into the garden.

At the foot of the steps, she paused a moment and stared intently at the blackness in the right hand corner of the garden. The shadows started to move towards her.

'George!' she cried in delight as loudly as she dared, and she caught up the skirt of her nightdress and ran forward in glee.

Lewis stepped out of the darkness and stood before her.

She stopped abruptly.

'Lewis!' she exclaimed. She let the skirt of her nightdress fall to the ground. 'What're you doing here? I thought you were George.'

He took a step closer to her.

Instinctively, she inched back.

A look of puzzlement crossed his face.

'I don't know why you're so surprised to see me,' he said. 'After all, you told me to come here at night, so that we could meet without anyone else being present.'

'No, I didn't!' she exclaimed. 'I wouldn't have done such a thing. It would have been wrong.'

He shrugged. 'Wrong or not, that's what you said at the club on Saturday.'

'Oh, I see,' she said. Her face cleared, and she gave an awkward laugh. 'I wasn't suggesting you come to see me— I'm marrying George, aren't I? I was talking about Lizzie. I thought you wanted to meet Lizzie away from the watchful gaze of a chaperone. I was suggesting you do what George and I used to do.' She pointed to the path on the left. 'He'd come along there.'

Ignoring her invitation that he look at the path that led to Lizzie's, he stared at her, bewildered.

'What made you think I wanted to talk in private to Lizzie? When have I ever shown any interest in her other than ordinary friendliness? She's perfectly pleasant to talk to, but I joined you both because it was obvious you wanted me to.'

She frowned. 'I don't understand. She said she's spoken to you after church when I wasn't there, and you were extremely friendly.'

'That's because she was a link to you. But it's you I want to be with. Not Lizzie.'

'Me?' she echoed in surprise. She put her hand to her throat. 'But why?'

He took a small step forward. 'Because I love you, Clara,' he said, his voice filling with emotion. 'I've done so since the day I met you at your sister's. And I instantly sensed that you felt something for me, too. Since then, I've not been able to get you out of my mind. And each time I see you, my feelings for you get stronger.'

She stared up at him, her eyes wide. 'But I'm getting engaged to George.'

'It's not official, though. And until it is, you're free to consider if you mightn't be happier with someone else. And I'm at liberty to encourage you to see that I'm that someone else.'

Bemused at her misunderstanding of the situation, she let him take her hand in his.

'Dear Clara,' he said, emboldened by the lack of any resistance. 'I know I'm only a company agent at the moment, but I've never intended to stay that forever. I've been working towards having a business of my own. I already own a boatyard, a godown and a boat. It's a good start, and I'll build on it, you can be sure. I'll be able to keep you in the way you deserve to be kept, whether I stay at Saunders & Co or whether I set up on my own. I very much want to marry you.'

'No, Lewis. I'm sorry.' She pulled her hand free of his. 'This is a terrible mistake. It's George I want to marry, not you. I've loved George all my life,' she said, her face white.

A wave of anger swiftly crossed his face, but was gone in an instant.

'I could say that you haven't yet lived so much as half your life,' he said steadily. 'I could also say that you've spent so many of your eighteen years apart from him, that all your life doesn't mean very long. You will have come back from England a different person. As he will have done, too. It wouldn't surprise anyone if what you used to think you wanted, you no longer did.'

'But I *do* want to marry him,' she insisted.

'I love you, Clara. You've captured my heart.' He took a step closer to her. 'Please don't break my heart without giving thought to what I've said. If you were to think seriously about marrying me, I suspect you might find that you no longer feel about George as you thought you did, and that I've made at least a dent in your affections.'

She edged back a little.

'But I appreciate this has taken you by surprise,' he said warmly, 'and you'll want to go back to the house now and quietly think things over. Please consider what I've said. You responded to me the moment we met, even if you weren't aware of it, and that must mean something. And it must surely be a comment on the way you feel about George.'

She opened her mouth to speak, but he held up his hand to stop her.

'I'll come here at the end of the week when you've had time to think, and we'll talk again,' he said quietly.

She looked at him in naked horror.

'You mustn't come here again like this, Lewis. Most definitely not. What you've said is very flattering, but I don't need any time to know what I feel about both you and George. I like you, and I enjoy talking to you. You're obviously attractive, and maybe I did flirt a little. But I didn't intend to, and if I did, I shouldn't have done and I'm sorry. But this is all a ghastly mistake. I don't feel anything more than friendship for you, and I never could. I'm sorry, but that's the truth. I love George.'

He stepped back from her. 'I see,' he said, flushing in

discomfort. 'Well, you couldn't have been any clearer than that.'

'I'm sorry,' she repeated.

He shook his head slowly. 'There's no need for you to feel sorry. Your behaviour was above reproach. I'm the one at fault. I misread the situation. I'd be grateful if, for the sake of the friendship you say you feel towards me, you don't mention this to your parents, or to Lizzie or anyone, but that you try to wipe it out of your mind. I'd like to feel that it could be as if this evening never happened.'

'I promise I won't tell a soul. We'll both forget everything you said.'

'Thank you.'

'But don't forget Lizzie,' she said quickly. 'She isn't unofficially engaged to anyone, though there's talk of a widower in Madras. I think she might like you to visit her in this way.'

'I don't think so. How could I look at Lizzie, now that I've seen you?' He gave a dramatic sigh, and put the back of his hand to his brow. 'No, I shall have to get used to being a lonely bachelor for the rest of my life, to becoming as desiccated as the coconut used in just about every dish.'

She gave him a wan smile.

'That's better,' he said approvingly. 'I don't like seeing you looking so woebegone.'

And he leaned forward and kissed her cheek. Then raising his hand in a wave, he turned and made his way through the trees to the path on the right.

For a long moment, she stared at the darkness that had consumed him, and then, firmly wiping her cheek where he'd planted his unwelcome kiss, she turned and went back to her house.

. . .

NEITHER HAD HEARD the slight gasp that had come moments earlier from the path to the left of the house.

Nor had they realised that they were not alone.

And nor did either see Lizzie step out of the shadows, her eyes glinting coldly in the light of the moon.

From her vantage point in the shadows between two coconut trees that backed on to the path between her house and Clara's, Lizzie watched Lewis lean over and kiss Clara's waiting face, and then leave the garden, and go in the direction of the Saunders's jetty.

And she saw Clara going back to her house, caressing the place where Lewis had kissed her.

The bitch! The sly, conniving bitch!

How she'd restrained herself from going forward and slapping Clara's simpering face in the way she deserved, she didn't know.

All the while pretending to be her friend, making as if she was helping her to get close to Lewis, Clara had actually been trying to steal Lewis for herself!

All those looks of delight when Lewis had joined them, looks that she'd taken to mean that Clara was pleased for her, were in reality an expression of Clara's pleasure at Lewis's presence.

And Lewis had obviously realised that.

How they must have laughed about her, and congratulated themselves on their cleverness in using her to shield from others the feelings that they'd developed for each other.

What a huge relief that she'd found out before it had gone on for any longer!

It was unbelievably fortunate that she'd got so fed up with waiting for Lewis to come to her garden that evening that, certain that he'd be on his way to her, she'd started along the path, expecting to meet him coming towards her.

What she hadn't expected was to get as far as Clara's garden, and then when she did, find him there, kissing Clara.

How dare they!

Seething, she spun round and headed at speed back to her house.

How stupid she'd been, and how blind!

How two-faced, dishonest and nasty of Clara to have used her so!

Clara, who was meant to be her friend, and who was meant to love George.

What kind of friendship was that? And what kind of love?

Her poor brother, she thought as she sped across the grass to the steps leading to her house. He deserved better than to have a cheating wife, which Clara would be if she married George while at the same time betraying him with Lewis.

And she'd no doubt at all that Clara *would* marry George, whatever her preference might have been. Clara's father would make sure that the marriage went ahead. Henry Saunders would never let Clara's feelings stand in the way of what was best for the company.

She slowed her steps, and paused.

Could it be that Clara didn't realise that in this matter her father would prove immovable, and could she actually be harbouring hopes of marrying Lewis?

That could certainly explain why Michael had met Lewis at the club that Wednesday afternoon. At the time, she'd thought it unusual for him to go to the club in the middle of the week. But he could have been acting on instructions from Tilly and Clara.

Either Tilly could have suspected that there was something going on between Clara and Lewis, given that Lewis had turned up more than once at Old Harbour House when Clara had been there, and also that he'd also got into the habit of going to church and making a beeline for Clara afterwards. Clara's smiles of pleasure whenever she saw Lewis would have fostered that suspicion.

Or Clara could have confided in Tilly? Who better to turn to when she needed help than her sister?

She started walking again.

If Tilly knew of Clara's feelings for Lewis, she could be helping Clara by encouraging a friendship between Michael and Lewis as a way of integrating Lewis into the family before springing upon them that it was Lewis whom Clara wanted to marry, not George.

But if Tilly and Clara thought they could ever make Lewis acceptable to Henry Saunders, they were wrong, she thought bitterly as she reached the top of the steps and crept into the house. There was a crucial difference between her and Clara—Clara didn't have a brother.

It was why her parents might have accepted Lewis, but Clara's wouldn't.

Tilly had married someone who wasn't a trader, so it was essential that Clara marry a man who was able to run the company when Henry Saunders could no longer do so.

Lewis would have been able to run Saunders & Co, but he wouldn't be seen as a good marriage prospect in the way that George was. Lewis was lower in status in the community, and more important than that, he wouldn't bring with him the possibility of the hitherto undreamed of expansion that would be brought about by a union with Goddard & Son.

The only good marriage in the eyes of Henry Saunders would be the marriage with George.

But she had a brother, and he was the future of Goddard & Son, so she had more choice about whom to marry.

Her parents, being ambitious by nature, wouldn't have been overjoyed at the idea of Lewis as a son-in-law, but they would almost certainly have accepted him when they realised how much she loved him, and they might even have been quite pleased that there was someone else in the family who could, if they wished, work alongside George.

Drawing deep angry breaths, she ran into her bedroom, stopped in the middle of the room, and glared at her bed.

In the midst of the anguish, frustration and anger that enveloped her, she knew one thing for sure. If she couldn't have Lewis, and she obviously couldn't—she'd no intention of being second-best to anyone—Clara was certainly not going to have him.

But Clara wasn't going to have George, either.

Her brother deserved a wife who loved him with the whole of her heart. It was just too bad that Henry Saunders wasn't going to get the son-in-law he wanted—he should have taught his daughter to be a nicer person.

But how to thwart Clara, and make sure that she didn't end up with either George or Lewis, she wondered as she slipped off her shawl, went across to her bed and climbed in.

She could always tell her brother what was going on.

If she did that, he'd refuse to marry Clara, even if he was madly in love with her. He had far too much pride.

And she wasn't sure that he *did* love Clara to that extent, anyway.

He certainly liked her, but he hadn't seemed in that much of a hurry to spend time with her since she'd returned to Cochin. And whatever he'd told Clara, she knew that there'd been a number of occasions when he could have dropped in on her, but hadn't.

And if George no longer wanted to marry Clara, either he or she would have to tell their parents about Clara and Lewis. Her parents would be appalled, and as they didn't need Clara in their family, not in the way that Clara's family needed George, that would be the end of any suggestion of Clara marrying George.

But Clara's parents, too, ought to know about their daughter's secret liaisons with Lewis.

The timing of the revelation was acutely important, she mused, and the order in which people were told.

There was no way she was going to sit back and watch Clara and Lewis get what they wanted, which was each other, while she was hurting so much at her so-called friend's betrayal.

This meant that Henry Saunders would have to have sacked Lewis before she told George and her parents about Clara's licentious behaviour.

When Clara's parents knew that Lewis had been sneaking into their garden at night, and meeting up with their daughter when she was in her nightclothes, they'd be horrified, and no matter how good he was at his job, he'd be dismissed, and Clara forbidden to see him again.

And that would serve him right. He had to pay for

running after Clara when he could have had her, and for joining in the deceit against her.

Henry Saunders would, therefore, be desperate that George and her parents didn't find out what had been going on, and he'd almost certainly try to bring forward the announcement of Clara's engagement to George, just in case anything got out.

That wasn't going to happen.

As soon as Lewis had been dismissed, her parents must be told. They'd immediately withdraw from the proposed engagement, but by then it would be too late for Henry Saunders to turn to Lewis, rather than have no one.

She lay on her side, her pillow damp with her tears.

Losing both George and Lewis would make things difficult for Clara's family for a while, but it wouldn't shame them for their daughter's deception in the way that they should be shamed.

As far as the British community was concerned, there'd been no official engagement, so it would be assumed that once Clara had returned from school, while she and George still regarded each other as friends, they'd felt no more than that for each other. That they weren't marrying wouldn't cause so much as a stir, and Clara wouldn't be seen to be at fault in any way.

But her shameful behaviour *should* be publicly known.

And in a blinding flash, she knew exactly what to do!

She sat up and wiped her eyes.

It meant that she'd have to bide her time until the right moment to strike, but she could do that.

And she'd have to say nothing to George, and hide her hatred of Clara and Lewis—but she could do that, too.

She'd carry on suggesting coffee mornings, thereby ensuring that Clara continued to believe that she was ignorant of the truth, and that she still entertained hopes of a future with Lewis.

If she could bring herself to feign friendship in the way that she'd have to, and she was sure that she could, then she'd be able to pay them all back in exactly the way that would hurt most.

26

W*ednesday morning*

AS THE *KETTUVALLAM* glided through the slow-flowing water, Lewis perched on the edge of a rattan lounger shaded by the boat's arched roof of thatch, and stared towards the riverbanks, his expression hard.

On both sides of the river, the banks were lined with slender dark green betel nut and palm trees, the reflections of which sliced through the water.

Every so often, the rows of trees were fractured by small pastel pink and green houses, or by a church, or a brightly coloured temple that was announced by the incense that drifted across the water.

Or by people.

Women could be seen rinsing their cooking pots in tin bowls that they'd set on the ground in front of their homes, or down at the water's edge, washing their clothes, often knee deep in the water, their brightly coloured saris gathered above their knees and twisted between their thighs.

Children not yet at school clambered with skinny legs and arms over the knotted tree trunks that grew from the sides of the low marshy banks, while in the shallows, solitary fishermen, sometimes standing in the water, sometimes in a small boat, were trying to net a meal for their families.

As were herons, kingfishers and sea eagles.

Stretching out behind the tall trees, the seemingly endless acres of flat paddy and rice fields were dotted with small figures, clad in white or light colours, who tended to the growing rice under the watchful eyes of the numerous white egrets pricking the shallow water with their long orange beaks.

Now and then, a canoe would pass between their *kettuvallam* and the shore, sometimes carrying a child on the way to school, sometimes taking two fishermen to their structure of nets and pulleys.

But as the waterway narrowed, people and houses were fewer.

Sanjay manoeuvred the boat towards one of the shallow side-streams that had been gouged out during the rainy season some years before at a time when the river was at its height, but which had continued to wind through the silver sandbanks long after the monsoon had passed and the river had subsided.

But Lewis didn't register the change of waterway, nor did he see any of the people they passed or the scenery.

Consumed by anger, bitterness and frustration, he could see only that Saunders & Co had slipped from his grasp.

In not much more than a couple of minutes, his dream of a shortcut to expansion had been shattered into a million pieces.

Moreover, it had been done in a way that humiliated him.

And the worst thing was, he had only himself to blame.

He'd never before misread a situation so badly.

Looking back with hindsight, he could now see so easily that Clara's response towards him on the day that they'd first met had been consistent with the way in which any young girl, newly released from school and out in the world for the first time, would behave towards any reasonable looking young man who wasn't a member of her family.

Yet he'd interpreted her blushing and flirting to mean that she'd found him so instantly attractive that in a trice, he'd supplanted George in her mind!

How could he have been so stupid as to have let the advantages of a union with the woman blind him to the probable reality of the situation?

His erroneous belief that she was attracted to him had coloured his interpretation of everything else that had happened.

Clara's delight at seeing him whenever they'd met had been no more than natural enjoyment at being able to talk to someone who wasn't her family. Or it could even have been pleasure on Lizzie's behalf, since it appeared that Lizzie, from what Clara had strongly implied, entertained amorous feelings for him.

And further building upon his initial error, he'd then misread the significance of Michael's visits to the club and the office. How stupid he'd been to assume that Clara had confided in Tilly her feelings for him, and that Tilly had charged Michael with getting to know the man her sister was hoping to marry.

Blinded by his ambition, he'd completely forgotten that Tilly had made it fairly clear on every occasion that they'd met that she didn't like him. That being so, she would've hardly promoted his marriage to her sister. On the contrary, she'd have tried to block it, if possible.

He couldn't have got things more wrong.

But that didn't excuse Clara. Nothing excused Clara's attitude towards him.

She should have shown some consideration for his feelings, and been kind in the way she'd responded to his mistake. Instead, she'd made him feel like a naughty child, who'd stepped out of line and been presumptuous in his hopes.

Presumptuous—yes, that was the right word.

She'd thought him presumptuous for having aspired to marry her. By the look on her face, she'd made it clear that she'd seen marrying someone like him as marrying beneath her.

It couldn't be because of his person that she'd rejected him.

She'd told him that he was attractive, hadn't she, and even though he'd read into it a significance that hadn't been there, he was sure that he hadn't been mistaken that when they'd first met, she'd been flirting with him, even though unaware of it.

And although he could now see that it was probably for Lizzie's sake that she'd wanted him to join them at Old Harbour House, if she'd found his presence repugnant, she wouldn't have wanted him there, no matter any wish to help Lizzie.

If she'd thought for a moment when they'd been together in the garden two nights before, she would have realised that he'd had good reason to believe she was encouraging him to think he stood a chance with her, even though that had been unintentional.

But she hadn't.

She'd been self-righteous and sanctimonious, and her sense of her social superiority had prevented her from considering that she might, at least in part, bear some responsibility for what he'd come to believe.

That readiness to look down on others must have come from her parents.

Yet who were they? They were no better than second-generation traders.

The cheek of it!

If he hadn't needed Saunders & Co in the way that he did, they'd instantly feel his wrath. And so, too, would Clara.

The moment he could see a way of punishing them for their snobbery, which wouldn't in any way hurt him, too, he'd take it. All three must be made to feel the intensity of pain that he'd been feeling for the past two days.

In the meantime, until he knew how he could best pay them back, he must convince Clara that he still valued their friendship, but that he accepted it would never be anything more.

Clara would be very ready to behave as if nothing had happened, he was sure.

She wouldn't want a visible rift between them in case anyone probed the reason why.

If what had happened got out, neither set of parents would be comfortable with the knowledge that Clara had been out in the garden in the dark, in her nightclothes, hoping to meet George. She'd know that she'd be diminished in the eyes of both families, and that might jeopardise her engagement to George.

And she wouldn't want to fall out with Lizzie, either, which would surely happen if Lizzie, whom Clara had said would welcome his advances, had any suspicion at all that he and Clara had met alone. That would without doubt put an end to Clara and Lizzie's friendship, and he wasn't yet ready for that to happen.

On the contrary, he'd do well to play up to Lizzie. If Clara saw him paying attention to Lizzie, it would destroy any concern that might have been lingering in her mind about him possibly harbouring a continued interest in her.

Until he'd decided how to punish the Saunders family, it was sensible to keep as close to them and their friends as possible, and to avoid doing anything that might rock the boat.

And he must keep Michael on his side, too.

At first, he'd let his imagination run away with him about Michael.

Ever since Michael had turned up at Henry's office at the end of a long day in which he'd been guiding people around Jew Town, answering their questions, and attending to their needs, he'd been curious as to why Michael hadn't instructed his driver to take him straight home, but had unnecessarily prolonged the day by dropping in at Muttancherry.

Unable to come up with a good explanation for this, he'd all but convinced himself that Michael's arrival at the Muttancherry office had been part of a plan that had originated with Edward and the Resident, rather than the spur of the moment decision that Michael had claimed, and this had put him on his guard.

But now he could see that, yet again, he'd been mistaken.

Michael was a man who enjoyed a game of billiards, and he, Lewis, was a worthy adversary. And it was in Michael's remit to go down to the wharves every so often. Of course, when he did so, he'd call in on someone with whom he played billiards, and on the man who was his father-in-law.

There'd been no more to it than that.

And that was backed up by a couple of things that Michael had let drop in their conversations at the club, which had alerted him to the fact that Michael wasn't too keen on Henry.

It was an antagonism that was easy to understand.

Henry had made it very clear, in public and in private, that he wanted a son-in-law with the interest and ability to take over the running of his company. Since Tilly's husband wasn't such a son-in-law, everyone realised that Clara's husband would have to step up to the mark. And that was an implied disappointment in Michael.

But it was more than that.

Henry never seemed at ease with Michael, nor interested in what he had to say—not in the way that he was with George.

Having a father-in-law who wished you had different talents, and who had no interest at all in your work, couldn't be very pleasant.

This was information to store in the back of his mind. It was just possible that Michael could prove useful to him in the future, which made their friendship something to cultivate.

And he was going to work at it.

27

O ld Harbour House,
Friday, mid-January

'I'M SO glad we could meet today,' Clara said, picking up her glass of pineapple juice.

Lizzie stretched her mouth into a smile. 'Me, too, Clara. And much as I like Tilly, I wasn't sorry she couldn't come with us today, and that it's just the two of us. Our *ayahs* are fine where they are, chatting to each other.'

Clara nodded. 'They're cousins or something, so they've got their families to talk about, and they won't be in a hurry to get back home.'

'That occurred to me, too. And it also occurred to me that if Lewis wondered whether we were here, it being a Friday morning, and came on the off chance, they won't think anything of it. Had Tilly been here, she might have begun to suspect that Lewis could be interested in you.'

Clara straightened imperceptibly.

Lizzie looked down at her drink in quiet satisfaction.

'Why would she think that?' Clara asked, her voice slightly strained. 'Lewis knows I'm with George. If Tilly suspected Lewis of having designs on one of us, that person would obviously be you.' She hesitated. 'D'you think he might come along this morning, then?'

Lizzie shrugged. 'I don't know, do I? You're more likely to know than I am.'

'Why would I?' Clara asked quickly.

'He works for your family, doesn't he? Your father could have told you what Lewis was doing today.'

'Oh, I see. Well, no, he didn't. And I wouldn't have expected him to. He's never done so in the past.' She hesitated. 'You're still very keen on Lewis, aren't you?'

Lizzie took a sip of her juice. 'Of course. Why wouldn't I be?'

Clara shrugged her shoulders. 'It's just that it's more than four weeks since the party at the club, and with Christmas in between, we haven't seen him for ages. I thought you might've lost interest.'

'Well, I haven't. I still feel the same as I did the minute I met him,' Lizzie said sharply. Regretting her tone of voice, she swiftly injected a note of wistfulness into her words. 'I can't wait to see him again.'

'Then I hope he comes along this morning.'

'And anyway,' Lizzie went on, adopting a mildly accusing tone, 'what about you and George? You've hardly seen him since the party. And when we called in on you on Christmas Day, I didn't see you talking to each other.'

Clara gave a heartfelt sigh. 'I know. It was so frustrating. Whenever we tried to talk to each other, someone interrupted. So many people visited us, and we called on so many other people, that no one really had any time to talk to anyone else. We just smiled and moved on.'

'It's always like that at Christmas.'

'I suppose so. And apart from not being able to spend time with George, I enjoyed Christmas. I ate far too much, of course. Our neighbours from further down the road did the traditional thing and brought us a decorated tray filled with sweets and cakes. I ate much more than my share, and felt really uncomfortable afterwards.'

Lizzie groaned theatrically. 'I was the same. After all that visiting, I don't know how I managed to eat any Christmas dinner, but I did.'

'Did you do as we did—have a mixture of Indian and British? We had a duck roast, a beef vindaloo and a ball curry. I'm not complaining—I love the balls of minced beef that float on top of the curry—but I'd got used to something different in England.'

Lizzie nodded. 'Ours was similar. When I saw the biryani that Cook had made, I actually found myself missing the Christmassy feel of the tasteless turkey we had every year in England. And I even missed the soggy boiled sprouts!'

They both laughed.

'You did more with your garden than we did with ours,' Lizzie went on. 'Your Christmas tree, if I can call a mango tree that, looked lovely with all those glittering ornaments. And so did the lanterns of stars you hung around the garden.'

'Amit organised everything, and our *mali* helped him.' She finished her juice, and sat back. 'Yes, I enjoyed our first Christmas back home, but it's nice getting back to normal. I'm glad you suggested coming here today.'

'I was desperate to get out,' Lizzie said, with feigned

lightness. 'You can have too much of my parents and brother. With George working with Father, the conversation at home seldom rises above coconuts.'

They both laughed again.

'Shall we have a hot drink now?' Lizzie suggested, anxious for more time in which to probe Clara about George.

Clara agreed. She signalled for the waiter, and they ordered a coffee.

'Coconut-obsessed or not, I've really missed seeing George,' Clara said with a sigh.

'So you *do* still want to marry him?'

When she saw Clara's look of surprise, she felt a moment's panic. Perhaps she should have been more circumspect.

'Of course, I do,' Clara retorted. 'You know I love him. So why wouldn't I?'

'It's only that you see so little of him. And I don't just mean over Christmas.'

'He works really hard,' Clara said defensively. 'You've said so yourself.'

Lizzie nodded. 'I know I have. I'm sorry if I sounded a bit ratty. If I did, it's because I'm jealous.' She forced a wry smile. 'It's not that I want to marry George,' she added, and forced out a giggle. 'But I'd love to be on the verge of marrying someone I adored, like you are. I'm sure it's the amount of work that George has got that's keeping him away from you. He really is busy. It makes me glad I'm not a man.'

'Me, too,' Clara said, visibly relaxing. 'If you were a man, we wouldn't be able to sit here on our own and talk.'

They smiled at each other.

Lizzie scowled inwardly.

Clara was a very good actress. If she hadn't known how

deceitful Clara was, and how disloyal to George, she'd never have guessed it from the way that Clara looked and spoke. At most, there was an occasional tinge of discomfort in Clara's expression, but no more than that.

'What's Tilly doing today?' Lizzie asked as the waiter approached the table with their drinks.

'She and Mama have gone for ideas for material. They didn't want to have to rush to get back to us. They're having a dress made for Edward's party. It's hard to believe that it's only three weeks away. Did you like the invitation?'

'Yes, I did.' She smiled at Clara. 'I noticed it's only silver and white—he didn't go for the black touches you originally suggested.'

The waiter put two cups of coffee on the table, and a plate of rice cakes, and left.

Clara nodded. 'I saw that, too. But his staff will have wanted to do it their way. To my relief, I might add. I'm glad that in the end, I wasn't involved in anything to do with the party. I'm far too busy at the moment.'

'Doing what?'

'Learning how to run a house, for a start. I'll have to do it before too long, so Mama's been teaching me.' She paused. 'Did you know that our parents are thinking of announcing our engagement on the day before Edward's party?'

No, no, no, Lizzie cried within herself. That absolutely must not be allowed to happen.

Making a conscious effort to steady her hand, she picked up her cup. 'I didn't realise they'd got as far as that.'

'Well, they have,' Clara said happily. 'Finally. It's been a long wait. The idea is to announce the engagement in the newspapers a day or so before the party, and then we'll marry in April before the rainy season begins.'

'You're so lucky—you'll soon have your own home.'

'I know. It's hard to believe, isn't it? Until now, it hadn't felt real, but now it does, and it's scary how much I'll have to learn in a short amount of time. I've not read a single chapter of my book since Christmas. And it's why I haven't been to see you, or suggested you come to me.'

'I hope you're going to ask me to be a bridesmaid,' Lizzie said, and she managed an excited giggle.

'Of course, I am. But what I want to know is, when am I going to be *your* bridesmaid? Are you holding out for Lewis, or do you think it might be the man in Madras?'

Lizzie waved her hand in dismissal. 'Forget Madras. An unknown man who lives miles away can't compete with a most attractive man who lives near by.' She paused. 'Have you seen Lewis recently?'

A pink haze spread across Clara's cheeks.

'No, not since the party at the club, back in December,' Clara said. 'He's probably working extra hard at the moment, taking advantage of the lovely weather. Like George and all the other traders.'

Holding herself in check, Lizzie bit back the desire to tell Clara that she was a blatant liar.

'I'm sure that's right,' she said. 'So, what are you going to wear for Edward's party? I imagine you're not having anything made or you would have gone with your mother and sister this morning.'

As Clara opened her mouth to reply, they heard the scraping of chairs being pushed to one side.

Lizzie glanced towards the entrance to the courtyard. 'It's Lewis,' she hissed.

Clara went a bright shade of red.

'Hello, ladies,' he said, coming up to them, and standing at the side of the table. 'I wondered if I might find you here.'

'You wondered correctly,' Lizzie said, and she gave him a wide smile of welcome.

He looked uncomfortable, she noticed with pleasure.

'Let me guess,' Clara said, with more than a touch of awkwardness in her voice. 'You've got your party invitation and you want to join in the discussion about what to wear?'

He laughed. 'You must be a mind reader.'

'In that case, do sit down,' Clara said.

Seeming a little more at ease, Lewis sat on the chair between them. He signalled to the waiter, who brought him a coffee.

'I notice you've got your *ayahs* with you today,' he said, indicating the two *ayahs* at a table on the other side of the café. 'Tilly's off duty, I take it.'

'She and Mother are hunting for material,' Clara said. 'Like you, they're thinking about party clothes.'

'And I'm sure we're not the only ones,' he said cheerfully. 'It's going to be the event of the season, one might say. Most of us have never been to Harrington's house. A number of people even assumed that he lived on Bolghotty Island. It'll be interesting to see his place.'

'From what Clara told us, it's lovely,' Lizzie said. 'But what have you been doing over Christmas, Lewis? You were noticeably absent during the inevitable round of social calls.'

He tapped the side of his head and grinned. 'That was the result of good planning, I must confess. I took myself off to the hills for a somewhat solitary Christmas, but one that was infinitely preferable to what I knew would be going on in Cochin. When it was safe to do so, I returned.' He paused, and glanced at Clara. 'How's George?'

She looked uncomfortable.

'As far as I know, he's fine,' she said. 'Lizzie hasn't said otherwise. He's working hard.'

Lewis nodded. 'I'm sure he is. We all are at this time of year.' He turned to look at Lizzie, and his eyes lingered warmly on her face. 'A trader's life isn't an easy one,' he said.

'I see you've found time to come out for coffee, though,' she remarked sharply.

'Ouch.' He grinned. 'All work and no play—well, you know how that ends for poor Jack. If Jack wants to avoid such a fate, he must be vigilant about taking time off to play. And when better to play than when you can do so with two beautiful women?'

He gave her a long, lazy smile.

Overcoming her desire to throw his coffee in his face, his response suggesting something she now knew to be false, she attempted a smile that was at the same time both flirtatious and flattered.

He was probably anxious to stop anyone from suspecting the truth before they were ready to tell Clara's parents, she thought angrily, and the best way to do that was for him to pretend to be interested in someone else, especially as—something he'll have known from Clara—the obvious someone else was already interested in him.

And Clara was bound to be in on it, too.

But two of them could play at pretending to feel something they didn't. She hadn't intended to go quite that far, but furious though she was, and much as she hated the idea, she was going to have to play along with their game.

If she didn't, Clara would wonder why she wasn't, since she'd professed herself keen on Lewis so many times in the past. And as recently as that morning.

The last thing she wanted was for Clara to suspect that

she'd discovered the truth about her and Lewis. Not with the plan for them that she had in mind.

Keeping herself firmly in control, she infused some longing into the smile she gave Lewis.

He looked pleased, and glanced swiftly at Clara before returning his gaze to her.

She'd probably never before have given a second thought to that glance at Clara, but her senses had never before been so awake. One thing was certain, she'd never let them go back to sleep again.

Gritting her teeth, she smiled at them both and prepared herself for an inane conversation over coffee, during which all three of them would be thinking the opposite of what they were actually saying.

28

L*ater*

THE CONVERSATION with Lewis and Clara in Old Harbour House had been light in tone and instantly forgettable. If anyone had asked them what they'd said to each other in the hour or so that they'd been chatting together, their words punctuated by laughter and smiles, Lizzie was sure that not one of them would have been able to come up with an answer.

But it had to be done, and at least it was over, she thought with a sigh of relief as she stepped down from the rickshaw, and went towards her house.

Now that her eyes had been opened, she could see so clearly how Lewis and Clara had been consciously hiding what they truly felt, and how they'd been using her.

But all that was going to end.

In three weeks, it would be Edward's party, and with

Clara busy at the moment, and with Lewis away on the several trips he'd mentioned that morning, there'd be no possibility of meeting during those weeks, even if they'd wanted to.

And she certainly didn't.

She needed that time to focus on making sure she got everything right.

That morning, Clara had told her that her parents were planning her engagement announcement to come out on the day before Edward's party, which would be a Friday.

But there wasn't going to be any such announcement, not if she had her way.

And she'd worked out just how to do that, and how to ensure that Clara would feel the contempt of not just both sets of parents, but also of the whole British community.

And how to make Clara's parents suffer, too.

With the first meeting of the three of them now thank-fully behind her, she thought as she went up the steps to the entrance to her house, through the open doorway and across to the sitting room, there was only one more thing to be done at the moment, and that was to suggest to her father that it would be no bad thing if he made contact again with the spice merchant in Calicut.

Purely for business reasons, of course, she'd tell him.

She'd plant the idea in her father's mind at dinner that evening, she decided, and as she sat down on the chair opposite her mother, she smiled in anticipation.

THANK GOODNESS THAT WAS OVER, Clara thought, going straight through the house to the back verandah and throwing herself on to the nearest chair.

In the last day or so, she'd become increasingly nervous

about meeting Lizzie in Old Harbour House again. The idea of acting as if everything was normal, which meant suggesting ways of pushing Lewis and Lizzie together, while knowing that Lewis hadn't been thinking about Lizzie in such a way, had filled her with dread.

It had been a relief at Christmas that with so many people around, there'd been no occasion on which she could have explained to Lizzie what had happened, and there'd been no urgency to do so as Lewis hadn't put in an appearance.

And after Christmas, with her plans for the engagement and announcement taking centre stage in her thoughts, the subject of Lizzie and Lewis had rather slipped to the back of her mind.

Realising that by now, it was probably too late to say anything, the best course of action, she'd decided, would be to follow Lewis's suggestion, and let it be as if nothing had happened.

It hadn't been a surprise, therefore, that soon after they'd met that morning, Lizzie had brought up Lewis's name.

In fact, the hope of seeing him had probably been the reason why Lizzie had suggested that they meet at Old Harbour House that morning.

From the outset, Lizzie had seemed a little on edge.

She'd put that down to Lizzie's anxiety to see Lewis again, and to her frustration at not knowing how she could do so. But her edginess, it transpired, was also caused by jealousy that Clara was about to marry the man she loved, whereas Lizzie was a long way from being in that position.

But she couldn't blame Lizzie for that. She, too, would have been jealous in those circumstances, had their positions been reversed.

Lewis, too, had seemed less relaxed than usual.

But she was pleased to see that he'd paid more attention to Lizzie than normal, which would explain why Lizzie seemed to relax as the morning went on, and Lewis, too.

So she, too, had felt herself gradually unwind.

Nevertheless, she wasn't in any hurry to repeat the morning, and she was very glad that soon after they'd met, she'd told Lizzie how busy she was.

Lizzie couldn't now expect her to accompany her on any Lewis-seeking missions during the next three weeks, or even after that. After Edward's party, she'd be far too busy with wedding arrangements to do so.

In future, with luck, owing to the lack of a companion to help her in her hunt, Lizzie's interest in Lewis would fade.

If only the man in Madras lived closer, she thought pulling off her ivory shawl. That would have been a welcome diversion for Lizzie, and it could have helped Lizzie to forget Lewis.

Perhaps she should try to get in a mention of Madras the next time she spoke to Lizzie's mother. But how?

'Would you like Amit to bring you a coffee, darling?' her mother asked, coming out on to the verandah to join her.

She looked up at her mother, and shook her head.

'I'll wait till after lunch,' she said with a smile. 'I've had enough coffee to last a lifetime.'

And she sat back in her chair, and wondered how she could prompt Lizzie's mother into immediate action.

WHAT A THOROUGHLY TEDIOUS MORNING, Lewis thought in irritation as he headed for his boatyard south of Muttancherry. It had to be done, of course, but he could think of so many better ways in which he could have used that time.

However, at least he'd achieved what he'd set out to do, which was to make things right with Clara.

It had preyed on his mind over Christmas, and spoiled what would otherwise have been a pleasant couple of weeks with Gulika, that if Clara took offence by what she saw as his presumption, she might decide to say something to her father about his behaviour towards her.

If she did that, Henry would be outraged that anyone would attempt to waylay his daughter when she was taking an evening stroll in the garden after dark, which would be how she'd present it, he was sure, and what's more, he'd have been even more horrified when it dawned on him that such a thing could have jeopardised the highly suitable marriage he'd arranged for his daughter.

And he would be appalled at the disgrace it could heap upon the family, should knowledge of such an unchaperoned rendezvous get out, no matter how unintentional on Clara's side.

He certainly wouldn't be best pleased, either, if he were to learn that she'd had such meetings with George in the past, but that would be different. He liked the Goddards, and she was going to be marrying George, anyway.

Having expressed his displeasure, he'd probably content himself by ensuring that in future she was more closely supervised whenever she left the house, and that the garden was watched at night.

But the outcome for him would be very different. Almost certainly, he'd be fired.

And he didn't want that. Not yet.

When he split from Henry, it had to be on *his* terms, not Henry's.

So joining the two girls that morning had been very necessary if he was going to maintain appearances for a little longer.

And the morning had gone well on the whole, he thought. He felt that he'd done what he'd set out to do. It had been a slow, slightly awkward start, but their conversation had started to flow after the first few difficult minutes. He'd gone out of his way to show an interest in Lizzie, and he'd been aware throughout that this had pleased Clara.

Lizzie, too, had seemed delighted by his attentions.

If Clara thought that he'd transferred his interest to Lizzie, in the way that Lizzie had seemed to want, she was bound to go out of her way to promote the friendship between the three of them, and the last thing she'd do would be to tell her parents, and consequently Lizzie's parents, anything that would cast him in a bad light, thus destroying Lizzie's chance of happiness, and Clara's hope of keeping Lizzie in Cochin.

With the threat of revelation now safely behind him, he could concentrate on the deals he'd recently made, and on their delivery.

He pushed open the gate and went through to the boatyard. His gaze immediately went beyond the open-fronted building to the godown behind it, and he paused.

In addition to restoring harmony to their group, that morning had been about one other thing, too.

In the heat of the moment alone with Clara, he'd told her that he had premises of his own and a boat. He'd been trying to assure her that he'd be able to support her. But it had been information that he'd intended to keep from Henry, and he now greatly regretted his moment of rashness.

He'd decided over Christmas that if Clara had remembered what he'd said, she would have been curious for more details, and would have asked him about it the next time she saw him, which had been that morning.

Had she done so, he'd been prepared to tell her that he'd been over-optimistic when he'd spoken—he'd been hoping to sign a deal for the premises plus boat, but it had fallen through.

But she hadn't said a word, and he realised that she must have been so appalled at the idea of marrying him that she hadn't taken in anything else.

That meant that he could relax, and allow himself the enjoyment of knowing that he was already making considerably more money than he would have thought possible two years ago, and he would soon be making even more. And that if anyone was ever to be held accountable for what he was doing, it wouldn't be him.

29

T*he following Thursday*

'I'VE ASKED them to bring our coffee to the verandah,' Edward told Michael as they walked up the marble staircase flanked by a carved hardwood balustrade, to the formal dining room in the centre of the Palace. 'While we have coffee, I want to hear how your investigation's going.'

They went through the double oak doors into the dining room, its walls the home of a dozen original etchings hung at spaced intervals, and paused to inspect the huge wooden table that stood on the old Indian carpet in the centre of the room.

Fifty chairs were positioned around the table, and fifty dinner places had been set. The silver cutlery and platters, and crystal glassware, sparkled in the sunlight that slid in strips through the shuttered windows.

Edward nodded. 'That's all ready for tonight, then. Let's

have our coffee.' And he led the way across the dining room to the verandah.

'I must confess, I don't envy you tonight's function, Edward. I'd much rather be having my considerably less elaborate dinner this evening, although it'll be a plentiful one,' Michael said cheerfully as they went through the double doors to the white wrought-iron table and chairs outside, and sat down.

'Where are you going this evening, then?' Edward asked.

'Tilly and I have been invited to my father-in-law's for dinner. He said it'll be a modest affair, since the main purpose is to bring us up to date with the arrangements for Clara's engagement to George. But as for the amount of food we're normally given—let's just say, Henry and Mary are the most generous of hosts.'

He paused as the servant put two coffees on the table, and a bowl of coconut cookies.

They each picked up a cup.

'I won't eat anything now,' Michael said, pushing the bowl closer to Edward. 'I need to prepare for tonight's onslaught on my stomach.'

Edward smiled.

'So, the investigation.' Michael settled comfortably into his chair. 'I've now seen Henry a few times socially since my visit to his office. I think he's exactly as he comes across—an easy-going, friendly man, very trusting of the people around him. He seems highly disorganised, though, and having someone like Lewis, who strikes me as very efficient, must be a great boon to him. But I recognise, of course, that his chaotic approach could always be an act.'

'If thieves and smugglers looked like thieves and smugglers,' Edward said drily, 'they'd soon get caught.'

'True. It's obviously also true that because of Tilly, I don't want him to be guilty of anything. But my instinct genuinely tells me that it's because of his honesty that he's successful, not because of anything illegal.'

'Who else works in the office?'

'Apart from Lewis, there's Nitesh, Henry's assistant. He's a sort of filing clerk, and he makes their tea and serves any guests. He's the type of quiet person you'd never notice. Because of the nature of his job there, I can't see how he could be involved.'

Edward stirred his coffee. 'Well, we're pretty certain that drugs are passing through Henry's wharves. If you don't think it's Henry or Nitesh, that leaves Lewis.'

'And Sanjay. He's the man in charge of Henry's workers on the wharves, and he goes on all of Lewis's trips with him, as far as I could gather. When we were walking around, we were trailed by Sanjay, and he was visibly nervous at my being there.'

'Which is suspicious in itself.'

'What's more, one of our undercover workers, a man called Jitu, told me that once or twice, after a trip to the backwaters, Sanjay had given him a small package or two to take elsewhere. They wouldn't have been signed for or recorded.'

'So it looks as if Sanjay could be involved,' Edward said slowly.

'He certainly isn't past stealing on a small scale, but that's a far cry from drug smuggling on a large-scale. And it's more important not to alert them to our interest in them than it is to go after a negligible amount of drugs.'

'I agree.' Edward took a sip of coffee. 'Sanjay's unlikely to be acting without Lewis's knowledge. So where are you with Lewis?'

'Well, as you know, I've now spent several Wednesday

evenings playing billiards with Lewis,' he said. 'He's a good player and I generally lose. Well, you saw at the party how he won every game. He's a man who likes to win at what he does, and I imagine he could be quite ruthless to get what he wanted, if necessary. And I'm not just talking about winning a game.'

'It sounds as if you don't like him.'

'It's probably truer to say that I don't trust him. He's easy to talk to and, in fact, is very good company. But there's something I don't completely trust about him, though I'd be hard put to say why. I've made a few negative comments about Henry, just to see if they led to anything, but they haven't.'

'But? I sense there's a but coming.'

Michael smiled. 'Lewis is clearly an ambitious man, and I can't see him wanting to remain a company agent for long, unless, of course, he's augmenting his income under cover of his position. And that could be through drugs. Though how he'd manage it, I don't know.'

'People can always find a way, if they're so inclined.'

'He brings in the produce from the backwaters, it's unloaded on the wharves and stored in godowns before being transferred to either Henry's ships or to others. And everything is documented and signed for. And there's no sign of him having an excess of money to spend.' Michael sat back, and shook his head. 'I'll encourage Jitu to get as close to Sanjay as possible, and I'll continue with Lewis, but it's mystifying.'

'What about Albert Goddard? You managed to get to his office, too, didn't you?'

'That's right. He's totally different from Henry in the way he goes about things. He's very organised and he keeps his office well. I suppose he'd have to, though, as he's actively teaching George the trading business. It would be hard to do that if you were operating out of a mess.'

'And your gut feeling is?'

'That Goddard could be unscrupulous when it came to advancing his own interests, but as far as his business goes, he wouldn't involve himself in anything illegal. I've never thought him as personable as Henry, but I'd be highly surprised if he were dishonest.'

'And what about George?' Edward asked. 'Although this will have started long before George got back from school, he could have become embroiled in it.'

Michael shook his head. 'It was George who showed me around their wharf. I can't see him taking part in anything to do with drugs. I think if he heard anything untoward, or suspected illegal activity, he'd rush straight to his father, who'd immediately contact the authorities.'

'I see.'

'All of Goddard's workers seemed relaxed and open. I didn't see a noticeable equivalent of Sanjay.'

'So, from the impression made on you by each of them, we should be watching Lewis more closely,' Edward said. 'And perhaps Sanjay, too.'

'Is it time we talked to the police about our suspicions?'

Edward shook his head. 'We don't need them at this stage. We still have soldiers stationed in Cochin, not as many as the ten thousand who came for Gandhi's visit last year, it's true, but more than we'll need for our purposes. Some of the police will certainly be in the pay of smugglers, and I wouldn't want anyone to be tipped off and thereby evade arrest. When we've apprehended the guilty party, we'll inform the police. But not till then.'

. . .

CLARA LEANED back in her favourite rattan chair and inhaled the evening air that was heavy with jasmine, mimosa and frangipani. Every so often, the scent of the sea was carried on the back of the breeze to the place where she was sitting with Michael.

'Are you planning to meet Lizzie for coffee tomorrow?' Michael asked, turning from the view of the moon-silvered sea, and smiling across the table at Clara. 'I know you often meet on Fridays.'

'Yes, we do, but we're not meeting in the way that you mean tomorrow,' she said. 'Mama and I are going to George's house. George and his mother will be there. And Lizzie, too. So Lizzie and I will be meeting, but not by ourselves. We're going to talk about the engagement announcement. And about the wedding. Papa and George's father have to work so they can't be with us.'

'It's getting quite close now, isn't it?'

'I know.' She beamed at him. 'The last few months have flown by. I may have moaned about having to wait, but looking back, I'm glad we *did* wait. If I'd come straight home from school and into an immediate engagement, and all the stuff that goes with it, I wouldn't have had any time to get back into the life in Cochin. I've enjoyed being able to do that, and just having a bit of freedom, I suppose.'

'I can understand that.'

'Annoyingly, Mama intended to ask you and Tilly this evening if you'd any suggestions to make about the wedding, but she forgot.'

Michael held up his hands in mock horror. 'Thank goodness for that! Tilly might have some ideas, but I haven't. It's a woman's thing.'

'But you help with events in The Residency, don't you?'

Michael raised his eyebrows in feigned surprise. 'I'd no

idea that your father was planning on such an elaborate wedding!' he exclaimed. 'Or is that Albert's doing? It does sound more like Albert than your father.'

Clara giggled. 'Papa would have a heart attack if I even suggested anything half as magnificent. But I'd hate that. I want a relatively quiet wedding. Lizzie thinks it should be grand, but that's Lizzie's taste, not mine. I know he's her brother, and she wants what she sees as the best for him, but George wouldn't like a huge wedding, either.'

Michael took a sip of his brandy, and returned the glass to the table. 'Poor Lewis. If you're not going to Old Harbour House tomorrow, he'll miss his Friday morning with you. Tilly said he occasionally joins you for coffee.'

She felt herself colour slightly. 'Yes, he does. It started because we thought he might be able to help us with ideas for Edward's party. And although that's not now necessary, he still comes at times.'

'I imagine he likes a change of scene,' Michael said with a smile. 'I've often wondered that he doesn't get bored here. Our community's very small. And some would call it inward looking, and oppressively traditional. And Lewis, being an employee, not a trader in his own right, is lower in status in the eyes of the British, which must be limiting. From what I've seen of him, apart from billiards, at which he's excellent, and I say that without rancour at having been resoundingly beaten by him—well, with only a little rancour—'

Clara giggled.

'—there's not much else for him in Cochin. I'm surprised that a life spent in either the club or your father's office holds any attraction for a young man like him.'

'Don't forget, he's already got his own premises, and a boat and godown, and that's an interest for him. One day he'll set up his own company.'

Michael stiffened imperceptibly.

In studied relaxation, he raised his glass again, swirled his brandy, and took a drink of it.

'Your father always gets the best brandy,' he said. 'I'm not surprised at Lewis's ambitions. He's always struck me as highly enterprising. Henry will miss him when he leaves.'

'Oh, I'm sure he's not planning to leave for some time yet. I probably shouldn't have said anything. It's something for the future. Don't tell Papa, will you? He doesn't yet know that Lewis has bought a boatyard.'

'I won't say a word to Henry; I promise.' Michael lifted his glass in salute. 'Well, good luck to Lewis, I say.'

As he finished his drink, Tilly swept through the open doorway on to the verandah.

'Mother's just been showing me her dress for Edward's party,' she said. 'She and Father are tired and have gone to bed. They asked me to say good night on their behalf.'

She sat down between Clara and Michael.

'Mother's dress is gorgeous, Clara, isn't it?' she went on. 'Don't worry, Michael,' she added quickly, putting her hand on his arm and looking at him with laughter in her eyes. 'I promise, I'm not going to bore you by talking about clothes. You can tell me instead what you and Clara have been discussing.'

'Since there are three of us, dear Tilly,' Michael said in amusement, 'it's important that we choose a topic of conversation that appeals to the majority. Since both you and Clara clearly want to discuss clothes—I saw Clara sit up in enthusiasm just now—I recognise that I'm outvoted and I shall sit back gracefully and allow you to bore me.'

He leaned back against his chair, folded his arms and embraced both with his grin. 'Right, bore away.'

30

T he Goddard house,
Friday morning

'SO THAT'S ALL the decisions made,' Julia Goddard said, smiling around the table in satisfaction.

'And amazingly easily done, if I might add,' Mary said.

Julia nodded. 'Indeed, yes. With Edward's party on the second of February, it makes sense to announce the engagement in the Friday editions of *The Malabar Herald* and *The Cochin Argus*, which appear the day before.'

'Most definitely,' Mary said. 'That way, everyone will know about the engagement before the party. It wouldn't have been appropriate, I think we're all agreed, to make an announcement at the party itself, but it'll be above reproach for you to go there as a newly engaged couple.'

Clara and George exchanged delighted smiles.

'And I think you might find that George will have your engagement ring by then,' Lizzie added.

Concealed by the rim of the table, George reached out and took Clara's hand in his. She lightly squeezed it, and hand in hand, they listened to the summing up of the morning's discussion.

'So we're going to send the announcement to the newspapers as soon as possible,' Mary said.

Julia nodded. 'That's right. Now that we've drafted what to say, there's no reason not to.'

'Why don't I drop it in?' Lizzie volunteered. 'Clara's going to be so busy between now and the party that I'll have more time than usual to myself. I can easily take it to the newspaper offices. It can be part of my bridesmaid's duties.'

Mary smiled warmly at her. 'That's very kind of you, Lizzie. Thank you.'

'Yes, thank you, bridesmaid,' Clara said with a laugh. 'As Mama said, that's really nice of you.'

'So that's decided,' Julia went on. 'Now that you know that your wedding present from both sets of parents jointly is to be a house, Clara, you and George will want to start looking. Either your mother or I will go with you when you look, and when we find something suitable, we'll ask the fathers to inspect our choice. After all,' she added with a smile, 'they'll be paying.'

'It's extremely generous of both of you,' George said, 'and we're very grateful, aren't we, Clara?'

She nodded vigorously. 'I'd had no idea that you'd give us such a wonderful present,' she said, pink with delight.

'Don't get too carried away, Clara,' Lizzie said drily. 'They just want to avoid you living with them, and having to see you drool over each other, and hear you giggle throughout dinner, and so on. Seeing you installed in a home of your own is an act of great selfishness, not unselfishness.'

They all laughed.

'I won't say that Lizzie hasn't hit on something that smacks of the truth,' Mary said. 'But be that as it may, we're going to miss you, Clara. And I'm sure your parents will miss you, too, George.'

'I shall certainly miss you, George,' Lizzie said cheerfully. 'At last, we'll be able to have a proper conversation at dinner, rather than listen to a nightly discussion between you and Papa about one aspect of work or another.'

'The best way to have your choice of discussion at the table is to have a home of your own, Lizzie,' Julia said sharply. 'Your father and I have asked repeatedly whether you're ready for us to invite Mr Lansdowne to spend a weekend with us. It would give you a chance to get to know him, and to see whether you'd like to marry him. But it's proving impossible to pin you down to anything.'

'Put it down to my consideration of your nerves and Papa's,' Lizzie said lightly. She smiled at her mother. 'As soon as I got back from school, I heard about the plan for George, and I decided there and then that I didn't want anything done about a marriage for me until after George's wedding. You can't be working on two family weddings at the same time.'

'That's true, Lizzie, but only to a certain extent,' Julia said firmly. 'It's Clara's family who'll be arranging Clara and George's wedding, just as we'll be the ones to arrange yours. You're going to have to decide what you want to do, or you'll miss any chance of a union with him.'

Lizzie gave a dramatic sigh. 'If I must.'

'It's up to you,' Julia continued. 'Given that he's in possession of a large house and an excellent job, and has the prospect of further career elevation, he'll be seen as a good catch, and now that he's out of mourning, he'll be the target of many a family. If you're hoping to lose any chance of marrying him, you're going about it the right way.'

Lizzie held up her hands. 'All right. You can invite him here. But not till after Edward's party. One thing at a time.'

She looked at Clara and rolled her eyes.

'DOES that mean that you've abandoned all hope for Lewis and you?' Clara asked later, her voice low, as she and Lizzie trailed behind their mothers as they returned to Lizzie's house, having said goodbye to George, who'd had to leave for the office.

'I may have to,' Lizzie said. 'I don't want to, but with you tied up for the next few weeks, I don't see when I'll be able to speak to him. Not in the way I need to if I'm going to let him know how I feel. There's always someone around after church and in the club, and anyway, Lewis doesn't go to either place every week. And I had to say something just now to my mother, didn't I?'

'There's always Edward's party,' Clara whispered.

'I know,' Lizzie said, and she giggled. 'Why d'you think I told Mama not to contact Mr Lansdowne till after that? I fully intend to wear a dress to the party that will make Lewis notice me. And if that doesn't work, I'll accept defeat.'

Clara glanced at her in amusement 'Good luck with getting past your father in such an outfit.'

'Even in February, the night air's been known to cool a little. A shawl will be very necessary. I shall be wrapped in it when I leave the house.'

Clara laughed. 'I'd have a spare dress to hand, if I were you. I can't see you getting away with that. D'you want to meet up the day before the party?'

Lizzie looked at her in surprise. 'But your announcement will be out that morning.'

'That doesn't matter. We could go for a walk by the Chinese fishing nets, and then have coffee. We won't have done that for a while. And we could talk about how we're doing our hair for the party and what we're wearing, and important things like that.'

'I'd love that.' Lizzie gave her a wide smile.

'Hurry up, Clara,' Mary called. 'Julia and Lizzie have things to do, I'm sure, and it's time we were headed back.'

'I'll have a word with Tilly, and we can decide whether to go for a walk or just sit with a coffee,' Clara said quickly.

HAVING SAID goodbye to Clara and Mary, Julia went back into the house.

Lizzie stood outside a little longer, watching until they were out of sight.

When she was certain that even if they'd turned, they wouldn't have been able to see her, her smile vanished, and a gleam of triumph took its place.

Yes, the focus was going to be on George's marriage before any more thought was given to hers, as she'd told Clara. And that was, indeed, the order in which things were going to happen.

But perhaps not quite in the way that she'd implied to Clara.

31

F riday,
      the day before Edward's party

'WHAT IS IT, HENRY?' Mary asked. 'You've gone very quiet.

Henry lowered *The Cochin Argus*, and stared in bewilderment above the paper at Clara and Mary.

'There's no announcement in the *Argus*,' he said. 'Nor in *The Malabar Herald*, either.' He indicated the newspaper on the table next to his breakfast plate.

Mary gave a half-smile. 'You must be mistaken, Henry. You're probably looking in the wrong place. Give me the newspapers while you eat your breakfast. If you're not careful, it'll go cold. I'll find the announcements.'

Henry handed her the papers and picked up his knife and fork.

Motionless, a piece of toast in her hand, Clara watched her mother go carefully down the columns on each page.

Mary lowered the papers, perplexed. 'You're right, Henry, the announcement isn't there. They've not printed it.'

Clara looked from one parent to the other. 'I don't understand,' she said. 'Lizzie was going to take the announcement into the offices of *The Cochin Argus*, and post the one for *The Malabar Herald*. That's what we decided, isn't it?'

Mary nodded. 'That's right. And Julia said she'd give Lizzie the money she'd need.'

'So why wouldn't they put it in?' Clara asked, her face ashen. 'Have they stopped posting such announcements? Is that it?'

Henry shook his head. 'No, it can't be that. There're a couple of other engagements there.'

'You'll have to speak to Albert, Henry,' Mary said decisively. 'See if he can throw some light on this.'

Clara drew in a sharp breath. 'That won't be possible.' She put her hand to her mouth, and stared at them both in alarm.

'Why not?' Henry asked.

'They're away. When we were leaving the Goddards that day we made the plans, I asked Lizzie if she wanted to meet up this morning, just to talk about how we were going to do our hair and things like that. She said she'd love to. But she sent a message by her *ayah* yesterday, saying she couldn't meet as they'd be away for a couple of days. They were leaving early this morning, and wouldn't be back till late Saturday afternoon.'

Henry frowned. 'Did Lizzie say where they were going?'

'Not really. Just that Mr Goddard was thinking of buying some land and wanted George and Mrs Goddard's opinions about it. And he wasn't prepared to leave Lizzie on her own, not even with her *ayah* and the servants.'

'How very strange,' he said slowly. 'He didn't say anything to me about any land. And why would he want Mary's opinion about a company purchase? It sounds highly unlikely.'

'I think you should both relax,' Mary said calmly. 'There's bound to be a simple explanation for the lack of any announcement. It's more than likely, for example, that Lizzie put them in her bag, and then forgot about them. Girls of her age are very easily distracted.'

'Not all of us,' Clara said. 'And not when we're doing a favour for a friend.'

'And as for going away today,' Mary continued, ignoring Clara's interruption, 'I can easily think of a reason for them to take a trip at such a time—Albert has found a possible house for Clara and George, and is exploring the area it's in, and seeing the house at different times of day.'

Henry's face cleared. 'You could be right, Mary.'

'I'm sure I am. This is something about which he'd need a woman's advice. Lizzie would be of help because she knows your taste, Clara. He'd want them to see it before tomorrow evening, so that he could tell us about it at the party.'

'D'you think so?' Clara said, sounding doubtful.

'I most definitely do, darling,' Mary said. 'Now rid yourself of that frown, or you'll have lines on your face tomorrow evening, just when you want to look at your most beautiful.'

A CUP of coffee in one hand and his newspaper in the other, Lewis walked straight through his house to the verandah, and sat down on the wicker chair closest to him.

Well, that was a surprise, he thought, in suppressed excitement.

The way Henry had been talking the night before, he was sure he'd see an announcement in the newspapers that morning. But not so. He'd gone through both of the papers twice, just in case he'd missed it the first time. But he hadn't —there was nothing there.

He took a drink of his coffee.

He hadn't mistaken what Henry had been hinting at ad nauseam the day before. Of that he was certain.

So what had gone wrong, he wondered.

Who had called it off? Because one of them must have done.

Clutching his cup in both hands, he leaned forward and stared ahead of him with unseeing eyes.

When he'd got home the night before, he'd fully intended to give the office a miss that morning, having already heard more than enough from Henry on the subject of George Goddard getting engaged to the woman who should be his. And he'd planned on making sure that he didn't see anyone from the Saunders family, or any of the Goddards, until they were at the party and couldn't be avoided.

He was still so angry at the way he'd been led on by Clara, and then so disparagingly treated, that he'd even been tempted to give the Harrington party a miss, rather than be caught up in the general congratulations, but his business sense had taken over.

As a result of the Clara fiasco, he'd be working for himself considerably sooner than he'd intended, and the party would be a good place to firm up old contacts and make new ones, and he'd reluctantly decided that it would be business folly not to go.

But now he wouldn't be going reluctantly—he'd be going with great enthusiasm.

Unless he was very mistaken about the significance of there not being an announcement, Clara would not now be marrying George.

In such a situation, in a community where it was generally known that an understanding existed, even though an unofficial one, no matter which of them had called off the engagement, nor for what reason, the woman always came out of it worse in society's eyes.

Clara and her parents would have to go to the party or the family would further lose face. But she would be feeling forlorn, no doubt, and highly embarrassed. He would be there, however, to comfort her.

And to offer an alternative to George.

And Henry, who was certain to be grateful to him for helping them through an awkward situation, would probably soon reconcile himself to welcoming him into the family. He might not have been Henry's first choice for Clara, but he met the essential requirement for a son-in-law of one day being able to take over the business.

So marrying Clara was once again his plan.

Clara, of course, who'd made it clear that she loved George, not him, would possibly be less than willing to transfer her affections.

But her father, out of self-interest, would push her into this, and her mother was certain to point out that Clara had been cast in a bad light in the eyes of the community, which made her a less desirable prospect for marriage, and she'd have to agree.

He would not forget Clara's scornful words, however.

And he wouldn't be in the least bit bothered if she never felt any deep affection for him. He despised her for what she'd said, and how she'd said it, and he always would, and in marrying her, he'd merely be using her.

But by the time she realised that, there wouldn't be much she could do about it.

TILLY HURRIED past a colourful array of shrubs and flowers to the steps that led up to the front door of the Saunders house. She tapped on the door, and waited.

As Amit was showing her into the house and taking her *topi*, her mother came hurrying out of the dining room into the hall.

'I thought I heard your voice, Tilly. You don't know how pleased I am to see you. Will you bring us more coffee, Amit, please?'

Seeing her mother's strained expression, Tilly tucked her arm into her mother's, and they went together into the dining room.

Her father made as if to stand up, but she gestured that he stay sitting, and she sat down at the table next to Clara. She reached across to Clara and squeezed her hand.

Clara gave her a tear-filled smile.

'Looking at your faces,' Tilly said, 'you didn't realise that there'd been a change of plan, and that the announcement wasn't going to be made today, after all.'

'We most definitely didn't,' Henry said. 'The Goddards didn't tell us in advance. Can you believe that?' His voice started to rise in anger.

'Calm yourself, Henry,' Mary said. 'We think Lizzie must have forgotten to post the announcements, Tilly. It's easy to overlook a thing like that when you're not directly concerned. And Lizzie has always seemed a somewhat self-centred girl.'

'What about Albert and Julia? What did they say?' Tilly asked.

'Nothing,' Henry said bluntly. 'We haven't seen anything of them since we discussed the arrangements with them. Although Albert must have been in the office yesterday, he didn't come and see me. This really is highly embarrassing. Most people had a pretty good idea that the engagement was to be announced today. What will they be thinking now?'

'They won't be thinking anything,' Tilly said firmly. 'They've probably forgotten all about it. The party's the biggest social event of the year so far, and that's what people will be focused on. And the fact that Albert didn't drop by the office yesterday suggests that he didn't realise what had happened. It bears out what you said about Lizzie forgetting, doesn't it?'

Henry nodded slowly. 'Yes, perhaps it does.'

'And you can go and see them now, can't you? I'll come with you, if you like.'

'They're not there,' Clara said, and she explained that Lizzie had said that the whole family would be looking at land somewhere, and wouldn't be back till just before the party.

At Tilly's look of surprise, Mary explained that they were wondering if the Goddards were looking at a possible house for George and Clara.

Tilly sat back in her chair. 'Well, I suppose they could be,' she said. 'But shouldn't both families look at possible houses, not just them? And who would do so on the day of a long-awaited party?'

'I can understand them not wanting to drag us to houses that wouldn't be suitable,' Mary said. 'It would make sense for them to find properties worth looking at, and then that we look at them together.'

'Albert is quite dogmatic as a person,' Tilly said thoughtfully. 'He's the sort of man to want to take control, and I can see Julia also wanting to lead the way. I dare say, given the sort of people they are, that it's something they could have done. And if they left before they received their newspapers, they wouldn't know that the engagement isn't in.'

Mary exclaimed in relief. 'Of course. I hadn't thought of that. It just means that if Edward's willing, we can announce the engagement at the party tomorrow night.'

Tilly turned to Clara, and smiled brightly. 'You see, there's no need to worry about this. When you meet Lizzie tomorrow, she'll be greatly distressed at letting you down in such a way. Now, let me see a smile.'

Clara gave her a ghost of a smile.

Tilly took her hand again. 'It'll be fine, Clara. All you should be thinking about is how lovely you're going to look tomorrow night—you're going to be the belle of the ball. And really, it doesn't make any difference whether your engagement is made official today or tomorrow, does it?'

32

The silence in the Goddard dining room weighted the air.

'Well?' Albert thundered.

He stood by the table, glaring at Lizzie, his legs astride, his clenched hands on his hips.

She hovered in the entrance to the dining room, her cotton day dress hastily donned as she'd rushed to answer the summons to appear before her parents at once.

She saw that *The Cochin Argus* was open on the table where her parents and George had been breakfasting. *The Malabar Herald* had fallen to the floor.

'Well, what have you got to say for yourself?' he shouted in fury, the veins on his forehead straining. 'And don't lie to me, Lizzie. The absence of any announcement, not in either paper, speaks for itself. You forgot to deliver them, didn't you? How could you be so selfish and so irresponsible?' He thumped the table hard with his fist. 'How, Lizzie? The Saunders are our friends. George is your brother.'

'Do calm yourself, darling,' Julia said, going up to Albert and putting her hand on his arm. 'Sit down, will you?

There'll be a reason for this. Won't there, Lizzie? It's not just a matter of forgetfulness, is it?'

To Lizzie's great relief, faced by her father's palpable anger, and suddenly scared that she might have gone too far, tears welled up, and she began to cry.

Tears would help her cause, she was sure.

Wiping his brow, Albert sat down heavily, and Julia took the chair next to him.

George twisted round in his chair and stared at Lizzie in anger.

'I'd like an explanation, too, Lizzie,' he said, his voice ice-cold. 'So stop snivelling and tell us why you didn't do what you'd promised to do. There'd better be a good reason for it, and for why you didn't think to tell us. Well, what is it?'

Lizzie's tears fell even more rapidly.

'If you had a good reason, no one is going to be angry with you, Lizzie,' Julia said impatiently. 'But you need to tell us what it is.'

Her tears slowed, and she gulped. 'I did have a reason,' she said, her voice shaking.

She wiped her eyes with her sleeve, pulled out a cotton handkerchief and blew her nose.

'Well, tell us then,' George said, rising to his feet, his voice shaking with rage. 'And then I'm going to Clara. What must she be thinking?'

Lizzie managed to squeeze out a few more tears.

'I suggest we all sit down and let Lizzie explain herself,' Julia said. 'Sit down, George, and you, too, Lizzie.'

She rang the bell on the table as Lizzie went to her seat.

The head servant appeared, and she asked for fresh coffee for them all. 'We'll wait until we have our drinks,' she said when the head servant had left the room, 'and the servants are out of earshot, and then Lizzie will tell us exactly what's going on.'

When their coffee had been served and the head servant dismissed, Albert folded his arms and looked again at Lizzie. 'Well?' he said, glaring at her.

'I deliberately didn't deliver the announcements,' she said, her voice low.

'Speak up, will you?' Albert raged. 'What d'you mean, you did this deliberately?'

'If you'd intended not to take them, don't you think you should have told us?' Julia said sharply.

Lizzie gave a loud sob.

'I was going to take them,' she said through her tears, 'but something Clara said made me stop. I thought I must be mistaken, and must have misunderstood. But if I wasn't wrong, then I didn't want the announcement to be made. I needed to know, though.'

'Do you have the slightest idea what she's talking about?' Albert snapped at Julia. 'She's your daughter.'

'And yours, too, darling, I might remind you.'

'Cut the riddles, Lizzie, and tell us what you mean,' George said coldly.

She looked at George with tear-filled eyes. 'A chance remark made me think that Clara was involved with someone else. There, I've said it.'

There was a moment's stunned silence.

Julia and Albert exchanged bewildered glances.

'I'm sure you're mistaken, Lizzie,' Julia said, turning back to her, a frown on her face. 'Clara's a well brought up young girl. And she and you have always been chaperoned whenever you've been out. It's out of the question that she's been seeing someone else. And we know she loves George. That's been obvious all along. It's never been in doubt.'

Lizzie nodded. 'That's what I thought.'

'Well, obviously you didn't think it hard enough,' George exclaimed. 'I've even got the ring so that Clara can wear it tomorrow night. What's she going to think when she sees the papers today?'

'I'm so sorry, George.' Lizzie gave another loud sob.

'Suppose you tell us exactly what's been going on, Lizzie,' Julia said firmly. 'You're obviously now convinced that there *is* something untoward, or there would have been an announcement today. There was plenty of time for you to get them there, even if you'd delayed for a day or two.'

Wiping her eyes on her handkerchief, Lizzie gulped.

Three pairs of eyes stared at her.

'Like I said, I thought Clara might be seeing someone else,' she mumbled, clutching her handkerchief.

'Do speak up,' her father said irritably.

She cleared her throat, and said more loudly, 'I thought Clara was seeing someone else.'

'Well, was she?' Julia prompted.

'Of course she wasn't, Mother!' George exclaimed. 'This is Clara we're talking about.'

'Yes, she was, Mama!' Lizzie countered at once. 'I couldn't believe it, either, George, but I was wrong. We both were. I'm so sorry.'

'What man? Who are you talking about?' Albert asked.

Lizzie hesitated.

'There isn't anyone, Father,' George intervened angrily. 'Is there, Lizzie? Be honest. You're just jealous that Clara and I love each other and you've got no one. But to lie like that. My own sister,' he added in disgust.

'It's because I care about you, George, that I wanted to make sure I wasn't mistaken. The announcement's not important—that could be made tomorrow. What mattered was whether or not she *was* seeing someone else. And I didn't have any evidence until a couple of days ago.'

George glared at her. 'And what does that mean?'

'It means what I said. I watched Clara, and finally discovered for sure that I was right.'

His forehead creasing, George looked towards his father. 'Father?' he said hesitantly.

'Who did you say the man was, Lizzie?' Albert asked.

She bit her lip. 'Lewis McKenzie.'

'Lewis!' George exclaimed. 'I don't believe you.' He paused. 'Although,' he said slowly, frowning, 'there was a time when I thought her too friendly with him. I even said so at one point. But no, it can't be. I refuse to believe it.'

'I'm so sorry, George,' she said, allowing a tremor to enter her voice.

'How d'you know that for certain, Lizzie? What is this evidence you're talking about?' Julia asked acidly.

'I saw them together,' Lizzie said, injecting a note of reluctance into her voice.

Julia made an impatient gesture of dismissal. 'They met in the Old Harbour House. We all know that. You were there, too. And you were always chaperoned.'

'I don't mean like that,' Lizzie went on. 'I mean at night, by themselves.'

'And you really expect us to believe that Henry and Mary countenanced that, do you?' Albert asked angrily.

'Of course not. They didn't know, did they? Lewis met her in the garden when she was supposed to be in bed. Something she let slip by mistake made me think that they were going to meet that way, so I went along the path to her house after dark—I know I shouldn't have done, but I had to know—'

George gave a loud exclamation.

'What is it, George?' Julia asked.

George stared at them, his face white. 'It's just that when we were little, before we went off to school in England, Clara and I occasionally met like that.'

For a long moment, no one spoke.

'In that case,' Albert said finally, 'I believe you, Lizzie. You've done the right thing in preventing an announcement about George's engagement to a woman who was betraying him, and who might have continued to do so after the wedding. But you should have told us before now what you'd discovered. The wedding is clearly off.'

George put his head in his hands.

Julia looked at Albert in alarm. 'What do we say to the Saunders when they come round, demanding an explanation?'

'They won't,' Lizzie said quickly.

All three looked at her.

'A while ago, Clara and I arranged to meet for coffee this morning. Two days ago, when I realised what was going to happen today, or not happen, I sent her a message saying we'd be away from this morning to tomorrow afternoon. I said that Papa wanted our opinion about some land he was thinking of buying.'

'I see,' Albert said slowly. He looked around the table. 'I see,' he repeated. 'Then I think that's what we'll do—we'll go away for a few days.'

'What about the party?' Lizzie asked. 'Won't it look strange to miss it? People are bound to know about the engagement. They might think badly about us breaking it, and think we're too ashamed to go to the party.'

'Not at all,' Albert said. 'There's a difference between knowing for certain and suspecting something. The engagement was an agreement between friends. It's never been made official, so there's nothing to break.'

'That won't stop them thinking we've behaved appallingly,' George said anxiously. 'They'll all be feeling sorry for Clara. Oh, God, I can't believe this.' He put his hand to his head.

'I don't think they will, darling,' Julia said calmly. 'I've a hair appointment this morning, which I now won't be able to keep. I appreciate that we'll have to leave as soon as possible, but if we could stop quickly at the hairdresser's on our way out, I could cancel the appointment.'

'If you must,' Albert snapped.

She gave him a half-smile. 'I would explain, in the strictest of confidence, of course, that the discovery of Clara's betrayal of George was such a shock, and caused such distress to us all, that we're leaving town for a few days. By this evening, the matter will be the sole topic of conversation in a large number of British homes.'

Inwardly, Lizzie smiled in delight.

'But where can we go?' she asked. 'We haven't made any arrangements.'

'Lizzie's right,' George agreed.

Albert stood up. 'We need to put this behind us as quickly as we can. I can see one way only of doing that. We'll instruct the servants to pack a few clothes for the weekend, and leave. We'll stop at the hairdresser on the way and then go down to the office. From there, I can contact our friends in Calicut—'

'Calicut!' George exclaimed.

'I can't think of a better course of action, George, can you?' Albert said quietly. 'One of my boats can take us up the coast to Calicut.'

George stared at his empty plate, and shrugged.

'I'll tell them we'll be arriving this evening,' Albert went on. 'And I'll contact the British Club—we'll stay there. Given what we now know, it's a great relief to me that I maintained my ties with my Calicut colleague, certainly until George was officially engaged to Clara. But with that now out of the question, we need to look to a different future.'

George rose unsteadily to his feet. 'I won't pretend that I'm not desperately upset about Clara's deception, because I am. She's so beautiful, and I'd so wanted to marry her,' he said, his voice breaking. 'But with what I now know, well... well, I'll just have to get over it, and I'll fall in with your choice for me, Father.'

33

T he Harrington house,
Saturday evening

AMID A BUZZ OF EXCITEMENT, the party guests left their cars alongside the white stone wall in front of Edward's house, and made their way through the wrought-iron gates to the path leading across the enclosed courtyard, to the distant strains of a Haydn string quartet.

Looking around eagerly to see who else was arriving at the same time, they called out to each other, and waved to their friends in front and behind them.

From the moment that Clara stepped out of the car and saw Edward's house ablaze with light flowing from every window, and heard the cheerful hum of the guests and the mellow music coming from within, the anxiety that had dogged her all day, drained away, and a burgeoning excitement took its place.

As her mother had said repeatedly, there'd be a simple explanation for what had happened.

She'd been telling herself the same thing throughout the day, but until then, had failed to convince herself of its truth.

But now, surrounded by the beauty of the evening, and knowing that soon she'd meet up with George and his family, who would clarify everything, she was confident that if it wasn't what her parents had speculated the day before, it would be something very similar.

Smiling at each other in relief that they'd soon be seeing the Goddards again, a relief tempered by an unspoken shapeless anxiety, she and her parents followed the glittering guests across the courtyard.

Everywhere sparkled. The profusion of silvered leaves hidden among the abundant jasmine shone in the light thrown out by lanterns of glittering stars.

'William!' She heard her father call to a fellow trader who was walking with his wife a few paces ahead of him.

Both the man and his wife turned and looked towards Henry.

Henry raised his hand in greeting and smiled. Both turned back without acknowledging Henry and continued to the steps leading up to the entrance.

Surprised, Henry lowered his hand.

'I wonder what's got into William,' he muttered to Mary as they followed the man up the steps and through the arched front door into the house. 'Perhaps he didn't see me.'

White-turbaned servants, standing just inside the entrance, guided the guests towards the majestic teak staircase that led to the first floor. As they went up the stairs, the guests were excitedly exchanging words with those who were nearest to them.

But no one spoke to Henry, Mary or Clara.

As they went up, Henry gave Mary a slight shrug of bewilderment.

Clara was so busy looking around that she failed to notice that no one was speaking to her family.

At the top of the staircase, a servant stood on either side, holding a silver tray on which there were flutes of champagne, glasses of fruit punch and of lime juice.

They helped themselves to a drink, and walked with everyone else across the polished teak floor to the large salon on the right.

As they entered the room, Clara gasped at the sight of the crystal chandeliers sparkling from the ceiling, and the mass of white roses and silvery leaves that surrounded the room, enhancing its elegant beauty.

Walking further in, she glimpsed through the wide arched doorway leading to the dining room that long buffet tables had been set out by the dining room wall, and that at the far end of the dining room, a string quartet was playing.

Edward was in the middle of the salon, surrounded by a group of people.

He saw her, smiled broadly and promptly waved.

He took a couple of steps towards her, but his progress was stopped by a large florid man, and she saw him drawn once again into the group.

'Let's find Albert,' Henry said, and the three of them moved forward, each looking around for the Goddards.

But they were nowhere to be seen.

'They can't be here yet,' Mary said at last. 'They probably got back after they'd intended, and will be late getting here.'

'Maybe,' Henry said. 'But it seems to me, there's something funny going on. There's a lack of friendliness, and for the life of me, I don't know what can be behind it. I suggest we have a word with the people who *are* here, and see if we can get to the bottom of this.'

'I'll check the verandah, just in case George is out there,' Clara said.

Henry nodded, and then headed for a cluster of traders he knew, while Mary went across to the group of women with whom she occasionally played a game of bridge.

As Clara went out on the verandah, she glanced in both directions, but the Goddards were nowhere to be seen. Stepping up to the balustrade, she looked down into the garden.

There were a number of guests chattering and laughing down there, enjoying their champagne beneath the stars, and surrounded by star-filled lanterns that twinkled among the trees and foliage.

But there was no sign of the Goddards there, either.

She raised her eyes to the glistening sea that lay beyond the white stone wall surrounding the garden.

Perhaps they'd been so badly delayed that they wouldn't be back in time for the party at all, she thought, trying hard to push down her rising fear.

FROM HIS POSITION just inside the salon, Lewis watched Henry go up to his trader friends, and saw them turn their backs on him.

He glanced across to Mary, who was approaching her bridge friends. As she neared them, her friends moved closer to each other, excluding her from their now tightly knit group.

He'd heard the rumours when he'd popped into the club that lunchtime. There was no one there who hadn't! The man involved hadn't been identified, but names had been bandied about, and one of the other company agents had actually suggested that he, Lewis, might be the man.

He'd had a lot of fun, laughing that off.

It hadn't occurred to him to make up such a rumour, but he was extremely grateful to the person who had. That person had done him a favour—things couldn't have turned out better for him.

That the Goddards hadn't yet turned up, and were probably unlikely to do so now, meant that they, too, must have heard the rumour. Someone aspiring to a seat on the Legislative Assembly wouldn't want his family to be associated with a woman of such loose morals.

They could have even known about it before that day. It would explain why the planned announcement hadn't been made.

There was definitely no way now that Clara would be marrying George.

She wouldn't just be feeling forlorn, she must be feeling desperate.

Aware that the shame that had been falsely attached to her was widely believed, she'd be feeling utterly disgraced, and possibly afraid.

And when Henry heard the rumour, so, too, would he.

Facing the loss of a number of contracts, and concerned about his company, there was no question of Henry refusing Lewis's offer to marry his tainted daughter, an offer made even more persuasive by him promising that when the time came, he'd continue trading under the name of Saunders & Co.

He wouldn't, of course.

Seeing the inevitable embarrassment on Clara's face as she was forced to agree to something about which she'd recently been so dismissive would be the icing on the cake.

As soon as a date had been set for the wedding, he'd buy a suitable house for a trader of his status, with a wife to maintain, and the first thing he'd do after that would be to install Gulika in his household.

WHILE OSTENSIBLY TALKING with Tilly and three other couples, Michael surreptitiously kept his eyes on Lewis, who was standing in the salon, staring towards the verandah.

One of the servants moving silently among the guests with trays of cocktails and canapés appeared at Michael's side. He exchanged his empty glass for a full one, and made a fuss of deciding which of the canapés to take. Doing so meant that he had a legitimate reason to turn from the group with which he'd been talking, and face Lewis.

As he did so, he saw Lewis turn back into the room, smiling in a way that could only be described as triumphant, and join a nearby group of men and women, which included Tilly.

He and Tilly had become aware that Henry and Mary were being shunned, and they intended to find out why. But whatever it was, it looked as if Lewis might well have been involved.

And if he had, it wouldn't surprise him.

The men who were watching Lewis had established that he did, indeed, have premises of his own, just as Clara had said. By following him, they'd discovered the whereabouts of his yard.

But it wasn't so much that he had a place of his own that was suspicious—other company agents had done the same —it was Lewis's secrecy about the whole thing that was the concern.

If he could be sly about withholding harmless information from Henry, he could be sly about any number of other things.

He decided to try to give Tilly a better chance of finding out the reason for what was happening, by getting the men away from the group that she and Lewis were in.

Taking a sip of his drink, he went across to Lewis and made a comment about a recent billiards' game.

In a matter of minutes, Lewis and the other husbands had moved slightly away from the women, and Tilly was able to turn her attention to persuading her women friends to tell her what was going on.

GLANCING TO HER RIGHT, Clara saw that a waiter was standing at her elbow, offering her a tray laden with a selection of drinks, including champagne, and small dishes of cashew nuts and of crunchy spiced savouries.

Impatiently, she indicated that he leave.

'Clara!' she heard her mother call.

She turned as her parents came out on to the verandah, their faces white.

Her heart started racing.

'Have you spoken to anyone yet?' Henry asked.

She shook her head. 'No. But I've not really tried to. I've been looking for George, but I don't think he's got here yet. Why d'you ask?'

Henry and Mary exchanged glances.

'Your father and I are being ignored by our friends,' Mary said, her voice shaking. 'And we don't know why. People we've known for years have turned their backs on us. We wondered if this was your experience, too.'

Clara's hand went to her throat. 'Why would they do that?'

'We don't yet know, darling,' Mary said quickly. 'I've just dragged Michael away from Lewis. He's gone to see if Edward knows anything. And he said that Tilly is trying to find out what she can. They're going to join us here as soon as they've any information.'

'What on earth can be going on?' Clara said, feeling dangerously close to tears. 'D'you think this could be anything to do with yesterday? Most people knew it was to be in yesterday's papers. Maybe they're blaming us for some reason.'

'I don't see how it can be,' Mary said. 'You'd expect an outpouring of sympathy, not to be ostracised.'

'I can't wait for George to get here. I'm sure he'll be able to tell us what's going on,' Clara said. 'You'll see. I don't—'

She broke off as Edward and Michael came out on to the verandah. She turned to Edward and managed a smile.

'Hello, Edward,' she said with forced gaiety. 'You're to be congratulated on the way you've decorated your house—it looks beautiful. And the party seems to be going very well. Lizzie and George are going to be really disappointed at missing so much of it.'

'They're not coming, Clara,' Edward said quietly.

'Not coming.' She vigorously shook her head. 'No, you must be mistaken. They wouldn't miss this for anything.'

'Albert's valet delivered a message this morning with their apologies. Apparently, the whole family has gone to Calicut for a few days.'

'To Calicut,' she whispered.

The blood drained from her face.

She looked from Edward to Michael, who was standing behind him.

'That's right, I'm afraid,' Michael said.

Edward stared at Clara's pale face. 'I'm not surprised that

you're taken aback, Clara,' he said, his voice warm with sympathy.

'I know that you and George had wanted to make this your first appearance as an officially engaged couple,' he went on, 'and now you're not able to do so. But if Albert had pressing business in Calicut, he wouldn't have had much choice. The note said he'd be seeing friends while he was there, so it's not surprising that he wanted his family with him.'

Henry slowly shook his head. 'I don't understand,' he said in puzzlement. 'That they've gone to Calicut today of all days can mean one thing only. Can you explain this, Clara? Did you and George quarrel perhaps, something that seemed of no importance to you, but might have meant more to him?'

'No,' she said, her voice a frightened whisper.

Edward looked from Henry to Clara's stricken face. 'May I ask the significance of Calicut?'

'Albert knows a trading family there, Edward,' Henry said. 'Before Clara returned from school, he'd been talking to the merchant about his daughter marrying George. And then Clara came home.' He shrugged. 'But the lack of announcement yesterday... and not being here today, and no word from them... And going to Calicut, of all places. It can mean one thing only. But why would they turn against our family in such a way?'

'Ah, here's Tilly,' Michael said with some relief as Tilly approached them. 'Perhaps she can shed some light on this.'

'Did you find out anything, Tilly?' Mary asked anxiously.

Tilly glanced quickly at Clara, and then back at her mother. 'Yes, I did. But it doesn't make any sense.' She looked back at Clara. 'Could I have a word with you, Clara, please?'

Clara stared at her in misery. 'Whatever it is, you can say it in front of Mama and Papa, and also Michael and Edward. Edward's our friend. I haven't done anything wrong so there's nothing I wouldn't want any of them to hear.'

'Well, if you really want that.'

'I do. Why has George stopped wanting to marry me?' she asked, her voice catching. 'If it's that he realised he didn't love me any longer, why didn't he tell me?'

'This is about something you're supposed to have been doing, Clara,' Tilly said gently. 'Are you sure you don't want to step to one side and let me tell you privately.'

'Quite sure, thank you.'

'Well then, just about everyone seems to have heard a rumour to the effect that you've been meeting a man—not George, but someone else—late at night in your garden, unsuitably dressed, when Mama and Papa thought you were in bed.'

'But I haven't!' she exclaimed.

'Of course, you haven't. But in the eyes of those in the community who believe this rumour, you've compromised yourself and tarnished your parents. The Goddards will almost certainly have heard about this, and that'll be why the engagement has been so abruptly terminated.'

'But it's not true!' she cried. 'It's a lie, Papa!'

'Of course, it is,' Henry said. 'Where could anyone have got such an idea? And why didn't the Goddards come to us as soon as they heard this. By acting as they've done, they've given substance to the rumour, and they've shown themselves to consider our friendship to be of no account.'

He looked at his wife and daughter. 'I think the best thing to do would be to go home now.' He glanced at

Edward, 'I'm sorry, Edward. It's clearly going to be a wonderful party, but not for us, I'm afraid.'

'I understand,' Edward said quietly. He paused. 'You can tell me to mind my own business, if you wish, but I think you should stay.'

'Stay?' Mary echoed. 'With everyone being so unpleasant to us? Except you, of course.'

'If you leave now, you'll be seen to be running away, and that will confirm for the scandalmongers that the rumour is true. Clara's reputation would not recover. However, if you remain here and withstand the hostility directed towards you, without any rudeness, or any aggression, you might find that people start to question the validity of what they've heard.'

'But it would be so awful for Clara,' Mary began.

'I think that the sight of Clara—' he smiled warmly at Clara, '—a sweet, gentle girl, who's clearly been well brought up, might also give them cause to doubt the truth of the rumour.'

Mary looked at Henry. 'It wouldn't be easy, darling, but I think Edward might be right. If we leave now, the rumour will stick to us forever. If there's a chance of encouraging people to question what they've heard, both for the sake of the business and our place in society here, we should take it.'

'Edward's right, Father,' Tilly said. 'Michael and I will do all we can to help.'

Henry nodded. 'All right. I agree. Thank you, Mary, for your strength.' He turned to Clara. 'As your mother said, this will be particularly difficult for you, Clara, but you know that there's no truth to this rumour, so you can look everyone in the eye.'

'Of course, she can,' Tilly said cheerfully. 'Come on, let's go in and get this over with. Follow us.' She took Michael's arm and led the way through the doorway back into the salon.

Henry and Mary followed Tilly and Michael.

Clara started walking after them, with Edward at her side.

Then she gave a sudden gasp, stopped abruptly. Her hand flew to her mouth. And she turned towards him with anguish in her eyes.

'What is it, Clara?' he asked.

'Oh, Edward,' she breathed. 'I've just thought of something. I wonder if it's the reason the rumour started.'

'Sit down and tell me,' he said quietly.

She shook her head. 'I can't.'

'If you don't tell me, I can't help you,' he said. 'I promise, I won't judge you.' And he pulled a rattan chair across to her, and indicated that she sit.

When she'd done so, he sat opposite her. 'Now, tell me what you think might have given rise to the rumour.'

Haltingly at first, she explained how she and George used to meet, and then, gaining strength as there was no sign of shock or condemnation in Edward's eyes, she told him about the confusion over Lizzie and Lewis, and how she'd assumed that Lewis was George.

'Someone must have seen me with Lewis. Someone in a boat maybe. Or Lewis could have inadvertently told a friend what had happened, and they told someone else. Maybe he was boasting. I don't know. And it got round.'

'I see,' he said slowly.

'So, how can I now look anyone in the eye, knowing that the rumour's not a lie—just a misrepresentation about what happened. Oh, poor Papa. His business will suffer dreadfully because of me.'

She jumped up and ran along the verandah, tears streaming down her cheeks. Reaching the balustrade at the far end, she stopped and stared with blurred vision across the lawn.

Edward came up to her and stood next to her.

'That does slightly alter everything. There is, however, a way out of this,' he said quietly. 'But I think you might not like it.'

She turned to him. 'I'll do anything at all to help Papa and Mama out of the mess I've created, no matter how awful. So tell me, what is it?'

34

Clara leaned against the balustrade and stared ahead of her. Edward stood quietly at her side.

'Tell me what it is, please,' she repeated.

'You must let me tell you a story first. Once upon a time,' he began, his eyes on the view ahead of him, 'there was an older man, rather plain in countenance, with greying hair. And there was a beautiful girl some years younger, lovely to look at, and as lovely inside as out.

The older man fell in love with the girl the moment he met her, but he was realistic enough to know that she'd never feel anything more for him than friendship. For months, he struggled to quell his love for her, but without success. He did manage, however, to avoid letting the world see it.'

She looked at him. 'Oh, Edward,' she whispered.

He turned to face her. 'And then one day, something serious happened that threatened the happiness of the woman he loved, and of her parents, too. The man wanted to help, but could think of one way only of doing so, a way that he knew she wouldn't like. That was by marrying her.'

She opened her mouth to speak, but he raised his hand to stop her.

'The man was hesitant to ask her for her hand as she could do so much better than marry a plain man like him, but as he could think of no other way to help her, he knew he'd have to put aside his reservations and propose to her.'

She stared into his face.

'I've loved you for so long, Clara. But I knew your heart was engaged elsewhere. And I knew also, that even if it weren't, you would never look on me as more than a friend.'

He paused. 'I know you don't love me, and probably never will. But I feel that we're friends, and that's a sound basis for a comfortable marriage. As for anything more than that, friends don't impose on each other, and I would never expect you to do anything that made you uncomfortable.' He hesitated. 'Do you understand what I'm saying?'

She nodded.

'And one day, if you meet someone with whom you truly fall in love, I shall release you from the marriage in the way that causes you the least amount of harm. Given all of that, will you marry me, Clara?'

She shook her head. 'I can't, Edward. It wouldn't be fair to you. Look at the way everyone thinks I've behaved. They'll feel contempt for you, marrying a wanton like me.'

He gave her a wry smile. 'On the contrary, my standing in Cochin is more likely to go up. They'll think I was the man with whom you were secretly meeting. That someone so beautiful should have been drawn to an unattractive man like me will make them look at me with fresh eyes.'

'But why would we need to have been meeting secretly?'

'Perhaps because we needed to get to know each other away from the gaze of the public. And I wouldn't want everyone to start fawning over you, thinking you might soon be in a position of power. I imagine they'd see that as a highly romantic situation.'

She bit her lip.

'You haven't answered me, Clara,' he said gently.

Her face broke into a shy smile. 'You're too hard on your appearance, Edward. I think you have the nicest of faces, and I shall enjoy seeing it every day.'

His arms at his side, he stared at her in utter delight.

Both said 'Thank you' at exactly the same moment.

They looked at each other in surprise, and burst out laughing.

35

M*inutes later*

'Then let's go inside and make our announcement, shall we?' he suggested, his face glowing with his delight. 'The sooner your parents can start enjoying this party, the better.'

She nodded, and together they walked back along the verandah and went into the salon.

Henry and Mary were standing by themselves just inside the door.

Edward had a quick word with the waiter closest to the door, asking that all the waiters take trays of drink around the room, and make sure that everyone had a glass in their hands.

Then he put his hand under Clara's elbow and they went up to Henry.

'I apologise for ignoring convention, Henry, but given the strange circumstances of the evening, and the need to remedy the situation as soon as possible, I've spoken to Clara before speaking to you.'

Henry exchanged a questioning glance with Mary, and then looked back at Edward.

'What are you saying, Edward?' Mary asked.

He smiled at her. 'That Clara has done me the very great honour of agreeing to be my wife.'

Both Henry and Mary stared at them, open-mouthed.

'We're about to announce it,' Edward added. 'Perhaps you would like to follow us to the dance floor, which is where I'll make the announcement. I daresay, when the guests have got over their shock, they'll want to ingratiate themselves with you, all the more so after their earlier treatment of you, so you'll need to be close at hand.'

'Clara?' Mary said.

'I'm delighted to be marrying Edward, Mama,' she said steadily. 'After all,' she added with a sly smile at Edward, 'how else am I going to be able to read *David Copperfield* in peace?'

Edward laughed.

'You'll want tomorrow to recover, I'm sure,' Edward said. 'But perhaps you and Clara would come to tea with me at The Residency on Monday afternoon. There are some matters we'll need to discuss.'

Henry muttered something impossible to determine.

'Good,' Edward said with a smile. 'At four o'clock, shall we say? But there's something we have to do before that.' He smiled at Clara. 'Are you ready, Clara?' he asked.

'I suppose so,' she said, and she gave him a nervous smile.

With a nod at Mary and Henry, Edward started moving confidently towards the dining room with Clara at his side. Henry and Mary followed close behind him. As they walked, the guests parted to allow the group to pass between them.

As she followed her daughter, Mary caught Tilly's eye, and with her head, indicated that she and Michael should join them.

Past the long buffet tables they walked, the tables almost invisible beneath an array of silver dishes piled high with Indian food at one end and British food at the other, and past the arrangements of smaller tables and chairs in the centre of the room, each table topped by a white tablecloth, in the middle of which stood a small crystal vase filled with white roses and silvered leaves.

When they reached the dance floor, Edward led Clara to the back of the floor, to a spot just in front of the pianoforte and the string trio from the Cochin Musical Association.

He helped himself to two glasses from the tray of a nearby waiter, and gave one to Clara.

He then turned and spoke to the leader of the musicians, asking that they let the Schubert fade away, and that when the guests had had a moment or two to gather around the dance floor, the pianoforte give the equivalent of a short drum roll.

Numbed by the evening's events, and the speed with which everything was happening, and the shock of it all, Mary and Henry took a glass and went and stood quietly at the side of the dance floor.

As the melody died away, and the guests, realising that something was about to happen, gathered swiftly around the edge of the dance floor, buzzing with curiosity, Edward took Clara's hand, and they walked to the centre of the dance floor, and stood facing everyone.

All conversation stopped.

Edward glanced at Clara, smiled, released her hand and looked back at his guests.

'Don't worry, we won't keep you long,' he began. 'You'll soon be able to enjoy the buffet and to start dancing. But there've been a few rumours circulating this evening, and Clara and I have realised that something we've tried so hard to keep secret has somehow slipped out.'

He looked at Clara and smiled.

'We'd intended your invitations to be the first you knew of our plans. But clearly it isn't to be so. Secrets do have a way of getting out,' he added wryly, and he smiled again at Clara.

Then he turned back to the guests.

'But in case there's anyone here who doesn't already know this, I'm delighted to be able to tell you that Clara has done me the greatest honour of agreeing to become my wife.'

A stunned silence descended upon the room.

'You should all have a glass in your hand,' he continued. 'Would you join me, therefore, in drinking a toast to my beautiful fiancée?'

He turned to Clara, and raised his glass.

'To Clara,' he said. 'Who has made me the happiest man alive.' And he put his glass to his lips.

Glancing among themselves in total amazement and confusion, his guests swiftly held up their glasses. 'To Clara and Edward,' they chorused in unison.

A hum in the room swelled rapidly to a volume of loudly expressed surprise mixed with excitement.

Then William, one of Henry's fellow traders, went swiftly across to Henry. 'Dear friend,' he said, putting his hand on Henry's shoulder. 'May I be one of the first to congratulate you on your daughter's forthcoming marriage? What a proud man you must be.'

In a matter of moments, Henry and Mary were surrounded by the people who'd earlier shunned them, and Clara and Edward, too, found themselves at the centre of a large group.

'Where's the ring?' one of the traders' wives called to Clara.

'You'll see it soon enough,' Edward said cheerfully. 'Our hand was rather forced this evening. We hadn't expected to announce our engagement tonight.'

'Clara, darling,' Tilly cried, rushing up to her. 'I'm so thrilled for you.' She threw her arms around her sister and hugged her tightly. 'Thank you,' she whispered into her ear.

LOUNGING against the wall of the buffet room, shielded from Lewis's sight by the people between them, Michael's gaze was on Lewis, who'd been standing at the entrance to the dining room throughout Edward's speech.

When he'd spoken to Lewis earlier on, he'd been struck by the man's good mood.

Their conversation had been light-hearted and full of anecdotes, with no reference at all to the rumour circulating Cochin. Lewis had seemed to be totally unaware of it, in fact.

Yet from the general tone that prevailed across the room, and the disapproving glances thrown at Clara from every corner, her disgrace was common knowledge.

So Lewis must have heard the rumour, too.

Perhaps his restraint was out of consideration for the family connections, since the disgraced girl was Michael's sister-in-law. But somehow, he didn't associate Lewis with sensitivity towards others. No, there was almost certainly another reason.

He was still wondering what it could be when he'd taken up his position against the wall while waiting for Edward to speak.

Stunned by the announcement he heard Edward making, he'd started to turn away from Lewis to look at Edward, when he caught sight of Lewis's expression. He'd stopped abruptly.

Surprise was written across Lewis's face, followed swiftly by acute disappointment, and then by anger. Intense anger.

Lewis was clearly furious at Clara's engagement.

He'd taken a step back to ensure that he stayed concealed behind the guests, who were gathering in startled groups, some around Mary and Henry, and others Edward and Clara.

His gaze remained firmly on Lewis's face.

That Lewis was incandescent with rage was beyond any doubt.

The only explanation must be, he decided, that when the expected announcement of Clara's marriage to George had failed to materialise, Lewis had started to entertain hopes about Clara for himself.

Nothing else could account for such a depth of feeling.

And it wasn't so hard to believe that Lewis would welcome the chance to marry Clara.

It had long been clear that Lewis and Clara liked each other as friends, and with George out of the way, he could easily have thought that he had a chance of becoming something more to her.

But if, indeed, Lewis's expectations had been building throughout the day, while disappointment would have been appropriate, the degree of anger he'd exhibited wouldn't.

Could it be possible, he wondered, straightening up and frowning, that Lewis had engineered the whole thing with the view to securing Clara for himself—that it was Lewis who'd put the rumour into circulation when there was still sufficient time for Goddard to cancel the announcement in the newspapers.

Lewis knew the trading business inside out, and he'd know that in the absence of George, he'd probably be acceptable to Henry, although not what Henry would have chosen for Clara had she not disgraced herself in the eyes of Cochin society.

Gaining more power in the company would be Lewis's main reason for wanting to marry Clara, of that he had no doubt. He'd spent enough time with Lewis to know that Clara wasn't the sort of woman that Lewis would choose for anything more than friendship.

Assuming, therefore, that Lewis was behind this, and that taking control of Henry's company had been his purpose, and that had now failed, what would he do next?

He glanced towards Edward and Clara. Would he try to prevent that marriage? Surely not. But all the same, he'd give a word of warning to Edward.

He looked back at Lewis.

Anger had given way to hatred.

But Lewis wasn't looking at Clara and Edward. He was looking at Henry.

Michael felt a sudden ice-cold chill.

So that avenue was closed, just like that, Lewis thought bitterly.

What a moment before had looked a promising situation from which he could profit—Clara disgraced and seen by all as spoiled goods, and him stepping in to save the day —now lay in ruins.

It was Harrington who'd saved the day.

Well, he wasn't going to give up.

He'd now moved too far in his thinking to be able to step back from his hopes and continue as he'd been doing. He was going to take control of the company one way or another, and as soon as possible.

He had sufficient to buy it from Henry, but he knew Henry well enough to know that he wouldn't voluntarily sell. He'd said often enough that he intended to work for as long as he could, and being in his early fifties, that meant he'd be working for many more years.

So Henry would have to be forced to sell.

And he could actually see a way of doing that.

There were risks involved, of course, but it would be worth the risk as the prize was that he'd get the company for a fraction of what it was worth.

And if he timed it right, some of the disgrace that was going to fall on the Saunders family, would fall on Edward Harrington, too.

In fact, he'd make sure of that happening. It would be a fitting punishment for snatching Clara from his grasp.

He turned away, his lips in a sneer.

36

T *he following morning*

DAWN FINALLY ARRIVED.

Having been unable to sleep at all that night, her head being in such a whirl, at the first glimmer of daybreak, Clara jumped out of bed, threw a shawl around her shoulders and went out on to the verandah.

The air was already comfortably warm, and she leaned against the balustrade, and stared out at the view.

Slender shards of steely grey light had shattered the indigo darkness of night, and the sky was turning a silvery grey, streaked with primrose-yellow and apple-green. Beneath the sky, the crests of the waves glittered and danced in the burgeoning light of day.

All around her, birds were breaking out into a joyful early morning chorus.

It was a February morning like any other.

Yet it was a totally different morning from any other.

So much had happened in the last two days that she couldn't believe that anything would ever be the same again.

Two mornings ago, she was on the verge of becoming engaged to George, whom she adored.

Today, only two days later, she was engaged to Edward, a man about whom she'd never for one moment given any romantic thought.

Yesterday morning, her name was being linked throughout Cochin with disreputable behaviour, unacceptable to the British community.

Today, she was being feted for being on the verge of making a most prestigious marriage.

Edward had been right in saying that what had seemed a disgrace the day before, would now be explained away as a natural desire for secrecy by a man of his status. They could all understand that he'd want Clara and him to have a chance to get to know each other away from the community's watchful gaze. No blame, therefore, was being attributed to either of them.

From the moment that she'd learnt that her life, which had been in tatters, destroyed by a shame that encompassed her parents, too, had been rescued by Edward, she'd been in a daze.

All she'd been able to think about the night before was the phoenix. Her life had risen from the ashes like the phoenix about which her English teacher had so often talked.

She and her family had without doubt been given back their life by Edward's kindness.

But what did she feel about having him as a husband, she wondered.

She certainly liked him, and always had.

He was older than she was, but she'd never felt their difference in age. At least, not in an unpleasant way. He made her feel safe, as if he could handle any situation. But that wasn't necessarily a matter of age—it said more about his character.

He was good company in that he was interesting and he had a sense of humour, and like her, he enjoyed reading. By the sound of it, they had a similar taste in books.

But marriage involved a little more than that. She might not be very well informed about what went on between husbands and wives, but she knew enough to know that they didn't read books together throughout the night, discussing the characterisation and imagery.

A knot of apprehension stirred deep within her.

Edward had said that he wouldn't make demands upon her, but at some point, he'd surely expect her to be a proper wife to him. With George, who was so attractive, being a proper wife might have been quite pleasant.

But Edward wasn't George.

She shook herself. Yes, there were aspects of marrying Edward that she might not relish, but that was irrelevant. She'd unwittingly got her family into a mess, and it was up to her to get them out of it. Marrying Edward would do that. And that was all that mattered.

But she shouldn't have had to be rescued, she thought in a surge of sudden anger. Someone was responsible for the rumour that got around.

It didn't start itself.

So who would start such a rumour, and why?

It must be Lewis. Only she and Lewis knew that they'd met in the garden that night, so he must be responsible.

She wondered if he'd been angry at the way she'd spoken to him at the time. But he'd been fine when they'd met a few days later, and he'd actually shown an interest in Lizzie, so it couldn't be that.

And another thing, although she and her family hadn't known what was being said until they reached Edward's house the night before, the Goddards must have heard the rumour early enough for them to withdraw the announcement and leave Cochin.

As it turned out, therefore, whatever Lewis's intention in causing trouble for her and her family, he'd done her a favour.

The readiness of the Goddards to believe the worst of her, and their failure to at least come round before taking any action and ask if there was any truth to the rumour, showed the friendship between the two families to be a shallow one.

And it cast George in a bad light, too.

Even if his parents hadn't wanted him to visit her, George should instantly have come to her side. He was supposed to love her, after all. If he didn't feel he could openly support her in the face of his parents' wrath, and that could have been difficult as he worked for his father, he could have come secretly to the garden after darkness in the way that he used to.

She gave a sudden exclamation, clenched her fist and put her knuckle to her mouth.

There *was* one other person who could have known that she'd met Lewis. That person was George.

George might have finally been doing what she'd several times asked of him—gone to see her after dark.

Everything fell into place with a thud.

George could have seen her with Lewis and drawn his own conclusions based on his fears in the past.

He would have been so upset that he told his parents,

and the Goddards' servants could have overheard what he'd said and told their servant friends in other houses. It wouldn't be the first time that information had travelled through Cochin in such a way.

That would explain why neither George nor his parents had come to their house, asking to know the truth. And it would explain why George had gone to Calicut, apparently willingly.

Tears rolled down her cheeks, and the peach-coloured sky in front of her blurred.

ALONG THE CORRIDOR from Clara's room, her parents lay on their backs in their beds and listened.

Theirs had been a night of fitful sleep, too, and they'd been awake when Clara had got up and gone outside. A short time later, they'd heard her burst into tears.

'Is this because she's marrying Edward, do you think?' Henry asked anxiously. 'She's done nothing wrong, and she shouldn't be punished by having to marry a man she doesn't love.'

Mary turned her head and looked at him. 'I'm not sure that it is. She seemed bemused and nervous last night when Edward told us they were getting married, but not unhappy. And towards the end of the evening, I thought she looked quite radiant. She certainly didn't look like a woman who felt she was being subjected to a punishment.'

'That's hardly surprising,' Henry said. 'Anyone would look radiant if they were being showered with congratulations at becoming engaged to one of the most powerful British officials in the area. I'm not surprised that the good people of Cochin instantly fell over themselves to cancel the bad impression they'd made earlier in the evening, both with Clara and with us. But you can hear her now. That isn't the sound of a happy girl.'

'We don't know the reason why she's crying, Henry. It could simply be the emotion of knowing that she's to make an advantageous marriage, one that will benefit not just her, but the whole family. That could be enough to move to tears a girl as young as Clara.'

Henry rolled on to his side and faced Mary.

'There's one thing that's stopping me from going out to Clara right now and telling her that she can cancel the engagement if she wants. No matter the consequences.'

'What's that?' Mary asked in surprise.

'That on that Friday evening when Edward walked with us along the promenade by the fishing nets, I told you later, after Clara had gone to her room, that I thought Edward might have an interest in her. And you, too, on another occasion had wondered if that was possible.'

'Yes, I remember.'

'He's a good man,' Henry went on, 'and if he genuinely cares for her, which I think he may do, and he comes to realise that marrying him is going to make her miserable, he might release her without any suggestion of breach of contract.'

'You're assuming that she *will* want to end the engagement, darling. You may be wrong, though. She and Edward have quite a bit in common, and she clearly enjoys his company. Friendship is a good basis on which to build. And there's no other suitable husband for Clara that springs to mind.'

She paused. 'We're having tea with Edward tomorrow. We can observe the two of them together. For the moment, though, I think we should put any concerns out of our mind. Clara must be feeling as if she doesn't know whether she's coming or going. Voicing a concern is the last thing that would help her.'

'You're right, my dear. And we must be careful, anyway, what we say. I wouldn't want the servants to pick up on anything other than our delight at the engagement. You know how they talk among themselves.'

She nodded. 'That's a good point. And something else worth thinking about is that the Goddards will probably be back on Monday or Tuesday. Given the circumstances of their departure, and the fact that by then they'll have heard our news, I expect they'll call on us as soon as they can after their return.'

'You may well be right, my dear.'

'It'll be a very different conversation from the one it might have been. I imagine that with Clara engaged, when they've congratulated us, they'll feel comfortable enough to tell us about the engagement of George to the daughter of Albert's friend. I'm sure that such a goal was the purpose of the Calicut trip.'

Henry stroked his chin. 'I'm sure that's right. All I can say is, they're not the friends I thought they were, and if there was any way of avoiding seeing them again, I'd take it. But as fellow traders in a small community, I recognise that there isn't.'

37

The Residency, *Monday afternoon*

THE SUN WAS high in the cerulean sky. The lawn and stone-flagged terrace had been leached of colour in the mid-after-noon glare, and the distant shoreline of Cochin was no more than a lilac haze.

The table in the centre of the lawn was shaded by a large black umbrella, which ruffled slightly every so often in the light breeze that drifted in from the sea.

'The afternoons are warming up,' Edward said as his staff set a tiered cake stand in the centre of the table, with small sandwiches on one tier, and a variety of pastries and miniature cakes on the others.

When the servants had given everyone a bone china teacup and saucer, and put the silver teapot, milk jug and sugar bowl next to the cake stand, they went back to the building.

'I tend to sit in this spot for tea in the afternoon as it catches any breeze there is,' he said.

Henry nodded. 'It's very pleasant, very pleasant indeed.'

'Would you like me to pour the tea, Edward?' Mary asked.

'I was hoping you'd suggest that,' he replied with a smile.

They sat quietly while Mary poured filled each of the cups with tea.

'I imagine this feels somewhat awkward for you,' Edward said, picking up his cup. He indicated that they should help themselves to the delicacies. 'My engagement to Clara must have come as a huge surprise. I think it did to all of us,' he added drily.

He hesitated. 'Please, do speak as you think. I wouldn't want you to stand on ceremony. I hope we're friends, and friends can speak freely to each other.'

'Thank you, Edward; it's very good of you,' Henry said. 'I won't pretend that your engagement wasn't an enormous surprise. It was one of many surprises that we'd been faced with since Friday morning. Isn't that so, Mary?'

Mary nodded. 'That's right, darling. And your engagement on top of everything that had happened.' She looked at Edward with a degree of helplessness. 'It's all been a lot to take in.'

'We're tremendously grateful to you,' Henry said quickly. 'Your proposal to Clara, well, it's saved her, and it saved our business. I can't tell you how thankful we are. A reputation is easily lost, but not so easily regained.'

'I'm glad I was able to step in,' Edward said. He looked warmly at Clara. 'I feel that I'm the winner here,' he said, 'through no merit of my own.'

'Perhaps you should say something, darling,' Mary prompted, and she gave Clara an encouraging smile.

Henry grunted. 'Yes, what are you thinking, Clara? You've been unusually quiet since we arrived.'

'If you really want to know,' she said, amusement in her voice, 'I was thinking about the pictures we saw on the way in, and pitying poor Edward if he has to wear his regalia very often in the heat.'

'Alas, the regime for clothes is very strict,' Edward said. 'I wear normal suits for everyday use when there's nothing much on, a formal pinstripe suit for luncheon parties, a light formal suit for tea parties—as you can see, that's what I'm wearing now—a morning coat with striped trousers and top hat for garden parties, and I have the equivalent of a regimental full dress for the really official engagements.'

'Good gracious! Your valet must have his work cut out,' she said with a laugh. She looked around the garden, and her gaze returned to him. 'It's really lovely here. Will I be able to come across and join you for afternoon tea when your work allows?' she asked.

He broke out in a broad smile. 'I can't think of anything I'd like better. And since we were talking about clothes, if it's just the two of us, and I have your permission, I shall be more relaxed in what I wear. When Michael and I have tea together, or morning coffee, for that matter, we're very casual in our clothing.'

'May I ask you, Edward, if your parents will be here for the wedding?' Mary asked.

He shook his head. 'It won't be possible, I'm afraid. I wouldn't want them here in the monsoon. Sensibly, they've suggested coming in December and staying for a couple of months, but this will depend upon Clara's wishes.'

'Of course, your parents must come, Edward. I'm very much looking forward to meeting them,' Clara said.

He inclined his head to her. 'Thank you.'

Then he turned to Henry and Mary. 'There's something I should like to give Clara, and some things I should like to say to her. Would you think me very rude if I asked her to go for a short walk with me? Within your line of vision, of course.'

Mary smiled. 'I believe that engaged couples are allowed to walk alone, and to spend some time together without a chaperone, provided it's in a public place. Please do go for your walk, Edward.'

Edward stood up, and held Clara's chair for her. He bent down and picked up a small package, and then they started walking towards the corner of the lawn. She saw that they were heading towards a distant bench, which would be visible to her parents.

When they reached the bench, they sat down.

He gave her the package. She looked at him curiously, and then felt around its edges.

'Is it a book?' she asked in amusement.

'You'll have to open it to find out.'

She unwrapped the patterned paper, and took out a book. 'Why, it's *David Copperfield*!' she exclaimed. 'I was going to read your copy when you'd finished with it. Now I shall have my own.'

'It means that you don't have to marry me in order to read *David Copperfield*,' he said quietly.

She put the book on her lap and stared at him.

'Everything I said about the nature of our marriage remains true,' he said. 'I would never impose on you. But you're not yet twenty. You're too young to be trapped in a marriage that isn't what you would've chosen. I want you to know that you can walk away from our engagement, if you wish. We could work out a way in which no blame would attach to anyone. I could go to London for a short visit, for example. I could—'

She put her finger to his lips to stop him.

'Thank you, Edward, for once again being so considerate. But I like you very much, and I should be happy to be your wife.' She gave him a sly smile. 'Does that mean I must return *David Copperfield* so that you can get your money back?'

He laughed, and impulsively reached across to her and hugged her tight. She hesitated, and then wound her arms around him, too.

For a moment, neither moved.

Then each tightened their hold on the other, before dropping their arms. Drawing back, they smiled at each other and then both turned to look ahead at the sea.

'If you agree,' he said after a few minutes, 'we'll marry in St Francis Church, have the reception here at The Residency, and then go back my house. Back to *our* house, I should say. It would be wise, I think, to leave the honeymoon till after the monsoon season.'

She smiled at him. 'I agree,' she said.

They turned again to the view.

'I suppose we ought to return to your parents,' he said at last. 'In the hope that you would confirm our engagement, I've a range of possible wedding invitations with me. You must choose what style you prefer, and the wording, and I'll have them printed, if you wish. In the interests of time, that might be a good idea.'

'I'm sure Mama and Papa will be happy to let you do that.'

'And we'll arrange for your ring. Then we need only decide whom to invite,' he said cheerfully, 'and also to fix the date. We should probably do that soon if we want to avoid the rainy season. We could even decide the date now, this afternoon. The end of March would be a lovely time to marry, being hot, but not uncomfortably so, and before the first rains. And it gives us time to have the banns read. What do you think?'

'It sounds perfect,' she said.

'Good.'

'There's just one thing,' she added. 'I imagine that the Goddards will be back later today. Albert and my father were friends. I wouldn't like their friendship to suffer for what was just a misunderstanding. A serious misunderstanding, but no blame should be attached to them. I should like the whole family to be invited to the wedding as if nothing had happened. Lizzie was going to be my bridesmaid, and I'd still like to have her as such, if she agrees.'

'Of course. I think that's the right thing to do.'

'Thank you, Edward,' she said.

He looked at her, his face suffused with love.

'You don't have to thank me, Clara. You know I love you. I want everything to be perfect for you. You've no idea how happy it makes me to know that I'll soon be able to call you my wife.'

His voice broke, and she saw that his eyes were moist with emotion.

She took hold of his hand, and picked up her book with her other hand. 'Dear Edward,' she said as they stood up

And hand in hand, they walked back to her parents.

38

T *uesday morning*

AMIT OPENED the door to the Saunders house. A look of surprise crossed his face, and he didn't move.

Julia, Albert and Lizzie stood in front of him.

'Please, inform the *sahib* that we wish to speak to him,' Albert said, his voice firm.

Leaving them standing on the doorstep, Amit went to inform Henry and Mary of their arrival.

A moment later, Henry came to the door. He and Albert faced each other in silence, and then Albert took a step forward.

'My friend,' he said.

Henry inched back.

'Have you behaved how friends behave?' he asked quietly. 'Breaking the engagement between your son and the daughter of the man you called your friend, without indicating any intention of doing so. And then engaging in matrimonial discussions about that same son with the daughter of a colleague elsewhere, which you've clearly been doing. That's friendship, is it?'

'Please, allow us to explain, Henry,' Julia said, moving to Albert's side.

Henry glanced round at Mary and Clara, who had followed him from the dining room. Mary gave him a slight nod.

'Well?' Henry asked, turning back to the Goddards and folding his arms in front of him.

'Do come in,' Mary said, gently moving Henry aside. 'Amit will bring us some coffee.' She glanced at the empty road behind them. 'Is George not with you?'

'He's coming to see Clara later,' Julia said. 'He prefers to speak to her by himself. Obviously under your supervision, of course. He's hoping you'll allow him to call upon her this afternoon.'

'He'll be welcome whenever he wants to visit,' Mary said.

'You'd better come in, then,' Henry muttered.

Lizzie followed Albert and Julia into the house, and they went across the hall to the sitting room and through to the verandah.

Amit closed the front door behind them and went to arrange for the coffees.

SITTING AROUND THE TABLE, they watched in silence as Amit served coffee, put a plate of mango and pineapple chunks in the centre of the table, and left.

'You called on us this morning,' Henry began, 'so I presume you've something to tell us that will help us to understand your behaviour towards Clara. And towards Mary and me. Such a public renunciation of George's engagement to Clara, unofficial though that engagement was, was bound to effect the standing of the family as a whole.'

Albert leaned forward and picked up his cup. 'I'm not sure that you can rightly claim that your standing has suffered, my friend,' he said. 'I would say it had gone up. Within minutes of returning from Calicut yesterday afternoon, we learnt that Clara is to marry Edward Harrington. Your standing could hardly be higher.'

'That's because Edward behaved like a true friend, and rescued the situation. It's now generally thought that he was the man at the heart of the rumour, but his engagement to Clara has absolved them of blame. Of course, he wasn't the man. There was no such person.'

'Regretfully, there was,' Julia insisted.

'Rubbish!' Henry exclaimed. 'There's never been a moment's doubt that Clara loves George. And we assumed that the same could be said of George. That you didn't approach us the moment you heard the rumour shows a lack of true friendship, and the shallowness of George's feelings for Clara.'

Albert flushed. 'George loved Clara. But I'm afraid you're mistaken about Clara's love for him.'

'That's not true!' Clara cried. 'I've always loved George, and you know it.'

'And we also know that you were secretly meeting another man, at night, in the dark, in your nightwear,' Julia cut in.

'How can you believe such a thing of Clara?' Mary exclaimed.

Albert and Julia exchanged glances.

'Because she was seen by an eyewitness who is entirely above reproach,' Albert said quietly. 'We were so angry at such a betrayal of George that we instantly withdrew the announcement and set off for Calicut.'

'If we hadn't been so certain that what we'd heard was true, we would have come straight to you,' Julia added. 'But knowing its validity, we couldn't do that. By going to Calicut we had an excuse to miss the party, which would have been an embarrassment for us all.'

'I would say that it was a little more than an excuse, as you put it,' Mary said evenly. 'I imagine you'll soon be announcing George's engagement to the daughter of Albert's colleague there.'

Albert nodded. 'That's right, we will. You can't imagine the hurt and distress that all this has caused George, and we're hoping that being engaged to another charming girl will help him get over it.'

'You need to talk to Clara, Mary,' Julia told her. 'I'm sure she'll admit the truth of the rumour. As I say, we know it to be true.'

Clara opened her mouth to speak.

'No, Clara,' Mary said. 'There's no need for you to deny this again. We're equally convinced that you're mistaken, Julia. And that one of you clearly made sure that everyone in Cochin learnt of what you believed.'

Julia flushed.

'I shan't attempt to describe our humiliation at Edward's party,' Mary went on. 'When Tilly told us what was being said, Clara denied everything. We believe our daughter, and that's all there is to be said about it.'

'As you wish,' Julia said, disapproval written across her face. She picked up her coffee and finished it.

'I hope this isn't going to stop our families from being friends,' Clara said anxiously.

Mary nodded. 'Clara's right. This is a small community, and we'll continually be meeting each other, one way or another. Clara and George are now both engaged, albeit not to each other, which rather brings that episode to an end, and I think we should try to put it behind us.'

'I can accept that,' Albert said.

Mary smiled with a degree of warmth. 'I'm glad you said that, Albert. You and Henry have become good friends, and I've enjoyed getting to know Julia better in the past few months. I would like to think that our friendship can continue, and that each of us can take delight in the fact that our children are making a good marriage. Would you both agree?'

'Readily,' Albert said. 'And you do, too, don't you, Julia?'

'Of course,' she said, and her smile embraced Clara as well as her parents. 'We're looking forward to hearing Clara's wedding plans,' she added. 'But I think we'll have to leave that for another time. Having been away, even for so short a time, Albert has much to do. As do I. And we're also about to arrange a visit to Madras.'

'I should like to stay on, Mama, if Clara doesn't mind,' Lizzie intervened. 'It's a while since we spoke, and we've a lot to catch up on.'

Mary turned to Clara. 'Well, Clara?' she asked.

'I'd like that, Mama. Yes, do stay, Lizzie.'

Mary rose to her feet, followed by Henry, and Julia and Albert got up, too. 'I'll ask Amit to bring you fresh coffee,' Mary told the girls. 'When we've said goodbye to Julia and Albert, we've things to do upstairs so we'll leave you on your own.'

. . .

THEIR COFFEE CUPS REPLENISHED, Clara sat across the table from Lizzie.

'Whatever you heard was wrong,' Clara said. 'I never arranged to meet anyone in the garden after dark, other than George, which you know about.'

'You were seen with Lewis, Clara,' Lizzie said.

Clara straightened up.

'And what made it worse,' Lizzie went on, 'is that you knew how much I liked him.'

'But that's a complete misreading of what happened!' Clara exclaimed. 'If you'd come to me as soon as you heard this, I could've explained.'

'I didn't tell you because I was so upset at you betraying my brother, as well as me,' Lizzie said angrily. 'Anyone in my position would've been.'

'But I wasn't betraying him. At first I thought it was a false rumour, and I said so when Mama asked me at the party. Later, though, talking to Edward, I suddenly realised that once—just once, Lizzie—as a result of a gross misunderstanding, Lewis came to my garden and called up to me. He was hidden in the shadows, and thinking it was George, I went down to him. It was a misunderstanding,' she repeated. 'That's all.'

'No, it wasn't. When we were at the club, I overheard you telling him to go to your garden,' Lizzie said accusingly. 'At first, I thought you were telling him how he could visit me, but now I know you weren't.'

Clara gestured her helplessness. 'You're completely wrong. Lewis asked me what women did if they wanted to meet a man without a chaperone in attendance. He said he'd asked you, too, but he'd been called away to play billiards so he hadn't been able to wait for an answer.'

Lizzie bit her lip. 'It's true—he *did* ask me,' she said slowly.

'I assumed he wanted to spend time alone with you, so I told him what George and I used to do. It was only when he came to my garden, not yours, that I found out it was me he was interested in. We'd got it wrong, both of us.'

She paused. 'I suppose George had finally decided to come along and see me, and saw me with Lewis. He must be the witness above reproach.'

'It wasn't George. It was me. Because I'd overheard what you said, I'd been expecting Lewis. I was impatient and went to meet him. I saw him kiss you.' Her voice rose in accusation.

'He was saying goodbye,' Clara said in desperation. 'I told him I loved George and had never had any interest in anyone else. I even tried to wipe his kiss off my face.'

Lizzie sat back, her face pale, and stared at Clara.

'So while you were trying to help me, I ended up hurting you. You must hate me,' she said at last. 'And you've now got to marry Edward. He's nice, but he's not young and hand-some like George. And George will have to marry the Calicut girl.'

'What's she like?'

Lizzie shrugged. 'She's our age, and she's pretty. She seems all right. It won't really affect me, though, as I'll be in Madras. I'm looking forward to living there. Whatever you say, I don't think you'll ever really like me again, not like you did before. Every time you look at Edward's face, you'll think of what you've lost through me.'

'How does George feel about the girl?'

Lizzie shook her head. 'I don't really know. He seems to like her. They were talking a lot about cricket. Her father's keen on cricket so she knows quite a bit about the game.

What about your father? Is he horribly disappointed? We all know that George would have run Saunders & Co one day, and now that won't happen.'

'He must be upset. After all, Edward's not another George. But he's not said anything. I'm sure he'll work something out, though. Maybe he'll sell the company when he can't run it any longer, but insist on his name being retained as part of the deal. Maybe Lewis will take it over. Who knows.'

Lizzie stood up. 'I ought to go, Clara. You'll soon be having lunch, and George is coming over later. I'll pass on to him what you've told me, and I'll take the blame I deserve.'

She gave her a wry smile. 'What about coffee at the Old Harbour House on Friday? Just you and me. No Lewis,' she added with a laugh. 'I could show my contrition by letting you go on about your wedding plans.'

Clara smiled as she got up. 'All right. I expect you'll have had your invitation by then. We're marrying in the first week of April.'

'Are we being invited, then?' Lizzie asked in surprise.

'Of course. We've established this morning that our two families are still friends, haven't we? Yes, it's a good idea to meet on Friday. We'll need to talk about your bridesmaid's dress.'

'I SAW LIZZIE LEAVE,' Mary said coming out to the verandah where Clara had just opened *David Copperfield*. She sat down next to her.

'I'm glad the Goddards came,' Clara said. 'It's cleared the air. And keeping Lizzie as my bridesmaid will further help to make things close to normal.'

Mary smiled. 'That's very wise. Personally, I wasn't the

least bit surprised that they visited, nor that they wanted to erase the whole sorry affair.'

Clara looked at Mary questioningly.

'I don't think you appreciate quite the status you'll have in the community when you marry Edward,' Mary told her. 'Nor the power. It's amazing what a woman can achieve if she plays her cards right. The Goddards will want to maintain as close a friendship with us as possible. You can be sure of that.'

Clara frowned. 'Does their self-interest make you like them less?'

'Not to any great extent. That's the way it is in both the political and the business worlds, I'm afraid.'

She paused, and turned to face Clara squarely. 'That you asked such a question shows me how much you've matured in the months since you've been home. We were right to defer the engagement, even though circumstances conspired against us and the outcome isn't what we expected. But I've confidence now that in whatever situation you find yourself, you'll make the most of it.'

'Thank you, Mama.'

'And did your talk with Lizzie go well?'

'It did. We've smoothed over everything, and we're putting it behind us. And just like old times, we're meeting for coffee in Old Harbour House on Friday morning. If you're unable to come, I'll ask *ayah*.'

'I'm glad that your friendship with Lizzie has withstood this.'

Clara smiled at her mother. 'I didn't quite say that. I'll never feel as close to Lizzie as before, but we'll be friendly enough while she's in Cochin. She'll be going to Madras, you know.'

She hesitated. 'I wouldn't want Papa to know, but I

suspect it was Lizzie, not their servants, who started the rumour. If so, it shows that she can be sly, and will act in a deliberately hurtful way if angered or jealous. I'll never again feel I can be completely open with her.'

'I KNOW Lizzie told you what happened,' George said, having gone through an explanation similar to Lizzie's that morning, 'but I'm desperate for you to believe that I never stopped loving you, Clara, no matter what you'd done.'

'Which was nothing,' Clara said sharply. 'Lizzie was going to explain how it was all a misunderstanding. Didn't she do that?'

'Yes, she did,' he said quickly. 'I expressed myself badly. But seeing you again...' he inched closer to her, '... looking so lovely. Is it any wonder that my words are not coming out as I intend? I love you, Clara. I can't believe that you're marrying Edward, not me.' He shook his head. 'I can't bear the thought of it.'

'I understand your Calicut girl is very pretty,' Clara said tartly. 'I'm sure she'll help you to bear it.'

'I deserve that,' he said, his voice contrite. He leaned towards her. 'But it's not her I love—it's you, Clara. Is there any chance at all of us getting back together? I love you so.'

'I'm sorry, George, but there isn't. We were finished the moment you believed what Lizzie said, agreed with your parents' change of plan for you, and went to Calicut without attempting to hear what I had to say.'

He gestured his despair.

'We aren't the only ones involved now—there's Edward and your fiancée,' she continued, 'and both sets of parents. This isn't a game. We're both involved in agreements that

can't be broken without repercussions, and more importantly, without hurting people.'

'You don't know how much I regret not coming to you.'

'If I'd had a chance to explain, things would be very
different today. But having said that, in the last couple of
days, I've had time to think.'

'What about?'

'You say you love me, but does a man who truly loves a
woman believe the worst of that woman without question?
And does a man in love help to bring disgrace to not just the
woman he claims to love, but to her family, too? A family
who's always been very kind to him? I don't think so. Your
instant belief in Lizzie's accusation tells me, George, that
you don't really know me at all.'

He sat back. 'I *do,* and I love you. But I can see that you
no longer believe that. And I have only myself to blame,' he
said miserably. He glanced dejectedly across the garden to
the deep blue sea, and then looked back at Clara. 'D'you
think you'll be happy, married to Edward?'

'I'm sure I shall,' she said quietly.

'But he's not very sporty, so I can't see you going to many
of the games on the Parade Ground. And the people he's
friendly with at the club are older than we are. And they're a
bit stuffy, if I'm being honest. So's he, for that matter. I like
him, though,' he added quickly. 'I just can't see the two of
you together. You and I are a much better fit,' he added with
a smile.

'Are we? I wonder if that's true. Edward and I have interests in common, you know? We both like reading, for a
start.'

He burst out laughing. 'You might read magazines, for
all I know, but I can't see you reading books, or at least, not
the sort of books he'd read.' And he laughed again.

'Actually, I don't really like magazines,' she said. 'But I suppose that over the months, you and I never really talked to each other, so you wouldn't know that.' She paused. 'How does your Calicut girl pass her time?'

He shrugged. 'I don't really know. Like any other girl, I suppose. And when we marry, she'll have the house to run. Mother and Father are getting us a house near theirs, so we won't be far from here. And she'll help with the cricket teas. In fact, she knows a lot about cricket,' he added, his voice brightening. 'Her understanding of the game is quite impressive.'

'A good fit for you, then,' Clara said with a smile.

And an unexpected wave of relief swept through her.

39

W *ednesday afternoon*

HIS HANDS THRUST deep in his trouser pockets, Lewis walked up to the high stone wall that surrounded his house, and went through the narrow gateway that was supported on either side by a massive pillar.

His head bowed in thought, he crossed the compound to the steps leading to the entrance. When he reached the top, he walked past the four lazy chairs with wide arms and wicker backs that were grouped in a circle on his small verandah, and went into the house.

Pausing in the front hall, he called to his head servant to bring a whisky to the office, and then went through the large sitting room that had been divided into two by a screen, the back half of which he'd made into an office, and it was into his office that he went.

He sat down behind his desk, beneath the square *punkah* fixed to the whitewashed ceiling.

His head servant followed him moments later, placed a glass of whisky next to him, and left.

Leaning back, he locked his hands behind his head.

Everything that had happened since Saturday had made him more determined than ever to get control of Saunders & Co, and to do so as soon as possible. There was now far too much money at stake for him to delay any longer before taking action.

Nothing would give him greater satisfaction than assuming control of the company in a way that caused the maximum disgrace possible to both Edward Harrington and the Saunders family, and that was going to be his goal.

Yes, Edward Harrington, too, must be caught up in the scandal that he intended to bring about.

It was because of Harrington that he'd lost the chance of marrying Clara Saunders, and was having to get what he wanted by a more tortuous route.

But he was mindful of the fact that none of the mud he'd be throwing would stick to Harrington if he hadn't yet married Clara.

This meant that he'd have to hold off acting until the moment she had a wedding ring on her finger.

But soon after he *did* act, Harrington would find himself on a boat heading for England and ignominy, his wife at his side, both of them weighted down by the shame of her family's disgrace.

While he, Lewis, would be flourishing in Cochin and, under the cover of running the company as it had always been run, would be adding some highly lucrative commodities to their range and opening up new sea routes.

He dropped his arms and picked up his glass.

Of course, he'd have to buy the company first. He'd no intention of merely managing it on Henry's behalf—this was going to be *his* enterprise, and his alone.

But Henry would be so taken by surprise at the situation he suddenly found himself in that faced with an offer from a buyer, who would be assuring him that his family would be provided for, who knew the company inside out, and who'd promised there'd be no change of name or alteration in the way of doing things, he'd be bound to take the money offered, no matter how low that offer.

By the time that the other traders had positioned themselves to make the sort of offer the company merited, it would be too late.

He glanced at the calendar on his desk. Harrington and Clara would be married in just over five weeks. So, in just over five weeks, he'd put his plan into effect.

But first things first, he thought, finishing his drink.

He was obliged to go to the backwaters the following Monday.

He needed to collect the peppercorns that had been harvested three day earlier, when they'd started turning red. Since then, they'd been laid out in the sun, and they'd be blackened by now and fully dry, and ready to be stored in airtight containers, and then shipped.

In addition to collecting the peppercorns, he had some small consignments to collect from his village contact, all above board, and, most importantly, for the first time he'd be ordering a large quantity of opium for himself.

But that would be a deal between the two of them, and no one else, not even Sanjay, would know that he'd placed such an order. Not at that stage, anyway.

Sanjay would obviously accompany him on the Monday trip as usual.

But with the plans he had in mind, he was going to have to take on another person, too, to work for him, and the Monday trip would be a good time to try out a possible addition to his workforce. It would obviously have to be someone who was already working for Henry as he didn't have much time in which to find a suitable candidate.

Sanjay rated a man called Jitu, and he might just be the man he needed.

Apparently, this Jitu had carried out a few small illegal transactions for Sanjay, his interest being solely in what he was paid, and that put Jitu at the top of the list.

But he'd have to size up the man for himself.

Although most of the workers on the wharves would probably be delighted to have an extra source of income, he wasn't prepared to take on just anyone. It had to be someone he could trust, who knew how to keep his mouth shut. Taking Jitu with him the following week would give him a chance to see what the man was made of.

So the trip the following week would be for strictly legitimate goods. He'd no intention of taking a risk by doing anything illegal with an as-yet unproven man in the boat.

But the trip he'd be making two weeks after that was a different matter.

On that second trip, they'd be going to his boathouse and godown, and that would reveal to Jitu, or whoever he hired, that he had his own property. And the man would also realise that the purpose of the trip was different from what Henry Saunders had been told.

Both men would know that Henry thought he was taking the large *kettuvallam* into the backwaters in order to pick up another consignment of coconut shells. But, in fact, they'd be going no further than his boathouse.

About six weeks earlier, he'd relayed to Henry a conversation he'd had one Wednesday afternoon at the club. The owner of a factory making ladles and spoons from hard coconut shells had casually mentioned that he'd be needing more shells before long, and he'd seen his opportunity, and offered to supply the shells at an unusually good price, and ship them to the man's factory.

The contract had been agreed, and recorded in Henry's ledger, and the shells had accordingly been collected and delivered. But not all the shells he'd brought back with him had been delivered. He'd ordered a larger number than was required by the contract.

Unknown to Henry, he'd held some back, storing them in his godown.

He'd instinctively felt that there could be an occasion at some point in the future when he'd want it to appear that he'd been to the backwaters, but hadn't.

And that occasion had come considerably sooner than he'd expected.

The sole purpose of the second trip would be to adapt the *kettuvallam* so that drugs could be secreted within the base of the boat, and behind the cupboards. As soon as they reached the boatyard, the local men he employed would get down to that.

To make it look as if they'd genuinely been to backwaters, they'd bring back the coconut shells he'd stored in his godown. They could be heaped in one of the Muttancherry godowns until he found a buyer for them.

It was essential, therefore, that he had complete confidence in the men he took with him on that second trip.

And also for the third trip, two weeks after the second, which would bring them back to Cochin on the evening before the Saunders wedding.

On that occasion, he'd ostensibly be doing the company's work—fulfilling the orders for the last of the hillside-harvested peppercorns, and checking that all newly planted vines had been tied to the supporting trees to stop them touching the soil. But he would also be taking possession of the large quantity of drugs he'd be ordering for himself on the first trip.

He sat back and looked around his office.

There being no time like the present, he'd check on that Jitu's background—one could never be too careful, not with so much at stake—and if that didn't throw up any reason not to trust him, he'd take him along with them the following Monday, and see what he made of him.

And if everything was satisfactory, Jitu would accompany him and Sanjay on all his trips after that.

Yes, he thought in grim satisfaction, Clara Saunders's wedding day was, indeed, going to be memorable, but in a way she could never have foreseen.

40

T*he wedding day*

THE DAY CLARA had been waiting for with a mixture of emotions—her wedding day—had at last arrived.

The past weeks had, at one moment, seemed to fly by in a whirl of pre-wedding activities, and in another, had seemed to drag slowly by.

At one moment, she couldn't wait for the wedding to arrive and be over with. And in another, she dreaded the day, and would have loved to have been able to curl up in her bed and not emerge until the day had passed.

Her only certainties were that she would definitely be marrying Edward, and that she liked him, and was lucky to be marrying such a good friend. He was such pleasant company that recently, every time they'd parted, she'd found herself looking forward to seeing him again.

She woke earlier than usual that day, threw back her

covers, jumped out of bed and went outside.

She wouldn't ever be doing this again, she thought in a rush of sadness as she leaned against the balustrade and watched the advent of dawn. At least, not on her verandah, not looking at the view that she'd loved for so many years.

Of course, it wouldn't be the last time that she watched the day unfurl before her eyes—Edward, too, loved to see the colours of day take shape, and from that night on, she'd be on Edward's verandah, looking at his view.

He'd told her that she must think of his house as her house, too. But she couldn't—it was Edward's, and it would feel thus until she'd lived in it long enough to feel at home in its contours.

The night sky was growing pale in the first light of dawn, and the sky and the sea had shed their mantel of sombre grey and taken on a soft luminous light.

As she stood watching, the sun rose in the east, turning the sky from silver-grey to the colour of ripe mangoes, and sheening with gold the water that lay beneath, bringing the events of the day that much closer.

A shiver ran through her.

Edward had made it clear in the past few weeks in his discreet way that he'd meant what he'd said when he'd proposed to her, and she knew she'd have her own bedroom, dressing room and bathroom.

Knowing that she liked him as a friend, but felt nothing more than friendship and gratitude for his many kindnesses, she'd felt great relief at this.

But separate though they would be during the night, their rooms would open on to the same side of the verandah, and she'd be able to step out and join him before they went to their rooms, and first thing in the morning.

She would want to do this, and she would also seek

occasions in the day, such as at afternoon tea, to join him in the way that a friend would do, and she knew that she'd look forward to his return in the evenings so that she could have the pleasure of talking to him over dinner and afterwards.

She could most definitely see them having a comfortable life together, and to her amazement, there'd been moments recently when she'd felt herself actually looking forward to the start of her new life.

She'd expected to feel a strong reluctance at having to leave behind the family home she loved, and her special part of the verandah, and the memories of George that would forever be ingrained in the wood of the furniture and walls.

But now that the day had come, she felt no more than the normal nostalgia at the thought of leaving the familiar and embracing the new.

She turned away from the view and went back into her room.

It was going to be a busy day. Tilly, her matron of honour, would be there in about an hour, and Lizzie, too. They'd bring their clothes and dress at her house, and they'd leave from there to go to the Church of St Francis.

The church would be full of orange blossom, a few ribbon-tied sprigs of which had been attached to the end of every pew, and the scent from which would fill the air.

At the end of the ceremony, a convoy of launches would take her and Edward, and their many guests, to a reception on the lawn of The Residency.

With all the thought that had been put into the occasion, the whole thing should go like clockwork, she thought, slipping into her day clothes and preparing to go downstairs for a quick breakfast.

There was a soft knock on the bedroom door.

'Come in,' she called.

Mary came in.

Seeing her mother, she laughed. 'Since when did you wait to be told to come in? You always knock at the door, open it at once and enter.'

Mary smiled. She saw the tension behind her mother's smile.

'What's the matter, Mama?' she asked in sudden anxiety.

'Nothing, darling. At least, not in the way you mean.' She went across and sat on Clara's bed, and indicated that Clara should sit next to her.

'Just in case you feel that there are things you should talk to me about,' Clara said, sitting down next to her mother, a pink haze spreading across her cheeks. 'Tilly's told me everything I need to know. You're off the hook,' she added with an embarrassed laugh.

'It's not that,' Mary said with a smile. 'I did know that Tilly had spoken to you. No, this is about something that's been worrying me. I woke very early and couldn't get it out of my mind.'

'What is it?' She bit her lip.

'Your engagement to Edward has happened so quickly. Your father and I were aware that Edward liked you, but had never seen anything to suggest that you felt more than friendship for him. All the signs were that you loved George. Your father and I are worried that you've agreed to this marriage because you think it the only way to salvage a difficult situation.'

Clara opened her mouth to speak.

'Before you say anything,' Mary went on, 'we want you to know that if you prefer not to marry Edward, we will support you in this, no matter the outcome. Tilly and Michael love each other and are very happy, and we want the same for you, dear Clara.' She paused. 'There, I've finished.'

'It's very kind of you and Papa to say that, but I'm perfectly happy to marry Edward. We've met a number of times over the past few weeks, and each time, I've thought what a very nice man he is, and how lucky I am that he loves me.'

Mary gave her a warm smile. 'I'm so glad to hear it, darling. We'd been so afraid that you were sacrificing your life for us.'

She laughed. 'How very dramatic, Mama! But since we're having a heart to heart, I shall tell you that I'm so very grateful to you and Papa, and to George's parents, for insisting that George and I didn't make our engagement official for six months.'

Mary looked at her in surprise. 'But you love George,' she said.

'Actually, I don't. I thought I did, I will admit. But I was wrong. I loved the George who was my childhood friend years ago. I like the George of today, but I don't love him. I was so in love with the idea of loving him, if that makes sense, that I didn't really see him as the adult he'd become.'

'I see,' Mary said slowly.

'When I *did* start to think seriously about him, after he'd gone to Calicut and I knew I'd lost him, and after Edward had proposed and I was able to think more clearly, I actually felt overjoyed at the way things had turned out.'

Mary frowned in surprise. 'Did you really?'

Clara nodded. 'I was amazed that I felt that way, but I did. I'd realised by then that George and I have nothing in common. I'm sure we'd have been quite happy together, but I'm even more sure that he'll be happier with the girl from

Calicut, and that I'll have a more enjoyable life with Edward.'

Mary gave a sob, and put her hand to her mouth. 'I can't tell you what a relief that is.'

Clara hugged her. 'You can tell Papa that the friendship with the Goddards will remain strong, and I look forward to meeting George's fiancée when she moves here. With Lizzie in Madras, an addition to our community will be most welcome. I hope she and I will be friends.'

Mary stood up, and Clara did, too.

'You're going to make Edward the most wonderful wife, darling,' Mary said, and with tears in her eyes, she kissed Clara's cheek.

CLARA STOOD on Henry's arm at the entrance to the church, a slender figure in a simple floor length bias cut white satin dress, with a high neck and long sleeves.

Each of her long fitted sleeves ended in a line of small pearl buttons, and in each ear she wore a single pearl earring. A tulle veil hung from a tiara of orange blossom, and fell to the floor behind her. In her hand, she held a bouquet of white lilies.

Henry turned to his daughter. 'You look very beautiful, Clara,' he said gruffly. 'Edward is a lucky man. As I was when I married your mother. I wish you the same great happiness that I've had with her.'

'Thank you, Papa, for everything,' Clara said quietly.

They smiled at each other, and then turned to face the crowded church.

In front of the altar, facing her, was Edward, in a black cut-away morning coat over a silver-grey waistcoat and pinstriped trousers. Next to him stood Michael, his best man, similarly dressed.

Wearing a pale blue dress, Tilly moved forward and took her place a little way in front of Clara, holding a prayer book and a white lily, and Lizzie, dressed in the same outfit as Tilly, stood behind her holding a sprig of orange blossom.

The organ sounded Wagner's bridal chorus, and Tilly started walking down the central aisle.

A sea of faces on either side turned towards Clara as they slowly progressed to the place where Edward waited.

HARDLY ABLE TO CONTAIN HIS excitement as the fruition of his plans grew increasingly imminent, Lewis fidgeted at the aisle end of a pew halfway up the church.

The organ music washed over him, and he hardly glanced at Clara as she passed him by, his eyes being firmly fixed on Henry's back.

Soon, Saunders & Co will be mine, was all he could think.

He'd move house soon after his purchase, find someone to marry and then bring Gulika in from the backwaters.

He might even take over the Saunders house, he thought wryly. They wouldn't be needing it, after all.

Once or twice, he glanced round at the entrance to the church. There was nothing yet to be seen, but the police would surely be there before too long.

Jitu had proved extremely reliable, having been tried out with several packets of drugs, and had shown himself to be very willing to take on more such tasks.

But the only task he'd been given that morning had been to go to the harbour police at sunrise, and alert them to the presence of drugs on Henry's *kettuvallam*.

At first, he'd intended to ask Sanjay to go to the police, but a throwaway remark by Jitu, about Sanjay's closeness to him, had made him rethink that.

Sanjay had gone on most of the trips he'd made over the past couple of years, and they were connected together, therefore, in people's minds. As he was anxious to be as distanced as possible from the whole thing, he realised that it would be wiser if Sanjay weren't too closely involved.

Accordingly, it was Jitu he'd asked to alert the police. He and Jitu wouldn't have become associated with each other after so short a period of time.

The police would now have had time to organise themselves, get to the wharves and do the search. They were bound to have found the drugs, and would probably arrive at the church at any minute.

The only possible delay would be if they'd forgotten that Henry's daughter was marrying that day. But if they had, someone would direct them to the church. It wasn't very far from the house, so any delay would be slight.

He stared ahead at the altar. Clara and Edward were exchanging vows.

He glanced behind him again. Still no sign of the police, but it couldn't be much longer.

It looked as if the timing was going to be perfect, he thought gleefully.

Edward and Clara were moments away from being declared man and wife. And by the time that the register had been signed by all concerned, the police would be there, arresting Henry. By then, Edward Harrington would be married to Clara, and the shame that was about to befall the Saunders family, would besmirch him, too.

From the hum that rose from the congregation, he realised that they were now married.

He smiled at those around him, nodding to indicate his pleasure.

Edward gave Clara little more than a peck on the cheek. Both turned and smiled at the applauding congregation, waved to them, and then made their way to the sacristy in order to sign the register.

He glanced again behind him.

Several harbour police and a couple of British soldiers stood at the entrance to the church, black silhouettes against the bright light of day.

His heart racing in excitement, he turned to face the altar.

Minutes later, the organ sounded again, and bathed in the soft glow of candlelight, Clara and Edward started walking down the aisle to Mendelssohn's 'Wedding March'.

Those smiles were soon going to be wiped off their smug faces, he thought in satisfaction as he turned slightly with the rest of the congregation to watch them pass, followed by Henry and Mary Saunders, Tilly and Michael, and Lizzie.

Then he filed out into the aisle to join the rest of the congregation in following the bridal procession.

Craning his neck, he tried to see above the heads of those in front of him, and he saw two policemen move to the side, allowing Clara and Edward to pass, and then step forward again. They gestured to Mary and Henry to approach them.

He saw Mary glance at Henry in surprise, and both go across to the police.

As he was so close to leaving the church, he might just be in time to hear what the police told Mary before they took Henry away, he thought, and he tried in vain to move ahead more quickly.

When he was finally able to step through the archway

into the bright light of day, he glanced towards Henry and Mary, eager to see what was happening.

But his view was blocked by a soldier in front of him.

He moved to one side to see beyond the soldier.

The soldier moved with him.

Before he realised what was happening, a policeman was standing at his other side, and two soldiers had positioned themselves behind him.

'Would you kindly come with us, sir?' the policeman asked.

'For what reason?' Lewis tried to smile his bewilderment at the man.

'A large quantity of drugs has been found in a godown south of Muttancherry, which, we believe, is owned by you, sir. Drugs were also found in the *kettuvallam* and launch on the premises, which, I believe, are also owned by you.'

A wave of fear shot through Lewis.

He suddenly felt very cold.

He shook his head vigorously. 'No, this is a mistake. You've got it wrong. It's Saunders who trades in drugs. You'll find them on his boat.'

'We don't think so,' the policeman said steadily. 'When we discovered the drugs on your property, we naturally conducted a thorough search of your employer's godowns and boats. There were no drugs at all to be found anywhere on his property. We're confident, therefore, that in this you were acting alone, with the aid of some employees of Saunders.'

'I don't understand,' he said in rising panic. 'You've made a terrible mistake.'

And then he turned, and saw Edward, and the expression on Edward's face.

And in a blinding flash, it all made sense.

41

L*ater that day*

THE MOMENT that Clara and Edward stepped on to the jetty on Bolghotty Island, an unseen band struck up the dance-tune 'Charmaine'.

'I would have liked the band to have played a song called Clara, but I couldn't find one,' Edward said as they walked along the path through The Residency gardens, Clara's arm tucked into his. 'But 'Charmaine' begins with a C so I hope that's close enough for you.'

'And there are two letters A in each name, too,' she added lightly.

Both laughed.

'They'll all be here in the next few minutes,' she said, glancing back at the water when they reached a large clump of bamboos that were absorbing the rays of the early after-noon sun, and she paused.

She looked up into his face. 'I just wanted to thank you again for everything you did to protect Father. I can't tell you how grateful I am.'

'It was a pleasure. Even if Henry and I hadn't been about to be related by marriage, I wouldn't have wanted to see an innocent man imprisoned. I'm just relieved we could prevent that from happening. In part, that was thanks to you.'

'Me?' she questioned.

'That's right. Once we knew that Lewis had property of his own, and it was you who told Michael that, it was just a question of finding out where it was.'

'How did you find it?'

'One of the men we'd placed on the wharves had been hired by Lewis, who trusted him, and he alerted us to Lewis's scheme. As a result, we were watching the wharves, and saw Lewis and Sanjay planting drugs in Henry's boats and godowns. After they'd gone, my men transferred the drugs to Lewis's property.'

'Thank goodness Lewis mentioned he'd got a place of his own, and I told Michael without realising its significance.'

Edward nodded. 'Michael deserves a lot of credit. He's worked very hard on this.'

'I'll thank him as soon as I see him.'

'And then I think we should forget all about Lewis. This is a happy occasion, after all, and we mustn't let Lewis spoil it for us. All that matters now is that your family is safe, and they are, and that Lewis and Sanjay are locked up, and they are. And with what Jitu will tell us, we'll be able to cut off one avenue of drug trafficking.'

'You're right.' She put her hand up to his cheek, rested it

there, and stared hard into his face. 'Dear, dear Edward,' she said. Her voice caught.

For a moment, neither moved.

Then she lowered her arm.

He gave an awkward laugh. 'I expect you'll want to remove your veil. It'll be a little while before all the guests are here so you've time. My suite of rooms has been furnished with anything you might need.'

'Thank you,' she said. 'Yes, I want to be able to circulate easily, and I'd hate anyone to trip over my veil. I won't be long, though.'

'Tilly's near the entrance. She's going to go in and help you.'

'You've thought of everything, haven't you? I'm so very lucky, Edward.'

'No, I'm the lucky one,' he said quietly. 'I'm going to be able to look at your beautiful face every day for the rest of my life, and I'll have someone to talk to whose conversation I enjoy. You can't get much luckier than that.'

She leaned up and kissed his cheek.

He coloured slightly.

Then she took his hand in hers and they walked across to The Residency entrance, smiling at the first groups of arrivals as they passed them by.

Some were gathering in the gardens, some standing in groups staring at the imposing building, some sitting at small circular tables covered in white cloths and shaded by large dark umbrellas.

At the far end of the clusters of tables and chairs, there was one long table, covered with a pristine white cloth, which had been set out for the wedding party.

Waiters had started circulating with trays laden with flutes of champagne and glasses of lime juice and soda water. Others carried platters of pre-lunch canapés, which they offered to the guests.

'Edward!' they heard a voice call just as they reached the building.

Turning, they saw Henry hurrying towards them. He waved at them to stop.

'Right, Mrs Harrington,' Edward said, turning to Clara with a smile. 'Your father is heading for me, and I can see Tilly coming across to you. I'll wait for you here. And when you're ready, we'll go together to greet our guests.'

EDWARD LEANED against the balustrade outside his bedroom, and stared ahead of him as the sun sank into the horizon, throwing a film of molten red-gold across the sea, and setting the tall dark coconut trees against a flaming backdrop.

All around him, the warm night air, scented with jasmine, tea and cardamom, buzzed with the songs of cicadas.

And in the house behind him, the house that was now Clara's home as well as his, he could hear her getting ready for bed.

He'd have given anything for them to have been about to spend the night in bed together, but he'd known from the day that they'd met that he wasn't the sort of man she'd willingly choose for a husband.

To encourage her to accept his proposal, he'd promised that he wouldn't expect that sort of closeness with her, and he intended to keep his word.

Even if it hurt.

And it was going to hurt.

It did already.

She'd had to know from the very start of their marriage that he was a man of his word, and having bid her good-night at the door of the room that was to be hers for the future, he'd kissed her on the cheek, and had then gone along to his room and prepared for bed.

As he did every other night, he'd put on his dark green silk smoking jacket, stepped out on to the verandah, and stood there surrounded by the beauty of the dying day, watching the rebirth of the star-filled night.

He glanced wistfully towards Clara's end of the verandah, and then looked quickly back at the view.

The first thing he must do was banish any feeling of regret at not being able to hold Clara in the way that a man would wish to hold his wife, he resolved. To do that, he must focus only on the many ways in which she was going to enhance his life.

When he could do that, he'd be perfectly happy.

There was a slight sound at his side. He glanced to his left.

Clara was standing there, ethereal in an ivory silk negligée.

He caught his breath.

'I thought you might be asleep by now,' he said awkwardly, tightening the belt of his smoking jacket. He cleared his throat. 'You must be tired. It's been a long day and so much has happened.'

'I feel quite awake, thank you,' she said brightly, and she turned to look at the sea. 'I used to go outside my room every night before I went to bed, and I'd look at the view, just as you're doing now. My view wasn't so very different from yours.'

'I, too, come out here every night,' he said, a trifle self-consciously.

'That's another thing we have in common,' she told him with a smile.

Both turned back to the view, and stared at the moon and the sea.

'I'm not surprised that your view was similar to mine,' he said after a few minutes. 'After all, Cochin is surrounded by water and sandy beaches, and coconut trees abound.' He hesitated. 'Why are you out here, Clara. I hadn't expected to see you again tonight.'

She leaned on the balustrade, turned her head to look at him, and smiled.

'When I was little, my *ayah* used to read to me before I went to sleep, which helped me to love stories. At your party, you told me a story that began Once Upon a Time. It's now my turn to tell *you* a story. And my story, too, begins with the words Once Upon a Time.'

He looked at her in amusement. 'I'm listening.'

'Once upon a time there was a girl, just out of school, who fell in love with the idea of being in love. She lived near a handsome man, and her parents and the parents of the handsome man decided that she and the man should marry. But what appeared to be a disaster struck, and when all seemed lost, out of the mists rode a radiant knight in shining armour.'

'I thought you might be talking about people I knew,' Edward murmured, 'but when I heard you mention a radiant knight in shining armour, I decided I must be mistaken. I'd been expecting a frog.'

'At first, the girl felt gratitude and relief at being rescued,' she went on, 'and was content to be marrying a man she liked so much, who'd done so much for her and her family.'

He smiled. 'For the sake of the girl's happiness, I'm glad she felt that way.'

She turned to face him, her eyes filling with tears. 'But gratitude and relief slipped into the past as she came to see the man for himself. And she knew, oh, Edward, she knew how much she loved him. Not for what he'd done for her and her family, but for him. For everything about him. Every time she left him, she found herself counting the hours till she'd be seeing him again. It wasn't a disaster that had struck that day, it was a stroke of amazing good fortune. She ended up, dear Edward, marrying the man she truly loved.'

He turned towards her, with hope and disbelief in his eyes.

She took a step closer to him. 'Now that she can be with him not just every day, but every night, too, she's not going to give up a single precious minute of that time if she doesn't have to.'

She moved still closer to him.

'I love you, Edward. Before I met you, I thought I understood what passion was, but I didn't. Throughout the past six weeks, though, I've learnt what it means. It's what I feel for you.'

'Clara,' he breathed. All the love he felt for her overflowed into her name. 'My Clara.'

He pulled her towards him and buried his face in her hair.

And then his lips found hers.

They drew apart, breathing heavily, each staring at the other in wonder. And then she fell into his arms again, and he hugged her tightly.

Her heart beating fast, she pulled slightly back and looked up into his face.

'We've established that I'm familiar with a sea view just like yours,' she said, her voice shaking slightly, her eyes full of love. 'But I'm not familiar with the landscape inside your bedroom. If it doesn't sound too forward of me to ask this, I should like to see it now.'

'Oh, Clara!' he cried.

And he swept her up in his arms, swung her round in an ecstasy of delight, and gazing down into her face with the ardour of love, he carried her into the room that would be their bedroom ever more.

AUTHORIAL NOTE

As its name suggests, British Cochin, a small enclave in the Indian state known as Kerala since 1956, was ruled by the British at the time of the Raj, 1858 to 1947.

Cochin, one of a cluster of islands, is surrounded by tropical jungle, which is criss-crossed by narrow waterways known as the backwaters. The fertile soil is ideal for growing spices, and it's the cultivation and trade of these which shaped the history of the area.

The Portuguese were the first to establish a colonial presence in Cochin. Then came the Dutch, and finally the British, who governed British Cochin until 1947, when India gained independence from the British colonial rule.

With so many foreign influences in Cochin before Indian Independence, it isn't surprising that the names of the towns, villages and roads have changed over the years, and determining the names in 1934 was difficult. Maps from that period are vague and full of gaps, and different documents from that time spell the names in different ways. And they have changed again today.

I've read, for example, that The Cochin Club was called

that in the 1930s, as it is today, and I've also read, in what seemed equally authoritative, that it was called The English Club at that time. This is one of the areas in which Mr. Gonzaga was most helpful—it was called The English Club at the time of my novel.

In deciding upon the names to use, I've drawn upon the spelling that appears to be most widely used in the 1930s.

Until Indian Independence, Bolgatty Palace, on Bolgatty Island, was the home of the British Governor, and was frequently referred to as The Residency. There are several variants of the spelling of Bolgatty during that period, but the most frequently used would appear to be Bolghotty.

Similarly, with Mattancherry.

I've opted for Muttancherry, which is the form I saw more frequently than any other. It should not be confused with the village of Muttanchery, however, which is located about 25 km east of Kozhikode, which is known also today by its English name, Calicut. Calicut lies 180km north of Cochin.

Madras has been known as Chennai since 1996.

IF YOU ENJOYED COCHIN FALL

It would be really kind if you could take a few minutes to leave a review of the book.

Reviews give welcome feedback to the author, and they help to make the novel visible to other readers, both through the review and because a number of promotional platforms today require a minimum number of reviews before they'll accept any publicity for that book.

Your words, therefore, really do matter.

Thank you!

LIZ'S NEWSLETTER

Every month, Liz sends out a newsletter that tells you about her work in progress, and any travelling and interesting things she's done in the past month. You'll be the first to see the cover of the next book to be published, and also to receive advance information about forthcoming promotions and special offers.

You can be sure that your email address would never be shared with anyone else, and if you write to Liz, which you

can do through her website – www.lizharrisauthor.com –
you will always get a reply.

As a thank you for signing up for Liz's newsletter, you'll
get a free download of her almost-contemporary novel,
Word Perfect, which was inspired by Liz's six years in
California.

DARJEELING INHERITANCE

Each novel in the series, The Colonials, is a standalone and is complete in itself.

If you enjoyed reading *Cochin Fall* – and I hope you did – and haven't yet read *Darjeeling Inheritance*, the first book in the series to be published, you might be interested in reading the Prologue to *Darjeeling Inheritance*.

In the next few pages, you'll read the opening of *Darjeeling Inheritance*.

DARJEELING INHERITANCE: THE PROLOGUE

In the foothills of the Himalayas,
  Darjeeling, April, 1919

The early spring sun beat down on the back of the seven-year old girl as she struggled to keep up with the man in a worn safari suit who was striding ahead of her up the steep path.

Every so often, the girl slipped and fell on the red earth, picked herself up, brushed the dirt from her dress and hurried more quickly after the man.

But Charles Edwin Lawrence, lines of grief etched deep into his sun-browned face, neither turned to his daughter nor paused to wait for her. His eyes fixed in front of him, he continued resolutely up the narrow path that led between the tiered rows of tea bushes, the tender young leaves of which shone brilliant green in the light of the sun.

When he arrived at the summit, he stood in the cool breeze and stared down at the neat rows of terraces that fell away beneath his feet.

His vision blurred with unshed tears, he turned to face

the mass of dark green forested slopes that rose in layers beneath the clear blue sky, and the range of mountains behind them, their gold-tipped peaks linked in a chain of gold above the snow-covered slopes, as if suspended in nothingness.

The girl reached the place where her father stood, slid her arm round his leg and put her thumb in her mouth.

He glanced down at her, bent slightly and gently pushed her thumb away from her mouth. 'Only babies do that, Charlie. You're not a baby any longer.'

'I'm seven now.'

He nodded. 'That's right. So you're not a baby any longer, are you? You're a big girl, who'll soon be off to school.'

Biting her lower lip, she stared at the ground and nodded.

She sensed him smile his approval.

Glancing up, she saw tears on his cheeks, and she frowned. 'You're crying. You've got a wet face.'

He shrugged his shoulders dismissively. 'It'll just be perspiration. I suggest you look at the view instead of looking at me.' Picking her up under her arms, he swung her high up above his head, and slid her on to his shoulders. Her legs hung down in front of him on either side of his face, and he took hold of each foot.

Clutching his forehead with one hand, she ran her other hand down the side of his cheek.

'You *are* crying, Papa,' she said, her voice accusing, and she wiped her wet hand on the skirt of her dress. She pulled the *topi* from his head, let it fall to the ground, wrapped her arms around his chin, leaned forward, and rested her cheek against the back of his head. 'Is Eddie ill again? I haven't seen him today.'

She felt him tighten. He pulled one of her feet closer to the other so that he could hold them both with one hand, and she wobbled as he swiftly ran his free hand across his face. Then once more, he held a foot in each hand.

'Yes, he's been ill again,' he said after a short pause.

Her forehead wrinkled with puzzlement at the strange note she heard in his voice. She inclined herself sideways in an attempt to see his face.

'But not any longer,' he added quietly. 'He's gone to join your brothers.'

She straightened up and let out a wail of misery. 'I don't want him to go. I want him to play with me.' A sob rose in her throat, and she screwed up her face, ready to cry.

'You're not going to cry, are you, Charlie? Remember what we said about you being a big girl. Well, I need you to be big. Kick your foot against me if you're going to be big.'

She swallowed her sob, and with his hand still tightly holding her leg, kicked his chest with her right foot.

'Good girl,' he said. 'You see, it's just you and me now. And all of this.' Slowly he turned in a full circle, with Charlie sitting high on his shoulders. 'Just look at it all. Sundar is Hindi for beautiful. You can see why my father called it Sundar. We love it here; it's where we want to be. My grandfather and father both loved Sundar, and so do we, you and me. Isn't that so?'

She nodded.

'Say it, Charlie. Say, It's where I want to be.'

'It's where I want to be,' she echoed.

'Good girl. Look around you. I bet you've never noticed that tea bushes don't grow all year round—they're asleep from late November to early March. They won't wake up and start growing again until the first rains of spring have fallen and the sun has warmed the air. But then they'll grow so quickly that they'll need to be plucked every four to five days. Did you know that?'

She shifted her position.

'Hold tight,' he said, 'and I'll get you down.' He raised his arms, lifted her up over his head and stood her on the ground next to him.

Then he knelt down beside her and stared into her face.

'There's only you left now, Charlie. There won't be any more.'

She felt a momentary fear at his serious expression, and put her thumb back into her mouth.

'But I know that Sundar's in your heart, just as it's in mine, and when the time comes I'll do my very best to make sure you have a husband who'll be able to run the garden when I've gone, and who'll continue to grow the very best tea that Darjeeling can produce. There'll always be a Lawrence at Sundar. That's what we both want, isn't it?'

She could tell that he wanted her to nod, so she did.

He gave a dry laugh, and stood up. 'You've no idea what I'm talking about, have you?' he said, his voice relaxing. 'But one day you will.' He gave a playful tug on the long auburn hair that hung from under her *topi*.

She stared up at his face, and saw that his eyes were red and he still looked sad, even though his mouth was shaped into a smile.

'It's where I want to be,' she repeated.

His smiled broadened, and this time his eyes smiled, too, and she felt a glow of happiness spread through her.

She was very sad that Eddie had gone to join the two older brothers she'd never met. She'd loved Eddie and had been looking forward to him being old enough to play with her, and now she was left with only the servants' children to play with and her *ayah*.

But she was happy that her father thought that she and he were alike. She wouldn't have wanted to be like her mother, who always seemed angry.

'I want to grow tea, too, Papa,' she said.

Her father laughed. 'Like I said, you're a Lawrence through and through, Charlie.' He leaned down and hugged her. Then he straightened up and stared again at the terraces that lay below them and on either side.

His gaze drifted across the verdant bushes to the house where the last of his sons lay, silent ever more, and his smile faded.

ACKNOWLEDGMENTS

Yet again, I have to say a huge thank you to my amazing cover designer, Jane Dixon-Smith, for another truly striking cover, and to my superb editor, Jane Eastgate. Also, a massive thank you to my Friend in the North, Stella, who sees my completed manuscript before anyone else, and who never fails to give me constructive criticism. Her comments are invaluable—every author should have a Stella!

A thank you also to the many writer friends I've made over the years—too many to mention. You've helped to make the writing process such an enjoyable one. I shall never tire of chatting about plot lines and characters over a writerly lunch.

In writing *Cochin Fall*, I drew upon many different sources, which are too numerous to list. I must, however, mention *Fort Cochin: History and Untold Stories*, by Tanya Abraham, and *British and Native Cochin*, by Charles Allen Lawson. Both of which were particularly helpful.

I should like to thank, also, Mr. Ivor Gonzaga, the General Manager of The Cochin Club, Kochi. I'm most grateful to him for answering the questions I sent him.

A few years ago, I had a wonderful stay in Fort Cochin, now known as Fort Kochi, but I didn't know at the time exactly what information I'd need when I came to write my novel. When I did discover the gaps in my knowledge, the covid situation prevented me from returning to India. Therefore, I'm extremely grateful that Mr. Gonzaga furnished me with the information I'd been unable to uncover during my extensive research. Any mistakes I've made are down to me.

Lastly, a heartfelt thank you, as always, to my husband, Richard, who keeps the real world at bay while I live in my fictional world.

ABOUT THE AUTHOR

Born in London, Liz Harris graduated from university with a Law degree, and then moved to California, where she led a varied life, from waitressing on Sunset Strip to working as secretary to the CEO of a large Japanese trading company.

Six years later, she returned to London and completed a degree in English, after which she taught secondary school pupils, first in Berkshire, and then in Cheshire.

In addition to the thirteen novels she's had published, she's had several short stories in anthologies and magazines.

Liz now lives in Oxfordshire. An active member of the Romantic Novelists' Association, the Historical Novel Society and Writers in Oxford, her interests are travel, the theatre, reading and cryptic crosswords.

To find out more about Liz, visit her website at: www.lizharrisauthor.com

ALSO BY LIZ HARRIS

Historical novels

Darjeeling Inheritance

Cochin Fall

Hanoi Spring (early 2022)

The Linford Series

A sweeping saga set between the wars

The Dark Horizon

The Flame Within

The Lengthening Shadow

Historical Novels

The Road Back

A Bargain Struck

The Lost Girl

A Western Heart

Contemporary novels

The Best Friend

Evie Undercover

The Art of Deception

In large print only

Word Perfect

Printed in Great Britain
by Amazon